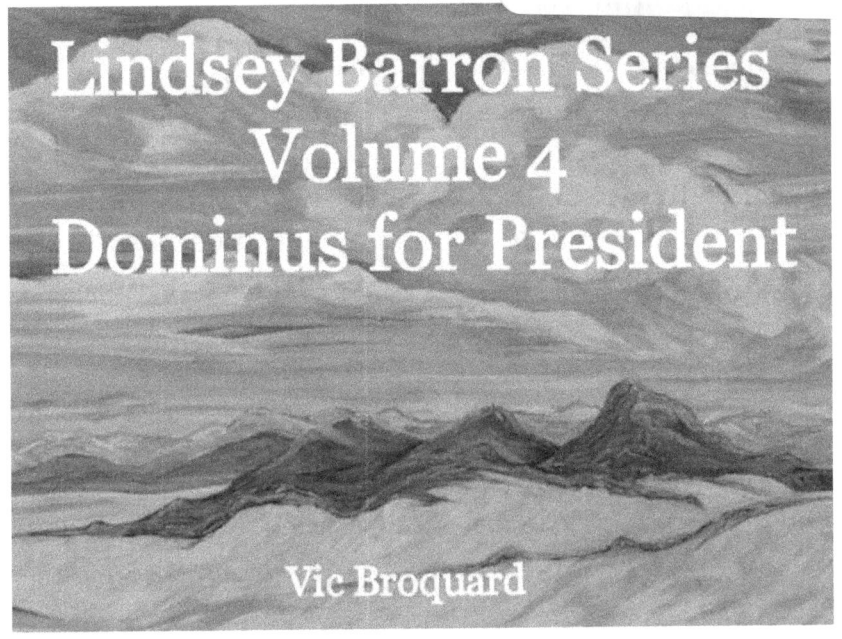

Lindsey Barron Series
Volume 4
Dominus for President

Vic Broquard

Lindsey Barron Series
Volume 4
Dominus for President

Vic Broquard

Artwork by Crooked Willow Studios.

Published by:
Broquard eBooks
http://Broquard-eBooks.com
author@Broquard-eBooks.com
103 Timberlane
East Peoria, IL 61611

For Morgan and L. Ron Hubbard

Table of Contents

Chapter 1—Home at Last

Controlled chaos, Lindsey thought to herself as her group watched their bus leave. It was June 1, they had finally returned to Lindsey's ranch home for summer vacation. Lindsey and her family's newly adopted sister, Ashley Stokes-Compton, stood by their large pile of duffle bags, containing their school book and clothes. Their good friends had also gotten off with them; Audrey Lemon and Pam Betts were now living with Lindsey here at her ranch, while the four Whitewater children, Tom, Jim, Amanda, and Fern, lived a few miles from here at their adjoining ranch. Sandy, Tom's fiancé, and her brother, Andy, lived in the small town of Arapahoe, just a few miles further south from the Whitewater ranch. All their bags had been deposited here on Lindsey's doorstep; a veritable mountain of bags lay at their feet.

Lena and Lloyd Compton, her parents, rushed to meet their returning daughters, Lindsey and Ashley, hugging both, as well as Audrey, for whom they were being unofficial foster parents. Running Bear Whitewater and Lucinda Morning Dove, or R. B. and Luci for short, hugged their four children, as well as Sandy who was about to become their daughter-in-law a few days from now. Tom and Sandy were getting married before heading off to college in Denver. Fred and Polly Betts were also present, since their family was now living here with Lena and Lloyd, and they hugged their daughter Pam.

Adding to the confusion were Amanda's Aunt Monane Tumble and Pam's Aunt Wilma Weltsi, both of whom had come to live with the Compton's for the summer. These two older women were part of the famous Rat Pack, who had been responsible for apprehending the evil wizard, Dominus Malefic, who had waged a campaign of terror across the world some fifteen or more years ago. He'd escaped and was back at it again, murdering and stealing once more. Additionally, two gangly, tall twins, Bill and Ted Weltsi, Wilma's older boys, were also present. Both stood behind the large group and watched the giant confusion before them. Lindsey had no idea

1

why the twins were here, however.

"Lena, you'd best get inside out of this hot sun," Wilma advised.

"Mom, you are so big!" exclaimed Lindsey. Indeed, Lena was nearly nine months pregnant.

Lean smiled, "Tell me something I don't already know!" Everyone chuckled, and the young wizards and witches hastily cast their Move Object spells, depositing their many bags either into their rooms or on the floor just inside the front entrance, where the teleport pad was located. R. B. had created a permanent teleport pad between his home and the Compton's home, and their children were constantly going back and forth between the two homes. This method ensured a safe, secure travel in these ever-growing dark times.

"Okay, kids, let's get your things over to our ranch and unpacked. You can come back here later on. Give Lindsey time to unpack as well," Luci ordered. Hastily, the Whitewaters obeyed, but it took three turns on the teleport pad for all them to exit with so many bags.

"Cya in a little while," Amanda called out as she suddenly disappeared from Lindsey's front room area, materializing in her own front room.

"Kids, let's sit in the living room a minute," Lena suggested. "I've got some things to tell you about right away. Polly's bringing us all a lemonade and sandwiches." Hastily, everyone found seats on the sofas and couches.

"Bill and Ted are going to be with us all summer and early fall," Lena explained. "With the baby due in two weeks, I'm not going to be able to work the ranch this summer. They've graciously volunteered to help out in the fields for me."

"Perfect for us," Ted broke in. "We plan to hit the Casino on Saturday nights. Bill and I have all sorts of schemes to win big. So don't look for us to be around those times." Both boys nodded, but Wilma rolled her eyes and shrugged her shoulders.

"Anyway," Lena continued, "what with having so many others around this summer, Lloyd and I decided to expand the house a bit. We've added a side wing for the twins, just off our bedroom wall. We turned it into a small apartment arrangement, including a tiny kitchen, so they can have their own independence."

"Yeh, we won't bother you folks. We promise to keep our stereo down at night," Ted added. Wilma glared at him, but said nothing.

"Yeh, but if trouble comes, you can count on us," Bill added. "Though it might take us a bit if we're out in the fields." This appeased Wilma, who ceased glaring at her boys. "Excuse us. We also just got here an hour ago, and we need to unpack too. Cya." The boys left out the front door.

Polly brought in their light lunch and the group rapidly gave an account of all that had gone on at Bradbury's School of Magic since their Christmas vacation. While Monane and Wilma had been actually involved in protecting the children when they won First Place at the National Track Meet in May, they were pretending to be Able Monument and Bill West, the Rat Pack members who were pretending to be themselves. Few knew their secret identity. Here at this house, Ashley, Lindsey, and Pam knew it. Amanda and R. B. also knew their secret identity. After all, R. B. was Monane's brother. Until now, both Wilma and Monane had to pretend to all these others that they only knew what they saw on TV or what they had learned from the girl's phone calls.

Lloyd, Fred, Lena, and Polly actually greatly desired to know all the details of that horrible affair. An hour later, their curiosity was finally satisfied. Lindsey now turned it around and wanted to know how her mother was doing. "When's the baby due mom? Have they given you a better estimate?"

"Two weeks, dear. If all goes well, you two should have a little brother. When I had my last checkup, the sonogram revealed it's going to be a boy. I wanted to be surprised, but I accidently saw the images. There's no doubt about it," she grinned.

"What do you girls think of the name Jonathon Samuel Compton?" Lloyd asked proud as can be. "After my father and yours, Lindsey," he added.

Lindsey beamed, Samuel Barron, or Rabnor actually, had been Lena's earlier husband, before he had been assassinated when Lindsey was five. Sam had also been a key member of the famous Rat Pack.

"Cool!" exclaimed Ashley, beating Lindsey.

"I love it!" Lindsey replied. Both proud parents smiled and relaxed. They had hoped their choice of a name would meet with their daughters' approval. "Well, I guess we better get unpacked and settled in, mom." All four girls headed to their rooms to begin their unpacking chores. Ashley and Lindsey shared the corner bedroom, while Pam and Audrey shared the end room, so that Audrey could grow her plants in the side walls. A spare bedroom separated them.

This new ranch house, designed and modeled after R. B.'s home, was forty by twenty on the outside. Its walls were three feet thick, earthen walls. Their roof sloped back and met the ground at the rear and now sod grew thick all over the roof. It was an energy efficient home, cool in the summers and warm in the winters, with nearly no heating or cooling needed. A set of solar panels on the roof generated electricity to run all their appliances. Their two water wells had been expanded to three. One provided the irrigation needed for the three one-mile in diameter crop circles. One provided water to the large barn, where their many horses and farm animals were kept. One provided their household water needs.

Inside, the space was magically enlarged to two hundred feet by one hundred feet. Here at the rear were five large bathrooms paralleling down a small hall opposite the six bedrooms. Besides the huge kitchen, pantry, and spacious dining room, they had three very large studies and two even larger workrooms. Up front, the enormous front room doubled as their dance floor, while the somewhat smaller family room held their entertainment center.

Lindsey finally finished unpacking, though Ashley, who had no arms, was only about half done. Pam stuck her head in their room, "I've worked out a schedule, Lindsey. The big wedding is only forty-eight hours away now! We have to get ready in a hurry, you know. Then, on the eleventh, we have to go to Denver to pick up our foreign exchange students. I've put in the fourteenth as being the baby's due date, though that can change at any moment. Gosh, I hope she doesn't have it at the same time as the wedding or when we have to go to Denver!" As usual, Pam was organizing things properly.

Lindsey didn't get the chance to reply. Just at that moment, a Message appeared in front of all four girls.

You have to come over real soon! Guess what dad's made us? A large pond! Now we can go swimming, fishing, and ice-skating in the wintertime! You have to see it! A.

The four girls stared at each other. "Wow! Super cool!" Pam exclaimed.

"Neat'o!" Audrey added.

"Come on! Let's go see it," Lindsey added. Ashley forgot about the rest of her unpacking, and the four dashed to the front room's teleport station. Lindsey called out, "Back in a bit! Gotta go see their new pond!" Lena, Polly, and Wilma all grinned.

"Told you," Polly whispered. She'd just won their wager over how long it would be before the four dashed over to the Whitewater's to see the pond. "Were we ever like that?" she asked jovially.

"Oh no!" exclaimed Wilma, pretending to be deadly serious. All three women cracked up and roared with laughter.

Amanda was waiting for them and hurried them outside to see. Tom, Jim, and Fern were standing on the small dock that stretched out some twenty-five feet over the clear, blue waters. Monane, Luci, and R. B. stood near the shore, watching the excitement of their children. "It's huge," Amanda explained, though she need not have. They could see that it was several hundred feet across.

What also got their attention was the second building that now stood next to R. B.'s sod home. "Dad's built a new underground home for others who may need a safe sanctuary later on. He decided we needed a better water supply, though I don't understand that part," Amanda explained.

As they passed by R. B., he said calmly, "My latest digging invention. I seemed to have gotten a bit carried away with using it." Luci chuckled. She had had to stop him playing with it; otherwise, he'd have made five ponds!

"Hi! This is so cool, darn shame that I have to leave in a few days," Tom lamented. He added quickly, "We're holding the wedding ceremony here by the dock. You can come by tomorrow and help us set up the huge tent, if you like."

"Way cool!" Pam exclaimed. "You must be a little upset that you are now moving away, though. I know I would be." She sympathized with Tom.

"Yes, no kidding. Ah well, Sandy and I are ready to move to the big city, Denver. Still, why couldn't he have made it six years ago? Nevertheless, Sandy and I can use it when we come back for visits. Next summer, we hope to spend all summer here, probably Christmas vacations too. We'll make good use of it, Pam. Guess you can really have fun this summer." She grinned.

"Oh, Lindsey, you've just got to see my new dress for the wedding!" Amanda suddenly remembered. All six girls were going to be Sandy's bridesmaids. However, only Fern had met her maid of honor, Adel Softwood, also an Arapaho. Jim felt left out as the six girls raced back into the house. He had hoped to snuggle a bit with Ashley. After all, in his opinion, this pond was the greatest invention of his dad's yet. He didn't see what the fuss over the sky blue dresses was all about anyway.

After many oh's and ah's, Lindsey realized that Lena probably had their dresses waiting for them to try on as well. Not long after admiring Fern and Amanda's new dresses, the four dashed back home.

Looking at her watch, Lena commented, "Right on time." Polly and Wilma chuckled.

"What do you mean, mom?" asked Lindsey, who had dashed into their living room, followed by Pam, Ashley, and Audrey. She'd overheard her mother's comment.

"I gave you about ten minutes before you all would come dashing back here wondering about your new bridesmaid's gowns. I was right," Lena answered with a teasing smirk. Lindsey faked a shocked surprise, but all four began giggling. "This way; they are in the workroom."

They dashed down the hall ahead of the three women. "Oh my! Beautiful! Incredible, perfect mom!" Lindsey declared as she saw the four gowns waiting for them. Each had matching sky blue heels as well, but only about an inch high.

The next two hours were spent with last minute adjustments. All four girls had grown significantly since Christmas, as expected by Polly and Lena, the two dressmakers.

As the dinner hour approached, Fred Betts took Pam aside for a long chat. "I'm taking the next two days off from work, Pam, so I can attend the wedding, providing some security for R. B. Will you please raise your right hand and repeat after me?" Pam had no idea what her father wanted, but did as he said. To her utter amazement, he swore her in as an official deputy in the Department of Magical Misuse!

"There, now it is official. You have complete access to our servers, Pam. No more needing to, well you know what I mean. No one can ever question your accesses of our databases. If you need to check on fingerprints, you have complete access to the UFDB." This was the Unified Fingerprint Data Base. Flabbergasted beyond works, Pam could only hug her father tightly.

At last, she whispered, "Thanks dad!" He smiled and held his daughter tightly.

Just after the large group finished their supper, the telephone rang. Lloyd took the call. Of course, everyone tried to listen in to figure out who was calling. Rarely did the phone ever ring around here. With everyone except Lena being a wizard or witch, no one needed to use the norm phone system. Lloyd motioned for Lena to come to the phone. He whispered to her, keeping the others in mystery. Lindsey strained to hear, but decided against casting an eavesdropping spell.

Lena nodded yes, and shortly thereafter, Lloyd hung up. "Well, who was it? What was that all about? More trouble?" asked Fred, worried that Dominus had caused yet more deaths.

"Sort of, Fred. Looks like we will have more company over the summer," Lloyd explained. "It was Doctor Blackburn."

"Oh no! Monique's not hurt again is she?" Pam gushed, suddenly terribly worried.

"No, no," Lloyd hastened to calm her fears. "Monique is having a bad reaction to living in their house. She took such a horrid beating there over the holidays. Psychological, he presumes. He has asked us if it would be all right for Monique to spend the summer here with us. It seems that they have been getting other threats while you kids were off at school, and Henry is worried about his family."

"We've asked them all to come down here and spend the summer with us," Lena added. "So for tonight, we'll put Monique and her sister, Ellie, up in the spare bedroom. Lloyd, you can fix up one of the study rooms for Lottie and Henry. I think that R. B. will put them up in his spare new home that he's just built, once the big wedding is over. I hope this is all right with Pam and the rest of you."

"Thank you! Thank you! Thank you!" exclaimed Pam, wild with anticipation of spending the whole summer with Monique. "Is she in pain? Do we need to go help her with things? I wondered how she would feel going back to her home to live. She was nearly killed in her own front room, you know."

"Henry has it under control, he said," Lloyd said sympathetically. "Perhaps you can lend a hand getting their rooms ready. I don't want Lena over-exerting herself or little Jonathon may arrive earlier than expected." He grinned at Lena, who tried to make light of his pronouncement, though Lindsey could see that she was very grateful for his insistence that she take it easy.

Around eight, the magical alarm sounded in a monotone voice, "Blackburn's are arriving." Pam dashed to the front door to meet them, followed by everyone else. They had all worked hard fixing up the nearly unused study behind their bedrooms for the parents. The spare bedroom required nothing; it was already to go. Lena was prepared for the arrival of their foreign exchange students in eleven days.

When Pam opened the door, a very subdued family that met her eyes. Monique was actually crying and did not have on her trademark cherry red lipstick. In fact, she wore none at all, highly unusual for this Red Hall girl, who was now entering her sixth year, as Pam was entering her fourth. "I'm so sorry," Monique wailed as she saw Pam. "I'm a complete basket case now." Pam just pulled her inside and forced her head onto Pam's shoulder, patting her gently on her back.

"It's okay, Monique. Come, I'll take to your room; it's right beside mine," Pam whispered and led her down the long hall.

Lottie and Ellie followed her inside. Doctor Blackburn lugged a number of suitcases inside. Lindsey saw that Ellie looked very frightened, and Lottie's face showed definite signs of stress. Henry had bags under his eyes.

"What's this world coming too?" Lottie said, as she shook hands with Lena. "I can't begin to thank you for putting us up, and you so close to your time. I'm so sorry that we are barging in on you like this."

"It's okay, really it is Lottie. Come on in. Lloyd and the others have fixed up one of our spare rooms for your bedroom. Ellie can sleep in our spare bedroom with her sister. It's no trouble at all," Lena answered her.

Lloyd and Fred helped Henry with the many suitcases. "So good of you to open your home to us. I really was at my wits end, you know. I can't tell you how much I appreciate this, Lloyd. Monique's face is still not fully healed. She's terribly sensitive to heat and cold. Today, we got another threatening phone call, and unfortunately, Monique answered it. She nearly had a psychotic break afterwards. Even Ellie is scared. Lottie has fielded dozens of threatening calls during the spring. I know it has upset her too, but she's said nothing about it."

Fred replied, "There just are not enough Security Forces to provide all the protection that we need. I'm so sorry, Henry. I did my best to get more into your hospital, but there's just none to be had any more. I've put in a request to station some from other states out here in Colorado, but no luck with getting it approved yet. I'll keep trying, Henry."

"Thanks, Fred. At least, Greeley Hospital is secure now. That's something. Really, the whole staff there is most appreciative of that!" Fred smiled.

Since only Monique had been here before, Lena and Lloyd took the three others on a grand tour of their home. All three were most impressed with the spaciousness and comforts of this home. Just as they finished their tour, R. B. and Luci appeared in the front room. They had insisted the children remain home, under the watchful eyes of Monane. They discussed the situation and R. B. said, "Our guest rooms will be ready for you on the fifth, after the many wedding guests have left. Early morning tomorrow, you can get a tour before the hectic wedding's last minute preparations get underway." Both thanked him for everything.

Meanwhile, in Monique's new bedroom, Pam had her sit down on the bed, and she sat beside her dear friend, still holding her in her arms. "Tell me about it," Pam asked softly.

Sometimes crying, sometimes shaking like a leaf in a summer's breeze, Monique told her about how fearful she was just being in her own home. "Then I heard that nasty man's voice on the phone, threatening me and Ellie. I don't know what happened, Pam. I just broke down. I snapped, somehow. I'm so scared—terrified, really, like the spell you learned this past year. I, I can't bear to live there anymore! I'm a total basket case!" She began sobbing once more. Pam continued to hold her tightly, but said nothing. What could she say anyway?

When she calmed down, Pam said, "You are safe here, Monique. No one's going to hurt you while you are here." Monique finally stopped shaking, realizing Pam spoke the truth. Here, she felt safe. At last, she hugged Pam. Just then, Ellie knocked and joined them.

Monique calmed down and said, "Sis, we need to unpack a bit and take a bath before we turn in," Monique advised her sister. "We should be safe here."

"Pam, I'm scared too; so is mom," Ellie ventured. "I only know Grade 1 spells. I can't even protect myself."

"Hey, don't make less of yourself, Ellie," Pam countered. "Look, Lindsey only knew Grade 1 spells when she had to face Dominus and Rubius in that cabin. Remember, they even had her mouth sewn shut and her hands cut off. So don't ever think that you can't do anything because you only know Grade 1 spells!" Ellie brightened up considerably, even managing a fleeting smile. "I'll let you two unpack and take a bath. I ought to take one too. We've five bathrooms on this end and one way up front."

By ten that night, everyone had retired for the night. Monique and Ellie fell into a deep sleep almost at once. Pam stared at her ceiling for a time, worrying about Monique, before she too fell asleep.

Ashley finally had time to relax. Until now, she had so little private time for herself. As she lay there listening to the steady breathing of her sleeping sister, Ashley's emotional troubles finally boiled over. Yes, she had much to ponder. Tom and Sandy would be getting married in two days; her mother would be having a baby any day now, and in ten days, she would be going to Denver to meet her foreign exchange students.

Those were not her worries at all. Here she was sleeping in her own bed, but now she was somehow vastly different from when she had first come here last summer. Last fall, she thought nothing about having no arms. She was antagonistic and easily fought back against any conceived insult towards herself. At that time, she had completely accepted herself as she was. Now, something had changed. She was sitting on grief that she did not know existed. She now wanted arms; she wanted to be like everyone else, and she didn't want to be so different, so helpless, and so dependent on others. Worse, she now thought of herself as a worthless cripple, something that she had never done before. It didn't matter in the slightest to her that others thought very highly of her. She knew the only thing that did matter was her own opinion of herself.

Then, there was Jim. Her heart continued to skip a beat every time she saw him. Though he doted on her, she couldn't imagine why he did so. If she were him, she certainly would be completely revolted by her sight. Ashley knew that she was a complete mess, but while at school, what with all the schoolwork and so many roommates, she had no private time. Now, it swelled to the forefront, threatening to overwhelm her completely. She longed to talk to her new mother about it, but Lena was going to have a baby. She'd have little time for Ashley. The mere thought of the infant brought on more surges of helplessness in her mind. How could she do anything to help with a baby? She had no arms and now in her mind, that was everything.

Tears began flowing down her face. At last, afraid that she might wake up Lindsey, she got up and stole out of their bedroom on her tiptoes. She just couldn't face Lindsey right now. What could she possibly say to her? How could she possibly explain what she was feeling? The house was very quiet. Ashley silently walked down to the kitchen, tears still flowing down her cheeks. She felt around for her tall stool and sat down, not even attempting to cast her Light spell. She thought of getting a glass of milk from the fridge, but decided against it. She could not lift the pitcher and would have to get the glass with her feet and open the door with her foot. Just now, the thought of using a Levitate spell and her feet only brought on more tears.

A bit later, she heard soft footsteps coming and tried in vain to halt her tears, hoping that whoever was coming might not see her. Lena turned on the dim nightlight. "Oh, I see you can't sleep either. Me, it seems I have to go pee every forty-five minutes. I just get comfortable, and I have to go. Ah well, only a few more days of this, and it'll be over. Dear, what's the matter?" She spied the wet cheeks. Ashley said nothing; she couldn't speak. If she tried, it would all come out. She valiantly tried to hold it all inside of herself.

"There, there, I suspected something was wrong, dear, when I saw you get off of the bus today. So much was going on then; I couldn't ask you about it. Besides, it should just be the two of us talking. Come on. Let's go sit in the front room. No one will hear us, just you and me. I do need to sit down. Jonathon is quite heavy now." Ashley managed a slight smile and followed Lena into the front room, where she turned on a nightlight only, just enough so each could see the other. Lena had her sit down on the sofa and promptly sat beside her, cradling her in her arms. She kissed her daughter on her head softly and said, "Tell me all about it, please."

Ashley was short, though she had grown three inches since Christmas. Thin and wiry, she had the looks of a teen fashion model, with hazel eyes and short, light brown hair that she had allowed to grow this past term. Soft natural curls fell to her shoulders. Lena, in contrast, had just turned forty. She had blue eyes and long brown hair, tied back in a ponytail usually. Her frame was well muscled, having worked her ranch all her adult life. As she listened to her new daughter, she rubbed her hands slowly over the teen's back, providing the motherly support that Ashley had never had.

"Something's happened to me. I'm all screwed up. I mean I'm so different now than I was this time last year. Like I used to be perfectly happy with myself, the way I am, and nothing can be done about it anyway. I just forced myself to find alternate ways to do things with my feet. That's all gone now. I don't know how or why, but it is! I feel like a hopeless cripple, mom. I just want to be normal, like all the other kids. I know I can't be but I can't help it any more. I can't hide it from myself. I don't want to be like me. I want to have arms just like everyone else!"

"Well, I don't think that anyone on earth *wants* to be like you are, without arms, Ashley. Something has happened to you, hasn't it? I know everyone thinks very highly of you, and you've earned the total respect of so many people in so many places I can't name them all just now. Yet, that isn't the problem, is it, dear? You've lost your own self-respect, haven't you?"

Ashley stopped sobbing and looked up at her mother. "You, you understand! I have. I mean I've lost count of the number of times others have said that to me—you know, like 'Ashley, you are the greatest,' but I don't care about what they think anymore. I care about myself, and I don't like myself anymore. I can't *do* anything. How am I ever going to *hold* my little brother? I mean, Lindsey and I worked on changing her doll's diapers. I can do that. But I want to hold him, *hug* him. I want to hold Jim too," she admitted. Lena smiled, realizing that there was a lot more to all this.

"When did you first notice that you began to feel this way—that you had to have arms to be happy with yourself?" Lena asked. "I find that it is helpful to find when one first had such ideas, such notions."

"Well, I had it on the bus coming home today. I imagined you had Jonathon, and I couldn't even hold him."

"Good, but is this the first time you had these feelings about yourself?"

"No, I felt like this at the Nationals when the bombs went off. Even though I was morphed into Cho Lin and had arms, I couldn't do anything. I just stared at the horrid scene. Hank had to teleport us home. I couldn't do anything at all.

"I see. That was an awful time for sure, dear, but is this the first time you felt like this?"

"Well, no. When we all went off to rescue Alister—when he was tied to the rock in the sea—we all landed on these huge boulders. I could barely stand up. Jim had to hold me to keep me from falling! Then, we got attacked, and I had an awful time without arms. I kept nearly falling off the boulder into the sea. I'm nothing but a horrible liability to others, mom."

"Yes, I can see how that must have been, but is this the very first time that you had these feelings of inadequacy?"

Ashley thought for a moment. "No, no, when we were kidnaped by Dominus and taken into that rundown house. He cut off Lindsey's arms, blinded her, made Pam into an idiot. I could only stand there and vomit! I was so utterly helpless. They all said so too—the Death Stalkers and Dominus. They thought I was a pitiful thing, completely useless and pathetic. I did too. I wanted to help them somehow, someway, but I couldn't even help either of them to go pee! I couldn't get their panties down, mom. And I couldn't even help Lindsey walk to the bathroom when she was blinded! See, I'm so utterly useless!"

"Yes, that must have been absolutely horrid for you, Ashley, just awful, unable to even do the simplest thing for Lindsey when she desperately needed it. I can understand you fully. Yet, is this the earliest time that you had these feelings, dear?" Lena continued to probe. She was certainly getting an earful.

Ashley thought back on the last year. Suddenly, she brightened up, "No! No, the first time was back at the beginning of the fall term, right after Dominus began running for President. We were learning the Morph Oneself into Another spell! That's when it started. I remember now. I changed into Lindsey! There I was looking just like her, and I had arms!"

"Ah, I see. What happened there?" Lena asked her daughter, relieved that she had cheered up considerably.

"God! I've never used that spell, only casting it to get a

pass on Spell Casting! I stood there and had arms, real arms. I could feel things; they were real! Yet, I didn't know what to *do* with them! I couldn't cast any spells. I didn't know how to hold a wand in my hand or how to use them. I stood there like a total *idiot*. I felt so strange, you know. Here I finally had arms, but found I had no idea how actually to use them. I mean I've obviously seen everyone else using their arms, but I never had them and still don't know how to use them. This sounds crazy, doesn't it, mom."

"Not at all, dear. Suddenly, you find you have the arms that you've never had as long as you can remember. That must have been quite a shock. It's kind of like riding horses. I can relate to that. I mean you've seen others riding for years and years, but you've never even touched a horse. Then all at once, you find yourself sitting on a horse, and you have no idea what to do. It boils down to a simple matter of education, dear, that's all," Lena replied.

She then added, "I have an idea. Why don't you do your spell thing and experiment with using arms? See if that's what you really want, rather get used to having them. I don't know anything about this magic stuff. In the world that I know, honestly, there is no way to get new arms, real ones, I mean. Some do have prosthetic limbs, but I don't know anything about that either and that's probably not what you would want anyway. I will check with the others as see if there is anything in the magical world that could get you real arms. How's that? We both will do some research."

"Cool, mom. I feel so much better now. I've not told anyone else about how I have been feeling though. The trouble with that spell is that I take on the appearance of the other person. If I morphed into Lindsey or Pam, it would just be *too* embarrassing."

"Well, why not change into one of the other girls from your school, one who is not here with us?" Ashley grinned; she'd not thought of that. Greatly relieved, she headed back to bed.

"I feel so silly, so stupid," Monique explained over the breakfast table. She still wore no makeup; her face was still just too sensitive. Monique, now seventeen, was a gorgeous blonde, her straight hair falling to her shoulders. She had deep blue eyes and a well-formed body, all the right curves in the right places. Yes, she was a knockout. "I ought to have gotten control of myself."

"I don't think you were being silly or stupid," Pam came to her defense immediately, flashing a smile, which prominently displayed the wide gap between her two overly large front teeth. Pam was a rather homily young girl, with short black hair and an oval face, which only exacerbated her appearance. Pam, normally very shy and retiring, openly defended her best friend. "After all, you were nearly killed in your own front room, and now others are calling you up threatening your life again. There's nothing silly about that!"

"I agree with her, Monique," Lindsey added, tossing her long brown hair back over her ear. It had threatened to fall into her bowl of cereal. "We'd all rather you and your family be safe and secure than have to go to the hospital again or worse."

"They are right. I can feel it," Audrey added her opinion. She was an average looking brunette, short and curly, but with sad looking blue eyes. However, she had an uncanny carving ability, bringing out incredible animals from what appeared to be ordinary blocks of wood.

"Well, I do need to get to the hospital," Henry spoke up. "Lottie, why don't you head to our house and pack up more things that we will need and bring them here. Let the girls do all the unpacking and arranging here on this end. I know that the rest of you are going to have your hands full with all the advance preparations for Tom and Sandy's wedding tomorrow." Everyone agreed, and the two teleported back to Greeley.

Fred and Lloyd went over to the Whitewater ranch to help set up the heavy tent and arrange the heavier items. The kids promised to join them after they finished the many chores around the ranch. Secretly, Lloyd was glad to be relieved of those duties, if only for the summer.

As Ashley was heading outside to see if there was anything she could do to help, Lena said, "Oh, nearly forgot. Ashley, we've invited your grandparents to come for the wedding. We thought that they would really love to see you all dolled up in your new fancy dress." That brought a big smile to the young girl. "Should be here around suppertime."

During the long afternoon, the girls helped set up chairs and tables for the wedding. They were expecting around fifty guests all told. The chapel area had to be fancied up, including the arrangement of the flowers. A reception would be held immediately afterwards. Polly, Lena, and Luci had already baked a dozen pies, while R. B. had laid in a large stock of drinks and ice cream. This afternoon, Polly baked the wedding cake, while Lena saw to its decoration. The kids were kept busy carrying out plates, silverware, cups, and tablecloths. By dinnertime, everyone was quite pooped, but all was in readiness for the big day tomorrow. In the morning, last minute arrangements would be needed, but the real work was done.

Supper at the Compton's was purposely going to be late tonight, so that Ashley's grandparents, Samson and Bertha, could join them, along with Henry, whose shift at the hospital was not over until six. Samson and Bertha arrived about a half hour before dinner. He was now sixty-seven, with short white and very thinning hair, a protruding belly. He'd shaved off his moustache, however. Bertha, a year younger, also had short white hair and a heavily wrinkled face, but Ashley noticed right away that her arthritic hands were giving her more trouble than they had over the Christmas holidays.

She had them get comfortable in the large living room, all three sitting on the new couch. However, Pam, Audrey, Lindsey, Ellie, and Monique were also chatting with them as well, having been run out of the kitchen for snitching pieces of the turkey off the huge platter. "Dear, we were going through all your dad's old things, you know, cleaning house," Samson explained. "We came across this journal of your fathers. We don't understand much of it, but we figured you might like to browse through it. Bertha sorted out hundreds of old photos of Joshua and made you this album of memories, well, our memories anyway."

"Fantastic! Thank you. I have so very few pictures of mom and dad," Ashley gushed her enthusiasm. Pam and

Monique took the journal and began leafing through it, while the others crowed around Ashley, Lindsey flipping the pages, as Bertha gave a running commentary on the photos. The half hour passed rapidly.

The monotonous voice announced, "Doctor Henry Blackburn is arriving." Monique and Ellie went to the front door to welcome their dad home at last. "Hi kids, all settled in now?" he asked, smelling of hospital detergents, as he always did when he finally came home each night.

Ellie answered before Monique could, "Oh yes. Mom's brought all my stuff and Moni's too. We are all set. We have your room fixed up pretty good too, dad. Come on, and I'll show you." She tugged on his arm.

"Time for that later," Lena called out, "Dinner's ready." She also introduced Ashley's grandparents to Henry, as they all headed for the huge dining room. After a very filling supper, Lena ordered Ashley to take her grandparents into the living room and tell them all about her school year. Lena knew that both were keenly interested in hearing about Ashley's adventures. They'd seen her win First Place at the National Track Meet and had been petrified watching the explosion and aftermath. Lena's call telling them that Ashley was unharmed greatly relieved them. Those three disappeared into the spacious living room.

While the adults relaxed with tea and coffee, the kids began their clean up duties. Tonight, Lindsey took Ashley's place on the tall stool and did the Clean spells, while the others cleared the table and put the clean dishes away. Monique made countless trips back and forth and began overhearing Lena's conversation with her dad.

"Henry, I admit that I know nothing about the world of magic, but it's about Ashley. She really ought to have arms. I'm afraid that she's finally reached that point where she has admitted really wanting them and needing them. I know that Lindsey hands were somehow regrown, an incredible miracle, way beyond my comprehension, but is there anything that can be done for Ashley?"

"We work with potions, Lena. For them to work their miracles, something must remain of the lost appendage.

Naturally, I read over Doctor Caterwall's report in the Medical Journal of Colorado, in which he described what he had done. It seems that on the surface, Lindsey had no hands, but in fact, underneath the skin, she had tiny formations of her hands. I believe that he said they were about an eighth of an inch in size. More like a tiny bump. Thus, he was able to get the potions to work their magic. They can also work if someone has just suffered an amputation, as in the second case with her," he explained as simply as he could.

"I admit I've taken an interest in Ashley. I took the liberty of obtaining a copy of her medical records from Chicago General last December. Based on those records, when she was two and a half, the stumps had not healed properly, and the doctor was forced to remove them completely, ball and all, though her lymph nodes remain intact. I examined the after-surgery x-rays and can vouch for her situation. I'm afraid our potions would most likely do nothing for her, since nothing at all remains of either arm. I'm sorry, Lena. Magical medicine also has its limitations too." He seemed sincerely sad about it as well.

"Thanks, Henry. I would be shirking my duties as her mother if I didn't explore all avenues. She's now beginning to really feel the trauma and hardship of a life without them," Lena explained.

Monique relayed what Lena had said about Ashley to the others and what her father's reply had been. "So that's what has been bothering Ashley all these months!" Lindsey exclaimed. "I knew something was very wrong. I saw that she had been crying all night once. Her pillow was wet as we got up, and her eyes were red."

"When she came, she was so feisty, so, well you know what I mean," Pam said. "Maybe she had all of that hurt and sense of loss deeply hidden all these years, buried and dormant. After all, she's been bounced around from foster home to foster home, with no real love in her life."

"She's had to be fiercely independent just like I have been," Audrey added. "Until now, I've always had to look out for me, because no one else was. She probably never had the luxury of just relaxing and enjoying life. I've never been as happy as I am here, Lindsey. You all are just the greatest!"

"Psychological and physical trauma," Monique added. "She's undoubtedly suffered heavily in both areas." Suddenly, her face flushed. "Kind of like I have," she admitted. "We must do something to help her. I know what dad is saying about healing potions. I already knew that from potion making class. Say, I remember something from one of my theory classes. Pam, I think that there is some other way to re-grow lost limbs. We've got to find it."

"Well, the dishes are done," Pam replied. "Let's duck into my room and see what we can find." The two headed towards Pam's room, but Monique stopped at her new room instead.

"Here are all my notes. I used to have them arranged nicely, but that was before the hasty move. Look for Alteration Theory III. It has to be here somewhere," Monique exclaimed, going through stacks of notebooks. Pam set Ashley's father's journal down and began searching through another stack.

"Is this it?" Pam asked. It was. Monique began leafing through the pages of her notebook. Pam marveled at Monique's perfectly formed letters; she had an eloquent handwriting indeed.

"Ah here it is, Professor Arthur Thornby mentioned this only once in passing. I think in answer to someone's question. Quote: Another way to heal is by use of a Ring of Regeneration, which also regrows lost appendages. However, such rings are extremely rare and costly. It is a Grade 9 spell that is in operation, and I don't know of any living wizard or witch who can cast the spell. Unquote. That's it; we need a Ring of Regeneration for Ashley," Monique proudly stated.

Pam raced to her room and brought her computer back. Both girls began typing away, searching for information on said rings. Monique went in search of how said rings operated, while Pam looked for their availability. "Gosh, MagAmazon lists only one such ring! Guess what they want for it?" Pam said.

"Fifty thousand?" Monique guessed.

"Try ten times that! Five hundred thousand dollars! Incredible," Pam replied. Monique's eyes rolled.

"What's five hundred thousand dollars?" the voice of Aunt Wilma broke in on the two. She had just passed their door and was intrigued by such a heady sum.

"Hi, we were looking for ways to get Ashley's arms re-grown. Doctor Blackburn says that potions won't work, since she has nothing of them left, and it was so long ago that she lost them. Monique has just found that Professor Arthur mentioned that a Ring of Regeneration would re-grow lost limbs. I found one so far, on MagAmazon, but they want five hundred thousand dollars for it."

"Yes, they are very rare, Pam," her aunt replied. "A Grade 9 spell, if I remember right."

"Yes, I looked that up," Monique assured her.

"I had forgotten all about that, but now that you have reminded me, I seem to recall that Sam once mentioned that he was going to acquire one for us as a safety measure, back in the days when we were so active. I wonder where Lindsey is at?" Aunt Wilma very nearly spilled the beans on her secret identity to Monique. She hastily wandered off looking for Lindsey.

"What's she mean?" asked Monique, slightly confused.

"She knew Sam Rabnor when they were at Bradbury's ages ago, at least a decade ago. I'm surprised she even remembers it. Ah well, I guess we should keep our eyes open for such a ring, but at a lower cost."

"True, that is a whole lot of money for one ring," Monique agreed. The amount was beyond anything she could imagine.

"Say, let's look at this journal some more. It's incredibly interesting, but I haven't deciphered much of it yet. I think it is in some kind of code," Pam ventured. The two began pouring over the handwritten pages again.

"Ah, there you are," Fred Betts interrupted them. "I'm going to bed early tonight. I'm on security duty at the wedding tomorrow. You two should get some sleep as well."

"Say dad, we've been looking at this journal that belonged to Ashley's dad, Joshua Stokes. We think a lot of it is in some kind of code, but do you have any idea what this means? It's at the top of over half of the pages. ORD442."

21

Fred, who was half-asleep, suddenly perked up. "Let me see that!" Pam handed it to him. "Darn, it must be. Pam, don't let this out of your sight! That is a secret code used by the Department of Security! Here, let me at your computer." Pam got out of the way. However, both girls looked over his shoulders as he typed away. Suddenly, they saw the home page appear for the Denver Department of Security. He typed in Betts and then entered his invisible password, but Pam already knew what it was, "Pamela." She smiled; her father had no idea how to make a secure password.

She didn't expect to see the page that he next brought up, though. Covert Agent Code Prefixes. He scrolled down the page. "There, Pam, ORD is the prefix of the Chicago based agents. What you have there is a Chicago Department of Security Covert Agent Identifier. Now, let's see what that leads us to, shall we?" Fred was quite excited, forgetting entirely about sleeping.

Soon the entrance page for the Chicago Department of Security appeared, a moment later Fred entered the site and did a look up on that id number. He didn't expect the screen that next appeared! It read: Top Security Clearance Level 9 Required—enter login. "Whoa, this is highly unusual! Level 9 just to view these records? What is going on here?" He re-entered his clearance codes. Pam assumed that her dad must have at least Level 9. After all, he had just been appointed head of the entire High Plains Department of Magical Misuse; she filed this bit of useful information.

Up came the page with a picture of Joshua Stokes. "That's him, dad. Ashley has a photo of him in her locket that Bertha gave her." Three sets of eyes read the page. "Deep Undercover Agent Joshua Stokes. Current assignment: Investigation of the Simon Mac Fluide Enterprises. Code A1256 reported."

"What's that mean, dad?" Pam asked.

"Don't know," Fred replied, opening another window and doing a search on his own website for that code. "Ah, Industrial Irregularities that may bring federal criminal charges. It looks like Joshua was a deep undercover agent for the Chicago Department of Security. Look at the rest of it. No final report was ever given by Joshua. It reports the details of his death. See, accidental death. Steel cables broke sending a load of I-beams flying off the semi into his car, just as Ashley says. It shows a picture of the truck driver, John Bell. Accidental Death is listed as the termination cause. Investigation is still pending."

Pam's face turned white. "Dad, that face! I've seen it before! Move over!" Fred, taken by surprise, traded places with his daughter, watching her open a new browser window and hastily entering her new triple secure server in his computer lab. He smiled, knowing that he'd really given her a highly useful Christmas present with that server. Pam pulled up her files on known Death Stalkers and began scrolling the many pictures she had been slowly assembling from every known source that she had come across in her browsing.

"There, dad! I knew I'd seen those eyes before. That truck driver isn't John Bell! It's Fenwick Arnold, one of the Death Stalkers who was never apprehended when Dominus was captured fifteen years ago!"

"I bet that was not an accident at all!" Monique finally spoke what she had been feeling all along.

Fred looked at her and his eyes opened wide. "I'll bet anything you are one hundred percent right about that! Ashley's folks were murdered, a staged accident. Poor thing lost her arms there as well. I guess when they made that log entry so long ago, no one recognized Fenwick. I can see how they could reach the conclusion of accidental death. Perhaps you two should show this to Ashley and her grandparents." Pam started to dash off to find them and then returned, a silly look on her face. Smiling, her father handed her the computer. "Take this with you," he teased.

"Ashley! Look what your dad's journal has led us to find! Dad's been helping me. See this code here at the top of many pages? It's his Chicago Department of Security Covert Agent Identifier! Your dad was a deep undercover agent! And it wasn't an accident either! Here, look at the police report and take a good look at the face of the man, who was driving the semi!" Pam barely could stand giving Ashley and her grandparents time to look at the face, before switching windows.

"Now look at this face," she switched to her image. "That's Fenwick Arnold, one of the Death Stalkers who was never apprehended! Your mom and dad were murdered by a Death Stalker! That was no traffic accident! He was doing an undercover investigation of the Simon Mac Fluide Enterprises just before he was murdered! I bet this journal will tell us loads of secret information that your dad uncovered!"

Ashley's face went white. "You mean. . . I've no arms because of . . . Mom and dad were murdered. . ."

"Well, we never knew he was a secret agent, did we Bertha?" Samson broke in. He added, "Well, this makes everything make more sense. We never understood how a wizard could possibly have been in such a car accident, what with all the spells we know. Why, it seemed utterly impossible."

Bertha began crying, "Now it makes sense. Joshua was going after very evil men and was killed for it. I know it hurts, but I feel so much better about it now. Joshua was such a good boy." She wiped her nose on her handkerchief.

By now, everyone in the household had heard the news, crowding around Pam's computer to see the images and reports. "Oh Ashley!" Lindsey exclaimed and hugged her sister tightly. They shared an even tighter bond now. Death Stalkers had killed both their fathers, though Ashley bore an even heavier burden from that slaying.

The group chatted over this amazing and startling discovery for a while, before Fred yawned heavily. "We'd better get to bed, gang. Big day tomorrow." Reluctantly, everyone agreed. As they all began heading for their rooms, Wilma flashed Ashley and Lindsey a signal to stay.

When the three were finally alone, Wilma said softly, "Ashley, we have some news for you. Monique and Pam discovered another way that can be used to give you back your arms. It's a rare Ring of Regeneration, which Monique and I believe will do the trick. Pam found one on the Net for around two hundred thousand dollars. The spell it holds is a Grade 9 spell." Ashley's face went from one of hopefulness to total downcast. She had ten thousand dollars from her mother, barely five percent of what was needed.

"However, Sam Barron acquired a Ring of Regeneration, though Monane and I didn't know he had actually gotten it. He spoke of trying to find one on several occasions. Lindsey and I checked her list of items that Sam left her in the Secure Vault in Denver. Good old Sam, he must have found one. Lindsey has just such a ring, Ashley!"

Ashley's face lit up, her eyes radiated joy. "Wow! Lindsey!" She really didn't know what to say or how to respond.

Wilma did. "Ashley, this is a very, very heavy decision you must face. You have grown up without arms, learning alternative ways to do things. If you decide to regenerate your arms right now, you will have an awful lot of re-learning to do very quickly. Lena told me a little bit about how terribly hard a time you had when you used the Morph spell and became Lindsey and Cho Lin who have arms. Indeed, you will have a very rough time trying to re-learn all your spell casting skills, to say nothing of everything else. It may take you many months to get up to the skill level you have right now with your feet. I'm not sure that you would be fully ready by the time you need to go back to school. Please consider this decision carefully. When and if you decide to use this ring, Monane and I will take Lindsey to retrieve the ring from her Secure Vault. As long as we have the ring, Ashley, we can regenerate your arms at any time for you. I would advise that you plan to allow a good deal of time to get adjusted to life with arms, however. I just want you to be very sure that this is something that you really want."

"I understand, Wilma. I have to confess something to both of you. I've been, well, just plain bullheaded and stupid. Here I have been learning all these incredible magical spells and have been very unwilling to use any of them to help me do the normal things in life. I mean, I can actually cast Levitate as Lindsey does, silently and without my wand. Yet, I still let her cast her spell on my food tray. I could Morph and get some hands to help me dress or any number of other things, but I haven't. I've been really stupid about it all. I've had this crazy notion that my spells are only to be used to attack the enemy, never to just help me do things that others normally do in life. You can kick my butt if you like. I've been an idiot about it."

Both smiled along with Ashley, as she sheepishly revealed what Lindsey had suspected all along. She continued, "I really do see what you mean about needing time to learn and adapt to having arms and hands, Wilma. I've Morphed into Lindsey and Cho Lin. There I was with hands and continued to try to pick up Cho Lin's wand for her with my feet! I've never wanted to admit this, but if I did suddenly have arms and hands, I really don't know how to use them. That sounds silly, doesn't it?"

"No, dear child, it most certainly does not. I think we all agree if you want your arms back, you should have them. Only the timing of their regeneration remains the main issue. I certainly would not want you to return to Bradbury's and not be able to continue with your fourth year courses."

Lindsey added, "God, no one would want to sit through Professor Janice's Grade 0 and 1 spell casting class again!" Ashley and Lindsey both giggled.

"Yeh, I need enough time to learn. How long would I need, do you suppose?" Ashley asked the most important question that she needed to have answered. Unfortunately, neither Wilma nor Ashley had an answer.

"Best thing I can think of, Ashley, is why not try Morphing into someone with arms and then experimenting for yourself? That way, you might get a real feel for how long it might take you to learn another way of doing everything that you do," Wilma advised her.

"I should, Wilma. Honestly, that's the only way I am really going to know if I really want them back and how awful of a time I will have adjusting to them. I do so darn many things you know. I'd have to relearn how to shoot pool, even!" With that decided, the three then headed for bed themselves. For the first time in months, Ashley slept soundly and totally at peace with herself. She could have arms and hands. She could be "normal." But did she really and truly want that? How long would it take? Would she be forced to give up something in return, like her terrific skill in pool?

Chapter 2—The Wedding

"Sure glad that we have six bathrooms," Lloyd commented to Fred. He, Fred Betts, Samson Stokes, and Henry Blackburn sat in the family room watching the latest MagNews, sipping their morning coffee. The other men chuckled. With so many females in the house, lines were still forming.

"Sure don't know why they need to spend so much time in there," Henry replied. "Lottie convinced me to add a second bathroom when we had Monique. Glad I did; sometimes I can't get in there."

Fred commented, "We should have a law that there has to be one restroom per female in the household." All three chuckled again.

Henry added, "Plus one for us." They laughed again. It was now ten in the morning and still the women were going in and out of the restrooms, getting ready for the big day.

Around eleven, Lena came out and announced, "Gentlemen, I present your daughters and granddaughter." She had a big grin on her face, knowing how stunning the four bridesmaids looked. Ashley, Lindsey, Pam, and Audrey walked out wearing identical sky blue long dresses with matching shoes. Monique and Ellie, wearing their red lipstick followed behind, along with Polly, Lottie, Bertha, and Aunt Wilma.

Many, many compliments flew in rapid succession. "Ashley, Lindsey, you both look just gorgeous!" Lloyd exclaimed, rather surprised just how grown up and attractive his two looked today. Bertha and Samson had tears in their eyes. Their Ashley looked stunning. Both were incredibly proud of their granddaughter.

A long round of picture taking followed. Bertha wanted several good photos of Ashley and then the other girls. Even Fred and Lloyd wanted some as well. With that handled, everyone grabbed a quick snack, before heading over to the Whitewater ranch.

"Amanda, you look fabulous," Lindsey commented. No sooner had they arrived than Luci escorted the four girls into

Amanda's room, where Amanda, Fern, and the maid of honor, Adel Softwood, were making last minute adjustments to Sandy's long white wedding dress.

Sandy was, of course, getting nervous, but looked very happy and radiant. The eight girls spent the remaining time adjusting and readjusting their appearance and dresses. Luci, issuing orders to the others helping, stood before their door, keeping others out of Amanda's room.

"Looks like we can expect well over a hundred today. It's grown a little," R. B. commented to Fred. "Let me introduce you to the ten tribal rangers who will also be providing our security today." Not long after that, the eleven took up their stations around the ranch area. Fred positioned himself at the rear of the tent behind all the chairs. While the others fanned out surrounding the perimeter, he would act as the last resort, the one closest to the gathering. He hoped sincerely that no trouble would spoil the couple's wedding.

Meanwhile, in Tom's room, the fellows were killing time, playing video games. Fischer Roan, Tom's best man, challenged Jim to a shooter game. Andy looked on, as did four of Tom's cousins who filled out the remainder of the groomsmen. All wore blue tuxedos, though at this time, they were a bit disheveled. "Got my ring?" Tom asked Fischer for the sixth time.

"Yeh, in my pocket. Stop fretting," he called out, annoyed that this distraction allowed Jim to score another point over his on-screen character.

At 12:30, Audrey suddenly felt really badly. She looked over at Ashley, who was sitting on Amanda's bed watching Adel fiddling with Sandy's dress. "We shouldn't be here!" Audrey whispered. Wham! A premonition hit Ashley hard. She shrieked from the unexpected and shocking vision. Everyone stared at the two girls.

"A bomb is going to fall on us!" Ashley wailed.

"We need to get out of here!" Audrey added. "I can feel it's not right for us to be here."

Amanda knew better than to doubt either girl. She waved her wand and sent R. B. a Message. Pam waved hers, sending her dad a similar Message. Lindsey sent one to

Monane and to Wilma, then her dad as well. Seconds later, Fred, R. B., Monane, Wilma, and Lloyd came rushing into Amanda's room. "Let me, R. B.," Monane insisted.

She went and sat down beside Ashley, whose face was stark white, still slightly in shock from her surprise vision. "Ashley, what have you seen? Can you describe what you saw?" The overly crowded room was silent! Everyone just had to hear what the young girl would say.

"A bomb is dropping on us. We are out there doing the ceremony, and the bomb falls on us. It's horrible! We are all dead, blown to bits." She started crying. Lindsey scooted over to her side and hugged her, supporting her. Monane had heard enough, and the adults left immediately.

On their way out, R. B. ordered, "You all stay inside here until further notice!"

With so many people milling around awaiting the start of the wedding, the five headed into R. B.'s workshop. "What are we going to do?" asked Monane.

Grim faced, Fred replied, "Well, it makes sense. With so darn many wizards and witches gathered here, they cannot attack us overland, not unless they had an army. She distinctly said the bomb would be falling on us. That means it must be coming from a plane, helicopter, ultralight, some flying craft, most likely. A flying wizard would look way to suspicious."

Wilma agreed with his conclusion. "We should get everyone that's outside now to someplace that will be safe. Throw up an illusion of a well-attended wedding ceremony. If a plane comes, I will go after the plane and its occupants."

"Leave the bomb to me," R. B. added.

"I'll work on the illusion," Fred decided. "Perhaps, Lloyd and Monane can help me with it. This will have to be a rather large illusion. We had better move fast, though. We've maybe twenty minutes to get ready."

Just then, all their wives came charging into the workshop. Luci screeched, "R. B., what's this about a bombing about to happen? We should do something at once!"

"We're on it, Luci. Please, we need calm right now. First thing, we must go out and move all the guests into the two houses. Fast, but let's not start a panic. We have twenty minutes, more or less," he replied. At once, his group left the workshop to start the mass evacuation. Trusting R. B., Luci led the women into the front room, issuing orders for them to help everyone cram into the house.

"Come on in; squeeze in," Polly began directing the startled guests.

"Over here. Some of you can stand here in the hallway," Lottie gestured. Just then, Monique entered, holding on tightly to her sister's hand. Ellie looked very pale and scared. "Over here by me, girls."

"Mom, what's happening?" Monique urgently asked, her voice filled with fear.

"Ashley and Audrey. They've alerted us to an attempted bombing. They think it will be dropped from a plane or something like that. R. B. says we will all be safe inside the houses. Squeeze in tight, kids. Make room for the others." She put her arms around her two daughters, holding them securely to her sides.

By five minutes til one, the last had entered the second house. The reservation security men were the last to enter, standing guard by both doors. Now Monane, Lloyd, and Fred began casting illusions as fast as they could. Illusions of the crowd seated watching the ceremony came into being. Images of guards on patrol around the outer perimeter of this central area began pacing back and forth. Monane created a passable illusion of the actual ceremonial gathering of the couple, the bridesmaids, and grooms. They had only just finished, when R. B. heard the drone of a single engine plane coming up from the south.

There was no time for these five to seek shelter. Instead, each quickly cast Skin of Stone spells on themselves. Wilma cursed about not bringing her Staff of Power, only having her wand at hand. She readied her spells and then glanced at R. B.

He was studying the plane's movement. "Perfect trajectory," he muttered to himself, and he readied his spells.

"That plane is going down!" Wilma spat onto the ground. Monane just grinned at her companion. She knew that Wilma was exceedingly angry that this wedding ceremony was going to be attacked. "We can't even have a safe wedding anymore!" The five waited as the seconds ticked slowly by.

As the plane drew closer, Wilma estimated that it was around two thousand feet above them, way beyond spell range. This is what she had expected. "I'll wait until you handle the bomb, R. B. Then that plane goes down!" R. B. grinned. He knew Wilma meant it. After all, she was Bill West, the Rat Pack Eliminator, and about to eliminate once again.

As the plane flew overhead, R. B. spied a small black thing falling from it. He acted. His wand activated five times, his spells hit the bomb and began pushing the bomb much further north. Repeatedly, he Pushed on the falling projectile, forcing it far to the north of their home. Only when he was sure that it would land in the vacant arroyo north of their ranch did he finally stop his rapid-fire Push spells. Boom! The explosion shook the ground, but it was over a mile from the house, blowing up rocks, ground, and several sagebrushes.

Wilma then activated her first spell. A door appeared, and she stepped through it, stepping out fifteen hundred feet in the air just below the plane. Gentle Fall momentarily lessened the speed of her descent, followed by Fly. Now in position, she spelled to kill, not capture, as she had been wont to do fifteen plus years ago. Her first Disintegrate spell removed the plane's rudder. The second removed its left elevator. Her third, the right elevator. The plane began a nosedive towards the earth. Wilma flew along as close as she dared to the plane, ready to disintegrate more of the plane, should it threaten to land too close to the dwellings below her. The plane followed a perfectly defined parabolic arc as it plunged to the earth.

A huge explosion accompanied with a blazing ball of fire announced that the plane had landed about a mile away in the deserted arroyo north of the range proper. Satisfied that no one could have survived that blast and crash, Wilma then Teleported to the side of R. B. "Exit one idiot bomber," she said flatly.

"Well, done Wilma." R. B. complimented her.

"Superb job, Wilma," Fred added. "Are you sure that you do not want to come work for the Department of Defense?" He grinned.

"No thanks. I came for a wedding! Let's get on with it. Then, I want to go check out that plane. The fire should be out by the time the ceremony is over," she explained.

Twenty minutes later, though talking like mad, everyone was in their places for the wedding. Only when the stereo began the traditional wedding music did the chatting die down. In pairs, Tom's cousins escorted Audrey, Pam, Fern, and Amanda from the house to the back of the large tent and then down the red carpet to the front, just feet before the new wooden dock, which stretched out over the new pond. They were followed by Andy leading Lindsey, and Jim with his arm around Ashley. Finally, Adel, escorted by Fischer Roan came and took their places. The proud parents entered next, followed by Tom, suddenly very nervous, as he slipped into his position near the docks beside the tribal priest, Grey Oak.

Now the music changed to the "Here comes the bride." Everyone rose and stared back to the front door of the house, trying to catch a glimpse of Sandy as she began her long walk to join Tom. She looked nervous, but radiant. Her father, Jake, steadied her, his arm around his daughter's waist. Many cameras began snapping pictures, as Sandy and her father began the short walk down the red carpet. More than one older woman began crying, but Ashley couldn't figure out why nor could Lindsey. The two walked up to Tom at which point Jake handed Sandy's hand to Tom.

Ten minutes later, the happy couple kissed before their guests, and a gay song began. The two beat a hasty retreat back down the red carpet. Wands activated, and the tables appeared, tablecloths spread, and the food began flowing out of the kitchen, floating by themselves to their assigned positions on the table. Lena, mouth open, stared in disbelief at this show of magic. Everyone formed into lines, and the many guests began shaking hands, hugging the parents and the new couple. Once through the line, they helped themselves to the wedding feast.

As the last went through the line, Jim turned on the background music, and the party began. Not long afterwards, Andy and Lindsey began dancing. Jim pulled Ashley out, and they joined them. Soon, many younger couples followed suit, including Monique and Pam. Sometime later, the happy couple, now greatly relieved that the worst was over, wedding-wise, cut their cake, stuffing a piece into each other's mouths.

Wilma and Monane came over to Pam and Wilma said, "Pam, we are going over to the downed plane to search for clues. Would you like to join us?"

"Wow! You bet!"

"I'm coming too," Monique added, not letting go of Pam's hand. Fred and Lloyd joined the four and they all walked slowly past the ranch house and then down into the arroyo. By the time that they got to the scene, the fire was out. Smoldering remains were all that was left.

No sooner had they got to the site than a magical door opened and Amanda, Lindsey, Ashley, and Jim appeared. "We want to see too," Lindsey explained. Pam enlarged her computer, which she had shrunk into a tiny space, carrying it in her dress. She began taking notes. First, she jotted down the identifying letters of the plane, while Monique, got her computer up and running and began searching for the type of plane this had been. None of them knew anything about the norm's planes.

Wilma carefully searched for bodies, but found none. "Darn, he escaped! Must have teleported out as the plane went down," she cursed, infuriated that whoever it was got away. "I ought to have kept on disintegrating the plane piece by piece!"

Given her pronouncement, Monane and Amanda began searching the sky above them, looking for the telltale residual magical energies. After some study, Monane pointed out, "There, do you see it, Amanda? Teleport line. One person left when the plane was about five hundred feet from the ground."

"Yes, it's very clear, isn't it, Monane. I wonder who it was?" she replied.

"I need to search for fingerprints, dad," Pam offered.

"Honey, let me. You will get your pretty blue dress ruined," Fred replied. He began sifting through the debris near the cockpit. About fifteen minutes later, he lifted two sets of prints, sealing them onto a piece of paper with scotch tape. "Here you go, Pam. Let me know what you find out."

"How's she going to find out, Mr. Betts?" asked

Monique.

Fred smiled, "She's been sworn in now. She has total access. I've made her a deputy in my department."

"Whoa! Super cool, Pam! Way to go!" Monique replied, in awe of her girlfriend. Pam grinned.

A half hour later, they all left via a magical door back to the ranch. There really was not much else of value here. The plane was a total loss and yielded no further clues.

By five, nearly all the guests had left. Calm finally returned to the Whitewater ranch. Tom and Sandy went inside along with everyone else to change into normal clothes, as did the girls. Both Sandy and Tom took Ashley and Audrey aside. Tom said, "Sandy and I both want to thank you two for your timely warning. We owe you our lives. If you two ever need anything, just holler!" He hugged both girls in turn.

Sandy added, "Bless you both! Thank you, thank you for everything! We owe you really big time!" She hugged both girls tightly and kissed them on their foreheads.

Finally, a half hour later, it was relaxation time. Now wearing comfortable clothes, they all sat around the front room. Naturally, the conversation was about the attempted bombing, but soon even that was forgotten. All wanted to know the new couple's plans.

"Well, tonight after we sort everything out," Sandy explained, "Tom's taking us to Denver. We've a bridal suite waiting for us. Then, tomorrow, probably later in the morning, we are going to Tahiti for our honeymoon. Two weeks in paradise without a care in the world—that's what the brochure said anyway."

"Yep, then after that, we are going apartment searching near the campus. Once we find something and get moved in, we will invite all of you to come for a visit. We're supposed to get our books and stuff in mid-August. Classes start earlier than Bradbury's, like about two weeks sooner. However, we will be home for Christmas about the same time as you folks, but we don't have to go back nearly so soon. We get another two weeks into January before the spring semester begins."

"Yes, just think, four years from now, I'll be an elementary school teacher, and Tom will be a full-fledged engineer!" Sandy exclaimed, excited about what the future held for them.

A while later, their things packed, the young couple teleported off to Denver. The others took this as a signal to return home, saying their goodbyes for the night. Luci and R. B. thanked everyone for all their help. Fred and Lloyd promised to return in the morning to help dismantle the huge tent.

An hour later, the girls were home chatting about the day. Pam and Monique, however, were in Pam's room, sleuthing away. Monique had identified the plane's make and model. Pam finally found out to whom the plane belonged. "Look at this; it is registered to the Mac Fluide Enterprises!"

"Now that is a weird coincidence," Monique replied. "What has this company got to do with Dominus and his Death Stalkers anyway?"

"Dunno, but Ashley's dad was investigating them when they must have murdered him. There must be a connection, Monique, there just must be. Besides, this is the company that owns that house in Telluride, you know, where Dominus was at and we were brutally mistreated, the one where you all blasted away the entire front walls. Weird, isn't it?"

"This is strange too! Look at this report that just got filed, Monique," Pam pointed out a police report that had just arrived on her dad's server. "Mac Fluide Enterprises reports one of their single engine Cessna's was stolen from Lamar Municipal Airport this afternoon."

"Well, that makes sense, Pam. Lamar is maybe sixty-five miles south of here and a little more west. They said the plane came from that direction. Do you really suppose that it was stolen?"

"Who knows, but I bet it wasn't," Pam replied with a sigh. "Guess I ought to see if I can find a match to these fingerprints." Monique looked over her shoulder as Pam set about this task. Monique had never really seen this software program running. After all, Pam was running official Department of Magical Misuse programs now, the real thing. Monique was all eyes, eagerly watching everything that Pam did.

A half hour later, Pam had a match. "Len Striker, Death Stalker! Well, now we know who was flying that plane and trying to bomb us all." Monique went to inform all the others of their findings, while Pam sent all the results to her triply secure server, nicely arranged to prove her case against Len, should he ever be captured.

The next morning, Ashley's grandparents returned home right after breakfast. Everyone else headed over to the Whitewater ranch to help the cleanup efforts. The girls spent most of the morning cleaning up the enormous amount of litter left from the party. Around ten, Andy came by to say goodbye to his friends and especially Lindsey. "Dad's taking me to the airport in Lamar, and I get to fly to the Chaco Canyon dig. Be back in a couple months. I'll send you emails and pics as often as I can, Lindsey." The two hugged, and Andy was off, spending the summer months on the archaeological excavation.

The afternoon was spent moving the Blackburn's into the new guest home that R. B. had recently built next to his house. While everyone was helping them get moved in and settled, Ashley finally had some time for herself. She waved her wand with her toes and said, "Morph into Peggy West." Magical energies flashed. Ashley now looked precisely like this Red Hall girl. More importantly, she had arms.

"This sure feels weird to me," she said to herself. "But I have to experiment and see what it's really like to have arms." She spent the afternoon doing all sorts of things with her arms and hands.

Over supper, she brought it up. "I know you've seen me being Peggy today. I've been doing like Wilma asked, seeing just what it's like, you know, to be like you and have arms and hands." Lindsey and Lena paid very close attention to what she was saying.

"It's really weird you know! You all are just using yours without any thoughts about what you are doing with your arms and hands, feeding yourselves, drinking your tea, as if it's all the simplest thing, requiring not even the slightest attention on your part, sort of like on automatic. Yes, I found many things so much easier to do with my arms and hands, but I constantly and very slowly had to do each individual motion! I really had to pay attention to everything or I messed up. Worse, I couldn't get even one single spell cast using my hands and wand! Wilma, you are right! I'd better give this considerable thought. If I get my arms regenerated, I'm going to need a very long time to get used to them, and I'm going to have to learn how to cast every one of my spells again!"

"I was suspecting something of the sort, dear. Still, I'm sure that everyone will lend you assistance on relearning the spells," Wilma responded.

"I was that way too," Lindsey added, "when I first got my new hands. It was slow going for a couple of weeks, getting used to them. I expect I had it a lot easier because I had been using my illusionary hands for so long, that had to help me. I could cast my spells with them, you see. Wilma's right, sis, we all will help you with the casting."

"Say, I have a plan," Pam spoke up; her mind was analyzing all that Ashley had said. Now she worked out a way around it. "I can see your point, Ashley. Say, you got your arms fully back in say a couple of weeks. Probably by the fall term, you would be comfortable doing all the normal things with them, but what if you are only halfway through relearning to cast your spells? This could be just awful for you! So I've got a plan for you, Ashley."

Ashley stopped eating and put her full attention onto what Pam was about to say. She was at a loss, but maybe her friend might have a good idea. Strange, she thought to herself. Last year, she'd never consider listening to someone's ideas about herself. She had indeed somehow changed.

"Actually, it was Lindsey who gave me the idea. Suppose that you spend the summer using your Morph spell as much as possible. Each day, you can work on getting used to doing things with arms. Each day, we can all work with you on learning how to cast spell with hands. Then, by the time we get to go back to school this fall, you will know two things: how quickly you would be able to adapt to doing things with arms and just how the re-learning of spell casting is going. That way, you'd be able to judge just how long a time you would need to get up to speed with regenerated arms and hands. What do you think?"

"You know, it sounds pretty good to me. I have been worrying all day just how long it would take me to relearn three years of spells. Gosh, I hope not another three years. I see what you are getting at, Pam. After three months of working on learning how to cast them with arms and hands, admittedly those of someone else, I could at least estimate how many more months it will take to get them all down. Plus, I would likely be able to cast some spells if I had to Morph into someone else again, like I did with Cho Lin. I wouldn't be totally helpless like that."

Lindsey added her thoughts too, "Plus, when we are all learning our new spells this fall, we can drill you both ways. Then, you will already have those down for later, less to have to relearn."

"Cool, Pam. I think this is a good plan. I hope you all don't mind seeing me as Peggy West a lot this summer," Ashley grinned.

Wilma added one further caution, "I believe you girls have made a wise decision. Just don't neglect the distinct possibility that Ashley might catch on rapidly. You may find that she has all of her spells relearned in July. Just as it could go slowly, it could also go quickly. I've no way to predict it. I don't think anyone could predict this. It's probably never been done before. Don't set your minds on it taking years, just as you should not expect it will take a few weeks."

"Cool! And I promise to use my spells to help myself," Ashley admitted. "I know in the past I haven't, but now I should." Lindsey heaved a sigh of relief. Ashley was beginning to shoulder responsibility well.

"Eeu! That's gross," Ellie commented early the next morning. She and Monique had accompanied Lindsey and Pam into the barn, as the two began their morning chores. Lindsey began milking the first of their four cows.

Lindsey grinned, "Where'd you think your milk comes from? City slicker," she teased the second year student. Monique and Pam both laughed.

"That's not fair. Let's see Moni milk the cow," Ellie

protested.

"Well, I don't know how," Monique attempted to come up with a suitable excuse.

"Wash your hands, pull up a stool and a bucket, and I'll show you," Lindsey suggested.

"There you go! Now you do it, Moni," Ellie teased her older sister, knowing that Monique felt just as funny about it as she did and that she hated to be called Moni. Monique had little choice but to make the attempt; she was not about to let Ellie win.

"Come on, Ellie; you can help me get the eggs," Pam suggested.

"But the chicken is sitting on hers," Ellie protested a minute later, as the two carried their buckets to the chicken coop and faced egg retrieval from over a dozen hens.

"Well, you can gently push her off," Pam suggested, "or maybe wait until she moves off herself, but you might be standing there a while."

Ellie made flapping motions with her hands, as if scooting the hen up from her nest. "What if she starts pecking me? Oh!" The hen flapped her wings and flew down to the ground to peck at the feed that Pam just scattered. Ellie had several down feathers in her hair and on her face. She decided that she didn't like collecting the eggs either.

"Maybe you could help Audrey and Ashley with the gardening," Lindsey suggested. Monique nodded vigorously, hoping to get rid of her little sister shadow. Ellie did just that, preferring to pull weeds than to deal with these "wild" animals. As she left, the three older girls grinned at each other.

With the early morning chores handled, everyone pitched in to help move the Blackburn's over to R. B.'s new guesthouse. While everyone was busily engaged in the moving, Lindsey asked him on the sly, "Did you know that others would be coming here—I mean to live on your ranch? So you built a new house for them?"

R. B. smiled, "Well, I'm not a Diviner. Seriously, I'm not surprised that more folks have not come to stay. When Dominus was at his height of crime some fifteen years ago, many friends and relations were packed into our house. I figured this time I'd have a spare house. Looks like I need to make another house or two. What do you think?"

Lindsey twisted her long hair in her fingers, and then answered truthfully, "If that is not too much trouble—I mean to build another house that it—I think that I would do it. Dominus seems to be running wild and no one is able to stop him. If they cost a lot, perhaps I could pay for some of their constructions from my inheritance."

"Lindsey, you have a heart of gold, bless you. Thank you for making the offer. Norm houses, well yes they do cost a lot. My style homes are exceedingly inexpensive to build, most of the cost is in the wood for the interior. Don't be surprised if next time you come home you find a third home here on my ranch and a second one on yours," he chuckled. Lindsey did too.

Around noon, the extended family sat down to a well-deserved lunch, prepared by Lena and Ashley. They had barely finished their lunch when the monotone voice announced, "Mag Post Delivery is arriving."

"Well, I wonder what that is all about," Lloyd said. "Anyone order anything?" Lindsey looked around the large table, but everyone shook their heads no. "Hum, you all stay here. I'll go meet them. Alert for trouble."

The festive mood changed instantly. Hands reached for their wands, though the girls decided not to call for their staves of power just yet. After all, it just might be an unexpected Mag delivery. Lloyd watched as the enchanted Mag truck popped into view. It looked like the usual Mag Postal trucks. Lloyd saw no signs of any impending attack as the driver climbed out, clipboard in hand. "Compton ranch?" he asked.

"Yes," Lloyd replied.

"Big delivery for you; sign here please." Lloyd signed on the line, and the driver walked to the rear of the truck. "Three small boxes and a really big, heavy one. You'll need your Levitate spell, sir."

Lloyd sent a Message that it was a regular mail delivery and that he needed some assistance. By the time the driver had climbed into the back and started handing out boxes to

Lloyd, everyone else, wands at the ready, excepting Ashley, came out to see what was going on. "Here, Pam, this one is addressed to you." He handed her a very heavy box.

"Whoa, this is heavy!" Pam exclaimed very nearly dropping it.

"Ah, this one is for Lindsey," Lloyd called out, handing out a lighter box. Lindsey took it from him. "One for Audrey." Audrey stepped forward and took hold of the smaller box.

"I didn't order anything. Perhaps there has been some mistake," she explained.

"Oh my, you were not kidding!" Lloyd exclaimed, as the driver, using his own Levitate spell began pushing a huge box out the back of his truck. It was at least eight feet long and four wide and three deep.

Between the two, they got the box safely on the ground. Lloyd read the label and called out, "Ashley, seems this monster is for you."

Dumbfounded, she walked over to the enormous box. "But I didn't order anything."

The driver hopped back into the truck and pop! The van vanished, leaving the group staring at the enormous and heavy box sitting on the gravel driveway. "I'll lend you a hand with it," Fred volunteered. The two men, using several spells, managed to push and shove it into the house.

Pam was already tearing into her box. "Oh my! It's from Tom and Sandy! There's a card inside. Sandy says, 'Thanks for everything you've done for us, Pam. Hope this little thank you proves useful. Love, Sandy and Tom.' I wonder what it is?"

"Well look dear," Polly suggested, wondering what Sandy had given to her daughter. It was customary for the bride to give out little presents to their bridesmaids.

"Wow! Look at this! Six books on Sleuthing! Cool! Oh, well, I'll be!" Pam held up a smaller box which was inside the larger box. "Six Spy Cameras! One even has sound! Way cool!"

"Look what Sandy gave me," Lindsey butted in, very excitedly. "It's a large book of spells. It says, *Non-grade Helpful Spells for Teachers and Teacher's Assistants* by Eloise Armintrout. Oh Pam, you are going to have to learn this one spell with me, Correct Grammar Errors!" Pam dropped everything, and the two began pouring over the table of contents.

Audrey read her personal card from Sandy. "Words cannot thank you for saving our lives and everyone else as well. Hope this small gift meets with your approval. Love, Sandy and Tom." She looked inside. There were two identical sets of the highest quality carving knife sets, ten blades per mahogany box. Audrey hugged them tightly to her chest for a minute. To her, these were incredibly precious indeed, far better than the cheap knives she had been using.

Ashley stood beside Lloyd and Fred as they attempted to open the huge box. First, they found a card, and Ashley eagerly sat down, opened it with her feet, and read it. "Ashley, words cannot express how much we are indebted to your timely warning of the attempted bombing of our wedding. You have saved not only our lives but also many that we love. Please accept this token of our love and appreciation for you. Thanks. Love Sandy and Tom."

"Well, I'll be," Fred finally discovered what was inside. "Ashley, it's a top of the line pool table!" Ashley gave a shriek of surprise and joy! She now had her own pool table!

As the men began assembling it, they also discovered that Tom had inserted a very fancy pool cue, just right for her. She realized that Jim must have had a hand in picking it out for her. An hour later, the men finished assembling it in the girl's study room, where the Blackburn's had been sleeping. A wall rack held four regular cues and had an extra slot for Ashley's personal cue stick.

No sooner than they had it setup and the mess cleaned up, when Jim came by. He had a sheepish grin on his face as he walked into the study room, where everyone was now standing. "Hi everyone. Ashley, I see it has come."

Ashley raced over to him, bumping solidly into him, throwing one leg around him, her style hug. "You had to have helped them pick this out, didn't you? And you didn't tell me they were getting me a pool table!"

"Guilty as charged, my princess," Jim grinned, though his face was a bit pinkish. His arms found their way around her waist. "Hope you like it. I picked out the cue stick." She gave him a kiss.

"Go get me my stool, and let's play a game," Ashley insisted. Jim could not refuse. In fact, everyone gathered around the two to watch. None here had ever seen Ashley shoot a game of pool, though they had heard about her skill. "You crack," she teased, "cause I'm a gonna run the table on you!"

"Not if I can help it," he teased her back. Amanda and Fern came by to show everyone what Sandy had gotten them and to see what the others had received, though Amanda already knew. She had helped Tom and Sandy pick out appropriate thank you gifts.

"Sandy got me a magical ring, see. It prevents anyone from charming me with various spells," she proudly showed her new ring to the others.

"Audrey, you'll have to come over to see what they got me," Fern explained. "A bunch of cool plant books, all sorts of plant doctoring supplies, and a big can of rare wild flower seeds, like yours. Now I'm going to start my own wild flower garden!" Fern was quite happy with her thank-you presents. She also got a ring that stored three spells, which she now wore.

Ellie whispered to Fern, "I would never have thought that Ashley could play pool. She's doing really well; at least I think so. I don't know much about pool."

"She skunks Jim all the time. She plays close to the professional level, Jim says," Fern replied. Jim luckily managed to sink two balls before scratching. Now, slowly but surely, Ashley ran the table on him, and he could do nothing to stop her.

"If you make this next shot, I'm going to have to tickle you, Ashley," he tried to intimidate her. She stuck her tongue out at him, and then went ahead and made the shot. Everyone laughed. Not to be outdone, Jim began tickling Ashley, who could only manage to lay her fancy new cue stick down before erupting in laughter, as she tried to escape his clutches. At once, Amanda and Fern charged to her rescue, joined at once by Lindsey, Audrey, and Pam. Not to be left out, Monique and Ellie charged after them. Jim tripped, and the girls were all over him, tickling him back. Ashley discovered that Jim was very ticklish himself.

"Tom! Where are you when I need you?" Jim called out while laughing uncontrollably. "Okay, okay, I give up!" Finally, the girls relented. Ashley went back to the pool table and finished her turn and the game.

"That was an incredible display of pool shooting, Ashley!" Fred commented. "I've never seen anything like that. You are incredibly good at it." She beamed.

"Hey, how about us all going for a swim in our new pond," Amanda suggested. That hit the spot. Five minutes later, the gang of teens raced for the front room teleport pad. However, Monique had to wear a big hat to keep the hot sun off her face. It was still very sensitive to heat and cold. She was the last one to head over to the Whitewater's. She knew she would have to watch, well maybe wade a little, but she knew that she dared not get her face wet yet. Bummer, she thought.

"Well, I'm heading off to the office," Fred announced. "Sure is exciting with all our children around, isn't it? I've got to find time to spend here with Pam and the others." Polly agreed with him.

Once Fred had gone, Wilma commented to Lena and Polly, "You know, Ashley does fantastically well without arms. Sometimes, I wonder if she really needs them regenerated. What if she doesn't have the same pool shooting skills with arms as she does with her feet? She is one remarkable young woman indeed."

"Oh!" Lena grimaced from a sharp stabbing pain. The women looked at her. "He kicked. I'm beginning to think Jonathon may not wait another two weeks. Maybe he wants to play too." They all grinned.

"Where were you and Lloyd planning on having the baby delivered?" Wilma asked.

"We've decided to use Greeley General this time. Sam and I had Lindsey in Lamar, but under the circumstances in these times, we both feel Greeley is more secure. You know, Lindsey and Ashley will both want to be there with us. Lloyd checked on Lamar and says security there is very lax."

"She's right. What with all the troubles the Blackburn's

have had, Fred has greatly increased that hospital's security," Polly added.

"Good. Can you fill me in on your plans for when the baby comes? I'll let Monane know. We both wish to be present to guarantee everyone's security," Wilma requested. The women discussed what they should do when the time came.

Chapter 3—The Arrival of Jonathon Samuel Compton

"Only two more days until our foreign exchange students arrive," Pam learnedly pointed out to her friends. It was June 8. The girls were taking turns working with Ashley-Peggy, coaching her on how to make the proper wand motions so she could cast her spells using arms and hands. It was not going all that well, thus far anyway.

"This is taking forever," Ashley-Peggy complained. "Clean! Clean! Clean!" an exasperated Ashley commanded, waving her wand. It failed to activate just as it had for the last ten minutes.

"What's she doing wrong?" asked Amanda. "Whoa a minute, Ashley. Let's see if we can figure this out." She looked at Lindsey for help.

Lindsey scratched her head, puzzled by why Ashley was not getting the proper wand activation. It reminded her of her own first days at Bradbury's School of Magic, when she had no hands and was trying her best to cast her first spells. Ashley gave her a dirty look, as if to say, "Well???"

Not even Monique had any answer, though she had tried her best. Pam had already tried to change the subject a moment ago, but failed. She looked down at the floor instead.

Audrey, who had been sitting nearby carving a piece of mahogany, which had already begun to look like a rhinoceros, said quietly, "She's going too fast and too jerky. Slower motion, perhaps." Ashley glared at her, but she took no note of it, continuing to remove tiny pieces of the wood. "My new knives are just fantastic."

"Slow motion! That's it," Lindsey exclaimed suddenly very excited. "Slow motion. I saw that in my new book. Everyone, hang on a second." She raced to her room, grabbed her new spell book, and returned. "Look, this is a book of spells for teachers. I remember seeing one was called Slow Motion. Let's see, page 73. Ah, give me a minute." Lindsey

46

read the spell carefully and practiced the motions the wand would need.

"It seems a pretty simple spell. Okay, I think I have it. Ashley, I want you to try it again, only this time I'm going to cast my spell as you do it. Slow Motion," she barked and her wand activated. Everyone stared at Ashley, fully expecting to see Ashley somehow move very slowly. Instead, they saw her moving normally, her hand waving just as before.

"Guess it doesn't work," Pam admitted. Monique agreed with her. Lindsey's mouth opened.

"Oh yes it did! Didn't you all see that?" she said in awe. Everyone shook their heads no.

"I saw her in slow motion. I think the spell slows down her motion so I can see where she is going astray. Here, Pam, Monique, Amanda, you try casting it. See what I mean," Lindsey insisted. The three read over the spell, practicing the simple wand motions.

One by one, they cast the spell. Then, Lindsey had Ashley attempt to cast her Clean useful spell. "Wow! Incredible! Cool!" Pam exclaimed. "It works!"

"Hey, that is a useful spell, Lindsey. We can see every motion she is making," Amanda added.

"I see where she is going wrong," Monique pointed out. "Here, Ashley, you are making this motion, not this one." She slowly executed the motion that Ashley had just done, and then she did the correct motion. She repeated the two versions several times.

"Oh! I think I see. Let me try it again," Ashley said hoping that this was what was wrong. "Clean!" Her wand activated, and the pile of dirt vanished. "Eureka! At last!" Everyone cheered her success.

Ashley then looked a bit sheepishly at her friends. "Er, it is supposed to be a gentle action, but I keep using way too much force with my hands, like I'm punching out someone in a fist fight. It's more like finesse not harsh motions. Golly, I've so much to learn about this. I can do it so easily with my feet and toes, either ones, for that matter. Maybe I might be better at this with the left hand. Does it matter for you which hand you use to cast your spells with your wand?"

"Now there is something that we hadn't considered," Pam astutely pointed out. "We all cast with our dominate hands. Audrey casts with her left hand, and she is left-handed. Me, I cast with my right hand because I am right handed, you see. So do the rest of you. Let's do a little experiment. All of us, let's switch hands, and see if we can cast our spells using the non-dominate hand."

"It won't work," Audrey said softly, still whittling away. She didn't look up, though.

Pam, Monique, Lindsey, Amanda, Fern, and Ellie all switched hands and barked a chorus of "Clean!" Nothing happened, not a single wand activated. "Told you so," Audrey remarked, still not looking up at them. All the dirt remained just where it was on the floor.

Several of the girls continued to make the wand activate for several more tries, growing nearly as frustrated with their wand's failure to activate as Ashley had become. "See, if we use the wrong hand, we are just as inept as Ashley is," Pam concluded.

"But how do I know if I am right handed or left handed?" asked Ashley. "Besides, will it depend on who I have chosen to Morph into? I mean I'm Peggy right now. What if I become Audrey? Does that mean I have to cast with my other hand just because I've Morphed into her cause she's left handed? What if I learn these all right handed and then my regenerated arms and hands turn out to be left handed? Do I have to then start all over, as you all are doing now, when you use your left hands? Does this make any sense at all?"

"She has a point," Monique answered. "Look, we should answer that question first, before we do anything else! Ashley, you successfully cast the Clean using your right hand. I want you to Morph into Audrey and try casting the Clean spell with your right hand and then with your left hand. Let's see if it makes any difference."

"Hey, I want to try that too," Pam added, intrigued by the whole notion that one's dominant hand may play a role in spell casting. In fact, everyone was just as curious as Pam. Wands waved and spells energized. Audrey did look up this time and saw seven duplicates of herself standing before her.

She giggled and stopped to watch the show.

Pam-Audrey said, "Okay, everyone, let's cast Clean with our right hands first, since we are normally right handed." At once, seven Clean spells occurred. "Cool. Now switch to your left hand and try it again." Seven barked their commands. Ashley's wand activated, and the pile of dirt she was aiming at vanished, but nothing at all happened from the others, though Pam's wand did sputter a little, almost firing.

"Well, that clinches it, doesn't it?" Pam-Audrey declared.

"Huh?" Ashley-Audrey said very confused. "Mine still worked either way."

"Right. You see, none of us can cast at all using our non-dominate hand. We are just as bungle-fingered as Ashley has been. Further, notice it has nothing to do with the Morphed form that we take. Audrey is left handed, but none of us can cast left handed," Pam-Audrey explained.

"But I did," Ashley-Audrey replied, still very confused.

"Yes, that is to be expected, you see, because you have never had arms and hands. Thus, you don't have a dominate hand, yet anyway. However, you do favor your right foot; you cast with it more so than your left, and you shoot pool or rather use your cue stick as a right handed person would, not a left handed person," Pam-Audrey explained further.

"So what does that mean?" asked Ashley-Audrey.

"Say, this is just too confusing! Can we all go back to our normal selves? Ashley, you go back to being Peggy, please," Monique gushed, her mind was finding it terribly difficult to remember who was really who. Audrey giggled, continuing to whittle away.

"It means, Ashley, that since you don't yet favor one hand over the other, it makes no difference which hand you use. As I see it, you have two choices. One, you can decide that you will eventually be right handed, once your arms are regenerated and then do all this relearning using your right hand. Two, you can practice casting each spell with each hand, becoming ambidextrous, so when you do get your arms and hands regenerated you will be able to cast your spells with either hand." Pam had that satisfied look on her face. She'd completely resolved the whole problem.

Ashley-Peggy thought about this for a minute before answering. "I think that I will practice each spell with each hand, ambidextrous as you suggest. That way, if somehow regenerating arms and hands turn out to be, well you know, right handed or left handed, then either way, I will be prepared. I can't lose that way."

"Hey, I like the sound of that one," Lindsey grinned. "Let's get Ashley back on her practicing, but from now on, one of us should always cast the Slow Motion spell and watch her motions. It is very easy to spot what the incorrect motion actually is and get it corrected really fast." Everyone agreed wholeheartedly with her. In fact, this was their first real breakthrough with Ashley's relearning to cast spells.

She had relearned three spells in three days. This fourth day, Ashley picked up six more that she could now cast without thinking about them and do it successfully each time. At last, Ashley began to have some confidence that they were making progress.

She'd already begun making rapid progress using her arms and hands for normal things, such as eating and doing her chores. She enjoyed setting the table and then clearing the table after the meals. It was so much easier and efficient using her hands. Even running the vacuum cleaner was a breeze now, and her normal job of doing the laundry took her a tenth the time as before, when she only had her feet to assist her.

Just as Polly called for the girls to come and set the supper table, Lena raced to the bathroom. Lindsey saw her, thought that was unusual, and went to check on her mother. "Oh!" exclaimed Lena, holding her large belly. "Lindsey dear, please get Lloyd quickly. I think Jonathon is coming a bit early." Her water had broken, and she'd just felt the first contraction begin.

Lloyd came racing into the bathroom. Lindsey heard him command, "Clean! Dry!" and figured that he was helping her clean up. A bit later, Lloyd called out, "Baby time. Cancel supper everyone! It's time to get Lena to Greeley."

"Dear, they should eat first," Lena protested. "It'll be hours yet." Lloyd blushed. This was his first child, and he had no idea what to expect. He deferred to Wilma.

"Kids, let's eat quickly; leave the mess and then get your things together. We should leave for Greeley in an hour," Wilma advised. The girls were so excited that they could scarcely eat, choosing to wolf down their supper as fast as they could. Only Lena didn't eat; eating right now was the last thing on her mind.

Forty-five minutes later, each girl had a small backpack with their things, including a change of clothes and purses. Amanda, Fern, Monique, and Ellie wished Lena all the best and insisted that Lindsey Message them with news every hour. Monane, Wilma, Lloyd, Ashley, Audrey, and Lindsey accompanied Lena to Greeley General, while Pam and Polly remained behind, watching the ranch, along with Wilma's two older boys.

At one in the morning, Jonathon Samuel Compton entered the world, to the delight of his older sisters and father, who had been pacing the floors outside the delivery room for hours. A little while later, everyone gathered around the proud, but tired, mother and baby. Lindsey snapped a few photos of the little fellow.

"He's so tiny!" Ashley whispered.

"Nine pounds, four ounces, perfectly good sized baby," Lloyd whispered back, as if he was an expert in babies. He wasn't of course.

"He's so cute!" Audrey whispered.

"I'll second that," Lindsey whispered back.

"Okay kids, time to get you three home, and let your mother get some sleep," Wilma insisted. After several hugs and kisses, Wilma and Monane brought the three home. Lloyd stayed at the hospital with Lena.

On June 9, the girls uniformly slept in. They had not gotten to bed until two in the morning. Pam, Monique, Amanda, Fern, and Ellie attempted to handle the early morning chores. Amanda ordered, "Okay, Monique and I will milk the cows. Pam, you, Fern, and Ellie collect the eggs."

"But I want to weed the vegetable patch," Fern complained.

"Me too," Ellie added, remembering her last encounter

with the hens.

"Okay, okay, go weed the garden then. Pam, you get the eggs," Amanda said rather disgustedly. After the two left the barn, she added, "Little sisters can be a pain."

"No kidding," Monique replied, wholeheartedly. "But I love her anyway." Both girls grinned.

"Having Audrey around has been the best thing ever," Amanda chatted while milking one of the cows. "Fern is always with her, not bugging me like she used to do all day long, driving me nuts."

"Same with Ellie. She's hanging around with Fern now, instead of following me all over," Monique added. "I really don't like milking cows, though." Pam overheard her and grinned to herself. No way was she going to milk cows!

Around ten, the three girls finally woke up. They spent the rest of the morning looking over the dozen photos of the new baby and chatting about the experience. After lunch, Polly put them to work arranging the last minute baby things, getting the diapers ready, the crib ready, and so on. Then, they began working with Ashley and her spells once more. Today, the relearning went well and by supper, Ashley-Peggy had another eight spells down pat using either hand.

After supper the monotone voice announced, "Lloyd and Lena are arriving." Everyone made a mad dash to the front door! Cries of "Let me see him," occurred frequently, as Jonathon entered his home for the first time. He, of course, mostly slept through the whole exciting time. After a number of baby photos of him and his mother were taken, everyone wanted to be the first to change his diapers. Seldom had a newborn had so many willing hands to care for their little needs. Yes, this was one of the happiest evenings in the Compton household in memory.

Wilma and Polly merely commented together, "It'll soon wear off," and Lena merely chuckled.

The next day, Ashley received the okay to publish her spring Bradbury's newsletter. In it, articles described all the events that had happened, particularly Yellow Hall's winning of First Place at the National Track Meet. The catastrophic bombing as they were receiving their trophy was also discussed in detail. However, some details were not disclosed, such as just how Alister had thwarted the attempt on their lives. With great pride, Ashley hit the Send to All Students and Families button that Pam and Monique had created for her. Nearly one thousand emails with the newsletter were sent to the students and their families. As far as the young editor was concerned, this made one thousand plus people who had heard the truth of the bombing.

Part of the day was used to fix up the bedrooms for their foreign exchange students, who were to arrive tomorrow, June 11. Specifically, Ashley moved her things into the spare bedroom between Lindsey and Pam's rooms. Since both she and Lindsey were each playing host and mentor to one of the girls from Utrecht, Netherlands, both girls felt that it would be best if they roomed with them. Later, if the two visitors chose to bunk together, it would be a simple matter for Ashley to move her things back into the room she was now sharing with Lindsey. That took all of an hour.

Most of the day was spent playing with Jonathon, well not actually playing, but doting over him, changing his diapers, holding him, burping him, changing his baby clothes, talking to him, and in general fussing over the little tike. Ashley-Peggy had no problems handling his needs. She then practiced with a doll of Lindsey's to see if she could safely handle his tiny body using her Levitate spell and feet. She found that if she were exceedingly careful, she could lift him and snuggle with him, an action in which she took an immense satisfaction. All her pent up fears over not being able to assist with her little brother's care evaporated.

Chapter 4—The Foreign Exchange Students

"Hurry up. We don't want to be late," Lloyd called out to Lindsey and Ashley, who were trying to dress for the occasion. They had tried on several outfits, before finally deciding to go casual, shorts and blouses. Ashley decided to wear her fancy form-fitting blouse that Lena made her, the one that left no doubt about her arms. The only problem was that she had continued to grow, and her bust now looked rather prominent in this blouse.

"You look smashing, Ashley," Lindsey complimented her sister. "Really you do. Jeannette will probably want to dress like us, and we ought to be representative of usual casual summer wear."

"Well, I hope my appearance doesn't shock her. You know how first impressions go," Ashley replied. "What's she going to think when she sees that her mentor is like this?" She shrugged her shoulders, and Lindsey knew what she meant.

"She'll just have to get used to it, though don't be surprised if she stares a whole lot at you at first. Just don't go kicking her," Lindsey teased her sister.

"I'd better not. We're supposed to be hosts and mentors. I hope she doesn't feel, well, you know, like she drew the bottom apple in the barrel with me as her mentor," Ashley confided her biggest fear.

"Actually, she might have just the opposite reaction, sis. Think about it for a minute. Just how many armless witches do we have at Bradbury's, eh? In fact, have we ever heard of one? No, so she might think you are super-hot stuff, like I do, Ashley."

Ashley actually blushed. "Really? I guess I do look an awful lot like those teen fashion models in Kathy's mags, as long as you don't see my missing parts." She added that last as a reminder.

"We'd better get going. I think Lloyd is getting

impatient with us. Honestly, he doesn't have to look just perfect, now does he?" Lindsey stated flatly. The two double-checked that they had their wands and purses—Ashley's was more like a belt pouch—and headed out to the adults who were waiting on them in the front room.

"Ah, girls, you look great," Lloyd had the presence of mind to tell the girls what they really wanted to hear, a bit of validation that they were looking their best for their guests from the Netherlands. Both smiled.

"More like ravishing," Wilma added, a twinkle in her eye. She and Monane were accompanying Lloyd and the girls on the trip to Denver, providing an extra measure of security. Both women held their staves of power. Jim and R. B. were also waiting on them. Jim was to be a host and mentor as well.

Pam and Audrey waved goodbye to them, as Polly and Lena watched from the hallway. Lloyd held on to Wilma's hand; she then formed a hand chain with the others, ending with Monane's arm securely around Ashley's waist. With his free right hand, he waved his wand and commanded, "Teleport: Denver International Airport, Teleport Arrival Platform." Magical energies flashed and the five now stood on a large, black, circular area just outside the main entrance to the huge airport.

"Gosh, Ashley, we are going to learn how to do this spell when we go back to school," Lindsey realized. "Pam has already seen it in our new Grade 5 spell book! I can't wait."

"You bet; it's like really cool!" Jim explained. "Once you can teleport, really then you can consider yourself a full-fledged wizard or witch. Then, you can go anywhere you want to go any time you want to go. Like unlimited freedom of travel." R. B. glared at his son for taking such a light-hearted view of such a powerful spell.

"Kids, let's get inside and check the arrival TV screens, please. I hope the flight is on time." Lloyd took charge, leading them past the two security men. Lindsey remembered her history lessons. Back at the turn of the start of the twenty-first century, the norm's had a very suppressive organization in charge of airport security, the so-called Department of Homeland Security. These folks would search infants, young children, and even grandparents looking for bombs and other terrorist devices, all in the name of political correctness. Rather than checking out the more likely people, they mostly ignored these so as not to seem to be picking on one group. When the world had finally accepted wizards and witches, one of their first contributions had been to establish real airport security. In one year, the wizards managed to stop all terrorist attempts with this mode of transportation. After all, even the simplest spells would stop any terrorist in their tracks.

"Ah, here we are," Lloyd announced. All seven stared at the giant screen.

Lindsey looked at their guest's flight number on the paper that Governor Alister had given her back in May. "United Flight 1123 from New York," she announced. "There it is, gate A42, on time, 11:01. Where's gate A42? Gosh, this place is huge!"

"Lindsey! Hi there!" the voice of Deiter Cross broke in on their conversation. He was hosting another of the twenty students from the Utrecht School of Magic. The five turned around to see who was talking to them.

"Hi Deiter," Lindsey said, noticing that he had what must be his parents with him. "Their plane is right on time from New York."

"Cool. Mom, dad, you just have to meet my friends from school. This is Lindsey Barron and her new sister Ashley Stokes-Compton. Jim Whitewater, he's on the winning track team. Er, sorry, I don't know the others."

"My dad, Lloyd Compton, Department of Security," Lindsey hastily stepped in with more introductions. "Wilma Weltsi, Pam's aunt, and Monane Tumble, Amanda's aunt. They're here for our security. Mom's just had her baby! We've got a little brother, Jonathon."

"Cool! This is my dad, Herbert Cross and my mom, Zelda," Deiter quickly added. A round of hand shaking followed, though both Herbert and Zelda had no idea what to do with Ashley and so just nodded to her, which she thought appropriate.

"So you are this budding Dispeller that Deiter has been going on about so often," Herbert said as he shook Lindsey's hand. "Very pleased to meet you at last. I'm head of the Cross Aerodynamics Company; we design new airplanes for the government." Lindsey detected that he definitely intended to impress her with his important position, that he was a powerful man. He was a tall, thin man, but quite imposing. Lindsey realized that Deiter had probably gotten much of his "superior" attitude from his father and was glad that Deiter had begun to change since that first year at Bradbury's.

"So this is Ashley," Zelda said with a smile. "We've just read your latest Bradbury school newspaper. You've done an incredibly fine job with it, though I honestly don't know how you could possibly manage it. Yet, here you are a fourth year witch in training so you must be able to do it somehow." She had blue eyes and platinum blonde hair, highly coiffed and puffed out. Her cherry red lips suggested that she was from Red Hall.

Ashley didn't appreciate her comments, though, but remained civil, "My feet are my hands." She left it at that for fear of starting an argument.

Herbert was civil to R. B. and Monane, though Lindsey saw that he was definitely prejudiced against Native Americans. He paid them scant attention.

"Gate A42 is this way," Herbert took control of the situation, leading the group down one of the long corridors.

Deiter walked alongside of Lindsey. "Is this your first time here?"

"Yes, it is so huge! How do people find their way around here?" she asked.

"Hundreds of thousands of people pass through this airport each year. I've been here many times. Sometimes, Lyle and I come here just to watch the planes landing and taking off, kind of cool. My dad is giving me flying lessons this summer. When we get back to school, I might even have my pilot's license. It's really far out flying around the sky in one of the norm's planes, though obviously teleporting is a vastly superior way of travel. You know that we are going to learn how this fall?"

"Yes, Pam has been reading up on it already," Ashley answered. "Say, what's the secret project Pam is working on for you, Deiter? Pam won't tell us a darn thing about it." She hoped to get some key information from him. Her curiosity was aroused, when Pam would say nothing about it.

"You all will find out soon enough," he replied, being just as secretive about it as Pam. She gave him a playful bump with her hips. He grinned, while Jim wondered what that was all about. Wisely, he said nothing.

Herbert talked politely with Lloyd; Zelda, with Wilma. However, Deiter chatted away with his friends. "What do you suppose they will look like?" he asked.

"Dunno," Jim said, wishing that he had looked up Dutch people and culture with his computer.

The 947 Jumbo jet with four hundred passengers banked into its final approach to DIA. The group of twenty students from the Netherlands peered out their windows, catching glimpses of the Rocky Mountains in the distance. Mostly, however, they saw the relatively flat High Plains.

"What will they think of me?" Jeannette van Ravinstijn said nervously for the twentieth time to her dear friend, Katja van der Veer. Her brother, Hans was sitting on the aisle side of Jeanette. He leaned over and gave her a kiss on her cheek.

"Een mooi meisje—oops, a beautiful girl, that's whad I think," he encouraged, remembering to practice his English.

His sister, Katja, added, "Be brave, Jeannette. Think about all that we will learn and get to experience here in the USA!"

"Ja, that be'st why I came," Jeanette swallowed, relieving the pressure in her ears.

"Remember, we lets the others leave the plane virst," Hans added. "We hast easier time den."

Nearly twenty host families gathered around the door from which the passengers would soon be walking from the huge plane. Deiter conjured a large banner that read: Bale Volker, the name of his student. Not to be outdone, Jim conjured one for himself, Lindsey, and Ashley, getting them to crack a big smile. His read: Hans van der Veer, while Lindsey's read: Katja van der Veer, and Ashley's read: Jeannette van Ravinstijn.

Soon the passengers began coming out of the door. Most were other travelers, intent upon making other connections or who lived here or who were coming for a visit. Lindsey grew excited, but thus far, none of the hundreds of people responded to any of the signs held up on display. "They are probably letting everyone else off first," Jim suggested.

At last, one tall blonde boy around their age came out carrying a blue tote bag with Dutch markings on it. Lindsey knew that the students were coming, and her excitement grew. This boy waved to Deiter. He must be Bale Volker, she assumed. She watched as the two shook hands, and quickly Herbert led them off to the baggage claim area. More and more of the waiting groups met up with their students.

"Where's Jeannette?" Ashley said worriedly, dancing from foot to foot, anxious to meet her new companion. Just as the last group of waiting parents left with their guests, a tall boy walked out, followed by two girls. "It has to be them!" Ashley exclaimed, trying to get a good first look, wondering which of the two blondes was her Jeannette.

"Hallo," Hans called out. "We're here last. You Jim, eh?"

"Hi, Jim Whitewater. Pleased to meet you Hans," Jim held out his hand and the two shook. "Welcome to America and Colorado," he added.

At last, the group finally got a good look at the two blondes behind him. Evidently, he had been purposely attempting to keep them rather hidden behind him. "My sister, Katja and our friend, Jeannette," Hans said, at last stepping aside as the two girls approached their respective hosts.

"Oh!" exclaimed Ashley, her mouth open wide, but unable to get any other words out.

"Oh!" exclaimed Jeannette, equally startled at the appearance of Ashley.

"Way cool! This is incredible, wow. Well, Governor Alister sure knew what he was doing this time," Lindsey burst out. Jeannette stared at Ashley, who stared right back, only it was not the usual stares either girl received.

"You're like me!" Ashley finally found some words to

59

say.

"No, you're like me!" Jeannette replied, very excited. "No one told us. I mean I thought I was the only one like this."

"Same here. Hi, I'm Ashley." The two moved up close and hugged, with Ashley putting her leg around the back of Jeannette. On the other hand, Ashley felt as if someone with arms was actually hugging her.

"Zo pleased to meet you, Ashley. Dis eest incredible. Wow. I thaught dat I'd be so different," Jeannette tried to explain, but went faster than her command of the English language allowed.

Lindsey quickly shook hands with Katja, "I'm Lindsey Barron, my sister, Ashley. Our good friend and neighbor, Jim. Oh, yes, this is my dad, Lloyd Compton. Jim's dad, Running Bear Whitewater, only just call him R. B. This is his sister, Jim's Aunt Monane, and this is Wilma Weltsi, a very close family friend and an aunt of Pam, who is also staying on our ranch. Golly, this is a surprise. Well, Jeannette, you are certainly staying with the right family!" Jeannette grinned.

"Ja, dat's good. She's my girlfriend. I promised to look after her always," Hans replied.

"Hey, cool, Hans. Ashley's my girlfriend. I look out for her too," Jim answered.

"I'm her, how you say, beste vriend; I helps her much times," Katja added, wanting to make it clear from the start what their arrangement was. "I assigned to be wid her and helps her, but I donst think—vell, we so worried, you knows, wid her no arms. Is so good dis way, you alls understand us well, our problems, u see." She talked way too fast for her English skills.

"Sure we do. Jeannette will fit in perfectly; really, you will fit in very well with our families!" Lindsey tried to alleviate their fears.

"We so relieved, cannot find words to say," Katja added. The relief on her face was plainly evident, no more so than on Jeannette's. Katja had light blonde hair, straight, falling to her shoulders and had light blue eyes. Katja was tall and thin, probably as tall as Amanda, Lindsey thought, meaning nearly six feet, just a few inches taller than she was. She had a roundish face and was quite pretty. Jeannette was about two inches taller than Ashley, who had grown some now and was five foot two. Also very light blonde, Jeannette too had beautiful blue eyes, and she wore her straight hair identically to Katja. Both girls had very pale skin, compared to the sun tanned girls. Both were wearing their school dresses, a white blouse top and a pleated black skirt with the symbol of their Utrecht school boldly displayed on their skirt. Hans was six-two, wiry framed, with light brown hair and blue eyes as well. His face was angelic, and his skin was untanned.

"Zee, I told you not to worry, Jeannette. Dis eest perfect, don't you dink?" Katja said to her dear friend.

"Ja, eest amazing," Jeannette replied, her fears and trepidations rapidly vanishing. For the first time in a week, she began to relax.

As they began the long walk to the baggage claim area, Hans asked, "Dhose eest Stave of Power?"

"Good conclusion, Hans," Monane replied. "Yes, they are. Wilma and I brought ours along, just in case of trouble. The girls left their staves of power back at the ranch. You've heard about the evil wizard Dominus Malefic and his Death Stalkers?" She asked a pointed question, greatly desiring to know just how well informed these students were. After all, they were in a bit of a risk staying on their ranches in these times.

"Ja, we know Dominus. Bad wizard, very bad. Eighteen years ago, killed Jeannette's and our grandparents while they were robbing our jewelry store. Took many gemstones." He spoke slowly, making sure of each word. He wanted to make very sure that they all understood him properly. "Ja, we know him. Bad man."

"I'm so sorry for your both of your grandparents," Wilma said softly. "We too have had much tragedy in our lives from Dominus and the Death Stalkers. One of them killed Lindsey's father when she was five. Lindsey grew up with no hands, a birth defect. Recently, we've learned that another Death Stalker killed Ashley's parents and cut off her arms in a faked traffic accident, but it was murder really."

"Steel I-beams from a semi-truck came smashing

through our car when I was two years old. It severed my arms but I don't remember anything of it. I've always been like this," Ashley felt compelled to explain.

"I got my hands regrown when I was in my first year at Bradbury's," Lindsey added.

"You, you, you are *the* Lindsey? *De* Ashley, de ones dats been on the news?" exclaimed Jeannette in utter awe, falling back from the group a few feet.

"De explosion on de TV?" broke in Hans, also stopping in his tracks.

Jim stopped too, "Yep, the very ones. Lindsey has had several go rounds with Dominus and licked him each time. Ashley actually kicked him in his privates. Around school, Ashley has a nickname now, DK, for Dominus Kicker. You saw us winning the National Track Meet? We took first place and set a new track record for the first place race."

"Wow! Coolest, ja, we saw it. All over the news, the MagNews!" Katja explained. "At virst, we didn't believe dast you be de same Lindsey and Ashley. Jeannette, you got to put dis in de school news! Wow!"

"You can all read about it," Ashley replied. "I'm the editor of our school newspaper. I just sent the latest edition out to everyone a couple days ago. The MagNews gets everything all wrong; they lie and distort all the facts. That's why I started up our school newspaper last term so that all our students and their families could know what really happened."

"I edit our school newspaper too; we have in common," Jeannette replied with a big grin, but talking more slowly now.

"Yes, and one of the Death Stalkers tried to bomb us a few days ago, at my brother's wedding. Dad, Wilma, Monane, and Lloyd put a stop to it," Jim added, not wanting to be left out. "Wilma, she brought the plane down, while dad here got the bomb moved miles away from us, harmlessly blowing up some dirt."

"Wow! Way cool," Jeannette expressed her awe.

"Do all you teens always talk with 'way cools?'" Wilma jested. Lindsey, Ashley, Jim, and their three guests all laughed.

They arrived at the large baggage claim area. Ever since the wizard revamped the baggage system, it worked to perfection. Soon the many bags began coming off the conveyor, which was magically enchanted to move each bag to the side of its owner. While everyone was waiting, Deiter brought his new friend over to meet Lindsey and Ashley.

"Hi gang. This is Bale Volker. Bale this is Miss Lindsey Barron, Miss Ashley Stokes-Compton, and Jim Whitewater."

"Wow! Another one like Jeannette, cool. We all were pretty worried about how Jeannette would fit in, but golly she's in good hands," Bale said in much better English.

"Feet," Ashley corrected him. "In much better feet." Everyone laughed.

"Des are *de* Lindsey, *de* Ashley, and *de* Jim, from de MagNews, Bale," Hans added quickly, making sure that Bale grasped just who they were.

"Can I have your autograph, Miss Lindsey?" Bale asked politely.

Somewhat taken aback, Lindsey replied, "Sure, why? Sorry, I didn't bring a pen."

Bale produced a pen and asked her to sign his airline ticket stub. Five minutes later, all twenty foreign exchange students heard who these three were and formed a line to get their autographs as well. "Can you possibly sign?" Bale asked Ashley rather sympathetically.

Seeing the crowd coming with pens and papers in hand, Ashley chuckled. "Okay, okay." She sat down on the floor and removed her right shoe. "Hand me your pen. Oh here," she took it from his hand with her toes and proceeded to sign her name below Jim's.

"Oh, you write with your feet?" exclaimed a surprised Jeannette.

"Sure, how else? Don't you?" Ashley asked between signings.

"Er, no. I use my special magical spells." Lindsey and Ashley both wondered what she meant, but now was not the time to ask. Soon the student's bags began appearing at their sides, and finally the autograph session was finished.

"Weird! I've never had anyone ask for my autograph," Ashley declared.

"Me either," Lindsey assured her sister.

A few minutes later, all three verified that they had their baggage, three duffle bags each. However, it was lunchtime. "Do we see the city and eat at the Golden Arch?" asked Hans.

Lloyd, anticipating something like this, stepped in. "Not today, but soon. You've probably heard this a hundred times, but for your safety, we want to get you to the safety of our secure ranches as soon as possible. It's unlikely that Dominus or one of his Death Stalkers will be trying to harm us today, but with so few of us adults around, we'd rather not risk your safety. You have my promise that you can go to the Golden Arches one day soon. Now, let's get you all home safely. Lena, my wife, has lunch waiting."

The adults waved their wands and levitated the kid's bags, floating them along behind them. It was a short walk to the teleport pad. A minute later, they arrived at the front door of the Compton ranch. "Wow! Way cool!" were among the many exclamations of surprise, as the three got their first glimpse of the unique ranch home, the barn, and ranch. Lena, holding Jonathon, opened the door to greet them.

"Oh yes, mom just had a baby two days ago. We've a little brother, Jonathon," Lindsey announced. "Mom, this is Hans and Katja van der Veer, and this is Jeannette van Ravinstijn. This is our mom, Lena Compton and Jonathon."

"Well, I'll be!" Lena could not hide her surprise at seeing Jeannette. "Welcome to our home; come on inside. Polly's whipped up a nice lunch. The rest are dying to meet you. R. B., your clan is here for lunch as well."

The three followed Lindsey and Ashley inside, gaping at the spatial distortion. "Yes, it's two hundred by one hundred feet inside, quite spacious, but small on the outside," Lindsey continued with the explanations. However, everyone else was lined up waiting to meet the three exchange students. Lindsey managed to get out, "Everyone, this is Hans and Katja van der Veer and Jeannette van Ravinstijn." After that it was mass pandemonium, as Audrey, Amanda, Fern, Pam, Monique, Ellie, Luci, Lottie, and Polly tried to introduce themselves.

Of course, the kids surrounded Ashley and Jeannette, marveling over how well they were matched and how they thought Ashley was the only witch in existence without arms.

As they were about to sit down, Lena announced, "Everyone, find the seat with your name. You see, with such a huge crowd, Pam thought it would be wise if we sat in our family groups. The Whitewater's, you are all down on that end. This way, our guests can see who is who and who is living where. I know, this must seem awfully confusing to you," Hans smiled. It certainly was.

Lena whispered to Jeannette, "Do you prefer a tall stool like Ashley does? I mean, we didn't know about, well, you know what I mean." She didn't want to offend Jeannette.

"Why does she need a tall stool? I eat like everyone else does, vell mostly," she added a little confused.

"Ashley uses her feet, so she needs to sit up higher to reach things more easily. Well, then, here's your spot for lunch. After this, you can all sit where you want; we are always rather informal around here," Lena added, somewhat unsure how Jeannette would eat.

As the large group dined, the three guests could not help but steal glances at Ashley. They had never seen anyone eat with their feet. Ashley and the others stole glances at Jeannette more than a little curious about how she would manage to eat. All were quite startled to see her food moving up to her mouth, as if invisible arms and hands were in operation. At last, with everyone staring at the two, both Ashley and Jeannette began to laugh.

"We sure do things differently," Ashley teased.

"Ja, ve do at dat," Jeannette replied with a big grin. This was so different than she had ever imagined. Jeannette had been terrified that everyone would be staring at her constantly because she was so different from everyone else. Yet, here was Ashley, managing so differently than she did. She was laughing at herself because she was doing just what she had feared others would be doing to her.

After they finished, Hans asked, "Can I please zie de room dat Jeannette has? You zie, I am supposed to ensure she be fine. My responsibility, Katja's too."

"Sure thing. This way," Lindsey motioned. "Around here, notice that there are no doorknobs, just these sliders down low. That's so Ashley doesn't have to deal with doorknobs." Jeannette found this very strange, but highly useful. We didn't know what you girls wanted for sleeping arrangements, so we decided that since we are your mentors, you probably ought to sleep with your mentor. That means, Katja, you are in here with me; that's your bed. Jeannette, you are bunking next door with Ashley, but if you want different arrangements, just say so. We can move Ashley back in here with me, where she normally is. Whatever you two find works best for you." Lindsey was trying to be as diplomatic as possible.

"Zo big a room! Cool! Fine, I be with Ashley," Jeannette replied. "She eest my mentor. I should be wid her."

"You sure dis is fine wid you, my love?" Hans asked.

"Ja, perfect, Hans. Now you go met dem, zee your room, unpack." Jeannette gave him a loving glance.

"Okay, Hans, come on; let's go see our ranch and your room. You get my brother's old room. He's just gotten married and is on his honeymoon trip before they are off to college in Denver." Jim chatted away, leading Hans to the front room teleport pad.

Lena spoke up, "Fine, I'll let you girls get acquainted and unpacked. By the way, what you would like for supper? Tonight, your first night in the USA, you can have whatever you most desire for supper."

"Dank u," Katja exclaimed, surprised by the kindness and the offer. She looked at Jeannette and the two grinned. "We like have dis famous Domino's pizza. We heard is very good."

Lena smiled, "Domino's it is. My, kids everywhere love pizzas, Polly. Amazing." They chuckled and left.

Pam, Monique, and Amanda sat on Lindsey's bed, while Katja began unpacking, and Lindsey began going over her checklist of things to verify upon arrival. "Governor Alister, he's head of our school you see, he's given me this list to make sure everything is in order. I mean these look a bit silly, but I'm supposed to check them off. Passport, wand, spending money," Lindsey began running down the list. Katja waved each as Lindsey called them off.

"We'll get your school clothes, books, and fancy cell

phones when we go back to school in the fall. However, your new computer will be arriving as soon as I send in this checklist. Pam's our resident computer expert, along with Monique; she's in Red hall, sixth year."

"You look really pretty and older," Katja said to Monique. "Now that I'm not so nervous, how is my English? Hans and I were very worried for Jeannette."

"Thanks, but I'm still not fully recovered," Monique answered. "It's really good. We could tell that you were a bit nervous, but then who wouldn't be nervous, going to a foreign country to stay a whole year with people you've never met. You three are awfully brave."

"Honestly, I think that Jeannette is incredibly brave for coming," Lindsey added. "I look out for my sister, Ashley, so I have some idea how you must feel, Katja. Is Hans her boyfriend?"

"Ja, we never dreamed that her mentor here would be as she is. That is such a relief, you know, having her with someone like her. Hans is in love wid her, and she is smitten with him, but she is—how do you say it—shy, bashful about it. We three have grown up together, you see. Say, there is one thing that we all need. We were hoping to be able to get many new clothes. The weight allowanced on zee plane, you see, vas not big. We could only bring a few clothes, but I have a check from our parents to pay for our stay and clothes, we hope." She handed Lindsey two checks.

Lindsey took the checks to her mother, and Lena returned to see Katja. "My, dear, this is way too much money that your parents have sent along."

"We need more clothes, pays for our food and stay, Mrs. Compton," Katja explained.

"Okay, clothes it is then. I will send back whatever is not needed when you return. After you get settled, let's all talk about what clothes you two need." Katja flashed her a big smile.

Audrey sat on Ashley's bed, chatting with Ashley and Jeanette and watching how Jeannette managed, ready to offer any help, should they need it. "You know, Jeannette, being here with us and all, this feels very right."

"She can sense when things are right or wrong. She was the first to sense that someone was going to bomb us at the wedding," Ashley explained.

"Oh, like a Diviner?" Jeannette asked, using her invisible, phantasmal hands to put away her school clothes.

"Not exactly, I can sense what is right and wrong. Ashley is the real Diviner. She may even be a class 4 Diviner," Audrey said quietly. "Say, you and Ashley, you do things so very differently. I was expecting that you two would be doing things about the same way, you know. Vastly different, that's for sure."

Jeannette flushed, "Wat you mean different?" She was unsure of what Audrey meant.

"Ashley, she does absolutely everything that she can using her feet as hands. Remarkable flexibility and agility, just incredible. Is it a spell that you use? I mean, to unpack your clothes and to eat at the table like the rest of us?"

"I don't know how Ashley can do all those things wid her feet. I amazed at how she could sign her name dat way at the airport. I don't know how to use my feet as she does. No one taught me dat. My vader, he taught me dis spell ven I was six. He's vorked wid me every day. It's like I create dis invisible, arms and hands, but not really arms and hands." She sighed, realizing her English was being mixed up with her native language more so than she wanted. She was still a bit nervous about everything. Slow down, she reminded herself of the advice her English teacher had kept telling her and everyone else, for that matter.

"It's like a Move Object spell. I imagine I have these long arms and hands and use them as you would your arms and hands. I cast my spells with them, hold my wand, eat, dress, and brush my teeth. Everything I do with this spell. Oh, I don't need to use wand nor say anything. I just do it, maybe a hundred times a day I use the spell. Make sense?" Jeannette hoped that it would.

"Wow, your English is nearly perfect when you go slowly," Ashley complimented her. "Yes, now it makes sense. I grew up all by myself, going from one bad foster home to another. No one taught me any magic, so I had to use what I had, my feet. Only now, I'm learning magic spells and can see just how useful they are for us. Gosh, Jeannette, since you do things more like normal people, I mean those with arms anyway, you must have had an easier time of it. Me, everyone always stares at me, like they've never seen anyone use their feet before. It really used to bother me. I felt really humiliated and embarrassed."

"Not very easy. People always stare at me too. I hate it. Den there are those that think I am so helpless. Those are de worst, for me, anyway. I do just fine, well most of the time," she added. "I should admit to you, Ashley, I'm helpless when it is too dark for me to see. I can't see what my invisible hands are doing. I drop my wand, and then I can do nothing. I am den truly helpless and scared too. Did you learn the Terror Killer spell? We did last year. No one could understand dat my greatest fear is going blind. Den I am very helpless. I am scared to death of that."

"Wow! Yes, we learned that one too. I was terrified of falling off this tall cliff. There were all these ropes, trees, branches, many things to grab hold of to keep from falling, but I couldn't grab anything. I just fell off the cliff. That terrifies me more than anything else does. Yet, I don't mind the dark since I do most everything with my feet anyway. I cast with my right foot so the dark is nothing to me. We are so alike and yet so different!" Jeannette grinned widely.

"You don't mind if I sleep with a nightlight on?" she asked what she most needed to know, the one thing that had scared her since she asked to go on this year long trip to the States.

"Sure, we always have a little nightlight on, but if you need a brighter one, just ask us," Ashley answered. The relief that shone on Jeannette's face said mountains to Ashley and Audrey.

"Say, I noticed that you don't have very many clothes," Audrey pointed out.

"No, parents sent along money for to buy us your kind of clothes. Plane had weight limits. Ve were limited on how much ve bring vid us, you see. Gosh, Ashley, your top, your blouse, I never seen anything like it. I try to hide my misshape.

You don't, very visible. I love your look. You are not feeling funny wearing it?"

"Not at all. Why pretend? I, well, we, are not like everyone else. Actually, all my tops are like this one. No dangling sleeves to get hung up on something. Mom says that I should be proud of the way I look. Jim loves it. I love the way he runs his hands over my shoulders," Ashley admitted.

"Cool! We must look the same! Can I buy some like yours?"

"Polly and mom have made mine, but I'm sure they will be very happy to make some for you. Do you have a fancy formal ball gown for the school dance?"

"No, we need to get most clothes here, your styles, please."

"Great! We can look alike!" Ashley exclaimed. Both girls giggled, both quite pleased.

"Mom, Jeannette needs a whole lot of clothes, like mine, no sleeves," Ashley said to Lena, with Audrey and Jeannette right behind her.

"I know. Katja already told me. Polly is whipping up a blouse for Jeannette right now. However, girls, tomorrow, you are all going to go clothes shopping. How's that?"

"Whoopee!" Audrey and Ashley cheered.

"We are going shopping tomorrow, Ashley," Lindsey announced; she and her group had just joined them here in their front room. The three giggled. They had just heard it from Lena.

Polly came in holding a sky blue silk blouse, "Ah, there you are, Jeannette. Would you like to try this on? I believe it ought to fit." Her eyes opened wide as she saw at once it was identical to Ashley's. While Lindsey usually had to help Ashley into hers, Jeannette needed no help, using her spell to dress herself. A bit later, she came out of her bedroom wearing it.

"How do I look?" she asked, extremely pleased with her new look.

"You look just like me! Way cool!" Ashley exclaimed.

"Now I don't have to hide myself. I show myself as I am," the young girl announced, pleased with her appearance. Katja wiped her watering eyes. Her dear friend was so happy, happier than she had ever expected.

"It's a perfect fit," Polly replied. "Now then, girls, tomorrow, we are going into Sterling and do some clothes shopping. Ashley and Jeannette need their tops specially made, so one stop we will make is at Monane's daughter's dress shop. Louisa sews custom-made dresses and things. You two will be able to get some very high quality, handmade clothes from her."

"Say, Kathy wanted us to all go shoe shopping this summer," Lindsey remembered. "I wonder if there is any way she could join us? I know that she lives in Limon, but maybe she can figure out some way to join us. Is it okay if I ask her?" Given the go ahead, Lindsey sent off an email to Kathy.

Next, they gave their guests the grand tour of the ranch. Jim brought Hans over as well. The plan was to show the three guests both ranches at one time. When Hans saw Jeannette in her new sky blue blouse, he, like Jim, couldn't keep his hands from sliding over her shoulders and back. "Very sexy," he whispered to Jeannette. She blushed and gave him a kiss on his cheek.

The three city dwellers found everything about the two ranches extremely fascinating, never having seen anything like this. Yet it was the teleport pad between the two front rooms that impressed them the most. "Like every day, we are over here or they are over at our place," Amanda explained. "This makes it so convenient."

Most of the afternoon, the kids spent telling each other about their lives. The three guests wanted to know all about Lindsey and Ashley and their adventures. Thus, the afternoon passed rapidly, as the large group hung out in the Whitewater's front room, sipping sodas and sampling Luci's fresh baked cookies.

Several hours later, it was their guest's turn to tell the large group about themselves. "Compared to you, we must be the dullest people around," Katja began. Slowly their story emerged. Their grandfathers had opened an upscale gemstone cutting and jewelry making business in Amsterdam, Veer and Ravinstijn's. They made exceptionally high quality, cut gems and jewelry. Then, around eighteen years ago, Dominus

Malefic and a half dozen of his Death Stalkers robbed their store, killing the two older men.

After that, the kid's fathers inherited the business and moved it to Utrecht. The memories in Amsterdam were too painful to endure. Both of their families were now quite wealthy, having done well with their business. Of course, everyone naturally wanted to know about Jeannette. Her story was simple. She was born with a birth defect. Her arms had never developed, though the doctors had no idea why, just one of those fluky birth defects.

When she was young, her parents took her to see many specialists. She remembered having to drink all sorts of magical potions, most of which made her sick and vomit. The doctors were unable to regrow her arms, stating that there just wasn't any trace of arms left to regrow. When she was five, her parents finally gave up trying and accepted the fact that Jeannette would never be normal. Instead, her father began teaching her the Move Objects spell. She had no wand and no magical training. Her father, a wizard himself, was very patient and worked with her daily. Slowly, she began to catch on how to cast this spell. By the time she was seven, she could slowly do what everyone else could do by using her spell and making it serve as hands.

The group learned that these twenty students were the top four fourth year students in the five halls of the Utrecht School of Magic. Since this year they needed to study the cultures of other countries and learn a foreign language, their Governor chose to utilize the Foreign Exchange Student Program, sending the top four from each hall abroad. It seems that Governor Alister Broadwell heard of his intention and extended the offer for his students to spend the year at Bradbury's School of Magic. Their Governor had accepted readily, since Bradbury's was the most exclusive magic school in the United States.

Jeannette wanted to be a writer of children's books and was editor of her school's newspaper. "Really, Jeannette ought to be a Nous!" Katja protested. "Honestly, she's the smartest person in our school! A Nous is highly intelligent and use their mind philosophies to solve incredibly complex problems. She's a super whiz at math; you won't believe it until you see it! Naturally, people pay highly for such solutions, I keep telling her."

"Wow!" exclaimed Pam, most impressed.

"Look, be realistic, will you? Anyone coming to me as a Nous is going to take one look at me and just leave," Jeannette protested. "I'd better just be satisfied writing uplifting children's books." Lindsey filed this away, intending to ask either Alister or Professor Cho Lin about Nous training for Jeannette, as one of her electives.

Hans wanted to become a professional hockey player, but he was interested in all sorts of sports. Katja, on the other hand, was a chemistry whiz and was keenly interested in becoming a professional potion maker, assuming that she did well in her first class in potion making this year.

What surprised them all was the fact that all three were excellent swimmers, divers, cross country skiers, and ice skaters. That Jeannette excelled at these four things, especially the water sports, Ashley found unbelievable. She remembered the awful time she had passing the swimming test and her terror of diving.

All three were very disappointed to hear that Bradbury's had no swimming or diving teams. Lindsey made another note to ask about these two items as well. "When winter comes, we can ice skate on your pond," Hans suggested. "Maybe we can get Klaas to come for a visit and all go skiing." He then explained that Klaas Stuben, their fourth Yellow Hall student, was staying with someone called Emilio Lopez in a strange sounding place, Pueblo.

"Well, I'll be! Emilio is on our track team; he's a good friend of ours," Jim exclaimed. "I'm sure we can get him to come over the holidays! If nothing else, I can teleport the two here." Hans thanked him profusely, leading Lindsey to conclude that Klaas was a close friend of theirs.

Pam commented, "Gosh, Jeannette, your services will be greatly appreciated at school. We all study together, this big group of us. I end up having to correct nearly everyone's math papers; I will put you to good use!" Everyone chuckled.

"So do we, study together," Katja announced. "Do you

think your group would mind if we four joined you? I think we will be needing lots of help; our English is not so good."

"We would be offended if you didn't join us!" Pam exclaimed. "Besides as long as you talk slowly, you are doing superbly." The two girls grinned.

"Hey, Hans, do you play soccer? Tom, my brother, just graduated, and we desperately need to find a replacement for Yellow Hall's soccer team," Jim asked.

"Ja, love it, be cool."

"Tom was our long distance relay runner," Jim added hopefully.

"Na, I don't run long ways well; ask Klaas, he is our long distance runner," Hans replied.

"Lindsey, I need Emilio's email address pronto!" Jim teased. She smiled and sent it to him that night.

Fred Betts and Henry Blackburn joined them for supper this first evening, though had they known it was pizzas, they might not have been so eager. Then again, they felt obliged to meet the foreign exchange students. Hans and Katja were quite interested in hearing all about Fred's job as the head of the entire High Plains Department of Magical Misuse. He was very eager to talk about his favorite thing.

Meanwhile, Doctor Blackburn just had to examine Jeannette's shoulders. "I owe it to you, Jeannette, professional courtesy, and all that. When I first met Ashley, I examined hers as well, just to make double certain that we cannot regrow her arms and yours."

"But I've seen so many doctors," she protested slightly. "They all say the same thing, there is just nothing there but sockets." A few minutes later, he agreed with their findings.

Later that evening, Hans and Katja decided to go for a walk around the ranch. While most went with them, Lindsey, Ashley, and Jeannette did not, going instead to Ashley's room. "We've been working with Ashley on her spells, Jeannette. You see, I have a Ring of Regeneration that my dad left me. It's in one of Lloyd's Secure Vaults in Denver. We've all worked out that this ring may be able to regenerate Ashley's arms and hands."

"Oh, that would be about the greatest thing I can think

of," Jeannette replied.

"Yes, but there is a complication. You see, Ashley does all her casting with her right foot. We've discovered that when she Morphs into someone with arms, she has been unable to cast any spells. The wand doesn't activate. We've been working with her, and just yesterday, we finally got it going well. We don't dare try it, not until she can cast all the spells she knows by using hands."

"I can see why. If she is stuck half way, what a mess having to do some with her feet and some wid her hands. Awful mess," the Dutch girl replied. "I suspect it doesn't matter much which hand she uses to cast the spells, does it?"

"Wow! How did you know that?" Ashley asked, very impressed. "We only yesterday figured that all out. Trial and error, experimenting you know."

"Reasonable conclusion. You grew up vid no arms and used your feet for all dings. Zo you not prefer right or left hands. Like me, I don't either," she replied.

"You are very sharp, Jeannette," Lindsey complimented her. "Have you learned the Morph spell?" Jeannette nodded. "Can you cast spells when you are Morphed into someone else?"

"Sure, is easy, either hand," she replied.

"Well, this is very encouraging, Ashley. We must be on the right path," Lindsey concluded.

"She should use Move Object like I do," Jeannette suggested. "Den Ashley would be more normal-like. I should learn to use my feet, den I would not be so terrified of the dark."

Ashley replied, "You know, sis, she is probably right. If I could learn to do things the way she does, I certainly would have so much less trouble at school. You know how I am dreading Potion Making I. If it wasn't for your helping me in the lab, I'd have flunked chemistry."

"Jeannette, how about a trade? You help us with Ashley, and Ashley can help you learn to use your feet properly?" Lindsey suggested.

"Deal!"

Lindsey looked at the pretty face of Jeannette and

added, "When we finally retrieve my ring and try to regenerate Ashley's lost arms, would you like us to also try to regenerate your arms as well? I don't know if it will work on either of you, but it is the only thing that Pam has been able to find that might work for Ashley. It might work for you too."

Jeannette's blue eyes opened wide. "U bedoelt het? U zou dat voor me doen?" She was so surprised that she forgot to speak English. Her face flushed as she realized it. "You mean it? You would do that for me? That must cost a fortune!"

"No cost at all. The ring is just sitting in my dad's vault doing nothing. I suppose that you ought to give it some thought. I mean, you might like yourself just as you are. You don't have to decide right now."

"If it would work, I would have a real life, not like this half-life," tears trickled down her cheeks. She was so surprised that her Move Object spell failed. Ashley pulled out a tissue with her toes and handed it to her. She managed a grin, kicked off her shoe, and fumbled to take it with her toes. A bit later, she dabbed her cheeks and managed a smile.

"There, you just did your first thing with your feet," Ashley validated her. Jeannette flashed a smile. "Come on; we ought to get practicing. We both have a lot to learn from each other. Let's start with pulling down our bed sheets." Lindsey quietly left the two alone, figuring that way, Jeannette would be far less embarrassed with her awkward first attempts. At least, Lindsey felt that that would be how she would be feeling if she were in her shoes. She spent some time with Jonathon, changing his diapers for her mom.

By then, the others returned. "You have such a huge ranch, Mr. Compton!" Hans said exuberantly. "Never seen such open spaces. Not like this in the Netherlands. Every few miles down road is town. Here, nothing but crops as far as can see!"

He smiled, "All Lena's doing. I'm not a rancher. She is, and it's just Lloyd, please." Hans grinned. "Say, where is Jeannette? She all right?" He noticed she was absent.

"She and Ashley are teaching each other how to do things. We should let them have some private time together, Hans," Lindsey explained.

"But we want to give our girlfriends a good night kiss," Jim teased.

"Well, you can do that in the morning. We are all going shopping at ten tomorrow morning," Amanda teased him back. With that, since the hour was getting late, those staying at the Whitewaters headed there. Pam returned to her computer and her research; Audrey, to her carving. Lindsey decided to play with Jonathon, since he was awake for a bit, though she most just held the newborn infant before Lena had to feed him.

"So you can cast some spells without your wand or saying the words?" Jeannette exclaimed rather awed at Ashley's statement.

"Yes, I can do Move Object that way. I just don't know how to make it do things as you do. Ordinarily, I just move my duffle bags, stuff like that. Lindsey, she can cast nearly all our spells from Grade 0 through 4 this way. She's going to be a Dispeller, after all. She worked with me last fall, and I can do seventeen, no eighteen, spells this way. We ran out of time to try for more."

"All them! Dat's, dat's, that's unheard of! Ve try to do them in sixth year. Me, I can do just dis one; my dad taught me, Move Object," Jeannette replied, very surprised by this revelation. Her respect for her mentor and Katja's rose enormously.

"Okay, now it's your turn," Jeannette decided. She'd successfully pulled down her bed for the night and made it again, several times. She'd even folded up her bath towel only using her feet. "Stand in front of your mirror and see if you can undo the buttons on your blouse. Go slow; make sure of each motion you want to make. I kind of imagine there are fingers there, you know, where you make contact with the buttons."

"Oh, this is so hard!" Ashley exclaimed. She got confused by trying to look down in front of her and then up into her reflection in the mirror. Only when she finally just focused on her image in the mirror was she able to undo one button.

"You did it!"

"So darn hard!" Ashley replied.

Jeannette moved up close to her, and they hugged. She whispered, "Everything is very hard for us, but ve manage, don't ve, Ashley?"

"We sure do! How do you say thank you in Dutch?"

"Dank u."

"Dank u!" Ashley gave her a hug, using her leg to hold them tight.

Chapter 5—The Shopping Day

At ten, after the girls raced through their morning chores and got ready to go on their shopping trip, Monane went down her checklist. "Girls, you have your rabbit's feet?" All three nodded.

"Hey, why do they need lucky rabbit's feet? Isn't that a silly norm custom thing?" asked Katja talking slowly. The three guests had funny looks on their faces.

"Oh, these are highly enchanted objects that will start jumping around whenever danger is near. R. B. made them for the girls; it runs off of a Grade 9 spell," she explained.

"Grade 9!" exclaimed Katja, quite impressed. She'd not thought very much at all about R. B. Neither had Hans. Now, they saw the Native American in a completely new light.

"Okay girls, get your staves of power," Monane went on with her list.

"Cool!" Lindsey said. "Margarete: Come."

"Zappo: Come." Ashley called out.

"Little Wolf: Come" Amanda said.

"Alf: Come." Pam commanded.

Staves of Power came flying into the room, three landing in the outreaching hands of the girls, but little Zappo had its harness on it, and rapidly fastened itself onto Ashley's back. The three guests stood staring at the four girls, their mouths open, unable to articulate an intelligent sound. While several of their professors at Utrecht had such a staff, certainly no student did.

"You've, you've all got them?" Katja finally managed to make a coherent question.

"Well, yes. My dad, Sam Barron, left me mine. Ever since Dominus and the Death Stalkers have been after us, R. B. thought that we needed better protection when we are out and about. Mine is really designed for a Dispeller, naturally, because that's what dad was. Amanda's Little Wolf is attuned to a Tracker, because that's what she's studying to become. Pam's Alf is designed to fit the needs of a Sleuth. Ashley's

Zappo is designed to protect her and allow her a way to easily attack. After all Dominus surely wants her dead, since she's studying to become a Diviner."

Monane spoke up, "We are going out in public in a good sized town. If we run into trouble, the girls can suck up harmful spells, while Wilma, Lloyd, R. B., Jim, and I deal with the aggressors. But don't worry, I can't image that we will run into any real trouble shopping for clothes. It's just that we want to be prepared. Next, on the checklist, Lindsey, do you have your ring and pin on you?" She nodded. "Prevents someone from spying on her. Ashley, your pin?" Ashley nodded. "Prevents someone from trying to charm her. Okay, everyone, no other items of any great value on you? We don't want to tempt pickpockets and the like. We adults will handle the actual purchase transactions for you. Okay, then let's get shopping. According to Lindsey, we must first pick up Kathy and her mother at Columbine Park. Wands ready? Everyone in contact?" Three cast their Teleport spells, and the group found themselves standing in the center of a large triangular park on the south side of Sterling.

Kathy and her mother were waiting for them. Kathy exclaimed, "Wow, Jeannette, you do look so similar to Ashley. You know, you too have the looks of a real teen fashion model. I brought along the latest edition that shows what clothes are in for this fall. That way, we are assured to be in style. You are with the best group, Jeannette. We all work together at school. You can count on us for everything. Where are we going first? Shoes or clothes?"

Lindsey was glad that she finally stopped for air. "We need to get them everyday summer clothes, at least three sets. Then, they need four sets for school, and they need their formal ball gowns. Plus, they want to get some extra things, souvenirs of the States. Then, we can go shoe shopping. I've never been to Sterling before. This is Pam's hometown. Where first, Miss Betts?"

Pam grinned. "We should get the outfits first and check on the ball gowns. Since Jeannette wants her tops to match Ashley's style, we then should go to Monane's daughter's shop. She is going to custom make them for her and Ashley. Jim, you have that map I made for you?" He waved it about. "Good. I don't expect that you guys are going to want to go with us girls, so Jim and R. B. will take Hans to several men's shops. We rendezvous back here at the park and then go to lunch. Questions?" Pam had the entire day mapped out, if only everyone stuck to the plan.

Sterling was where both Wilma and Monane lived, though actually both had small ranches on the western outskirts of Sterling. Hence, R. B. was also quite familiar with the town. "I'll take the boys, Monane. Cya at lunchtime," R. B. announced. Shortly, Lloyd, Jim, Hans, and R. B. vanished.

"Aunt Wilma, we should go to Elaine's first; they have the latest fashions, I think," Pam suggested. A minute later, the women walked into the large women's clothing store.

"Oh look, Jeannette! It's Amani's!" exclaimed an excited Katja.

"Ja, and look at de price! Fabulous. Ve pays three times dis amount in Utrecht! Dis is great shop!" Jeannette replied. Even Kathy was impressed; the two girls certainly knew the latest styles.

"Remember, when you find the right tops, blouses, and dresses you want, I'll take pictures of them. Then, we can show Louisa what you want her to make," Pam explained.

"Ja, but I want to get the real thing too. That way I have both," Jeannette replied.

Two hours later, Wilma and Monane teleported them back to the park to meet up with the men. The three women and all the girls were heavily laden with various packages. Even Monique had bought several new outfits, but no new dresses. In contrast, the men had empty hands. "Vat Hans? You finds nothing?" asked Katja rather worried that her brother had come up with empty hands.

Jim spoke up, "We already teleported our stuff back home. We're hungry. What's for lunch?"

"De Arches, Golden Arches, please. Ve wants zie burgers," Katja said too quickly, messing up her English.

Pam looked crestfallen, "But I have the perfect place for us to eat. We can always eat at the Arches; they are everywhere."

"Ja, we have them in Utrecht too," Hans replied. "Katja, Pam's right. We can always go to the Arches. Let's see what Pam has."

Katja grinned, "Okay. Okay. But I want to eat at the Arches soon. I promised everyone back home, you remember, Hans. We have to tell them if the burgers are the same as in Utrecht." Pam let out a sigh of relief. Her great plans for the day were back on track.

"Thanks. Aunt Wilma, let's all go to the Old Corral. It's just a few blocks from here." Wilma smiled and led the way. Pam had good taste, she thought.

"You will get the atmosphere of the Old West in this restaurant. Great decor and good, hearty food. I love this place. It's my favorite place to eat out. Well, except for Domino's," Pam admitted sheepishly.

Indeed, the decor was carefully reconstructed to resemble as close as possible the Old Western days when Sterling was founded. The waitress was dressed in an authentic cowgirl outfit. "May I take your order?" she said pleasantly.

"You should try the roast beef special," Pam suggested to her friends. In the end, the kids all did as Pam suggested. While they waited for their food, Wilma and Kathy's mother teleported their many packages back home. By the time they finished, their order came.

"My gosh!" exclaimed Amanda. "You get all this for only five dollars? Incredible. It's huge!" She stared at the oversized plate heaped with roast beef, real mashed potatoes, both swimming in brown gravy. Even the bowl of peas was also very large.

R. B. who knew better, watched Jim as he looked at the steak that he'd ordered for eight dollars. The oversized plate just barely held the steak. "Told you," Pam snickered. "You will need a doggie bag, I expect." The girls giggled, though they knew that they could not possibly eat this much food.

Lindsey kept a sharp eye on Ashley to see if she would need any assistance. "Well, here goes, Jeannette," Ashley whispered to her new friend sitting beside her. She cast her Move Object spell and carefully lifted her fork, scooped up a bit of the succulent beef, gravy, and potatoes and headed it for her mouth. It worked! A bit slow, but it worked.

Jeannette, who was eating as fast as the others, said, "You got it, Ashley. Perfect! Pam this is so good! It melts in your mouth!" Pam beamed, pleased that her diner was well-liked. Monique stole a glance at her girlfriend, Pam, and mouthed, "Super, my love!" Pam blushed, very happy that she had been able to share this with Monique.

A half hour later, everyone was quite stuffed, though virtually no plates were entirely empty. Poor Jim could only finish half of his steak. "Pam, that was one superb steak. I admit, I need a doggie bag, please." Ashley giggled at his embarrassment. So did R. B.

The three then took several photos of the diner to show their friends back home. As they left, the men went in search of sporting goods, while the women headed for Aunt Monane's daughter's dressmaking shop. Lindsey noted that Louisa looked very similar to her mother. Native American traits were prominent, from her long, thick black hair to her sharp eyes. "Hi mom. You've brought me a crowd?"

After the many introductions, Monane explained what they needed again. Earlier she had phoned her daughter, and Louisa was expecting them. While the others wandered about the shop looking at the gorgeous dresses on display, Monane had Ashley and Jeannette show Louisa what they wanted made especially for them. Ashley ordered three new blouses and one gown, but insisted that Jeannette get six blouses and a gown.

However, Kathy spied the most elegant gown she'd seen. Amanda, Lindsey, Pam, Monique, and Audrey came over to see what she kept ooing over. "Wow! Now that *is* a fabulous gown indeed! Pam, you would look stunning in it," Monique spoke what everyone was thinking: this was by far the best-looking gown they had seen today.

Lindsey had an idea, "Say, what if we all had the same gown, but in different colors, you know, to wear to our formal ball and dances? We'd look the same, but not the same." It took all of one minute for her idea to hook itself solidly in everyone's heart. "Okay, then it's my treat! I'll buy each of you one, just to say thanks for everything. Louisa, can I bother you a minute?" She refused to listen to the other girls protesting that she would pay for them.

"Yes, Miss Barron," Louisa greeted her.

"I am buying us all this dress, one for each of us, and Katja, Ashley, and Jeannette too. No, let's get Fern and Ellie in on this too. The other three had followed Louisa over to see what the others were doing. At once, they too fell in love with this dress on display. "Now all you have to do is pick your colors. I want mine in pale yellow, please." Louisa's mouth opened; her lips wiggled several times, before she could speak.

"Wow! Okay! That, by the way, is my own design. You are really honoring me. Really, this many gowns? Wow. Okay, pale yellow." She signaled one of her assistants who came rushing over, tape measure in hand. She carefully measured Lindsey and made the notations opposite her name and dress color. "You are all growing, I will leave in extra allowances so that you can alter them later on as needed," Louisa explained.

"Thank you, Lindsey," Amanda said next. "Light blue please."

Monique chose bright red, but Lindsey already guessed that would be her choice. Audrey chose a light brown. Pam picked a light pink. Kathy chose a light green dress. Ashley wanted a deep rich blue one. Monique picked a lighter shade of red for her sister, Ellie, while Amanda chose a light green for her sister, Fern. Katja and Jeannette were the last to choose. Finally, they decided on sky blue, identical colors, though Jeannette's would be sleeveless, matching Ashley's. Later at home, Lindsey had just spent two thousand dollars, but sent a check for two hundred more to thank Louisa.

Louisa promised that the special blouses would be delivered in a week, while the dresses would take longer, but she promised to have them as soon as possible. After they left, Louisa cheered and danced around her store, happy as a lark. She'd made more money in this short hour than she had made in a month. Further, Lindsey would tell others at Bradbury's about Louisa's shop. Her future had just taken a huge upswing!

"Now for shoes," Pam announced, looking over her

methodical list. Its heading was List of Things to Do in the Proper Order. She had not forgotten Kathy's burning desire to go shoe shopping. However, they had to visit two stores. First, the guests needed regular shoes. They insisted on getting two pairs of Nike's, which back home retailed for nearly triple the prices that they saw here in Sterling. Next, the two got a pair of dressier shoes.

"Okay, Kathy, Barkers is up next." Kathy giggled. Now they could look at real heels—the kind that all the teen models wore—the kind that she knew would make them look so grown up.

"We need to get heels to match our new gowns," Kathy took charge, since the others had never been in such an elegant, fashionable shoe store before. Pumps came in many heel heights; some were toweringly tall. "Mom, I am going to treat everyone to their ball gown shoes," Kathy insisted.

Her mother put her foot down, "Kathy, under no circumstances are you wearing any heels higher than three inches. So stop drooling over those! They must be at least five inches!" Indeed, Kathy was. She sighed and began looking at the lower height heels. An hour later, an elated Kathy left the store with everyone else. Now they would all look stunning at the formal balls wearing three-inch heels! They were looking like grown up teens now, no longer children, in her mind at least.

They met up with the fellows at the park once more. Again, none of them were carrying packages. "Here, Jim, Hans, make yourselves useful, carry our shoe boxes," Aunt Wilma said.

"Next, we are close to my home. I thought we could take a walk by my house, though our family is not living in it just now. What with dad's new promotion and Dominus coming after me, it isn't safe for us to live there anymore. At least, we can walk by my house. Besides, it is on the way to our last stop, Jeans and More Jeans. We all need jeans and shorts for this summer." Pam did want to show Monique where she had grown up.

As they approached her old house, Audrey said, "We should not be here. It is not a good idea for us to be here."

Almost at the same time, Ashley turned white. "Lindsey, I'm having a vision. Someone is following us and will try to kill me!"

Lloyd and R. B. sprang into action. Lloyd moved casually out in front of the group, while R. B. dropped to the rear. "Keep walking. Monane, Wilma, keep your eyes peeled," Lloyd said. "Kids, just keep on walking; act like nothing is wrong."

"See True!" Amanda's staff energized. At once, Pam and Ashley commanded their staves to cast the same spell on themselves. Trying not to look conspicuous, the three glanced at the many people walking the sidewalks around them.

"Here's my house," Pam said belatedly, wishing now she had never had the idea to show Monique her old home. What if she got everyone killed? It would be all her fault!

Amanda turned to the guests walking behind her, "There's Pam's old house, where she normally lives, before all this Dominus trouble began. Don't look back! There is someone following us who is using a Morph spell!" She quickly turned and faced the direction they were walking.

Pam could not keep herself from looking, though she attempted to disguise her actions by saying, "Yes, that's our house there. We've a big back yard. That's a Death Stalker behind us. One of the newer ones. I've seen his face in dad's recent files! Oh no! He's looking right at us!"

The whole group turned to face what appeared to be an old man walking down the street some hundred feet behind them. "He's casting!" Amanda called out, though Pam and Ashley both saw through his illusion with their spells. To the other's, it appeared that he was merely picking up a stick from the ground.

The magical attack lasted barely ten seconds, but quite a lot happened in that fleeing span of time. Ashley yelled, "Absorb it!" The Disintegrate beam headed directly toward her was sucked into her staff. Lindsey's Dispel Magic failed, but Pam's worked. Everyone caught a glimpse of their real attacker. His Morph spell was gone. Monique shot a bolt of lightning at him, but it was nullified by his protection spell, though it nearly knocked him off his feet. Audrey shot a mass of webs over him, hoping to pin him down, but his protection again allowed him to elude them.

Lloyd cast a giant hand that grabbed a hold of the Death Stalker and firmly held on to him. Lloyd was intent upon capturing him. Monane cast her Silence spell over the entire area around the man. Unable to hear, he would have a much more difficult time casting his spells. Wilma, unwilling to kill this man right in front of these children, cast a Paralyze spell on their attacker who suddenly stood bent over like a statue. The effect of R. B.'s spell could not be seen. However, the Death Stalker found himself wandering around in some other dimension, a maze perhaps, he thought to himself as he searched for the way out and back to his body.

"Well done. Looks like we've captured ourselves a Death Stalker," Lloyd spoke first. "You all stay back, let me arrest him. My job." Wand at the ready, he began moving closer to the frozen statue-like man. "I'll take that wand." He reached to take the man's wand from him so that the Death Stalker could not escape once the holding spells were canceled.

R. B. yelled, "Stop, Lloyd! Don't take. . ."

Too late, Lloyd pulled the wand from the man's grip. Instantly, a magical contingency spell activated, and the body simply vanished. Lloyd cursed.

"He had a contingency spell on him. Removing the wand triggered it, likely a Teleport spell," R. B. explained. "Sorry I spotted that too late, Lloyd."

Wilma muttered to Monane, "I ought to have spelled to kill, but the girls and guests. . ." Monane nodded, grateful that Wilma had not killed him right before the children's eyes. They would get another chance at him one day; she was sure of it.

"You okay sis? He tried to kill you, didn't he? That was a Disintegrate spell Zappo sucked up wasn't it?" Lindsey asked.

"Yes, I'm fine, bit frazzled, but okay. Golly, we can't even walk down the street without Dominus' men attacking us!" Ashley growled in anger.

"Well, Pam, your father was very wise in having you all staying with us," Lloyd said. "We can report to him that your home is most definitely being watched. Well, we've given them something to think about, Pam. Good idea of yours to come by here. Now they think that you are still living here. They will be wasting valuable manpower watching the place night and day. Good thinking, Pam." He praised her, but that was exactly the opposite of what she had been thinking! Pam didn't quite know what to make of it, and so said nothing. Lloyd was right. Now they would be certainly watching the place, wasting manpower.

"Shall we get our jeans now?" suggested Wilma.

"Way to go, Audrey, Ashley," Kathy finally spoke. "Gosh, I didn't even get the chance to get a spell off. You are way too fast for me. See how valuable having Audrey and Ashley around actually are?" She wanted the three guests to appreciate her two friends. She need not have worried, however. All three were staring in awe at both girls.

"Yes, Peaches said nearly the same thing, after that mock battle Professor Delius had us do at the end of May," Lindsey explained. "Actually, almost none of the ten who were supposed to get me really knew what to cast or when. Professor Delius said that we all need attack training in mock battles. He told me he was going to try to get some set up for us all this next term. I'm beginning to see that he might be right. We are far too slow. I mean that lasted only a few seconds, and I couldn't think of anything better to cast than Dispel Magic. I think we all need some kind of practice."

Wilma replied, "Well, I would second Delius's idea. To stay alive when being attacked by these evil men requires split second thinking and acting. You can't get that from books, only from actually doing it." She was about to say more about the many practice sessions that she and Sam had done to get her attacking skills honed to a fine edge just before they went after Dominus so many years ago, but quickly shut up. "To the jeans; lead on Pam."

"Mom! We found fabulous dresses and things. Got great looking, matching heels, and a Death Stalker tried to kill Ashley!" Lindsey blurted out what had happened to Lena, the second they all arrived back home safely.

"What? Ashley, are you all right?" Lena rushed to inspect her daughter.

"I'm fine. Zappo saved me. We nearly caught him, only he had an In Case Someone Takes My Wand, Teleport Me Away spell on him. R. B. spotted it a second too late, when dad tried to take his wand away from him," she explained.

After a lengthy discussion, Hans changed the subject. He said, "Katja, Jeannette, you must come over to Whitewaters and see what we got for us all."

Curious, the girls left their massive piles on the front room floor and dashed to the teleport pad to go and see. All were curious about just what the men had been buying. Hans proudly showed off a new archery set that Jim had gotten for him. "We went a little overboard," R. B. admitted to everyone, including Luci, who stood by watching the excited children.

They had bought a number of water toys for their swimming in the pond and a small canoe for the pond as well. R. B. insisted it was going to be useful if someone needed rescuing. Luci didn't buy that explanation at all. Each teen had a pair of cowboy boots for riding, a compete ski outfit, complete with skis, a pair of ice skates, and winter parkas for the three guests. "Now we have lots of fun here," Hans replied with a broad grin. Obviously, he was thinking ahead to the winter holidays, and so were Jim and R. B.

Chapter 6—Summertime

Pam dug into her research projects, considering she now had the luxury of time on her hands. True, she did her part with helping Ashley relearn spells, but she avoided the long horseback rides and other outdoor activities that Lindsey, Amanda, and Jim did with the three guests.

Besides getting and keeping her extensive database of the criminal activities of the Death Stalkers and Dominus up to date, she had the Restricted Wish spell to research, a project given to her by Governor Alister himself! Then, she had the request from Deiter Cross to research what happened during a Teleport Spell. Since she had not yet learned that spell, she doled that one out to Monique, who spent all of her time alongside of Pam.

Then, there was the secret code writing in Ashley's father's journal to decipher. Although the information was obviously quite dated, at least thirteen years old, she nevertheless greatly desired to know what Joshua Stokes had found out about this Mac Fluide Enterprises. Indeed, that name kept coming up in the strangest places. For instance, that company owned the abandoned house in which Dominus had kept them last year, when he had his men kidnap Pam and her friends, casting that awful Idiot Mind on her. True, the others had disintegrated a large section of the home's outer wall, but she and Monique had checked on it twice since then, during their days in Telluride. It still showed no signs of being repaired.

Pam was also curious about the killings of the grandparents of the three foreign exchange students. Although this too was now history, she was curious since Dominus was behind it. She had to know all about what had happened.

Also bouncing around in her head was just why had Dominus kidnaped Governor Alister last spring. True, Pam and her friends had been instrumental in his rescue. Why did Dominus want to obtain the Crown of Moses once more? He certainly couldn't hope to use it to alter the weather as he had done last fall. To Pam's sleuthing mind, there just had to be some other reason behind this action of Dominus. She had to figure it out.

The bombing at the Nationals in May still held her interest. She was determined to find evidence to pin the bombing on the Death Stalkers and Dominus. True, she had positive ids from some of the professors that the Death Stalkers were on the scene, attempting to capture Lindsey and Ashley, but nothing directly connected them to the bombing. Indeed, if confronted with this, they could say that they wanted to rescue the girls during this horrid bombing episode.

Her stack of textbooks for the fall term sat on her desk as well. From all indications, this term would require far more homework than ever before. Pam desperately wanted to get a head start on all subjects, especially spell casting, since they were going to be studying Grade 5 spells, really powerful ones, including Teleport! She wondered why Bradbury's didn't offer summer school so she could get a head start.

Also sitting on her desk was the book Tom and Sandy had gotten for Lindsey, who was sharing it with Pam, Teacher's Spells. Already the Stop Motion spell had proved invaluable in diagnosing how Ashley had gone wrong on her initial attempts at spell casting using arms and hands. Pam desperately wanted to learn all the spells in this book as well. So did Lindsey, for that matter.

Finally, Pam was worried about using Lindsey's Ring of Regeneration on Ashley and Jeannette. Would it work? Was this the best avenue to follow? What were the repercussions of using it? Would arms and hands be regenerated and be normal hands or would they be some kind of freakish thing that would horrify both girls? What about the psychological impact of suddenly having hands and arms? She sighed, "I have way too much to research, Monique!"

"Come here," Monique replied lovingly, her red lips smiling. "I know just what you need!" Pam moved over to her desk and Monique pulled her down into her lap. She hugged Pam, who found herself hugging Monique back. Then, they passionately kissed. Rejuvenated, Pam asked, "What have you found?"

"Well, I wish we were at Bradbury's. I really need to check the library. It is so hard to tell fact from fiction from wishful hoping here on the Net. Anyone can say anything about anything, whether it is true or not. I'd rather wait a bit longer; otherwise, I may just be filling your head with incorrect data. How about we work on another problem?"

"Okay, let's see if we can come up with plausible reasons why Alister was kidnaped, love?" Pam suggested. The two began to draw up charts, outlining possible explanations.

Middle of the afternoon, Jeannette wandered in to see what they were doing. Lindsey was working with Ashley and her spells, and Jeannette, not interested in the gardening that Audrey and Fern were doing, went in search of other things to do. "Hi, what are you doing? Can I help?" she asked slowly, especially since Katja was not around. She and Hans were assembling some of the new pool and swimming toys. All were going swimming later on this afternoon.

"We are working out the reason why Dominus kidnaped Governor Alister and tried to kill him slowly, while he tried to recover the Crown of Moses," Pam explained.

"Ja, interesting. Tell me about it," Jeannette replied, sitting down on Pam's bed. Pam and Monique spent a half hour going over all that they knew about the incident and the related events, including the hurricane disaster and the abduction and attempted slaying of the Diviner, Millicent Prague. "Ja, ve studied Dominus in World History class," Jeannette replied, remembering to slow down and get her English correct.

Next, Pam showed her the large chart of possible explanations behind this abduction of Governor Alister. They had ten reasons why drawn out. "Let me think a minute. Some of des are good reasons, but ve must look at the, how you say, ah, whole picture of Dominus. She laid back on Pam's bed, closed her eyes, and thought.

"Ve must look wide view; oh no, you say broad view; that's it, broad view. What scares Dominus Malefic most? Asks that as de first question, because that's de most important question to asks. Fear often underlines a man's actions and decisions, you see, especially de criminal types, who do wrongs. Wat vreest hij de meesten? Oops, what does he fear most?"

"Well, probably getting caught again," Monique replied without hesitation.

"Right, the Rat Pack were the ones who captured him the last time, but only Bill West and Able Monument are still alive. His minions killed their Diviner Mabel Pruit and their Dispeller, Sam Barron, effectively crippling the Rat Pack. Today, the Rat Pack doesn't have enough clues about what his plans are or where he may strike next to get there ahead of him and lay a trap for him," Pam elaborated.

"Yet, dis Bill and Able, they have been present several time when you encountered Dominus and the Death Stalkers," Jeannette continued her analysis. "If I were him, I would be very worried or scared with their reappearance. After all, no one heard from them the last many years, have they? No, they have scared Dominus. He is very intelligent. I think he thinks if the Rat Pack gets another Diviner, he would be in serious troubles again, in danger of being captured, maybe killed this time. I think we can say he most fears a replacement Diviner. Dat makes Ashley a prime suspect, does it not? She is Diviner. We saw it in Sterling the other day. She knows things or senses them. I think Dominus fears that Ashley may become the Diviner who will get him caught dis time."

"That makes sense," Pam followed her argument and added to it. "So if I feared Ashley and her Divination powers, I would want to make darn sure that Ashley was behind the divinations of his actions and plans. Ah ha. I would set a trap for her. Arrange something bad and see if she divines it, particularly bringing in the Rat Pack to handle it. Jeannette, I think you have solved this puzzle! Dominus went after the Crown of Moses and Governor Alister only to see if Ashley would divine what was happening and send the Rat Pack to rescue him!"

"But Pam darling, he's already done just that!" Monique interrupted, rather startled where this was headed. "That means he *knows* for sure that Ashley is correctly divining his plans and actions! That makes Ashley his prime target. No wonder that Death Stalker tried to kill Ashley the other day in

Sterling! He didn't care at all about the rest of us, only Ashley!"

"That must make Ashley their prime target, number one!" Pam gasped. "I'd better email Governor Alister about this at once! Ashley won't be safe anywhere she goes!"

"I'll let R. B. know too, and everyone else," Monique added.

"Gosh, Jeannette, that was incredible reasoning. Thank you! You sure seem to be a budding Nous, don't you?" Pam said. Jeannette flushed and smiled.

A few minutes later, a MagMail delivery came, delivering three new computers for the Dutch students, compliments of Governor Alister. As usual, Pam went over each computer, setting them up for optimum performance and installing everyone's email addresses in the contact's database. She also added a few links to the more relevant Net sites that they would be likely to use.

The guests were kept busy with horseback riding, archery, swimming, and of course chores. By the end of the week, the first installment of their special clothing order from Louisa arrived for Ashley and Jeannette. Both had to try on each top and show it to their friends. They were very happy with their new looks. However, Lindsey wondered what would happen if the arm regeneration worked. All these specially made clothes would not then fit. She chatted with her mom, who reassured her that all could easily be redone either sleeveless or she and Polly could add some sleeves, whichever the girls desired. Lindsey realized that she ought to get some sewing lessons from her mother and Polly, only she didn't seem to have time right now.

During the week, Ashley's spell casting improved greatly. She had down pat all of her Grade 0 useful spells and was into the Grade 1 spells. Lindsey estimated that surely by the end of June, Ashley would have them all relearned and would be ready to attempt to regenerate her arms. Thus, she decided to talk to Governor Alister about this and she sent him an extensive email. To her surprise, he replied within an hour!

Dear Miss Barron,

Thank you for the detailed report on Miss Stokes-Compton

and on our new exchange student, Miss van Ravinstijn. I have been well aware that your inherited ring may be just what Miss Stokes-Compton would need. However, as you have so very well pointed out, a number of problems had to be worked out with her first, before any such attempt ought to be made. Do I detect the input of Miss Betts behind the scenes? (That's a tease, by the way.)

After her remarkable mental changes this past year, I conclude, as you have, that she is in the right mental state to have this procedure performed. Yes, she must be able to handle normal daily activities using her arms and hands. I am amazed that it took her this long to figure out that she ought to be using her Morph spell for this purpose. As to her spell casting, I must compliment you and Pam (?) on your thoroughness. Indeed, returning this fall with regenerated arms and hands, but unable to cast her known spells would be a disaster for her. I agree with you; no attempt should be made until she can routinely cast all known spells while Morphed into Peggy. Her wand held in her hands must activate properly, that is a given. Once that is achieved, I believe that she is psychologically ready for the regeneration attempt.

However, many things may go wrong with the attempt. Do not, I repeat, do not try this yourselves. When it is time, let me know, and I will send Doctor Caterwall to you. All regeneration must be done under his care and supervision. Give me as much advanced notice as possible, please, though I personally hope it may yet be this summer.

As far as Miss Jeannette van Ravinstijn is concerned, her Governor has assured me that she is very level headed and as well-adjusted to her situation as can be expected. She has no problems casting spells using her Move Object spell to control her wand. However, to be on the safe side, she, too, ought to practice casting them while Morphed into someone with arms and hands. However, as you probably have discovered by now, she has serious problems in the dark or when she cannot see, for whatever reason. She completely freezes up, drops her wand, and becomes "completely and utterly helpless." Those are the words of her Governor. She makes no use at all of her feet, I'm told, though I suspect you have already discovered this for yourself. If you can find a way to get her over this barrier, this hurdle, it would be wise for her sake.

When it is time, please make very sure that both girls really want this regeneration for their own sake, not for some other reason, such as just to be normal, like all the other kids. Doctor Caterwall can assist you in making this determination. If Miss van Ravinstijn wishes to have this attempted on her, I will inform her parents in Utrecht for their permission to go ahead with it.

Keep up the admirable work, Miss Barron. I look forward to seeing you all back here soon.

Sincerely,

Governor Alister Broadwell

Arthur Bradbury School of Magic

While Ashley, Jim, and Hans were shooting pool, Jeannette watching, Lindsey showed the email to Pam and Monique. "Ah just as we thought, there can be bad side-effects! We had better get researching them," Pam declared.

Just then, Audrey came by their room carrying her latest carving. "Hey, can you look at this newest piece I've made for Jeannette and tell me what emotion you sense from it? I'm not totally sure I got it completely right."

Lindsey looked at the mahogany carving of a mother horse nuzzling her newborn colt. Instantly, she replied, "I see love, Audrey. I think you've outdone yourself with this one. It's fabulous."

Monique and Pam looked at it as well, and then looked at each other. In unison, they said, "Love, Audrey, love." Monique added, "It's what love is all about, deeply caring for another. You ought to be in Red Hall. You can put emotions into mere carvings."

"No, I don't put them there. I just find them there, in each piece of wood. Thanks, I guess it's okay. I'll go give it to her. Is she with Ashley?"

"Yes, last time I saw them, they were playing pool," Lindsey replied.

"Okay. Oh, by the way, Pam, I think you ought to look into what happened to her grandparents. I think it may be important. It feels like it to me." She didn't say anything else or elaborate. By now, everyone knew that she would have said all she did know and that they ought to trust her intuitions.

Monique looked at Pam, who said, "Well, okay. Let's sleuth that one next. At least, we have one research project finished." Monique chuckled. The two began typing away on their laptops.

"Excuse me, Jeannette. I have a small present I made just for you. Here. I hope you like it," Audrey said meekly.

Jeannette was so excited that she had Hans hold it for her, afraid that she might lose control of her spell and drop it. "It's so utterly beautiful! You can just see the love the mother has for her baby," she spoke as slowly as possible, very unwilling to chance messing up her English. "Thank you! Thank you!" She pressed forward into Audrey's body, as if hugging her, and used her spell to hold her tightly. Audrey blushed, but was pleased that she liked it.

"Understand: Dutch!" Monique commanded and her wand flashed. "That's better, I'm into the newspaper accounts of the robbery and murder, Pam. Blah, blah, the usual stuff. Nothing I see useful. I'll keep on it."

"Well, I wonder what was stolen?" Pam said.

"No way to find out, I suppose, unless we can contact their parents. Perhaps they might know. Do you suppose we could write to the insurance company that underwrote their loss?" Monique asked.

"Let me see if there is anything in the Interpol file first."

"What? You have access to the Interpol databases?" Monique asked, a bit annoyed that Pam had such access, and she had yet to figure out how to hack into their site.

"Via dad," Pam said, sensing what was going on in Monique's mind, a tad bit of jealously. Monique relaxed, and Pam smiled; she had been right in her guess. A few minutes of digging through web pages of files, Pam finally homed in on the reports of the correct year of the robbery and murders. A bit later, she found the actual final report. "Understand: Dutch," she commanded and began reading.

"Here we go. I've got it, the official list of all stolen items. I'm making a copy for us. Is your printer hooked up? Perhaps we ought to have a hardcopy printout to look over,"

Pam asked. A bit later, the pages came out of her printer, and the two, sitting close beside each other, looked over the three pages of stolen items.

"This is weird, Pam. Look, they stole only the Grade D diamonds. The GIA classifies their color on an alphabetical scale from D-Z, with D being colorless. They stole only the very best diamonds. Plus, only cut diamonds, ready for mounting and then only diamonds that weighted 2 carats. A carat is 200 milligrams. Nothing else at all. If we use their figures, one of the stolen diamonds would be worth about three thousand dollars. They stole one thousand of these. Hence, their take was about three million dollar's worth of diamonds."

"Wow. That is an incredible sum."

Monique went on, "True, Pam, but think a minute. They left everything else, which represented perhaps hundreds of millions of dollars!"

"That makes no sense. If they killed the owners, why leave the rest? Why take only one very specific type of diamond?"

"Dunno, but they only took the very best and of one size, a nice size for a ring," Monique elaborated.

"You know what is really weirder? None has ever been recovered. I mean, every jeweler had been on the lookout for them, but not one has ever been found! Fifteen years and not a one has surfaced. Why would Dominus steal three million in diamonds and then do nothing with them? Is he collecting diamonds? What would you do with a thousand diamonds anyway?"

"Dunno, mount them in rings I suppose," Monique replied. "At least that's what I might do with them. You could then sell them. Still, none has ever been found, so that must not be right. What is Dominus doing with a thousand diamonds?"

"Well, he didn't have them on him when he was arrested by the Rat Pack," Pam pointed out. "He must still have them somewhere. This only gets more curious."

"Say, didn't he rob Fort Knox of a bunch of gold when he first escaped from prison?" Pam asked. Monique agreed with her, and soon Pam brought up exactly what he had stolen.

"Two hundred ten-pound bars of gold," she announced. Monique had the conversion to dollars site up and entered the amount.

"At eight hundred per ounce, two hundred times ten times sixteen gives us a net haul of twenty-five million six hundred thousand dollars' worth," Monique stated, reading the enormous figure from her screen.

"How much gold does it take to make the average ring, I wonder," Pam mused.

"Probably around a quarter of an ounce, why?"

"Well, that means he could make around one hundred twenty-five thousand rings out of that amount of gold, maybe more. It would have been interesting to see the number of diamonds stolen being equal to the number of rings he could make from that gold," Pam admitted.

"You think Dominus is trying to make rings out of these?"

"I can't figure out what else he could be doing with them, especially the diamonds. I wonder if R. B. can shed any light on it. Come on; let's go see him."

Unfortunately, supper was now being served. After dinner chores were done, everyone headed over to the Whitewater's to go swimming. All except Monique, who dare not get her face in the waters just yet, and Pam, who really didn't like swimming and preferred to be with Monique. "You going swimming with us tonight?" asked Lindsey.

"No, we want to chat with R. B.," Pam replied.

While the others headed off to the ponds, Pam and Monique found R. B. back at work in his workshop. "Great minds think alike," he replied, after Pam explained her theory about the stolen gold and diamonds. "That's what I thought when I heard about the theft of the gold. Now that I know a thousand diamonds are also involved, it is highly likely that Dominus intends to mass-produce something of value, more than likely magically enchanted rings. Those with the diamonds on them would be highly useful."

"But what spells could he possibly want to put into a whole bunch of rings? I mean he cannot wear a thousand rings, now can he?" Pam said somewhat exasperated with the whole thing.

"Most any spell could be put into a ring's enchantment, Pam, though there is not much point in making a ring that simply casts a Light spell that goes out in ten minute's time. If he is making rings, Pam, he isn't making them all for himself. A few perhaps, but not thousands. More than likely, he'll give them to his closest associates, like the Death Stalkers. It would be clever to create an enchanted ring that would store the In Case of This Happening, Then Cast This Automatically, such as Teleport to safety. However, that is not likely because such a ring would have to be of the highest quality imaginable to hold such a powerful spell as that. I do believe that you are on to something, but we just don't know the purpose of the rings as yet."

Later, she explained her findings and theory about the rings to her father, who promised to alert his staff for any appearance of "rings." Additionally, Pam sent the facts on to Governor Alister to get his opinion on it as well.

Lindsey and Pam spent a little time each evening working together to learn some of the spells from the Teacher's Spell Book. In addition to the Slow Motion and Grade Paper, they found the Detect Plagiarism spell a fascinating one indeed and complex to cast. It took the two nearly a week to master that one. They skipped the Enter Grades in a Grade Book spell, figuring they had no use for that one at all. Find Related Material was a very useful spell, especially for Pam. When cast, one specified the topic on which one wished additional reference material and then specified the library to search. When the spell finished, a paper list appeared containing the related materials contained in the search library. When Monique heard about this spell, she also spent time learning it because this spell would help her in her studies at school. She was dreading the voluminous amounts of homework the professors assigned or so she had heard.

Two weeks after the arrival of the Dutch students, Ashley was ready to have Jeannette solo in the dark a bit. The girl had always been terrified of total darkness because she couldn't then cast any spells. She always collapsed into a helpless state, unable to do anything for herself. Having worked with Jeannette getting her to do some simple things with her feet as she did, Ashley thought that now was the time to begin to build confidence in her new friend. She proposed, "Tonight after dark, let's put Jeannette through her paces here in the house. She and I will start in our room, as if we were in bed say. Everyone else, turn off all the lights, even the night lights, so that it is pitch black in here."

"Then, Jeannette's task will be to get out of bed, find our door, open it, walk through the house to the front room, and turn on the big lamp there. I'll be right behind her all the way, in case she runs into trouble."

"But she gets petrified when it's totally dark," Katja protested.

"Everyone gets spooked when it's so dark they can't see anything. That's normal. I think Jeannette can now handle doing this much on her own. If she gets too spooked, I will use Emotion: Calm on her right away."

In their room, Ashley had Jeannette get into bed and pull the covers up without using magic, as she had been doing for the last week now. "Are you ready?" Ashley asked.

"I don't know if I can do this! I might freak out. I always do, Ashley. I'm scared already. I feel so helpless."

"That's just a state of mind, Jeannette. Remember: focus on the senses you do have. I know that you will do just fine! I know it." Ashley gave her a little pep talk. If she had fingers, she would have crossed them. "Okay, ready in here." One by one, the lights went out. Ashley turned out their nightlight herself. Their room was utterly black, as was the rest of the entire house. Outside their room, everyone else held their breath, though Katja fully expected to hear Jeannette scream in terror and panic. She had done so many times, especially in spell casting class when they were working on spells, which cost her her sight for a time.

"I'm scared, Ashley," Jeannette whispered, fighting to control the wave of terror floating over her.

"Everyone is somewhat afraid of what they can't see or perceive. You are doing fine."

"But I haven't done anything yet."

"Yes, you have; you haven't screamed in panic. Now see

if you can get yourself out of bed. Remember to keep your feet widely spaced; better balance that way. I'm right here with you. You can do it."

Her covers seemed like snakes, fighting to constrict her, to hold her to the bed. She fought against them and managed to sit up, finally free of their entanglement. "I'm sitting. Here goes. I'm on my feet."

Carefully, she slowly moved across the room to where she imagined the door must be. Naturally, she misjudged its location. "It's not here."

"Feel with your toes; see where you are at."

"Oh, the dresser. Door is this way." Now she found the door. She nearly fell down trying to slide the latch back with her foot. Jeannette got the door opened. Ashley moved to get behind her, and found it a tough act as well. Slowly, the girls moved down their long hallway. Jeannette continually felt along the wall, trying to find the opening to the longer hall that led to the front of the house. At last, she turned and headed towards the front. Her confidence rose now, and she made better time of it, until she bumped into the front wall.

Next, she had to feel her way to the entrance of the front room. A bit later, the two entered the front room. Feeling the sofas and chairs, she slowly made her way to the lamp. At last, she felt it and then began moving her head around it, trying to find the pull chain. Finally, she felt it hit her cheek, and she used her mouth to pull it down. The lights came on. The others then turned on many other lights and came to congratulate Jeannette.

"See you did it," Ashley exclaimed. Jeannette was incredibly pleased. Katja explained that this was the first time since she had known Jeannette that she had not freaked out when it was so dark. After this astonishing success, Lindsey suggested that they all play kick the can at dusk, so Jeannette could get more used to the dusk and early evening darkness. They started running around playing the game just after sunset, and Jeannette got so enthused about the game, she forgot her fears of the coming nighttime. She did as well as everyone else when it became too dark to continue to play the game. Bit by bit, she overcame her greatest fear, being helpless in the night.

During the last week of June, Lindsey had Jeannette Morph in to Pam and then had her begin casting spells using her wand in her right hand. To Lindsey's amazement, Jeannette had no difficulty with this at all. Spell after spell worked perfectly, from the lowly Clean to the Magical Missile to a Bolt of Lightning and Ball of Fire, of which the latter three and many others were cast outside. After three sessions of this, Lindsey verified that Jeannette could cast her spells with real hands. She sent her report on to Governor Alister.

The girls' formal dresses arrived the third Friday in June. After trying them on, Lena suggested that they have a fancy dance on Saturday night—yes, complete with Domino's pizzas. On Saturday morning, the girls raced through their chores so they could have as much time as they wanted to get fancied up for the dance. Pam grew very tired of the many "Now how do I looks" that were sent her way. She thought everyone looked great anyway. Much of the afternoon was spent getting used to walking properly in their new heels. This actually surprised all the girls, who finally learned that they needed to take smaller steps.

At six, all of those over at the Whitewater's came, and Jim hooked up the sound system to play the formal dance music. Indeed, for the first half hour everyone looked over the girls in their matching outfits and heels, marveling at just how fantastic they all looked. Fred and Henry had returned to see their daughters, primarily because Polly and Lottie had been insistent. Now they understood why. Their daughters were growing up rapidly and looked like young women, gorgeous young women.

Fred asked his daughter, in her elegant light pink gown with matching heels, for the first dance. Pam blushed and proudly danced with her father. Fred just beamed. He wanted to say, "Look at my daughter!" But held back for fear of embarrassing her. "Dad, I am still homely; it's just the dress." He ignored her protest.

"One day Pam, some young man is going to fall head over heels for you."

"But dad, Monique is already head over heels for me, and I, her."

He whispered, "Yes, I know. Just don't be too upset if one day a very handsome man falls for Monique. It's been known to happen."

Likewise, Henry took his older daughter, Monique, onto the dance floor for the first dance. She looked positively ravishing in her bright red, long formal gown and matching heels. Both men just could not believe the transformation of their daughters; only yesterday, they had been kids running around their backyards. Now, here they were so grown up!

Lloyd chose to dance with Lindsey first, who looked incredibly pretty in her light yellow gown and heels to match. He whispered into her ears, "Thank you for giving them such joy. I am so proud of you. If I were twenty years younger, I'd come after you." She blushed and accepted the compliment, though she got so many thank you's from everyone she lost track of them all. Lindsey was just happy that she could do what she did for all of her friends.

R. B. danced first with his daughter. Amanda in her light blue gown and matching heels, with her thick, long black hair, looked fabulous indeed. He told her so, and she blushed too. "I feel so grown up, dad," she whispered in his ear.

Jim whisked Ashley onto the floor before Lloyd could get the chance. Ashley's deep rich blue gown and heels only enhanced her radiance. Jim thought she was an angel. "I think I need to give you a better name than princess. You are more like a goddess. Yes, Goddess Ashley. I do love you so!" he whispered in her ear, and she crimsoned, but enjoyed hearing it. At this moment, she felt like she was a teen model in one of Kathy's magazines.

Following Jim's lead, though he didn't have to, Hans took his heart's desire onto the dance floor for the first dance. Jeannette in her sky blue, long formal gown, which really did highlight her shoulders and what was not there, and matching heels felt happier than she could ever remember. Hans, sliding his hands over her back and shoulders, sent tingles throughout her entire body. She never wanted this moment to end. "You are the most beautiful girl in the entire world, Jeannette, and I love you madly," he whispered in her ear. Now she knew she didn't want this ever to end.

Secretly, Katja, standing there in her matching sky blue dress and heels, longed for her heartthrob to see her like this. Klaas was miles from here with some other family, Mexicans, she recalled from his emails. Just then, the monotone voice announced, "Friendly arrivals."

Lena, who was in on the plan, was right beside the door, holding little Jonathon. She opened the door, "Hi, right on time, first dance. Come on in, Kathy. You must be Emilio and you Klaas. I'm Lena Compton. Come on in and find your partners." Indeed, Kathy's mother, Elinor, had brought the three teens. After all, Lena thought, Kathy was a big part of this.

Emilio led Kathy in her light green gown with matching heels onto the dance floor, blending with the others. Kathy just knew now that she had achieved a major victory; fashion reigned king here. She was incredibly happy.

Katja saw Klaas and waved to him. She wanted to run over to him, but found she had to walk carefully and slowly in her gown and heels. Klaas closed the distance rapidly. "Gosh! Katja, you look fabulous, fantastic. Sorry, I don't know more proper English words. You are stunning."

"Ja, I know!" She put her arms around her boyfriend, and they too began to dance. "I so wanted you to see me tonight! How did you know?"

"Lena, she told us about it and invited us. Kathy's mom, that's Emilio's girlfriend, she brought us."

Lottie asked her daughter, Ellie, in her light red dress and heels, for the first dance. "Ellie, you look so grown up!" Ellie smiled, stating that she was. Ellie felt extremely proud that she was now a part of this whole group of friends. After all, Lindsey had included her and bought her this fabulous dress so everyone could see that she was part of their group.

Luci took Fern onto the dance floor for the first dance. Her youngest daughter wearing her light green formal gown and heels looked so grown up that Luci was a bit shocked. "Fern, I didn't realize how much you have grown up. Look at you! You are going to wow all the boys when you go back to school. You look just terrific!"

"I know mom. I'm grown up, well almost anyway."

Polly chose to take Audrey onto the dance floor for the first dance. "Dear, you look incredible! Your choice of this light brown gown is just perfect for you. How did you ever find matching pumps? You are going to make some boy incredibly happy to dance with you."

The fathers switched partners on the second dance. Lloyd took Ashley out of Jim's arms, sliding Lindsey into her place. "My turn; you don't get to monopolize the prettiest girl at the party." Jim gave one of his fake looks of absolute shock and horror, causing both Lindsey and Ashley to break out into a laugh.

As they danced, he whispered, "Ashley, you are just plain stunning. So grown up. Gosh, you have your father wishing he were twenty years younger!"

Henry took Ellie away from her mother, "My turn. My little rose has blossomed into a magnificent young woman." Ellie blushed and held her dad tight.

On the next dance, Lloyd took Audrey from Polly, "You look stunning indeed, daughter. I love the color you chose. It suits you just perfectly." Audrey felt incredibly happy. The world was indeed a wonderful place in which to live, just now, anyway.

Ten o'clock came too soon. The girls swore that Lloyd had moved the hour hand up three hours, and Lindsey so accused him. Everyone laughed and sat down to gobble up the many pizzas that the Mag Delivery had just brought. Lena had timed their arrival perfectly. While they were eating, she said, "Listen up. I have a little announcement to make. Since Kathy, Emilio, and Klaas have never been here before, I thought that they ought to stay overnight so that they can properly see our ranch and the Whitewater's ranch in the morning. Elinor agrees with me, but says they need to return around four tomorrow afternoon. The ladies will be staying here, while the boys will stay at the Whitewaters."

The yells of appreciation and clapping, Lena did not expect. She now knew just how close these friends actually were. The dozen large pizzas vanished rapidly. Next, the girls decided to show the three new arrivals around the inside of the Compton home. Jeannette whispered to Ashley, "Have Jim put his arm over your shoulder like Hans is doing with me. Then, you can lead him around and show him things."

Ashley needed no second encouragement. Neither did Jim, who instantly duplicated the way Hans held onto Jeannette. Jim whispered, "Hans is sharper than I am. I wish I'd of figured this move out last year!" She giggled and began leading him after the others.

Finally, Kathy and Emilio saw Lindsey's, Ashley's, and Audrey's home, as well as where Pam was now living in safety. Both were impressed.

Klaas and Katja held hands the whole evening. Neither wanted to be parted from the other, not until the last moment. He did give her a good night kiss when they used the teleport pad to travel to the Whitewater's.

Lena fed Jonathon his midnight feeding and saw that the girl's lights were still on. She went to investigate. All the girls still wore their fancy gowns and heels, chatting together like there would be no tomorrow. "Okay, girls, time to change. Morning comes early in summer. Say, would you like to hold more Saturday night formal dances?"

"Could we mom?" Lindsey gushed. "That would be fabulous!" All the others echoed her sentiments. Lena chuckled and agreed to see what could be done. She didn't see why not. Only then did the girls reluctantly start undressing for bed. Lena smiled all the way to her bedroom, where she was attacked by Lloyd and pelted with loving kisses.

The next day, they raced through their chores so they could spend time looking over the Compton ranch and then the Whitewater ranch. Emilio was most impressed with both ranches. He had never dreamed they were this cool and wished he could come here for the summer. He and Kathy began a conspiracy to try to find a way to make that happen next summer. Four o'clock came much too soon for the three. However, with the prospect of returning next Saturday night now a reality, they didn't protest too much on having to leave and say goodbye.

Chapter 7—Regenerations

By July 4, Ashley had finished relearning all of her spells. While Morphed into Peggy, she was able to cast them all either left handedly or right handedly. Jeannette was getting along well. Her terror of being helpless in the dark was drastically reduced. Now was the time for decisions, since two more months of summer vacation remained.

Wilma, Monane, Lena, and Lindsey held a private meeting with Ashley and Jeannette, but only with one girl at a time. Monane spoke first. "Okay, Ashley, as far as any of us know, you are fully ready to make an attempt at the regeneration of your arms. However, now is the time that you must make this decision. It is your decision and yours alone to make. Do not make it out of an urge to be just like everyone else. None of us is like everyone else. We are all unique individuals. If you decide to try this and it works, there is no going back. No doctor would remove them for you, if you didn't like them. You would permanently have arms and hands just like the rest of us. This is a very important decision that you alone must make. None of us will think any less of you no matter what you decide to do, Ashley. We all love you and that will not change one iota because of whatever decision you chose to make. Is this clear?"

"Yes, Monane. I truly do like myself as I am. When I came back from school, I admit, I didn't, but that's changed. I'm me, and I like me. That's a good sign, isn't it?" she asked.

Lena grinned, "Yes, dear, a very good sign indeed."

"Well, I have been so stupid all these years in not using magic to help myself with things. I'm over that too. I've discovered that it is so much easier to do all the normal things when I am Morphed into Peggy. I really want to give it a try. If I could get arms and hands, things would be so much easier for me to do. I just have to try it. I know it might not work. Pam and Monique have shown me web pages of just awful results, but if it would work, my life would be so much easier to live. If it doesn't work, well, I can accept that too. I'm happy as I am and can get by so much better now, but I owe it to myself to at least try it."

"Good girl, that's the right attitude to take. We'll let Governor Alister know your decision at once. Now please send in Jeannette; she must make her choice as well."

A bit later, Jeannette came in, rather timidly. Monane gave her nearly the same speech she'd just delivered to Ashley. "I would like to try it. I know I'm doing just fine as I am, really I am, especially since Ashley has shown me how to do some things with my feet. I never thought I could face the darkness, but now I can. Honestly, life would be so much easier for me. I have to try it. Only," she didn't finish her sentence. She had purposely been speaking slowly, making sure of her English.

"Only you have a reservation?" Monane probed and encouraged her with a smile.

"Only, I don't know how to thank Lindsey for it. I mean if it would really work and I would get real arms and hands, how can I possibly ever thank her for such a gift? It would be the biggest miracle I can imagine. Yet, I can't find anyway to thank her for something so huge, so big, and so important."

"I understand. I thought that this might become a consideration. I will answer it this way, dear. These are very dark times that we wizards and witches are facing, very dark. By all indications, it will only get darker. Yet, if we are to survive, we must band together. United, we are stronger than the forces of evil. You saw that when we were in Sterling. You can thank Lindsey by always being there for her when she needs it, even though you will be going back to Utrecht next summer, Lindsey and the rest of us will have a strong ally in you. Dominus and his Death Stalkers operate around the world as you know more so than others. United, we have a chance. This, I know personally, means the world to Lindsey."

"I promise, whether this works for me or not, that I and all my friends will always be there for Lindsey and her friends! But this seems so minor compared to the gift she is giving me."

"What seems minor to you may be major to her. I think that Lindsey sees this gift to you as really a minor thing, a very good thing to do, but not as important as stopping Dominus. It is a matter of viewpoint."

The Nous in her kicked in, "Ja, ja, I sees it now. Wij werken samen. Oops," she got a bit too excited and slowed back down. "We work together. That is vital to her and all of us. I happy with it now."

"Good girl. So what is your decision then?"

"Let's give it a try. I won't get my hopes up. I can accept it not working, but I do hope it does work."

"Excellent. I will relay your decision to Governor Alister and the Bradbury Doctor Caterwall. They will contact your parents for their approval, since you are still a minor. I'm sure that your parents will be elated. As I understand it, Doctor Caterwall will try it with Ashley first, since she at least was born with arms. I think he will be using that as a measuring reference."

"Good, Ashley must be first. She's my friend now."

On July 5, Monane, Wilma, Lloyd, and R. B. teleported Lindsey to Denver to pay a visit to Lloyd's Secure Vaults. Governor Alister was waiting patiently for them just outside the entrance. With a ring of such immense power and value, the five adults insisted on providing a full escort for Lindsey. She too brought along her Staff of Power. Only Governor Alister and Lindsey had been here before, though this was only Lindsey's second time.

"Good day," Governor Alister said solemnly. "We shall talk once we are safely within the vault. Follow me." Memories of their last trip here two years ago came unbidden into Lindsey's mind. How she had changed since then, she reflected. A man pointed the way to the Vault officer. Lindsey stated that she wished to visit her vault, told him the number, and opened her mouth for the requisite DNA swap. Once she passed, a young man in an immaculate business suit escorted them to the elevator, which took them down into the vaults. One of the electric golf carts, as Alister jokingly called them, appeared and the young man drove them down to her vault, 716. There he left them, after instructing her to take another DNA swap and place it in the slot.

This she did and the massive tumblers made a loud noise as they unlocked the vault. The group entered. "Oh my, there's that desk and chair I made for Sam!" exclaimed R. B.

suddenly overcome with emotion. Indeed, Monane and Wilma began crying, as memories of their best friend returned.

"I remember how he used to sit at that desk and tease us so," Monane reminisced.

"Those cooking pots! Remember how we and Mabel used to cook our dinners with those? It seems like yesterday. I miss Sam so much!" Both women and R. B. were unable to stop tears from flowing.

"We'd best find the ring," Alister spoke softly.

"He always kept the valuable rings in the secret compartment," R. B. said. "Lindsey, here, tap this knot lightly. Yes, like that." She heard a faint click. "Now open the drawer." She did and the secret compartment had opened, revealing six rings in a velvet box. Each box was labeled. She recognized her dad's handwriting at once.

"This is it." She held the small box up for all to see.

"Allow me to double-check it, please," Alister said. She gave it to him, and he cast his spells on it. Lindsey immediately recognized the Identify spell. "Yes, this is it. Please put it securely in your pocket. Under no circumstances are you to let it slip onto your fingers, Lindsey." She did as he asked.

"Now then, we can talk. I will escort you out and wait until you have teleported safely home. Doctor Caterwall will be arriving outside the building shortly, and he will be traveling back with you. He does not know the location of your ranch and so cannot Teleport there safely. He will supervise the usage of the ring and will be reporting directly to me on the progress and results. Once you are finished with the ring, we must get it back safely to this vault. This secure vault is the safest place on earth for such a ring in these times."

"Lindsey, I must compliment you on your decision to make these attempts. You have the most generous heart I know. However, I will admit to you right now that I had hopes that this day might come for Miss Stokes-Compton. When I heard of her and did what I could to bring her to Bradbury's, I had an old man's hope that this day might come. Indeed, it has, but your kindness extends far beyond to a young girl you've only just met. When I heard of Miss van Ravinstijn, I saw two opposites, yet so alike in many ways. I admit that I had some hope that you might just offer it to her as well. Whether or not the ring works as we all hope it does, by doing this for Miss van Ravinstijn, you have forged new bonds that one day may play a vital role in defeating Dominus. Indeed, it might. I am very proud to have you as a friend, Lindsey. Thank you." Lindsey gave him a hug.

"Mind if I drive?" Alister asked, as they began their return journey. Lindsey had put another stack of bills in the emergency chute, to be drawn upon should her checking account balance require it. Even though she used half of the balance in her account to pay off her mother's ranch mortgage, she still had plenty, but didn't know when she would be able to return here.

Alister enjoyed driving them the short distance back to the elevator. "That was fun." A couple minutes later, they stepped outside the building. At once, all were on their highest state of alert. Even Lindsey cast See True on herself.

"Ah, there you are," Doctor Caterwall called out. He was leaning against the wall. "No signs of troubles out here."

"Let's make haste," Lloyd replied, his eyes looking about the area for anything out of place. Quickly the group joined hands. Governor Alister watched them disappear; only now could he relax. This ring was incredibly valuable and important, especially with Dominus on the loose. He waited another minute. Seeing nothing unusual, he too vanished from the streets of Denver.

"Very pleased to meet you Miss van Ravinstijn," Doctor Caterwall greeted Jeannette. "They failed to tell me just how pretty you are!"

She blushed. "Please, just Jeannette." He grinned.

"Your father, nice sounding man, wish I spoke Dutch though, he has given us his permission to make this attempt. He sent me the last set of x-rays of your shoulders to use as a guideline. So let's get this started shall we? Then, Lindsey can give me a tour of her ranch. Are you ready, Ashley?"

"Yes sir. What do I have to do? Will it hurt?" Ashley asked, a little worried, a little scared.

"Ashley, none of us knows how it will work. I do hope it

is not painful, but I am prepared. When I regrew Lindsey's hands, I gave her a strong sleeping potion, and she slept through most of it. Now, I want you to lay down on your bed. I will put the ring on one of your toes. The first thing we must watch for is the ring activating. According to everything we have read, you should feel an energy flowing throughout your body. Please tell us if you feel anything like that. Comfortable? All set?"

"Yes sir," she took a deep breath and held it expecting some kind of shock. Carefully, Doctor Caterwall put the ring close to her right middle toe. He watched in fascination as the ring expanded in size as it touched the toe. Soon he could slide it on to her toe.

"It tickles,. It's cold, kind of. Don't feel anything else yet." A minute later, magical energy flashed, completely hiding her body. Then, it cleared up. "What was that!" Ashley exclaimed. "I felt something all over me!"

"Wow! Look at that!" exclaimed Lindsey.

"What? What?" Ashley begged.

"Your whole body is kind of outlined in energy," Doctor Caterwall explained. "Only we can see ghostly images of arms and hands and fingers where they ought to be. This is very hopeful indeed!"

One by one, everyone came in to see for themselves the ghostly arms and hands just where they ought to be. Lindsey held up a mirror so Ashley could see for herself. "Wow! Way cool!" she exclaimed. "It doesn't hurt at all, Jeannette."

After an hour with nothing more really happening, the others went off to play at the pond, while Pam and Monique went back to Pam's room to work with their research projects. Doctor Caterwall and Jeannette stayed by Ashley's side until lunchtime. Even then, he was reluctant to leave her alone. Lena spelled him so he could eat. Polly then spelled her so Lena could give him a tour and show him where he would be sleeping.

Lindsey came to sit with her sister after supper. She took one look at the ghostly arms and exclaimed, "Ashley! It's working; they are getting more solid! Look!" She held up the mirror so she could see for herself.

"They itch and tingle. I mean I feel weird sensations where arms should be, but Doctor Caterwall insists I'm not to move a muscle. I wonder how long this will take. It is embarrassing to be using the bed pan and having others feed me. I seem to be ravenously hungry though."

Lindsey giggled, "I know. Mom said you ate twice what you normally do. I think that is also a very good sign." They chatted until Lindsey had to go to bed. To be on the safe side, Doctor Caterwall gave Ashley a sleeping potion so that she would sleep restfully through the night. Still, the adults took shifts sitting beside the sleeping girl.

Early the next morning, Doctor Blackburn, who had cancelled his appointments for the morning, popped in to see as well. He was just as curious as Doctor Caterwall. The two men had a lengthy chat. Henry then decided to cancel all of his morning appointments for the rest of the week, so that he could be here mornings to watch the progress. Both men compared notes daily. Their chart listed just how much food she ate, what type, along with what and how much she drank.

"Yes, she has cravings, Henry. Milk and meat predominate, but Oreos?" exclaimed Dr. Caterwall. Both shook their heads. One thing they were sure about, the regeneration required at least double the normal food intake. The appendages had to be built as part of the body. Thus, they encouraged her to eat whatever she felt a craving for and as often as she desired. Both men noted that she only expelled a small amount compared to the volume she ate.

Lindsey and Jeannette observed that each day, the ghostly appendages grew more and more solid, more and more real. In fact, Lindsey took a cell phone photo each day at the same time, putting them on to her computer for comparisons. Even Pam declared that the ring was working its miracle; it was quite plain by the photos.

Both doctors agreed that they had best not even touch the arms until the process was completely done. Neither knew if the mere touch of their hands might alter the results. Play it safe, was Doctor Caterwall's motto. Henry concurred.

On July 12, the ring suddenly and inexplicably fell off her toe, causing everyone great concern. Dr. Caterwall exclaimed, "Oh, maybe it's done. That's what Pam's research would indicate. Okay, Ashley, try to sit up and see if the arms and hands work for you. I'd rather not touch them just yet."

She sat up her usual way and felt her arms. She announced, "They seemed just like the arms and hands and fingers I feel when I'm Morphed into Peggy." Convinced all was well, the two doctors began to touch, feel, and examine them for themselves. After an extensive hour-long examination, both doctors could find nothing at all wrong with the arms, hands, or fingers. At last, Ashley was allowed to get up and move about.

She began experimenting with them to see if they really worked. Five minutes later, she let out a yell of pure joy. She had arms and hands just like everyone else. They worked! It was as if she had never lost hers in that accident when she was two years old. Ashley danced around the whole house, unable to contain her total happiness and excitement over this incredible miracle.

Jim came over as soon as he heard that she was up. He'd been by several times each day, however. "Wow! It worked! Fantastic."

"You going to still like me now that I have arms like everyone else?" Ashley asked. Lindsey, standing in the background, knew that there was an awful lot of emotion at stake in Jim's reply. She knew that Ashley had fallen in love with Jim, but would he still be attracted to her now?

"Yes, indeedy, as long as you are still wanting to be my mischievous, ornery, goddess. If you don't, then I'll have to tickle you until you do."

"Whoa, buster! Now I can tickle you back," she exclaimed and began chasing him around, waving her fingers about. At last, he let her catch him, and the two embraced lovingly. Lindsey heaved a big sigh of relief.

Meantime, Doctor Caterwall wasted no time getting Jeannette ready. Lindsey stuck her head in with Katja, who was at her friend's side. "Are you comfortable and ready, Jeannette?" he asked.

She took a deep breath and said, "Yes, I hope this works."

"So do we all," he replied kindly, and he put the ring onto her toe as well. As before, the ring expanded to fit on to her toe. Everyone held their breath. A minute seemed like an eternity. Then, came a similar blinding flash of magical energies. When it died down, Jeannette's whole body was outlined in a similar magical energy field. Soon, everyone saw the same ghostly outlines of where her arms and hands ought to be located.

"It's working! Het werkt goed!" Katja exclaimed. Lindsey held the mirror up so Jeannette could see the ghostly images as well. The smile on the girl's face gave Lindsey an incredible feeling. She was truly helping another in need.

Again, everyone pitched in to feed her and look after her needs. Lindsey took daily photos, sending them to her computer and to Jeannette's as well. Doctor Caterwall and Doctor Blackburn also asked to have a complete set of the photos, and Lindsey was happy to oblige. Since Lindsey felt it was her responsibility to sit with Jeannette as much as possible, Audrey, Pam, and Monique took over with Ashley.

"Now then, Ashley, we need to see you cast all of your spells," Pam said, looking at the lengthy spell list that she had made, check boxes beside each spell.

"With your new arms, that is," Monique teased her and both giggled.

Pam hoped that Ashley would not run into trouble—that their patient hours in June would pay off. It took several tries for Ashley to get the proper feel of her wand in her own hands, before her Clean spell worked. Pam breathed a sigh of relief as she checked that spell off.

Each morning, the two doctors re-examined Ashley's arms. Doctor Blackburn brought in a muscle chart one morning so they could compare how her arms were compared to normal girls her age. They concluded that they were just average and that she should probably work out, strengthening her muscles. Ashley's legs were strong and powerful, well-muscled. Her arms stood out in stark contrast. Hence, they devised an exercise plan for Ashley to follow. She grimaced at the thought of exercising, but went along with the doctor's orders.

Hans and Jim took her over to their new archery range to teach her how to shoot a bow. This also tended to exercise her arms as well, making it fun. "I can actually shoot a bow, Jim. I never could do that before. So many things I resolved to myself that I could never do. A whole new world is opening up to me!" Jim gave her a huge hug and kiss.

"I can hug you back, and oh how I've wanted to do this, Jim!" She put her arms around him and gave him a strong hug.

Meantime, Lena and Polly quickly began making the needed alterations to all of Ashley's tops and blouses. Her gowns, they waited to get her desires. Ashley looked them over and decided to show off her new arms and shoulders. All her gowns now were sleeveless, much to Jim's pleasure.

Finally, on July 19, the ring fell off of Jeannette's toe. Again, the doctors examined her completely. Both were concerned if the arms would work, given the unusual formation of her shoulder sockets. Doctor Blackburn brought along a small portable x-ray machine. The two compared the before and after images of her shoulders. Both were amazed at the results. Before, where a normal shoulder socket was located, the bone was flat and not concave, as one would expect. Now, it had been transformed and fit the ball of her arm bone perfectly.

Next, they checked the full range of motion of her arms and finally gave her the go ahead to get up and see how they felt and worked. Jeannette moved her arms tentatively at first and then began waving them all around. She began bawling wildly, scaring both doctors, who feared that something had gone horribly wrong.

"I can't believe I have real arms!" she finally blubbered. "It's the greatest miracle ever, for me." They were tears of pure joy and happiness, and the doctors relaxed. Again, neither could find anything wrong with Jeannette's new arms, other than the fact that they were slightly below the normal in terms of muscles. They gave her the same exercise program that Ashley was following.

That evening as Jeannette joined everyone else for supper, eating with her own arms and hands for the first time, she, Katja, and Hans all cried, and thanked Lindsey repeatedly. After they ate, Lindsey had Jeannette stand beside Ashley, and she took a photo of the two of them and then one close up of Jeannette. She then fixed up a photo series of Jeannette and said, "I've sent you an email of the pictures. You should call your parents and email them these pictures so they can see for themselves!" Jeannette hugged Lindsey tightly, and then danced off to do just that.

Later that night as they sat around chatting, the phone rang. Lena answered it. "Lindsey! It's for you. I think it is Jeannette's dad!"

"Hello, this is Lindsey Barron."

"Hallo, my English is not so good. I speak slowly. This is Falco van Ravinstijn, Jeannette's father. I just got the photos you took of her." She heard him crying and then sniffing. "I must thank you from the bottom of my heart, my darling Jeannette. I try all childhood get her arms made, no could do. I let her go to States, though I fear for her—how she get by; kids make fun of her. I learn she with Ashley, who like her. Now dis, I can never thanks you enough for vat you have done for my Jeannette. Ve will meet you all dis next summer, ven ve come to States to get her, bring her home. Thank you so much. You made me happiest vader in world. Dank u! Dank u! Dank u!"

"You are welcome, Mr. van Ravinstijn. I'm only so happy that it worked. Jeannette wants to talk to you. Hold on a second." Lindsey handed the phone to Jeannette, who was very excited to talk to her dad again, though she had just called them an hour before.

They talked rapidly in Dutch. Pam kicked herself for not having cast Understand: Dutch before Jeannette got on the phone. Katja and Hans understood it all, however.

"My vader says thank you again. He is the happiest man ever," Jeannette told Lindsey after she hung up.

"Yes, apparently, your folks are coming to the States to pick you up and take you home at the end of the school year," Lindsey explained.

"Ja, that is the plan," Hans replied. "Den you can meet all our parents." He grinned.

Starting in the morning, Lindsey and the others began putting Jeannette through her spells, using the checklist that Pam had printed off. Unlike Ashley who had to practice each spell a few times, because of the way Jeannette had always cast her spells, each one fired off as they came to it.

Later on, Jeannette decided that she wanted her gowns to look exactly like Ashley's, bare shoulders, proudly displaying her arms.

The next Saturday night formal dance, the two girls wore their slightly altered gowns for the first time. Kathy's comment to Ashley was simply, "What a brilliant fashion statement Ashley! You look sexy like this. Maybe we all should alter ours to look like yours!"

Lindsey vetoed it. She wanted the two girls to be in the limelight for once. Ashley's arms clung to Jim all evening. "You don't know how long I have yearned to have arms to hold you, Jim."

"Well, as far as I'm concerned, you can hang on to me forever." She gave him a loving kiss.

Nearby, Jeannette had similar feelings, only hers had been far longer in duration. She too clung to Hans all night. He looked more like a proud peacock, Pam thought.

Yes, the adults and Lindsey did take her precious ring back to the secure vault the day after Jeannette was done with it.

One final footnote on this whole process: Both girls discovered by accident when they were practicing the casting of their Morph spells that they could Morph into their previous forms. Ashley was the first to discover this, as she accidentally held in her mind the image of the way she used to appear when she cast it. She was surprised to find herself armless again, but Lindsey's frantic Dispel Magic brought her back into her new self. Ashley and Jeannette found this phenomenon most curious indeed.

Chapter 8—Dog Days of August

It was hot, very hot, and dry. Dominus sat sunning himself beside his pool. Nadia van Nye strolled out; her bikini left nothing for the imagination. Her high heels clicked on the concrete, announcing her arrival.

"Dominus, I bring good news indeed. The Death Stalkers have finally located where the Barron and Stokes kids live," she announced. He smiled. "On the other hand, their ranches are too well protected. We can't even get within five miles of their place without the alarm being raised. Many wizards and witches live with these Compton's and Whitewater's. It seems they have men from the Department of Defense and Magical Misuse there protecting the kids. Why are you worrying about some kids?"

Len asked, "We would have to launch an all-out attack to get to them while they are there. Should I draw up such plans?"

"Don't be silly, Len. At the moment, they are of little importance. Their day will come soon enough. Right now, it is the presidential race that really matters."

"I don't get it, Dominus. Surely, you don't think that you will get enough votes to win, do you?" asked Nadia, who seemed to always be on the outside of his plans. Why would he attack them?

"Oh don't be silly, Nadia. Of course, I won't get enough votes. That's hardly the point. I never expected to win. Besides, their silly norm rules preclude a convicted felon from taking office. No, the race is critical for an entirely different reason. Now, what is the report on the distribution? How goes that first batch? Wasn't it supposed to be six hundred?"

She replied, "Six hundred forty. One hundred have been given out. They report that the factory is gearing up to full production. I believe the figure they suggest ranges around a thousand a month. I think they'll make very nice presents, my love."

"Good, good."

"But I thought that you wanted to be President, dear," Nadia changed the subject.

"Don't be silly, Nadia. I don't want to be their President. After all, who would be? They have such a stupid system where their Congress can veto what the President orders or the judicial courts can overturn the President. How stupid can they get? No, I will be their supreme ruler, their king, once my Golden Path is walked to its end. When I become King, you, Nadia will be my queen, if you so desire."

"Oh yes, very much so, Dominus, your Fetish Queen," she grinned, wiggling her body before his eyes.

Dominus played his hands along her body. He didn't tell her the rest of what he was thinking, "Until I find someone prettier than you to be my queen."

"Oh no!" Jim nearly cried as he got the news. "Lindsey, they've canceled the National Track Meets until further notice!"

"Well, that's for the best, you know," Pam broke in. "After all, so many people were either killed or badly hurt last year. Obviously, they can't guarantee the security of anyone going to the Nationals, neither runners nor spectators. I'm surprised they took as long as they have to cancel it."

"Well, we still can try to win first place at Bradbury's," Amanda tried to look at what remained.

"Yes, we should make every attempt to take the school soccer cup and the track trophy," Lindsey agreed with Amanda. Jim was not cheered up and left to send an email to Jake, their captain.

Fern commented, "At least, sis, you won't have to practice running twenty miles this summer."

Amanda smiled, "Yes, little sis, you are right, but already I miss the running this summer."

"I'm not. I enjoy swimming in this heat. It's so much more fun. Come on in and join us," Fern suggested. Amanda and Lindsey waded out into the blue waters of the pond. Lindsey turned around and saw Ashley with her arms around Jim, lying on the shoreline. Jeannette likewise had hers around Hans. She rather wished Andy was here, but said nothing. Amanda found herself wishing Henry were here too. Audrey and Katja were splashing Fern and Ellie. Pam and Monique were back in Pam's room, probably playing with their computers, Lindsey thought. Still the summer was fun and relaxing. Just now, the world seemed particularly beautiful to Lindsey.

Pam just finished logging in all the currently available findings from the bombing at the Nationals in Des Moines last May. One set of unidentified fingerprints were recovered from one of the pieces of the detonator. While several witnesses identified several known Death Stalkers as being on the premises, specifically in the basement below the explosion site, there was no proof that would conclusively link Dominus and his men to the actual explosion. The Department of Law continued to put forth the hypothesis that the ex-Bradbury student had acted alone and was responsible, though none could explain why he would blow himself up or why blow the floor out from under the Bradbury track team. Their thesis had too many holes in it.

"Well, it comes down to one set of fingerprints, if we are to tie the bombing to Dominus. They can't pin the theft of the trophies on him either, and are looking to find some associates of Phillip Royster, claiming he robbed the factory, but so far, Phillip seems to be acting alone," Pam stated flatly to Monique.

"Darn, I was so hopeful. Well, perhaps in time more will be discovered, Pam. I think we're going to have to leave the Teleport research and the Restricted Wish research go until we can use the school library. What say you to having another go at cracking Joshua Stokes and his secret coded journal? Unless you want to go swimming. Honestly, Pam, you don't have to stay indoors with me just because my face is still too sensitive and all that."

"I don't want to go swimming. I'm not athletic—barely passed my swimming exams at Bradbury's. Besides, I look awful in a swimming suit and you know it," Pam declared.

"You do not! You just think you don't," Monique countered her, but Pam didn't listen to her.

"Okay on the Stokes code, what have we tried?" Pam

changed the subject. The two rattled off the schemes that they had already attempted to use to crack his code. None showed any signs of working.

"We must be missing something, Pam," Monique exclaimed, brushing her hair back from her face. The two opened the journal to the first page. The top portion of the first page read as follows, omitting the Chicago Secret Agent Id Code Number.

Code Number: xxx

Alice's Adventures in Wonderland—perfect for Ashley. 2105 edition.

Went to Ace Hardware today, bought Lisa her new stove.

P42

81, 82, points, 37, 81, Mac Fluide Enterprises, 28, being, 59, cover operation.

P182

15, 13-n't, 14, their, 80!

Tomorrow, install stove for Lisa.

Pam stared at the start of the page. Certainly, he was making notes on family details, but the rest was encoded somehow and had to do with his spy assignment. "These P numbers are all over the place, Monique. What if they stood for page and a page number in some book? Then, the individual numbers might refer to something on that page."

"Probably words, in that case, but what book? Were any other books recovered?" Monique asked. Pam shook her head; she had no idea.

Pam pulled her hair and mused, "Strange that the first entry is a book title. The P numbers occur shortly after that. Surely, he would want someone to be able to read his notes, if something happened to him. He would have to have a way to tell us to what book the P numbers refer."

"Hey, if you were going to get a book for your child, you would write down its title, right?" Monique asked, having a flash of insight.

"Yes, but I would never write down the edition year, rather its ISBN or MAGISBN number, maybe the author. Why did he write down the edition year? Unless, he is directing us to that specific edition! You found the key, Monique! Everyone knows the Alice book; it's been republished many times, so he would have to tell us which one. Otherwise, the page numbers would vary. I bet the numbers refer to words on that page. Monique, where can we get our hands on this old edition?"

"Leave that to me. Have it in short order." However, neither Wilma nor Polly would allow Monique to Teleport to Greeley on her own. Both accompanied her to their library. A half hour later, the three returned, Monique had a well-worn copy of the book.

Pam realized she really did need to know how to Teleport, for then she would have complete freedom to travel where she desired. Pam called out the page numbers and word numbers, Monique looked them up. It was incredibly tedious going, though. Slowly Pam wrote down:

The direction points to the Mac Fluide Enterprises as being a cover operation. I can't-n't prove their guilt!

"Wait, -n't means remove that from the looked up word," Pam called out and looked at the whole message properly:

The direction points to the Mac Fluide Enterprises as being a cover operation. I can prove their guilt!

"We've done it, Pam!" Monique exclaimed, looking over Pam's shoulder. "Perfect sentences. We have our work cut out for us; there's a hundred plus pages to decipher here."

"Wait a second. I've been an idiot!" Pam growled. She grabbed Lindsey's Teacher's Spells book and thumbed through the pages. "Ah, here it is. Reveal Secret Code." Monique leaned over to read along with her.

"Okay, it is simple enough," Pam declared. "Here goes." She waved her wand as if opening pages in a book over the first page of the journal and commanded, "Reveal Hidden Codes." Before her eyes, she saw an image superimposed over the writings, Page 42, word 81, word 82 and so on.

"Rats, that doesn't help a whole lot, but it would have gotten us to this point," Pam stated the obvious. "I guess we just have to do it bit by bit. Monique, something in here got Joshua killed. We must find out what that was!"

Painstaking, arduous, tedious. Many adjectives the two

girls used to explain their next week of nearly constant decoding. Pam began a full translation, but decided to use two different colored pens. The secret coded message portions she wrote in black ink, but used blue ink on what appeared to be simple household notes to himself, documenting what needed to be done each day or so. Wisely, she didn't discard these household notes as irrelevant. For all they knew, there could well be a code within a code.

Slowly, a picture of corporate crime became visible. One Simon Mac Fluide founded the original company. At one point, the Enterprise needed a small oil refinery. Joshua uncovered that their representatives secretly stole the company from its owners and murdered them. Later, the company needed some jets and tried to buy out a small private jet service, which had a fleet of five planes. The owner was coerced into signing the company over to them for a paltry million dollars. After taking possession of the funds, he was murdered, and the funds disappeared, only to be re-deposited in the corporate accounts. A bank was apparently needed at some point. A small bank in the Cayman Islands was again taken over. The owner had apparently signed the transfer of ownership papers, but he was found murdered shortly thereafter, and Joshua claimed he had proof that the signature was forged.

All told, Joshua claimed that he had proof that the Enterprise was guilty of at least seven murders, countless extortion plots, illegal off-shore banking practices, and income tax evasion.

"Gosh, if he really did have proof of one of these, that would be enough to put his life in danger," Monique stated the obvious.

"Yes, but look, he talks about trying to find out who this Simon Mac Fluide was. That was the topic of his last entries in the journal, presumably just before he was killed," Pam pointed out. "Stands to reason that's more likely when the company had to eliminate him."

"But if he had all this proof, where is it? You yourself said that the Department of Law in Chicago did nothing about this. It stands to reason that if they had the proof that Joshua claims he had, they would have taken action against the Enterprise."

Pam countered, "Unless they got to someone in the Department of Law, regained possession of the evidence, wiping out any traces that it had ever been given to that department. We are being hasty. Let's be methodical about this. I will have dad contact the Chicago Department of Law and see if they have any records of this proof of crimes ever having been sent in by their agent, Joshua. Go from there."

"Meanwhile let's continue our detective work here. Joshua claims repeatedly over many pages that he has proof of these crimes. What form would that proof take?" Pam asked.

"Eye witness accounts, perhaps. Fingerprints? Documents?" Monique attempted to hash out various forms proof of guilt might take.

"I doubt very much eye witness accounts. Fingerprints? Probably not, since those would have been found at the crime scenes. We should research each of these murders and see what was discovered in each by the authorities. If there were, for example, unknown sets of fingerprints found at a crime scene that did not match any on file and if Joshua somehow managed to lift a set that matched those, then fingerprints would definitely fit the proof criteria."

"More likely, he may have come across corporate documents, such as ordering the murders," Pam added.

"But if he got the physical proof, where did he keep them? He was deep undercover, so he would not be going into the Department of Law on any regular basis to hand them over," Monique theorized.

"No, you have a point. I mean if I was pretending to be deep undercover, I would stash them away in some secret, safe place, until I came out from the job. Then, I would recover them and turn in the lot," Pam suggested.

"But we know he was with his wife and daughter, at least part of the day. Where would he stash them?" Monique asked. Neither had an answer. A week later, Fred gave her his findings from Chicago. Joshua apparently never turned in any documents or proof of any wrongdoing before he died. Pam then knew that either men from or hired by the Enterprise stole the proofs back after they killed him or perhaps just before killed him or the proofs were never found and hence still likely stashed where Joshua had placed them.

One evening, Ashley joined them. She was interested in reading about her parent's home life, what little of it was in the journal. Because Pam had made the decoding document in two colors of ink, preserving the original layout of each page, Ashley became annoyed just trying to read about her parents. She wasn't particularly interested in the crimes that her father was investigating. After all, they were thirteen years old or older.

Growing more annoyed, she took some blank papers and began copying out just the family lines.

Went to Ace Hardware today, bought Lisa her new stove.

Tomorrow, install stove for Lisa.

Ran into flue troubles.

Stove doesn't draft properly.

Need to create a flue safe vault for stove.

Lisa is elated stove works properly now.

Kazam opens flue safe vault

so Lisa can cook when strong winds blow.

Ashley read back what she had copied. She imagined her mother so happy with her new stove, but then bewildered because it didn't burn quite right.

"Hey, Pam, what's a flue safe vault anyway? What's it got to do with making it so the stove can cook right when strong winds blow?" Ashley asked, rather annoyed that she had no idea of what her father had been describing. Well, she knew little about how stoves worked, probably Pam did.

"When strong winds blow over the exhaust pipe," Lena began to explain. She had been walking by the girl's room, heard her daughter's question, and saw Pam shrug. "The winds create a suction that blows out the flames or pilot light. So what you do is put a damper on the exhaust pipe. It goes downward and has a swinging flap in it. When there is no wind, the flap shuts and the exhaust goes up the pipe and outside. When the winds blow, the flap opens and the suction draws inside air on up the pipe, while not creating a stronger suction on the pilot light or the cooking flames; they then burn normally. That's what he was talking about."

Lena finished up, "However, there is no such thing as a flue safe vault, certainly not where stoves are concerned."

Pam sat straight up in her chair. "Incredible. Let me double-check that!" Hastily, she Googled for flue safe vaults and fond no relevant hits at all. Then, she tried MagGoogle, in case this might be a magical device of some kind. Even fewer hits occurred, all irrelevant.

"Lena, you've found where Joshua hid his proofs! He built a safe. Ah, Kazam is the password that opens the safe! It is probably somewhere around wherever the stove was located," Pam explained.

"Cool, but where was the stove?" Monique asked. Pam had no answer yet. "Ashley, do you know where your parents were living before they were killed?" Ashley shrugged her shoulders. She was only two and had no real memories of the place.

Pam had Ashley call her grandfather to see if he knew the address where Joshua and Lisa were living when he was killed. Ashley wrote it down for Pam:

12305 South Harmon, Apartment 6.

It was an apartment complex. Samson said that they were living frugally and planning to buy a home when Ashley turned three.

When Fred Betts came home for supper that night, Pam explained her theory. Joshua hid his proofs in a secret vault located somewhere in the stove or exhaust pipes of the stove. She just had to find a way to go there and see if the vault was still there. "Dad, if it still exists and the many proofs are inside, the Department of Law can then prosecute this Mac Fluide Enterprises. We just *have* to try, dad." She put on her most begging, pleading face, which he could never refuse. Pam had her dad wrapped around her fingers, when she wanted to do so. Fred relented.

Of course, Ashley wanted to go. She could see the old apartment where she and her parents lived. Thus, Jim insisted that where his little goddess went, so went he. Lindsey didn't want to be left out. If Ashley was going, she had to be there to protect her sister. Of course, where any of these three girls went, Wilma and Monane insisted on going with them, especially after their trip into Sterling!

"Now wait a minute, everyone cannot go. We need some here to protect all the others," Fred stated factually. "Here's how we work this. I will lead. Wilma and Monane will be with me. Pam, Lindsey, and Ashley can go with us, and Jim too. However, we do not want to hazard anything like the Sterling fiasco. Hence, girls, if you want to come, each of you will have to Morph into a boy. Since Wilma is going, Bill and Ted would be appropriate disguises for two of you. Let's see, how about Tom Whitewater for the third one of you?"

"But dad! A boy! You want me to become a boy?" Pam asked, infuriated at the idea of Morphing into a boy.

"If you wish to go, you will be Tom; Ashley will be Bill; and Lindsey, Ted. Then, if we are recognized, it will look perfectly normal: Wilma and her boys along with Monane and her nephew. Take it or leave it, Pam," Fred said sternly. Pam recognized that tone; she knew he was firm and could not easily be swayed. She agreed, though she knew she would just hate pretending to be Tom.

Fred continued, "Jim, careful, no holding hands with Bill. That will look awfully weird." Jim faked a moan, but realized he spoke the truth. "Good, then we go at ten tomorrow morning."

Shortly after ten, the group arrived before 12305 South Harmon, Chicago, Illinois. To their dismay, a work crew was scooping up the rubble of the building. Fred made some inquiries of the foreman. "Gang, the place was demolished two days ago, and they are clearing the rubble to build a new hotel here. However, he said that Ace Salvage Yard went through the building last week, removing anything worth saving. I asked about stoves and he said those were removed by Ace."

Ashley was crestfallen. Now she would never be able to see where she and her parents had lived. Pam insisted that they find this salvage yard, however. They walked a ways until Pam found a public phone booth and quickly looked up the location of this salvage yard. Once more, the group held hands and Fred Teleported them to the Ace Salvage Yard.

There, Fred made some inquiries, but got nowhere until

he flashed his Department of Magical Misuse badge. Then, the reluctant owner became cooperative. He led them inside his yard to where they had deposited all that they had salvaged from the apartment complex. At least he kept good records, Pam thought. The many piles were labeled with the apartment number from which they had come. Quickly, they found the pile for apartment 6. An old wood burning stove, well, a cheap knock-off of an old style wood burning stove, lay on its side in a bad state indeed.

Fred had to make a decision. He was out of his jurisdiction, but could try to bluff the man into giving him this stove and pipes. Fred was not one to lie to get his way. He could call for the local authorities to come and confiscate the stuff, but then if it turned out to be nothing at all, he would look like a fool. Instead, he said, "The boys here are looking for a summer restoration project. How much for the whole lot?"

He haggled a bit over the price and handed the owner a hundred dollar bill. At once, everyone began casting Shrink spells over the incredibly dirty pile of junk, placing the tiny pieces into a large sack. The spell also drastically lowered the weight of each piece, especially the heavy stove itself. A half hour later, the group arrived back at the Compton ranch.

Gleefully, the three girls cancelled their Morph spells. "That was awful, being a boy!" declared Ashley. "Yuck." Only Pam found the experience slightly amusing.

Now they all set to work trying to figure out where the secret vault might be located in all this junk. "Well, we could try to reconstruct the stove and its pipes," Jim suggested, "only we don't know what it looked like." An hour later, they still had gotten nowhere, only very dirty.

Exasperated with the whole reconstruction idea, Pam finally just called out loudly, "Kazam!"

To everyone's complete surprise, the side of one of the flue pipes opened up rather noisily, revealing a magical space inside the pipe. Many brittle and yellowed papers were inside, rolled and tied with a piece of string. The years and constant exposure to heat from the flue pipe had taken its toll on the acid content of the paper. Gingerly, Fred retrieved the roll. "I will get this to headquarters where we have the staff and equipment to attempt to recover what we can from these documents. Pam, I must thank you heartily on another Sleuthing job well done. These may well prove invaluable in bringing them to justice and cast more light on the who and why Ashley's parents were murdered. Well done, daughter! And yes, I will let you know about anything that we find." Pam grinned.

While she would have loved to examine them, she knew that merely opening the roll would likely begin the paper breakup, leaving her with tiny bits instead. Back in the lab, they may find scientific ways to handle these valuable documents. Holding the roll carefully in his hand, Fred teleported off to work in Sterling.

"What do we do with all this junk?" Jim asked, as they stared at the pile.

Monane stated, "Well, do something with it! Lena will have a fit if you store trash here on her ranch." Lindsey chuckled, knowing that she would. In the end, Jim shrank it down once more and hauled it to his father's trash pile.

With this line of investigation at a temporary end, Pam and Monique began to wonder just who this Simon Mac Fluide was and who was in charge of the Enterprise and just how big it was. They began an Internet search for all information on these topics.

"It seems that this Simon fellow is a modern-day Howard Hughes," Monique pointed out. "Wealthy, reclusive, no photos anywhere, lives alone, no one knows for sure where, handles all business via telephone, and then has a voice-disguiser distorting his voice. Must not trust anyone, though with all the murders and crimes, I can see why he would want to remain elusive."

Pam chuckled, expecting something like this. "Well, according to their latest filing, a John Prichard is the Corporate Executive Officer, the top dog, below this Simon fellow, who seems to be Chairman of the Executive Board only. Maybe we will have better luck tracking down John Prichard," she suggested.

Indeed, at once they found photos, comments, company descriptions, and many other documents signed by Mr.

Prichard on the Internet. He lived in Denver in a million dollar estate on the outskirts of the city, where the posh suburb was located. One photo showed him entering a huge limousine. Also apparent in the photo backgrounds were numerous bodyguards. Soon, Pam gave up on him, she found numerous lesser officials of the corporation also readily identifiable.

The two next turned their attention on obtaining a list of all the property holdings that the corporation claimed to have. The list was extensive! Yes, there was the bank and oil refinery, but also a yacht, jets, their own private airfield, numerous factories, warehouses in nearly every country in the world, and even a hundred homes, including the abandoned one in Telluride. When they finally finished their exhaustive research, they printed out a ten page document listing every known holding of Mac Fluide enterprises. The amount was staggering. Pam printed out two copies, one for herself and one for Monique.

The two sat back and looked at their lists. "Now what?" asked a bewildered Monique.

"Dunno," Pam admitted. "This is huge. I will need to think about this. This company has its hands in nearly everything imaginable, including making plastic explosives for the US Army. Weird. Ah well, we are also out of time. I'm a Floor Monitor this year and will be heading back to school next week. I guess we'd better wrap things up. Darn, I have not had any time to get ahead in any of my new subjects! I had it all planned out, too! By now, I was supposed to be in chapter six in each of my new courses." Monique giggled, glad that Pam had not put her nose in the books and had been with her this summer. She could not recall a happier summer vacation than this one spent so close to Pam, the girl she adored and deeply loved.

Chapter 9—Return to Bradbury's

Lindsey explained to the three foreign exchange students, "All new students go one week early, before classes start, for orientation week. We Floor Monitors go with you. It's our jobs to get you settled in, get your classes arranged, get you all the supplies, books, and stuff you are going to need, and take you all over the campus to your classrooms and such so that you know your way around on your own. Everyone else used to return on the last day of August, but with this nasty Dominus business, they will be returning three days early. That gives you four days to get used to everything before the campus becomes crowded. Questions?"

None of the three had any, but Pam did. She raised her hand as if Lindsey was her professor. Lindsey giggled, "Miss Betts?" Everyone roared with laughter.

"Why is Governor Alister coming here? He's never come to our homes before." She asked what everyone was thinking. Indeed, Lindsey received an email yesterday stating that he would be arriving around ten today and that Lindsey should get all the people at the Whitewater's and all of those staying at her place together for a short meeting. Speculation ran wild about the why last night. Pam wanted to see if Lindsey had heard anything else since then.

"I imagine that he wants to welcome Katja, Jeannette, and Hans," Lindsey replied for the tenth time. Other than that, she couldn't guess.

Their front room was packed. Polly and Lottie passed out tea and sodas to the waiting group. At last, the monotone voice announced, "Governor Alister Broadwell arriving." Everyone suddenly became serious, particularly Jim, who rarely was totally serious. Lindsey opened the door, and there stood Governor Alister. He was now in his early fifties, a hint of grey in his otherwise black hair and sideburns. He wore his school robes over his business suit. As he stepped inside, he handed his robes to Lloyd. "Miss Barron, good to see you once again. I see you have everyone gathered here together."

"Yes sir, as you requested. Please come in. Everyone is dying to meet you," Lindsey replied, very pleased that her mother and father would finally get the opportunity to meet him. Amanda wanted her father and mother to meet him, since he was her Tracking Theory teacher as well. Jim still could not believe Alister was here.

"Tea?" Lena offered. He graciously accepted a cup and took the open chair, which Lloyd had arranged such that he was facing the large gathering. "First of all, I would like to take this opportunity to personally welcome our three students from Utrecht School of Magic. I've no doubt who they are in this group," he teased them. "Hans and Katja van der Veer?" They stepped forward, and he shook their hands. Jim thought that little deductive work was needed to identify the twins; they looked very similar in many ways. "And this must be Miss Jeannette van Ravinstijn." Bursting with pride, she was able to shake his hand, something she had never been able to do before.

He sensed this too. "I am honored to be the first person you are greeting with your new arms, Miss van Ravinstijn. I am extremely pleased that Miss Barron was able to lend you a hand with them." Everyone chuckled at his pun, Jeannette giggled. She took an instant liking to him.

He chatted for a few minutes with the three Dutch students, asking them how their summer had gone, were they enjoying their stay, polite conversation. At last, he became more serious. "Now then, I had best get to the reason for this unexpected visit. If I don't say something soon, I do believe Miss Betts will have a fit." Pam flushed. She was wondering when he would say why he really paid them this unexpected visit. Everyone else giggled or chuckled, however.

"Lindsey has kept me fully informed concerning Ashley and Jeannette. I don't believe that there are words enough to thank Miss Barron for what she has done for these two students. Miss Betts has done, as always, a remarkable job of Sleuthing, revealing now for the first time that Ashley's father was an undercover agent for the Chicago Department of Law and that Ashley's parent's deaths were not an accident, but murders. The recovery and deciphering of his secret journal has led to the recovery of key documents, which Fred Betts is having analyzed in his lab. Time will tell whether or not they will lead to arrests of those responsible for the crimes."

"Which brings me to the reason for my unexpected visit, Miss Betts," he winked at her. "I take the security of all students while at Bradbury's very seriously. With that in mind, I have been working with Professor Mary Ann Thornby, who is a Class 3 Diviner. She and I believe that, at this time with Dominus and Death Stalkers running wild around the world, revealing to the world that Miss Barron has one of the extremely rare Rings of Regeneration would lead to major attempts to steal it from her by any possible means. This includes capturing her, kidnaping her family members or dear friends, holding them ransom in return for the ring. Dominus himself would most certainly desire possession of that ring."

"This is in part why I had not told you long ago, Lindsey, that via this ring, Ashley's arms might be restored. Professor Mary Ann believes that at this time, if you reveal to the entire student body that you have this ring and used it to regenerate both Ashley and Jeannette's arms and hands, then very bad consequences may result." Lindsey had not thought about the consequences of using the ring, only that she had to use it to help her sister and Jeannette. What had she done? Now, everyone she loved may well be in danger. Her face turned white.

"However, all is not gloom and doom. As I understand it from Lindsey's reports, Ashley and Jeannette, you can use your Morph spells to change into your previous bodies without arms. Is this correct?"

"Yes," Ashley replied, "It's awfully spooky though, I mean being as I was most all of my life."

Alister smiled, "Yes, I expect it is more than a little spooky. Yet, in this interesting anomaly, there is hope. Here is what I would like you to do. Let's pretend that Lindsey has taught you both a powerful spell that allows you to appear to have perfectly normal arms and hands. After all, this is only deviating slightly from the truth. It was a powerful spell that was cast on each of you girls. I will announce it to the entire student body, so any blame for the slight alteration of the truth can be laid upon my head. You go about your lives normally. However, perhaps once each week, Morph yourselves into your old shapes for a short time, but appear that way in a very public place, where many other students can see the 'old you' without arms. That will add credence to the fact that a spell may be in use at all other times."

"If you will play along with my little deception, we can throw off any criminal attempts to steal the ring and harm many of your family and friends. Trust me Ashley, once the newness wears off, that is, seeing you with normal arms and hands, everyone will simply forget about it, accepting the new you as normal, accepting the fact that you are the recipient of a very useful, powerful spell. Let's not give Dominus and the Death Stalkers more reasons than they already have to harm your family and friends or attack you while you are at school. Will you two do this for me?"

"Ja, I must. I not vant anything to happen to dis people, who have been so wonderful to me," Jeannette replied, talking too fast, messing up her English slightly. "But my friends, they already know, I emailed them."

"That is not a problem. I will speak with all them tomorrow when they all arrive for Orientation Week. I'm sure that we can trust them to be discrete about it," Alister suggested.

"Sure, I'll do it. Golly, Mary Ann has been having premonitions about me. I've been so excited about my own life that I haven't even practiced any divination the whole summer," Ashley realized as she spoke the words. She wondered if in her laxness she had missed something major that was to happen to her or her friends. Ashley vowed to ask Professor Mary Ann about it as soon as she could.

"Excellent, thank you both for doing this for me and for Lindsey. Now then, since I am here, I believe that everyone would like to show me around the two ranches. Yes, I would like to see R. B.'s teleport pad that I have heard so much about from the children. Lloyd, R. B., I would like to check on your various protective spells and devices as well. Perhaps, I can lend a little in that area."

Lindsey was very pleased to show him around their new

house. Lena, holding little Jonathon, kept saying not to mind the messes. He stayed for over an hour and visited the Whitewater ranch as well. Governor Alister had a brief but private conversation with Lloyd and R. B., but neither would tell the inquisitive kids what was discussed. Lindsey guessed it was about their security precautions.

The next morning, a little before ten in the morning, Lindsey, Pam, Hans, Katja, and Jeannette stood on her porch along with a giant pile of duffle bags. "Honestly, Lindsey, our bags seem to multiply each year!" Pam declared. This triggered Lindsey's memories of her very first bus trip to Bradbury's. She had no hands then and carried everything she owned in a tiny backpack. Now she had seven duffle bags all stuffed so that she didn't have to have an eighth one!

Lindsey also felt strange. Sandy would not be here with her, returning to Bradbury's. She'd graduated, gotten married, and was now somewhere in Denver. She missed Sandy already. Pam had taken her place as a Yellow Hall Floor Monitor, along with Lindsey.

Everyone had said their farewells already. The five waited patiently for ten o'clock to come. Right on the dot, according to Pam, who was timing the bus run this year, figuring a Floor Monitor should know the precise schedule of things, everyone heard the popping sound and saw the yellow school bus materialize just before their porch.

Two Security men hopped off first, followed by Jimmy, who still had not gotten his missing front teeth fixed. "Howdy, Miss Lindsey, Miss Ashley. 'hese mus' be our visi'ing s'uden's from Ne'herlands."

"What's he saying?" whispered Jeannette to Pam. "He's so hard to understand." Pam explained. Lindsey, clipboard in hand, led them onto the bus, while the Security men checked over their many bags. Satisfied the bags were okay, they loaded them underneath the double decker bus.

"Wow. Just like our school bus," Hans exclaimed.

Katja explained, "Ve like to sit up top, though it is only a short ride to our school."

"We always like to sit at the back so we can see better. Let's get the top back seats," Lindsey suggested, checking off the five names on her list of students to be picked up today. Pam did likewise with her checklist.

"Hey, look at this," Lindsey noted. "We get to go to Lamar and then La Junta this year, before we go to Limon. Got to pick up four new first year students." Indeed, they only got started when they stopped at Lamar, south and a little east of Arapahoe. A young boy and a scared looking girl climbed onboard. Lindsey got the new Blue Hall boy settled in and seat belt fastened, while Pam helped ease the new Brown Hall girl's fears. Pam decided to sit with her, at least until some other Brown Hall students got onboard.

Only a few minutes later, they stopped in La Junta, adding a Yellow Hall first year girl, named Frances Whiting and a Red Hall boy. Lindsey had Frances come up and join the other Yellow Hall students, introducing her to everyone. The bus shot almost due north for a time, before stopping in Limon. Kathy waved to them from the outside, as the Security men verified her and began searching her many bags. She brought another Yellow Hall boy along with her, Sam James. Kathy also escorted another pair of first years onboard, a Brown Hall boy and Blue Hall girl.

"How come you are going back so early?" asked Pam. Kathy was not a Floor Monitor.

"Oh, I forgot to email you all. I have been appointed the official school representative for all the Foreign Exchange Students. I get to conduct a number of school wide orientation meetings for them—you know, telling them about the history of Bradbury's and all that." Lindsey saw that she was very happy with her new assignment and not upset about having to go back to school a few days early.

The bus then headed southwest to Colorado Springs. When it stopped, Lindsey saw Deiter Cross and his foreign exchange student. However, Deiter spied her looking out of the window and waved his new Staff of Power in the air, then sent her a Message.

My new Staff of Power! D.

A bit later, the Black Hall boy joined Lindsey and her group, introducing his exchange student to the others, Bale Vokker. "Dad got me a Staff of Power for my birthday, Lindsey.

Now I can really help! Of course, I need some help with it. Perhaps when you have some spare time this week, we can get together and have a peek at my staff?"

"Sure, Deiter. That's great that your dad got you one too. I think the more protections we have, the better off we will be," Lindsey replied, unable to think of anything better to say.

Lindsey had to rush off and take care of four more first years, lending Pam a hand. Before they took their seats, they cross-checked their lists. So far so good. They had little time to chat before the bus stopped in Pueblo. Here Emilio and Klaas Stuben climbed aboard, joining the ever-growing group at the back of the bus. Additionally, Lindsey and Pam checked four more first years onboard, including another Yellow Hall boy.

The last stop was Canon City, where a Blue Hall monitor and another Dutch student got onboard, along with three more first year students. Pam and Lindsey verified their lists and returned to their group. Everyone was accounted for; now came the long haul to the campus.

All the Dutch students sat with Lindsey's group. For a time, everyone just had to see Jeannette and her arms. That was their sole topic of conversation for at least ten minutes. However, Deiter had to chat with Ashley about her new arms. He didn't believe that this was a mere spell, but Lindsey promised to talk to him in private about it later on. Only then did he relax about Ashley's arms.

During the next few minutes, the Dutch students exchanged stories about what they had done with their host families during the summer. Many were envious of Hans, Katja, and Jeannette, after they heard that these three had gone swimming nearly every day, horseback riding, had formal dancing parties, and even archery lessons. Uniformly, they all declared that they had had Domino's at least once.

Then came the expected oh's and ah's, as they entered the mountains of southern Colorado. Later, zipping through the streets of Durango at a hundred miles an hour, the bus traveled in twisted space. Still, it was creepy, as they apparently "moved" through other cars and trucks, as if they were not there. Not long after that, at Cortez, they took the state route 145 up towards Telluride. The Dutch students stared at the magnificent mountains, so close that you could almost touch them.

Going through the older student's minds was not the scenery, but the several ambushes of the school bus that they had experienced over the past three years. Lindsey hoped and prayed they would arrive safe this time. So did the two Security men. They sat at keen alert the whole drive up 145. Finally, the Ophir Loop came and went through the San Juan Mountains and Forest. Now, Lindsey relaxed, for there were no more likely spots where someone could ambush the bus.

"Lindsey, let me take care of the eight first years and you take care of our three exchange students, okay?" Pam volunteered, as the bus neared the school parking lot. Lindsey made sure that Pam really wanted to do it, this being her first time at it. Since Pam did, Lindsey explained to the three older students that they'd wait a bit and let the first years get off first. Katja smiled and enjoyed watching these beginning students stare in awe at their campus. She was remembering her first day at her school back in Utrecht.

As the bus emptied, Lindsey explained, "We are in the parking lot. There is only the one main gate that anyone can enter. There's this high stone wall encircling the whole campus, and it's enchanted to not allow anyone to climb or fly over it. Keeps the likes of Dominus out, usually. Our campus is in the shape of a large pentagram, and we are at the southeastern corner. The Admin building is just inside the gates. Okay, let's get off now."

As they stood beside their large pile of bags, Lindsey looked at room assignments. "Golly, we are in room fourteen this year. Okay, I'll first move our bags there." Jeannette watched but did not see Lindsey casting any spell. Yet to her amazement, group after group of bags suddenly disappeared.

"Coolest. You don't need your wand? Like me on this spell?" Jeannette asked.

Lindsey grinned, "Nope. Okay, Hans, your bags are in your room, number 15. You are rooming with Emilio and Klaas."

"How about moving my bags too, Senorita Lindsey?" Emilio begged.

Flushing, Lindsey replied, "There, sorry, I forgot to move yours. Now then, as your Floor Monitor, I'm supposed to lead you to the dorms first. Then, Emilio can take the boys to their room, and I'll take the girls. We are going to need to meet with Professor Cho Lin to finalize your schedules, so what say we meet in the commons in about a half hour?" Everyone agreed.

Lindsey led the small procession toward the dorms, explaining as she went. "Here across the bottom of the pentagram to your right is the Infirmary. We are heading down the middle of the pentagram. Here's our topside swimming pool. There are huge indoor pools below this one, including a diving one. Ahead is the dorm, also a pentagram building. You can see Black Hall is the bottom edge. Yellow Hall is on the northwest side."

Lindsey, have the Dutch students meet me in the cafeteria in an hour, please. C. L.

The Message fluttered before Lindsey's eyes. "Oh, change of plans, Cho Lin will meet all of you in the cafeteria in one hour. That makes it simpler. Here is our commons room. Back here is our study hall, where we meet to study." She explained about the two stairs, boys and girls. Then, she led her two up to the second floor room, Kathy and Ashley tagging along behind her.

Room 14 was over half way down the long hall. However, the room was identical to all the previous rooms that Lindsey had had. The only difference was that two more beds, dressers, desks, and chairs had been added for Katja and Jeannette. All their many bags lay neatly beside the beds. Since the bags were where they were supposed to be, Lindsey then led them down to the girl's bathroom, which was huge and very well equipped. Both Katja and Jeannette were very impressed with the restroom facilities, declaring them much superior to theirs back home.

The hour passed rapidly and was just enough to allow the three to get fully unpacked before seeing Professor Cho Lin. Just as they were leaving, Pam finally entered, declaring being a Floor Monitor was fun. When they arrived in the cafeteria, Professor Cho Lin, the Yellow Hall councilor, was waiting for them. Before long, all twenty of the Exchange students were here.

Naturally, most wanted to chat with Jeannette to see what had happened to her. Many were shocked to see that she had real arms and hands, and they chatted away in Dutch. Kathy also arrived and took a seat near the rear. Professor Cho Lin rose and got their attention.

"On behalf of all the faculty and staff, welcome to Bradbury's. I'm Professor Cho Lin Sung, Illusion Magic and Yellow Hall Councilor. Behind us is Miss Kathy Townsend; she is your Student Hostess for your stay here. If you need something, you can always ask her. She will be giving you a history of our school this evening right after supper. Now then, the first order of business is the finalization of your schedules. We offer many electives here; more than a few are not listed officially in the catalog. So please ask me about courses of study that you may be interested in pursuing this year. When I call your name, please come up, and we'll get your schedule finalized. Katja van der Veer."

"Your basic schedule looks fine, Katja. However, is there something you would prefer to take instead of a Study Hall?" Cho Lin asked. A bit later, grinning from ear to ear, she carried her finalized schedule back in her hand, waving it about.

"Jeannette! You will never guess what elective I got! Baroque harpsichord performance practices! Wow!" Lindsey had taken harpsichord lessons during her second year, and suddenly she remembered how much she loved its sound and wished that she had continued with it. Katja promised to give her more lessons. She'd been playing hers ever since her second year. Her father had bought her a fabulous, handmade instrument on which to practice at home. Lindsey noted that Professor Cho Lin would be her teacher.

"Katja! They have Nous Theory I course! Incredible, wow! Heaven! Unbelievable!" Jeannette was ecstatic over her elective course. Hans decided to stick with the study hall. He just was not as sharp as the two girls and wanted the extra time to study, so that he would have more free time for sports.

Lindsey and her group found their schedules

unchanged from when they received them at the end of last term. Most had to take their elective course after supper in a ninth hour. However, the Dutch students schedules substituted their elective for the nine o'clock English class and had no six o'clock extra class. Other than that, the schedules of Katja, Jeannette, and Hans matched Lindsey and her friends.

```
 8:00  PE
 9:00  English
10:00  Trigonometry
11:00  Physics
 1:00  World Cultures and Foreign Language
 2:00  Alteration Theory II
 3:00  Potion Making I
 4:00  Spell Casting Grade 5
 6:00  Elective
```

With schedules fixed, Lindsey took them to the penthouse to meet their House Parents and to obtain their fancy cell phones. Ashley couldn't help tagging along just to see the look of surprise on Ann Bitterroot's face when she saw Ashley with arms, Jeannette too. Indeed, Ann's matronly look gave way to surprise when she saw Ashley and gave her a big smile, not what Ashley had though she would do. Yet Ann was expecting Jeannette to be another Special Needs student and was even more shocked. Ann still wore her hair tied back in a tight brown bun.

Once they had their phones, Lindsey took them back to their rooms. Next, she traded places with Pam, so that the computer whiz could fix up all three student's cell phones to send photos back to their computers. Lindsey gathered up the twenty new Yellow Hall first years and took them to the bookstore to obtain their wands, books, clothing, and supplies. Halfway through the many long lines, Pam and the three joined her, and Lindsey then helped the three get their things, while Pam continued working with the first years.

Before they headed back to their rooms, Jeannette and Katja both had to buy a postcard containing a photo of the Bradbury campus. After jotting a quick note to their parents, they sent them off via MagMail, knowing their folks would receive them tomorrow.

By the time they got their books arranged, it was time for supper. Governor Alister gave his usual welcome address, which was nearly the same as last year. Hence, the twenty new exchange students met their professors. Indeed, Alister had each of them pass by the main table, where the professors met them and shook their hands, welcoming them. Lindsey thought this was a very nice touch indeed.

Ashley found nearly all the older Floor Monitors making an opportunity to come over to her table and examine her new arms and hands. "They look so real. They feel so real," were the typical comments from the girl monitors. "Cool Ashley" was the typical comment from the boys. She realized that when everyone else returned, she would have to endure yet another round of stares. However, this time it would not be so bad for her, not so embarrassing.

Just after dinner, Pam and Lindsey got a break from their duties. Kathy took over, giving all twenty a history lesson about Bradbury's. Just as Lindsey was leaving, Deiter showed up, carrying his Staff of Power. "Hi ya, Lindsey. I figured now might be a good time to get together, while our guests are with Kathy." Pam and Ashley left Lindsey with him and headed up to their room.

"Sure, let's head off to the gardens. We can probably find some peace and quiet there," Lindsey suggested.

A couple of minutes later, the two were nearly alone among the fragrant flowers. "Say, what's with Ashley and Jeannette claiming their arms are the result of spells. I swear they both have real arms."

"Safety Deiter. If someone outside Bradbury's finds out how I was able to regenerate their arms, Dominus and the Death Stalkers would probably stop at nothing to get it from me. Alister has asked them to say what they are saying. Promise me you won't go telling this to another soul, Deiter."

"Of course I won't. We are a team. My dad bought me this powerful staff. It's called The Dragon." Deiter was very proud of his new staff, rightly so, Lindsey thought.

"What are its spells?" she asked. Deiter thought that she would never ask that question!

"Well, it has the basics, Continuous Light, Dispel Magic,

Teleport, even the one yours has, the Big Globe of Protection. Dad says it is an attacking staff. It has Paralyzation, Lightning Bolt, Ball of Fire, and Hold a Person or Animal. I really wanted to ask you about charges. The Dragon holds twenty-five. Dad says that is the usual amount for a staff. What I need to know is at what level should I keep it? Dad says that the usual rule of thumb is fifty-fifty, or around thirteen charges in it."

"Well, that's what we do, Deiter, halfway. Then you can absorb as needed and still attack. However, I think that you are going to want to attack much more than absorb. After all, absorb is what I do. I know that Ashley wanted to shoot many spells from her staff when we were rescuing Alister. However, she got stuck having to absorb for you guys, and it filled up rapidly."

"Ah. Since we are a team, maybe I ought to keep it charged a little more, giving me more spells to shoot before I have to stop to absorb more magical energies. What do you think?"

"Honestly, Deiter, if you run into Dominus or a Death Stalker, they are going to be shooting at least Grade 6 or better spells at you. If you have to absorb, you best be able to absorb one of those biggies. How about keeping the ability to absorb a Grade 8 spell? So that means you could charge it to seventeen charges. That amounts to casting five lightning bolts or balls of fire, before needing to recharge. However, if you are by yourself, Deiter, I would highly recommend that you lower it to maybe ten charges, allowing you to absorb fifteen grades of spells, maybe a couple Grade 7 spells. That's what I do, shoot a bunch of protection spells to drain it so I can absorb like mad, but then that is my job, to keep everyone else alive and protected."

"Great, I'll do it. Thanks. Say, do you think we will get another cool opportunity to use them this year?" Deiter was itching to get into another fight with the Death Stalkers. Typical Black Hall person, she thought to herself.

"I sure hope not. We have all these exchange students now. I sure would not want anything to happen to them." Deiter looked crestfallen, hoping that Lindsey or Ashley would already have some new action to perform.

"Well, I will keep my eyes open, and let you all know if something comes up. Say, is it true that Pam has discovered that Ashley's parents were murdered, and it wasn't an auto accident at all?"

"Yes, he was a deep undercover officer for the Chicago Department of Law. We think that he may have gotten too close to someone or have found out something he wasn't supposed to and was murdered to stop him. Exactly what, we don't know yet."

"How's Ashley taking the news?" he asked sincerely interested. "I know it must have been a shock to find out that it wasn't a horrible accident that cost her her arms and killed her parents."

"I think that she took the news well, Deiter. She now feels that there was a reason for her parent's death, not some freakish accident. I think she'd have more trouble if it was the other way around." Lindsey then suggested that he chat with Pam about the care and cleaning of his staff. Pam knew more about that than she did. He promised to do so. The two chatted all the way back to the dorm. Lindsey marveled that he and she had just had their first *real* talk ever. Deiter was definitely changing his outlook and attitudes towards others.

The next day, Lindsey and Pam led the twenty first years along with their Dutch students on the grand tour of the campus. As expected, the magnificent buildings and the complex tunnel system awed them. Once they finished that, Pam took over the education of the first year students. While she had to walk each student through their schedule, going from class to class, she, as had Sandy, worked out all sorts of games they could play to better familiarize themselves with the campus. Pam had it organized down to the last minute. Lindsey let her have her fun and spent her morning walking the four through their daily routine, going from class to class.

Particularly, she drilled them on going from PE class to their elective class and to their trigonometry class, where they would meet up with Lindsey's group once more. After trig, all the rest of the classes were with Lindsey's group, and they could just tag along. Only on this one different class would they be totally on their own. Hence, she made very sure each could find their way there and then to trig.

After lunch, Lindsey let them do whatever they wanted. All four went swimming in the huge pool. Pam, dragging her tired body into the lunchroom, had discovered the fatal flaw in her carefully arranged orientation games. She had been run ragged. Lindsey spelled her during the afternoon while Pam sacked out in their room.

After supper, Deiter cornered Pam and pleaded with her to help him learn the proper care of his staff. Reluctantly, she agreed, returning after dark to her room. "Deiter was really very civil and nice to me, Lindsey. What's come over him?" The two giggled. "Say, what was Ashley up to at supper? I saw her talking very seriously to Professor Jasper. I think they left together. Is something wrong?"

"I think it has to do with her pool game," Lindsey offered.

Indeed, it did. "Professor Jasper, have you got some time to play pool with me after supper? I've got arms now, and Tom and Sandy gave me a pool table, so I have been practicing shooting pool with my arms and hands, but it isn't working out at all as I expected."

He grinned. "Certainly, Ashley. When I heard what Lindsey's ring did for you, I wondered what this would do to your game. Let's have a look at it, shall we?"

In the poolroom deep underneath the stadium, Jasper saw at once the problem she was having. "It's now a different game for you, isn't it?" She nodded, trying to keep her tears from coming. If she wanted to shoot well, she'd have to go back to shooting with her feet. She'd already decided that she could do that, because at least she'd have hands to move things around not wasting so much time between shots.

"Slow Motion," he cast and observed her make a number of shots. "Suggestion. When you go to shoot, forget about trying to use lots of force. Try to hit it with as little force as you would if you were using your feet." She tried his suggestion, though it felt as if she were forcibly holding back on her shots. Yet, she was nearly as successful now as she was with her feet. "Good. Ashley, my advice is to continue to practice hitting it as softly as you would with your feet. Once you have that skill level achieved again, then you can experiment using a bit more force. Gradually, work your way up to using more power in your strokes." She agreed to work on it, and they returned to the dorms.

The days were warm, and all had idle time. Hans and Jeannette spent a good deal of time in the formal gardens, while Katja and Klaas walked behind them. All four knew that soon they would be buried in homework, once the classes began, buried doubly because they had to study, read, and write in English, not Dutch. True, all twenty had worked long and hard last year on their English, but still it was not their primary language. None was truly at home reading and writing English.

On Friday, all the other students began arriving, and by noon over six hundred students walked the campus. Amanda joined Lindsey, Ashley, and Pam. "Deiter has a Staff of Power too?" she exclaimed, surprised. "Soon, all students will have one," Amanda teased. The others giggled.

"None at Utrecht has one," Katja said, a regretful note in her voice. "US students must have a lot of money."

"No, just powerful wizards for fathers," Amanda attempted to set the record straight. "My dad made or fixed up three of ours, and Lindsey inherited hers from her father. Only Deiter's dad bought him one. I don't think any other student has one." Katja seemed to alter her opinion, and Amanda dropped the subject. "Has anyone seen Henry yet?" No one had, she took off to find her boyfriend, whom she'd not seen all summer.

Andy, Lindsey's boyfriend, had spent all summer on an archaeological dig. Lindsey had met his bus as it arrived bringing both Amanda and Andy here. After she moved their bags to their rooms, Andy said mysteriously, "Meet me in the gardens in an hour."

Lindsey loved to walk the stone path among the flowerbeds of the Formal Gardens. The heady aromas threatened to swamp her sense of smell entirely. She paced the length of this section for the third time, anxiously waiting for Andy to come. Although they had exchanged emails all summer and he had sent several photos of the dig, including several goofy ones as a joke, her heart raced as she spied him strolling up to meet her.

"Hi Lindsey," he said, opening his arms for her. The two joined and exchanged a kiss. "Ah, you missed me." She blushed. "Well, I missed you. I got you a little something." He handed her a small box. Lindsey tore it open to see a beautifully made turquoise and gold horse broach. "I made friends with an Indian jewelry maker. I had her make this one especially for you. It's supposed to bring you good luck. It's a one of a kind." Lindsey gave him a very big kiss, and then put it around her neck.

"Thank you! How does it look?"

"Pretty, but not as pretty as you. Gosh, I missed you, Lindsey. I almost quit and came home after the first week. That's how much I was missing you, but I stuck it out. Glad I did. I learned lots, and we made some remarkable finds. By the way, Lindsey, that was absolutely the most monumental, fantastic, incredible, greatest thing ever that you did for Ashley and the Dutch girl, Jeannette! Between you and me, and I don't care what Ashley has to say, I think that you gave them back their quality of life!"

"Shh. Remember, we're supposed to be pretending it is just a spell, but really anyone would have done it if they had the ring," Lindsey couldn't think of anything to say other than reminding him of what she'd said in her email to him.

"Of course, it is just a spell," Andy teased her, "and a Grade 9 spell at that. Can you teach me to cast that one?" he jested. Lindsey grinned and poked him in the ribs. He responded by giving her another kiss. That they stayed in the gardens for over an hour was some indication how much these two had missed each other during the summer.

"This fall we will begin with tennis, so grab your rackets and balls, girls, and follow me," Betsy, their PE teacher explained. The first day of classes began on sunny September 1. As usual, Betsy waved her wand, changing each girl into her PE outfit.

"Oh no!" moaned Pam, "I just got up. I just ate, and we have to go running around!"

"Come on. I'll race you," Amanda cheerily teased Pam. Everyone knew that Pam and Kathy disliked anything athletic, Pam especially. For nearly an hour, they batted balls up against a wall, which had a net line painted on it. Betsy showed them how to hold the racket and execute a forehand drive and a backhand smash. None of the girls knew how to play tennis so they were all in the same boat. Few enjoyed PE this early in the morning.

Lindsey and Ashley made sure that Katja, Hans, and Jeannette knew where they were to go for their special next class and how to find the others an hour later. Then, they joined the others heading for English class.

"This term, we will be concentrating on writing," Professor Elaine Mac Elroy began. "There are many different kinds or styles of writing. For example, there is writing to persuade someone to accept your points." At least, Pam found this interesting, since she had been writing in this manner for some years. For her, the hour passed rapidly. For Emilio, who fell asleep twice and had to be poked awake by Ashley, time drug on endlessly.

Katja, Hans, and Jeannette rejoined them as they entered their math room for their trigonometry class. Professor Herbert Mac Elroy called roll promptly and then began at once. He drew a right triangle on the board. "Assume this is a right triangle; you remember those from your geometry class, I hope. Now if I tell you that these two sides are equal in length," he pointed to the two that formed the ninety degree angle, "who can tell me what these two angles must be?"

Pam's hand shot up, "Miss Betts?"

"Forty-five, professor."

"Precisely. Now then, suppose that I tell you that their length is five feet long each. Who can tell me how to find how long the longer side is?" Again, Pam's hand shot up, as well as Jeannette's.

"Miss van Ravinstijn?" He already knew that Pam would know the answer.

"Square root of two times five, professor," she replied.

"Excellent, correct again. Trig is the study of angles and

sides of triangles and the many relationships between them. This is a highly useful branch of math, one that we can use in our everyday world. Some of you play pool. Here are the cue ball and the eight ball. They are lined up here. However, the pocket in which you need to drive the eight ball lies over here, at a forty-five degree angle from the line of the cue ball and the eight ball. We can use trig to estimate where our cue ball must strike the eight ball in order to drive it into the pocket."

"You are learning to play tennis. The angle with which your racket hits the ball determines, in part, the direction the ball will travel. If you strike the ball with your racket slanted this way, the ball tends to go downward, yet if you reverse it, the ball goes upward. If you hit it square on, the ball flies straight forward. It is all in the angles, trig at work."

Kathy slowly drifted off into slumber land. However, for once Emilio managed to stay awake and listen to the math lecture. Pam thought this was a hopeful sign. Perhaps she would not have to tutor him endlessly in trig as she had done in the other math courses.

Next hour, they walked downstairs to their physics class. This was the class Pam was very eager to have, knowing that she needed to know as much physics as possible to help her sleuthing. Professor Jasper called roll and then launched into his introduction. "Wizards and witches, this is a most vital class for you. A solid understanding of the laws of motion, how objects interact, is critical for your survival. Suppose that you have made an error in teleportation, which I understand you will be learning this term. You have arrived sixteen feet above the ground. How long do you have to cast your Gentle Fall spell?"

"Andy?"

"One second, sir."

"Right, one second, because on Earth, the force of gravity in pulling objects down, and an object suddenly let go will begin to accelerate downward at a rate of thirty-two feet per second per second. In one second, you will have fallen sixteen feet. Now, suppose that you are lucky enough to have arrived thirty-two feet above the ground. How many of you believe that you now have two full seconds to cast it before you made a disastrous collision with the ground?" Many, many hands rose.

"I see. Maybe I'd better ask it the other way around. How many of you don't believe that you have two full seconds to get your spell cast?"

Ashley, Pam, Jeannette, and Lindsey raised their hands. No one else did. Jasper smiled, "Well four of you are right. Jeannette, perhaps you can suggest what makes you say that you don't have two full seconds."

"Sir, each second, you accelerate thirty-two feet per second faster than the second before, ignoring air resistance and friction effects. It's gravity times time squared over two," Jeannette answered.

"Precisely, in two seconds you would have fallen sixty-four feet. Now another example, as you can see, I have stacked six children's play blocks on my tablecloth here on my desk. The objective: remove the tablecloth without knocking the blocks over. Can anyone hazard a guess how this might be done?"

"Oh, I know that one!" Emilio muttered and shot his hand high, as though he was in competition with several others. For once, Professor Jasper allowed Emilio to answer it.

"Pull the cloth out really fast!"

"Right, like this." He jerked it out very fast, and the blocks remained standing on his lab table. "Now can anyone explain to us how that was possible?"

Andy knew he was going to love this class. So did Pam, Lindsey, Ashley, and many others. Finally, they were getting a valuable science class, Lindsey thought.

On their way to lunch, Katja stated, "I thought that physics was going to be a really boring subject, but it is just the opposite."

"See, I told you so," Jeannette replied to her friend.

At one, they filed into the Hall of Illusion for their World Cultures and Foreign Language class. Lindsey was elated to find the Cho Lin was teaching this class. That meant it would not be boring. "Good afternoon. Welcome to World Cultures class. This year we will be learning about the social customs, the culture, and the language of many other people of our world. This year we are honored to have twenty fourth-year magic students with us from the Netherlands, the Utrecht School of Magic. Why do we need to study the culture and languages of another country?"

Pam's hand shot up as well as those of Katja, Jeannette, Hans, and Klaas. Cho Lin ignored Pam and asked Klaas. "Ve come to the States to go to school. We need to speak English to read everything and to communicate with you. We need to know your customs so ve don't say something that will make you mad at us."

"Exactly, Klaas. You are going to be learning the Teleport spell this year. As you know, once you have mastered it, you can go anywhere in the world at any time, any place you desire. With this unlimited freedom comes much more responsibility on your part. Suppose that you teleported to the Great Wall in China. Once there, if you do not know the customs of the people there around you, it will be very easy for you to get into very big trouble very quickly."

"Now as part of our studies, each of you will get to choose a foreign language. You will be required to both speak it and read and write in that language. Of course, some languages are far harder for English speaking people to learn than others are. I will take that into consideration when I grade you on how well you perform. Of course, you are not allowed to use magical spells to do so. By Friday, each of you must make your choice of language to learn."

Of course, Lindsey's groups had already decided on the language, Dutch. Even Deiter chose Dutch for the same reasons; he was hosting Bale.

Professor Arthur Thornby called roll in his Alteration Theory II class. "Welcome to advanced alteration theory. Can anyone tell me why this course is so important to you at this time? Yes, Miss Betts?"

"We are going to learn how to Teleport soon. It uses alteration magic."

"Precisely so. If you do not have your theory down very solidly, you can end up your teleport spell by being very solidly within the ground. That's a joke, by the way, you know—you misjudge and materialize under the ground, solid." No one thought that sounded the least bit funny, however. Everyone paid very keen attention to his lecture, though, Kathy, more so than normal, fearing that she might mess up her spell and wind up as he said, deep underground and very dead.

Lindsey dreaded their next class, Potion Making I, primarily because it was being held in the Hall of Necromancy, the dark arts. Gloomy Professor Delius Dogs was their teacher. He was head of Black Hall. Still, Kathy was more excited about this class than she had been over any other class in her three years here. She wanted to become a Potion Maker when she graduated.

Ashley was very thankful that she now had arms. Last May when she learned she would have this class this fall, she was petrified that she wouldn't be able to handle it. Indeed, Lindsey had to do all her actual mixing in chemistry class because she was far too slow with her feet. Now, she was as able as everyone else was, though she knew nothing about the making of potions.

Lindsey was expecting some kind of quaint old musty room, black kettles bubbling, arcane bottles lying everywhere—just like the old time movies she'd seen. She walked into a modern laboratory, not unlike their chemistry labs in the science and math hall! Each student station had a Bunsen burner and sterile glass beakers just as they had had in chemistry class. True, along one wall were the wild ingredients, all nicely labeled in jars, thirty jars of each type. There were precisely thirty students in the class. The room was bright and well lighted. An exhaust hood was above each of the thirty workstations.

In stark contrast, Professor Delius walked in, dressed in his black robes, his well-oiled black hair shining in the light. "Welcome to Potion Making I. Some of you will excel in my class. Some of you will not be returning to this subject ever. I want to be frank and honest right up front with you. Potion making is both an art and a science. It is a science, because the wizarding world has now established 100% workable formulas for a wide number of magical potions. *If* you follow the recipe absolutely *exactly*, you have a potion that will perform precisely as intended."

"Miss Barron can testify to the precise workability of the healing potions that she was given to regrow her hands, twice now, I do believe." All heads naturally turned to Lindsey, whose face grew suddenly very hot indeed. She tried to skink as low as she could on her lab stool.

"Yet, potion making is also an *art*. Every year, great potion making artists are devising new potions, hither to fore unknown to the wizarding world. So let me be perfectly clear, in this class *no* points will be awarded for the creation of any new or variation of an assigned potion! This class is only concerning itself with the science aspect, perfect, workable, and known potions. If I assign you to make a healing potion and you turn in a potion that instead of healing accidentally turns all that it is poured over into pure gold, you will receive *zero* points for that potion!"

"Some say that routine, normal potion making can be done by an *idiot*. Well, I agree. All that you have to do is to *precisely,* and I do mean *precisely,* follow the instructions in your text book. If you do that, you will excel at potion making. However, I can tell you right now that many of you simply cannot or will not follow instructions precisely, much to your folly. Time will tell, as they say."

"Potions can heal the sick. Potions can regrow hands, as we all know. Potions can give you phenomenal luck. Potions can allow you to breathe underwater. Potions can change your body into that of another, much like your Morph spells do, only it does it far better. A potion can cause your body to become invisible for a time. A potion can cause someone to fall totally in love with you. Yes, there are hundreds of different accepted standard potions. In this course, I will be attempting to teach you how to make fifty of these potions."

"During the fall term, each class period you will work on brewing the next potion in your text book. When you have it finished, put a sample into one of the vials with your name on it. Write which potion it is supposed to be on the vial's label and hand it in to me to be graded. Then, go on to the next potion. Just before the Christmas holidays, I will be giving you a final exam. Each of you will be assigned to make one of the first twenty-five potions that you supposedly have learned how to make. You will have an hour to brew that potion, unless the recipe requires a longer period. Half of your grade comes from how well your assigned potion matches the known standard for that potion. In the spring, you will make the remaining twenty-five potions, and in May you will receive a similar test for the other half of your grade. Is this understood?"

"I have only one rule in this class. DO NOT EVER DRINK OR SIP ANY POTION THAT YOU MAKE UNLESS I GIVE YOU A 100% PASS ON THAT POTION! Why? If you have made it wrong, it can kill you, and I don't want to be activating you as a zombie in my next necromancy class." That cast a scary and nervous feeling among nearly all students, including Deiter.

"Open your text to chapter 1. We will be making an Anti-sneezing potion, one of the simplest of all potions to make. The supplies you need are on the shelves. The drawer beneath your workstation holds all the equipment you will need, including a measuring scale. Start."

Sometime later, Emilio whispered to Pam, "Mine seems to have turned yellow. That isn't right, is it? Or does it turn clearish like yours later on?"

Pam's brew was never yellow. She took a whiff of his boiling pot and asked, "How much alum did you put in it anyway?"

"It says 1 tsp. So I put one tablespoon in it, just like it says," Emilio protested.

"Oh no! That's the abbreviation for teaspoon! Tbs is tablespoon. I guess you have to start all over," Pam declared flatly. He groaned and turned off his burner, then dumped the contents down the drain. He disliked potion making already. Why didn't the author just say teaspoon anyway?

As the end of the period drew closer, Pam's nose became very dry. She looked up and noticed that many of those around her were fiddling with their noses as well. The cold voice of Professor Delius broke the silence, "Miss West, would you *please* turn on your overhead fan? Your potion is drying out the noses of the whole class. I believe you have made it strong enough for a *cow!*"

She hastily turned on her fan; she'd forgotten to do it.

From the vapors filling the room, she'd mis-duplicated the recipe rather significantly. A bit embarrassed, she decided to turn in her attempt anyway.

As everyone was finishing up, Professor Delius announced, "Those of you who wish to turn in your sample for grading may take your vial to that machine there. Press the Open button; place your vial inside; press the Grade button. Your grade will appear on the screen. Those who do not turn in a vial get zero points on today's potion, but you may try again tomorrow."

Soon there was a lineup for the grading machine. Kathy put hers inside and pressed Grade. Shortly, the screen displayed 100. "Yes!" she exclaimed. Pam went next, but the readout only displayed 95. Lindsey's read 90. Both Ashley and Amanda received a 91. Jeannette also got 100, but Katja, an 85. Emilio, 65. Andy's score was 92, while Deiter only had 85. Kathy, who also saw Pam's score, said, "Well, 95 is almost perfect, Pam." Pam glared at Kathy, a bit upset that Kathy had gotten a better score than she had.

"Well, finally, we get to the *real* magic!" Emilio declared as they left the spooky Hall of Necromancy, heading over to the Hall of Alteration and back with Professor Arthur Thornby for part of their Spell Casting Grade 5.

"That was *real* magic! If you had the sniffles, my potion would have cured it," declared Kathy, indignantly.

"Er, yes, I'm sorry, Senorita Kathy. I meant real *spell* casting," Emilio hastily tried to smooth over his major blunder with his girlfriend.

"Welcome you witches and wizards. Spell Casting Grade 5," Professor Thronby began the class promptly on time. "As some of you may have heard from upperclassmen, the first spell that we will be learning is indeed Teleport." He paused while the young teens reacted in various ways. This was the spell most had been waiting to learn. "Yes, once you have learned this spell, you have untold freedom. You can go to Tahiti in a blink, enjoying the tropical beaches. Or perhaps a quick trip to Cancun or the warm coasts of southern Spain. With this spell, you can travel to any location on this planet in the blink of an eye." Again, he waited for their enthusiastic reaction to die down. He knew that he had their full and complete attention now!

"Right here at the beginning, let me point out one ironclad rule. During the time that you are officially on the Bradbury campus, that is, from the time your bus arrives in our parking lot, until the time you step off the bus at your home, absolutely no one is permitted to Teleport outside of the walls of this campus, unless you are accompanied by one of the professors. I'm sorry if you are disappointed that you cannot pop off to Tahiti on Saturdays to enjoy some fun in the sun. Violation means instant *expulsion* from Bradbury's. Why? You are here to learn, and while you are here, your safety is the responsibility of this school and its faculty. Where you go during vacations and over the holidays is up to you. Save your excursions to Tahiti until then. Please note, you are allowed to Teleport anywhere you desire within the walls of our campus."

"Now then, Teleport is not a trivial spell. This is not some fun game that you are about to play. If you make an error, you may find yourself instantly dead! If you misjudge your arrival location, you may find your body is one hundred feet below the ground. That does save on burial costs, I'm told." No one laughed at his joke, however.

"The wand motion is perhaps the simplest of all wand motions, a decisive, downward flip, as if pointing to the desired spot. That, you will find, is nearly impossible to goof. This is one of the few spells that takes but a fraction of a second to cast, which is why so many favor this spell to extricate themselves from mortal danger. One flip of the wand and poof, you are out of the life threatening situation."

"However, great care must be taken in the selection of your arrival point. Two famous cases come to mind. One Phil Deringer inappropriately chose to arrive in the middle of one of the norm's expressways in southern California. He arrived precisely on target, but found himself five feet directly in front of an oncoming semi-truck traveling at sixty-five miles an hour. He was identified from his various pieces."

"Then there is the case of Mildred Weber, a most conservative witch. Her motto was always aim very high and Gentle Fall to the ground. While visiting the busy Los Angeles

International Airport, she arrived five hundred feet above the ground, her usual destination elevation. The only problem was she neglected to consider that other objects might also be sharing the same space. Half of her body materialized outside the plane, the remainder appeared inside the cabin, nearly frightening the passengers to death. She was very lucky; the Department of Magical Misuse was able to extricate her from this predicament."

"Remember, you must always think about what you are doing with this spell. If you find yourself unable to concentrate fully, for heaven's sake, don't cast your Teleport spell!" Lindsey noted that several girls were rather pale. She too wondered if perhaps they shouldn't learn this spell at some later time.

"The key to safe usage of this spell is to hold firmly in your mind and to concentrate fully and completely on your destination location. Once you are solidly holding the image of your location, you make your wand motion and speak, 'Teleport:' adding the destination point, which is firmly in your mind."

"Please take note of this admonition. If you make the wand motion and speak the command word, 'Teleport,' your wand will activate, and you will be teleported, whether your mind wavers on the destination point. If it does waver, you will still be teleported, but to who knows where. If you are very lucky and your mind is wavering from the destination point to somewhere else, you may find you still arrive at your destination point. However, it is more likely that you will arrive at the spot on which your mind wandered."

"A former Bradbury student is a perfect example of this. I won't mention his name, however. While practicing the spell, he was holding on to the desired destination point of the gardens, but his mind continually thought about his girlfriend, who was in the girl's bathroom. His spell activated, he arrived in their bathroom, much to his embarrassment as well as the young woman, who was using the facilities." Many of the boys laughed, and several girls giggled.

"The point is, if your mind is wavering, for heaven's sake don't cast your spell at that time. Focus; get your mind firmly on the destination location before you activate your spell. Is this clear?" Everyone nodded.

"There is one final caution that I must make. When you are in transit, moving between your source point and your destination point, do *not* open your eyes and look around. Allow me to explain more of the theory behind this spell, so that this caution may make more sense to you." He looked directly at Deiter Cross and then gave Pam Betts a passing glance. Pam sat up even straighter in her chair. This was going to be important. She just knew it was.

He drew a pair of axes on the board, just as they had done so many times in geometry, when they were about to plot a point or a line. "Here is the origin point. It is not an absolute origin point of the earth; rather it is where you are currently positioned on earth. I am using 2D space instead of 3D space to keep this more readily visualized. Now then, we will call this origin point where you are located O1. Over here, is your destination point, let's call it O2." He made an 'X' above and to the right of O1.

"When you teleport, you are merely changing the location of your personal origin point from O1 to O2. It is rather like backing out of the physical universe here at O1, and then reappearing in the physical universe at O2, which immediately becomes your new origin point and view point of the world." Everyone seemed to grasp this oversimplification.

"The philosophical question then becomes, if we are 'stepping out' of the physical universe during the tiny fraction of time that the spell requires, what then, if anything, lies outside of our universe? There have been many reports over the ages of strange things that inhabit that netherworld. Those that claim to have gotten a very good view of them have returned to this world temporarily insane. Frothing at the mouth, convulsions, and even total insanity has resulted from such attempts, intentional or accidental, of seeing what may lie in this netherworld."

"Indeed, by accident, Mr. Cross here had that misfortune last year when he was being teleported out of the Death Stalker combat by Bill West. Many of you saw the condition that he was in when he arrived here at the destination point. Now don't panic over this. Normally, when you are casting this spell, you have your mind totally focused on your destination point. Thus, you will never have sufficient time to view this netherworld as you travel to your destination point, as it is but a mere fraction of a second. I felt that I owed this explanation to Mr. Cross, after his unfortunate experience last year."

"Now then, open your spell book to the Alteration Section, page forty-two. Read and fully grasp the four pages of spell explanation. Once you believe you have that down, grab a pile of clay, and you are to make me a clay demonstration showing me just how a Teleport spell is accomplished. Make little figures representing yourself. Put small paper labels on each piece of clay, such as 'Me,' 'my wand,' 'my house,' and so on. Make the demonstrations on the trays, so that if you don't get it finished today, you can leave it over there until tomorrow."

"Before I let you near this spell, you must show me in a clay model that you fully understand what we are attempting with this powerful alteration based spell. Now let's get to work."

At supper, the entire topic of conversation among Lindsey's group was the Teleport spell. "I never dreamed it would be this dangerous," Ashley commented, "but think of the freedom we will have! Incredible."

On their way out of the dining room, Pam caught Deiter for a moment. "I'm still researching for you, only now I'm also researching it for me too. Did you see the way that he looked at you and at me?"

"Yes, couldn't miss it, Pam. It's intriguing—that there is some other 'world' or whatever when you step out of this one. Anything you can find out will be helpful, Pam. Thanks a bunch." She grinned and headed off to get her things for her "ninth" class, Sleuthing Theory II.

Around seven Lindsey and her friends returned from their special elective classes. Andy was very excited about his Archaeology II class; he was delving into ancient Egyptian sites. Pam felt challenged, "I can see that I'm going to have to study until midnight this year or I'll never pass any of our classes. Have you noticed how hard everything has become?"

Monique had wandered into Yellow Hall study hall to find out how Pam's classes had gone. "I tried to tell you, love. Now you see why you didn't see much of me in my forth year. Don't worry. It only gets worse with each year. I don't see how I'm to pass this sixth year!" Pam groaned, as did Emilio, who overheard them.

"Pam, those direction locating devices you gave us last year—those are working fabulously well. Governor Alister and I worked with them during my Tracker Theory II tonight. Wonderful invention, saves lots of work on our part," Amanda just had to thank Pam again, now that she and Alister had put them through a grueling set of tests. Pam smiled, pleased with her invention, really an adaption from the surveying people.

"Dispelling Theory II is going to be awfully hard," Lindsey commented. "Gang, listen up. Professor Delius told me that his proposal for mock combat battles got approved!"

"Well, we all really do need to get some training so we can defend ourselves," Pam declared. "Though I don't suppose that they will let any of us actually get hurt during these mock battles, will they?"

"We didn't actually cast the spells, only pretend," Lindsey tried to dampen Pam's concern. "He said that Governor Alister will announce it to the whole school on Friday evening." Even the three Dutch students were keenly interested in just what these mock battles might entail, but everyone just had to be patient until Friday.

Just then, Ashley wandered in from her Divination Theory II class. Lindsey asked her how it had gone. "Finally, we are getting me to have some control over these premonitions. At least that's the goal this term. She thinks I should be able to start being able to predict what others may do. I wonder if that is possible. Guess I'll find out."

The voice of Jake Rattlebeam broke in on their quiet conversations here in the study hall. "Ah, there you all are. Try outs for the track and soccer teams will be Saturday morning at ten. Let everyone know that they are welcome to try out. We need to replace Tom in the twenty-mile relay and his left forward position on our soccer team. Bummer that there's no

Nationals this year. Gotta go find Jim. You won't believe how heavy our course load is! Sixth year, they load it on like there's no tomorrow! It's only the first day!"

At Thursday's spell casting class, everyone gathered outside the Hall of Alteration. A bit of a chill was in the air as fall came early at this higher elevation. All had passed their clay demonstrations, eagerly awaiting their first attempt to Teleport, even if it was only a few feet away.

"One final word," Professor Arthur cautioned them. "When you first are successful with the spell, you can transport around two hundred-fifty pounds—that means you and another person. After you have used the spell frequently, you will find the total weight that you can take or the number of other persons you can take with you will increase. Fundamentally, that limit is solely dependent upon just how convinced you are that you can do it. The greater your conviction, the more people you can take with you. Now then, because this spell is so inherently dangerous, only one person at a time will attempt to Teleport. When I call your name, come to my side, and take my hand. You will be teleporting me with you. I will do my best to prevent any mishaps. Your destination will be that red 'X' I've placed on the ground over there." Lindsey noted that it was about ten feet away.

"Now do not expect to succeed on your first attempt. We will go through the class from A to Z and then repeat again and again. Each of you ought to be able to get several tries in today. Let's get started then. Miss Barron, you are up first."

Oh no! All eyes would be on her. That all eyes would be on each of them as they made their attempts eluded her, only that once more, she was in the limelight. Lindsey grew a bit nervous as she stepped to Arthur's side. "Emotion: calm." Professor Arthur cast his spell on her. Lindsey suddenly felt tranquil and serene. "Don't fret. I have to cast that on nearly everyone on their first attempt. Now get the target firmly in mind. Plan to arrive three feet above the 'X.' When you have it, cast the spell." He also cast Slow Motion and Monitor Thoughts on Lindsey. She relaxed even more, knowing that Professor Arthur would be watching over her in case she messed it up badly.

"It's hard to block all other thoughts," she whispered. He grinned and gave her more encouragement. At last, she moved her wand sharply downward, saying, "Teleport: three feet above the 'X.'" Magical energies flashed, and Lindsey felt herself falling down. She braced herself and landed on her feet, right on the 'X!' "I did it! I did it!" Lindsey was wild with excitement. Pam and several others began spontaneously clapping. Deiter was among them as well as Peaches.

"Miss Betts," Arthur called out. Pam nervously took her place beside him. Lindsey spied him casting Emotion: Calm on her as well. After what seemed an eternity, Pam and Arthur vanished, only to reappear five feet above ground. Before Pam could cast her Gentle Fall, Arthur did it for them. Pam's face turned a bit pink, but the group clapped for her anyway.

One by one, the young teens stepped up to attempt their very first Teleport. When Kathy did hers, she arrived fifty feet above the ground and hastily cast Gentle Fall on herself and Arthur. She was too frightened of picking any target location closer to the ground. "Better safe than sorry," she explained to the others as she rejoined the thirty.

Hans failed his first attempt. He explained that he kept having images of home appearing in his mind, blocking out the 'X.' Professor Arthur suggested that he practice focusing until his turn came around once more.

"No! No! Focus on the destination!" Arthur shouted as he brought Lyle back from the 'X.' If I had not intervened, you would have landed us thirty feet underground. Do you have a death wish, son?" Lyle's face was scarlet; he muttered something inaudible to the group and walked back to them his face staring at the ground.

"Don't worry, Lyle, you will get it next time," Lindsey felt she ought to give him an encouraging word, even though he had been the one who had cast the Trip spell when they were in their first year here, causing her to fall and break both of her handless arms in three places. He'd paid for that with an entire month's detention. Besides, that was years ago now, and he needed encouraging. Deiter mouthed, "Thank you" to Lindsey.

By the end of the class, everyone had successfully

teleported at least one time; even Lyle got it right the next time. As they headed off to supper, Pam told them, "According to Monique, each time we practice this, the destination point gets trickier. The final passing standard will be to land on top of a three-foot wide column that is ten feet above the ground. She said that indicates a precision landing, but it is hard to do the first time."

"Then, you get to solo, Teleport all by yourself," Pam continued. "Monique said that was the scariest part of it all, knowing Professor Arthur is not there with you!" Lindsey felt very sober when she heard this news.

The group congregated at the Yellow Hall tables for supper. Kathy asked, "You know we have to let Cho Lin know what foreign language we are going to try to learn by tomorrow. I think that we all should try the same one. Don't you think so too?"

"Sure, then we can help each other out," Ashley agreed. "Probably we should learn Dutch. That way, Hans, Katja, and Katja can help us out."

Lindsey said, "Okay, all those in favor of tackling Dutch say yes." Everyone in her group did so. "Okay, I will let her know that we are all going to try to learn Dutch."

"Way cool, so are we," Deiter Cross cheerily said. He'd just walked over from the Black Hall tables to see Lindsey. "Peaches and I are choosing Dutch too, mostly because we have Bale. Say, I was wondering if I could have a word with you and Pam? Kind of in private, please." Lindsey suddenly became very curious. This was not like Deiter at all. Pam raised her eyebrows. She still didn't trust him. After all, he was the one who teased and picked on Lindsey mercilessly their first year here.

The three stepped away from the tables. Deiter spoke softly so they wouldn't be overheard. "I was wondering, you know our homework, well, it seems to be growing, and I was wondering if perhaps Peaches, Bale, and I could join your study group in Yellow Hall study hall evenings. I mean it would look good for our exchange students if Black Hall and Yellow Hall were seen to be working together. Besides, Alister has said repeatedly that we are stronger if we stick together.

Peaches is pretty good in English, and I've always been good in math. Bale's a fast learner, at least what I've seen of him so far. I know I used to be a jerk, but I've been trying to change."

That last did it. Pam had been following his words carefully, figuring that the three really wanted to lean on them for homework help, nothing more. Yet he had admitted he'd been a jerk, and she couldn't argue with his attempts to change. He had sent the girls on the victorious track team a bouquet of roses when they had won First Place at the Nationals last May. She looked at Lindsey and gave her a slight nod.

"It's okay with me Deiter. Pam?"

"Yes, but you have to help others who need assistance. We all help each other out on things," Pam said, hoping that he might decide not to join them.

His huge smile convinced her otherwise. "Thanks! You won't regret it. We'll bring our things by this evening. I know you have special classes until seven, so we'll come by then. Thanks again!" They each returned to their respective hall tables. "Looks like Deiter, Peaches, and Bale will be joining us in study hall at night," Pam announced. Everyone had been straining to hear what they had discussed. He promised to help us with our homework, so it shouldn't be a one-way street. He says Peaches is good in English, and he is good in math, so we'll have to see."

"I don't know about him," Emilio grumbled a little. "After all, he's Black Hall."

"But Peaches was really nice to me in swimming class," Ashley countered. "We ought to at least see how it works out."

That evening, the three Black Hall students arrived on time, carrying their many books and computers. At first, conversation seemed a little strained, but soon, schoolwork broke down the last barriers. Deiter proved a valuable asset, helping Emilio with his trig assignment. Pam kept a sharp eye on him, half expecting Deiter to lose patience with Emilio, whose math skills were poor, due in large measure to the lower quality of his early norm school years. Peaches really proved her worth, helping all five foreign exchange students with their English work that they had in their special class, which was at the same time as everyone else's English class. Actually, all twenty Dutch students were in that same class designed for their special needs.

When they were taking a chat break, Ashley explained to Jeannette, "Peaches is a fantastic high diver. We had diving lessons last year, and I was terrified of diving. She really helped me out."

"You dive? Twenty meter board?" asked Jeannette.

"Oops, not sure how tall twenty meters is, but ours is twenty-five feet," Peaches replied. "I've been diving all my life. I've been working on all the official dives that one has to do if you were in a competition. I have them all down pat. I'm not so good on the free style dives though, been working on those a little each week."

"Ja, wid no arms, I couldn't do the technical dives, but I'm good on free style from the twenty meter board," Jeannette said quietly.

"What? You dive with no arms?" Way cool!" Peaches exclaimed.

Thinking that Peaches didn't believe her friend, Katja jumped in, "Ja, she says truth. Jeannette swims like fish. Good diver, we all are. Ve swim every day, even Hans."

"Coolest! I usually go on Saturday mornings, around nine. No one is around then, so we can have the whole pool to ourselves. Want to come along with me? I'll show you what I can do."

"Ja, sure ve would," Katja replied, knowing how much she and Jeannette loved to swim. Lindsey and Ashley made a note of the time, since as the two girls' hosts, they ought to go with them.

As they walked outside on Friday afternoon in spell casting class, Lindsey saw the tall pillars and knew that Pam's report of what Monique had told her was right. Indeed, today, they worked on precision landings. The top surface of the pillars was only three feet in diameter. More than one student missed the target, Gentle Falling once they lost their balance. By the end of the class, only Deiter managed to land squarely on top once. On his first try, Lyle actually missed the pillar by five feet, much to his embarrassment. Yet by the end of the period, he too was landing with at least one foot on top.

"These Grade 5 spells are much harder to master," Deiter commented as they all headed to supper. "I hope they all are not this difficult or we'll never get through them all." Pam had the same idea, though she had not vocalized it yet.

"May I have your attention?" Governor Alister spoke as everyone gathered for dinner. "Thank you. I have an important announcement to make. Professor Delius wishes us to hold mock magical battles, similar to the one you have all probably heard rumors about last May. In these dark times with Death Stalkers attacking seemingly at random, he and most of our staff feel that it would be wise for you to experience what a magical combat might be like. It is one thing to sit back and cast your Magical Missiles at harmless rotting pumpkins left over from Halloween and quite another to think of using that spell when you are facing your enemies."

"Indeed, several of you students have already been attacked by evil wizards and witches. Many of you know just how badly Miss Blackburn was injured by a Death Stalker last Christmas. We would like you to have a little firsthand training in a mock combat situation. Mind you, no actual spells are cast; it's all pretend. Nevertheless, the eleven who participated in the mock combat conducted last May had nothing buy high praise and thanks for it. Some of you may well decide that you do not want to fight back. Of course, that is your choice, though the Death Stalkers will still do what they intend to do. We feel if you have a little idea of what real magical spell battles are like, you are in a better position to make such decisions."

"The mock battles will take place on Sunday mornings at ten over in Black Hall, where Professor Delius has kindly created the battlefield. Each session will be recorded so that you can watch it and see what your performance actually was, as well as the others who are participating. In this way, you can learn your strengths and weaknesses. Due to the age disparity, to say nothing of the spells available by years, you will be fighting only members of your class. The sixth year students who wish to participate will take the field this Sunday. The following Sunday, those fifth year students who wish will battle, and so on each Sunday morning. However, the first years will not be allowed to participate until their second year. A Clean spell is not going to be very effective against a Death Stalker." Many first year students giggled, having just learned their Clean spell, along with Chill and Warm.

"Those of you who wish to participate, please sign up on the roster lists that are posed on the bulletin board just inside the main entrance of the Hall of Necromancy. Now, let us enjoy this fine dinner." Several dozen voices yelled out various supportive calls, including Pam's "Yes!" Emilio added his "Hurray!"

Saturday morning was going to a busy one for Lindsey and Ashley. They needed to monitor the diving meeting of their Dutch students at nine. Then, at ten, the tryouts for the track and soccer teams required their presence. As promised, Peaches met them at their dorm's door, and the five walked down to the swimming pool area, and then descended two stories underground, where the Olympic size diving pool was located. Betsy was there waiting them, holding a cup of coffee.

"Ah, I see you have brought company this morning, Peaches," she smiled. "Welcome. I spot for her every Saturday morning so she can practice her high dives. Come to watch?"

"No, Betsy, they both dive too. I'll show them some of my dives first," Peaches insisted. Ashley and Lindsey, wearing their swimming suits under their school clothes, quickly changed, as did the others. They sat on the side, dangling their feet into the warm waters. From here, they could see the dives perfectly.

Peaches went through her first five technical dives, letter perfect. "Ja, you are good," Katja said. "Very good."

"Okay, Katja, let's see what you can do," Peaches said as she slid up onto the side beside Ashley, who handed her a towel.

"Okay, I try to do the same you did," Katja explained.

"She good too, you see," Jeannette added, supporting her best friend.

Five perfect dives later, Peaches was ecstatic! "Incredible! Superb, Katja! Well done! Betsy, did you see her? She's great at this!" Katja slid out of the pool, and Lindsey handed her a towel.

"Danke," she said a little out of breath. "Jeannette, you show them free style."

"I've never dived with my new arms yet. I always dove with no arms, I'm afraid I will not do so well. Need to practice lots," Jeannette countered.

"Just imagine your arms are just your imaginary arms," Ashley suggested, trying to offer her charge something that might help.

"Ja, okay." Jeannette climbed to the top. Ashley watched her closely. She too took several deep breaths before making her sudden run down the board. She jumped high in the air and landed solidly on the edge of the board. At the peak of the upswing, she began her dive. It was a reverse back flip into a swan dive, executed with the grace of a swan.

"Beautiful! Wow! Incredible!" Peaches yelled when Jeannette broke the surface. She then did her triple forward roll, landing vertical, like an arrow piercing the blue surface.

"Here comes, how you say? Drill?" Jeannette spun her body around and around in a clockwise motion like a power drill bit, eventually drilling straight into the water, while still spinning.

"Unbelievable! I've never seen that one before," Peaches exclaimed, when Jeannette broke the surface once more.

"When she had no arms, this roll was the easiest thing for her to do," Katja explained. "Do your butterfly, Jeannette," Katja called out.

This time, Jeannette used a bit of magic in the dive. First, she arched her back and began a wide radius back flip, with her arms straight out from her sides, mimicking a butterfly's wings. As her body finally finished the circle, she appeared to float horizontally about six feet above the surface of the water, flying along in a straight path for about ten feet. Then, she finally pulled her arms in and forward, her body following a perfect arc into the waters, with only the slightest break in the surface marking her passage into the waters.

When she broke the surface, Peaches stood up and clapped for her. Lindsey and Ashley quickly joined her in congratulating Jeannette on a fantastic dive.

A bit later, Peaches suggested, "We should start a diving team. If we can get enough good divers, maybe the school will send us to the Florida National Diving Contest in May."

"I agree, you ladies have incredible talent!" Betsy added to Peaches suggestion. "If you can get three more divers, train all year, I will see if I can get Governor Alister to send us to the Florida Nationals in May!"

"Way coolest!" exclaimed Peaches. "Best news I have heard in four years! We will find three more divers somewhere. With six hundred of us, there just has to be three more good divers here!"

The three girls chatted about diving all the way back to the dorms, where Lindsey and Ashley hastily changed into their track outfits and raced to the stadium for track tryouts. Amanda, Fern, Jim, Jake, and Emilio were already there ahead of them. They were talking with Hans and Klaas. Andy was the last to arrive, about five to ten o'clock. "Hi Lindsey, how many do you think will show up to try out, besides our Dutch friends?" he asked.

"Don't know. Honestly, with Nationals cancelled, I don't know. I had hoped that with us winning First Place last year, more of our classmates would try out. You know, now that I think about it, each year, we've only just had enough players to field the team, never had anyone on the bench to help out when needed." Lindsey realized how down to the wire they had always been.

The group waited until ten o'clock, before starting. Much to everyone's surprise, right at ten, two Yellow Hall students dressed in track outfits walked up. The older boy, Lindsey had seen around but didn't know anything about him. He was not in her classes. He spoke hesitantly, "Yellow Hall track tryouts?"

"Hey, welcome!" Jake took charge. "I'm Jake Rattlebeam, captain. Yes, you came to the right place."

"Dirk Dentwood, fifth year," the tall boy with brown hair cut like a soup bowl replied.

"I'm Lil Ames, fourth year," the light brown haired girl added, rather meekly. She had long hair tied back in a ponytail.

"Great! Glad to have you tryout! Do you know everyone here?" Jake asked. Naturally, they knew the names of the former Yellow Hall team members, but not the new Dutch boys, whom Jake promptly introduced.

"Well, we are desperate for another twenty-mile relay race runner to take Tom's place. He played left forward on our soccer team. Hans here only wants to play soccer, not run. Klaas only wants to run and not play soccer. How about you two? What are you good at, if you know?"

Dirk spoke first, "After seeing your incredible victory at the Nationals, I spent the summer practicing running five miles. I don't think I'm up to your standards. I've played a lot of soccer, though. Just don't put me in as goalkeeper, terrible at that."

"How about you, Lil?" Jake asked.

"I really don't think I'm much of a runner, but I will try. I've played a lot of soccer with my brothers. They would use me in whatever position they had open, goalkeeper to forward. I don't know if I'm good enough for you all though," Lil replied.

"Andy is our short distance runner, mostly because we don't have anyone else. He's a good goalkeeper though. Let's see Lil race Andy," Jake wisely suggested.

Amanda and Lindsey moved to the finish line of the 100-meter dash. Jake gave Andy and Lil the start signal and the two sprinted towards the two girls. No contest, Lil beat Andy by ten feet. "Hey, great, Lil can take my place in the sprint!" Andy suggested.

"Okay, let's see how the longer runners fare," Jake didn't want to commit just yet. "We have to find someone to take Tom's place in the twenty-mile relay, so everyone, except Lil and Andy who are going to man the stop watches, let's race five miles. If you need to fall out, just do so. I know Emilio, Fern, Ashley, and I will probably fall off after a mile, if we get that far," he teased, making it acceptable for Hans, Klaas, and Dirk to do so as well.

Off the group went; the Apaches set the pace at six-minute miles as usual. For a short time, everyone kept the pace, but by a half mile Emilio and Hans began falling behind, soon stopping altogether as this was further than they were used to racing in their mile relay. At the mile point, Fern pulled out, as well as Klaas and Jake. Jim, Amanda, Lindsey, Ashley, and Dirk continued.

After two and a half miles of this grueling pace, Dirk finally dropped out. Jake's heart sank, he had so hoped one of these would be able to fill Tom's shoes somehow. They just had to have someone who could run the five-mile leg.

This was the first time that Ashley had run since she had arms. Now she fully realized just how much having arms really helped her run. In fact, she wondered how she had ever managed to run fast before? She'd spent too much effort on just maintaining her balance. Now, it was second nature; the arms helped completely, and she ran far more effortlessly than she ever had before.

Though she had never run the five miles before with the Apaches, she found that she was able to keep pace with them for three miles before she slowly began dropping back, unused to such long runs. However, she doggedly kept at it, for she also realized that someone had to replace Tom, and she was the only one left who could. As they headed down the last half mile, Jim, Amanda, and Lindsey poured on all that they had, each one determined to beat the other. Neck and neck, the three sped towards the finish line, marked by Andy and Lil.

As they drew even closer, Amanda began to move out in front, while Lindsey fell behind Jim. Once again, Amanda beat her brother, and once again, Jim beat out Lindsey. However, all three, while jogging to cool down, cheered Ashley who crossed the line about a thousand feet behind Lindsey.

"Way to go Ashley!" Jake yelled. "You've been promoted to the twenty-mile relay!" Gasping for breath, she nodded. She'd accomplished what she set out to do and was pleased. "Klaas, you take her place in the mile relay. Andy, you are Lil's backup and Dirk, you are the back up for the four of us in the mile relay race. Now let's play some soccer."

"Give us a break!" Amanda called out.

Jake looked a bit sheepishly at her, "Oh yeh, forgot, you just ran five fast miles. Well, the rest of us can work on soccer until you four rest up a bit."

While the four cooled down and rested up, they watched the soccer simulations that Jake put the others through. Lil surprised them all, easily adapting to whichever position Jake had her play, except goalkeeper. Hans and Dirk also played well, but Dirk did better in any position other than forward, while Hans did better as a forward.

Jake finally announced, "You four are all on the soccer team! We'll try starting Hans at left forward, but Klaas, I promise not to use you unless we are in a dire emergency. Lil, Dirk, I promise to get you into the game often. For the first time in six years Yellow Hall actually has a reserve player, someone on the bench! Glory hallelujah! Miracle! Lil, you can play any position except goalkeeper, so you can replace anyone of us. Dirk, I promise not to put you in at forward. You do exceptionally well at middle field or full back." Both Lil and Dirk looked very pleased and happy to be on the Yellow Hall team. Lindsey suspected that neither of them had much hope that they would be good enough to make the team.

"Now about practices," Jake continued.

Emilio groaned. "I know, I know," Jake went on, "this homework is something else. Just wait until you get to sixth year. You ain't seen nothing yet in terms of homework, and this is only the first week! What would you say to holding only one practice session a week, say ten on Saturdays? At least until the season ends when the snows come. After all, we don't have to worry about Nationals this year." Everyone totally agreed with this; the fewer drains on their study time, the better.

Chapter 10—Dominus for President

Sunday morning, Lindsey began work on Monday's English paper. The first paper of the year was to be an "informational" paper. "Just put down the facts, no opinions," Pam reminded her. She thought that should be easy, but the facts of what? Well, that was the very question most were asking.

"Hey everyone, Dominus is on TV again," Fern called out from the commons. Everyone dashed into the adjoining room, glad for a distraction.

"Our country needs a strong leader, one who will make sure that everyone gets their fair share. After all, how much of your tax dollars that you give to the government each year do you really get back? Think about that one. The government collects billions from us each year, yet what has your government actually done for you this year, besides taken your money?"

"A vote for Dominus is a vote for change. We need to make government responsive to the needs of the people that it represents. Congressmen with their bloated salaries pass more and more laws, so much so that even lawyers can no longer sort them out. A vote for me is a vote for change. Here is your opportunity to send a message to the clowns in Washington, DC."

"To help you send just that message, I have, at my own expense, had these fine rings of pure gold made, which I'm giving away free to my loyal supporters. Yes, you heard right. No silly campaign buttons. The basic ring is worth at least three hundred dollars. If you support my platform for change in government, visit your local campaign headquarters and ask for a ring. Wear it with pride and show others in our country that you have had enough of the same old same old, that you demand a change in politics and in government. Send those on Capitol Hill a golden message. Get your Dominus for President ring today."

"As the election is now only a couple months away, I will be bringing more of my campaign speeches to you on

Sunday mornings. Ignore the polls and vote for change. Thank you for your attention."

The camera zoomed in on a display case, which held some two dozen golden rings. Half were much like a wide wedding band, but the others had a fine diamond as well. "I bet you have to be someone really important to get one with a diamond," Emilio commented, disgusted with the whole Dominus for President Campaign. He, like the rest of Lindsey's group, had not paid any attention to the news during the summer. Hearing Dominus still running for president was like a cold slap in their faces.

"Hey, we can make our informatory paper on Dominus for President," Pam suggested. Certainly, this topic had a large body of facts associated with it.

Once the Dominus feature finished, the Sunday talks shows began. All were carrying discussions with various Senators, Representatives, and political thinkers, who began offering their take on this latest development.

"Well, this incredible move by Dominus Malefic has taken the campaign to a new level! Instead of the same old same old, as he says, he is giving away valuable golden rings. Now this is, to this political analyst, a brilliant, bold move on his part. We have checked on these rings. Yes, there are two types, with and without the two-caret diamond. I'm told that the KMAG studio has gotten their hands on one of each ring and had them analyzed. The basic ring is, as he claims, made of pure gold, a quarter of an ounce. The gold alone is worth nearly the three hundred dollars, ignoring the manufacturing costs. The diamond is real and very clear, probably worth three thousand dollars on today's open market. Can you imagine giving out such value to your supporters? Brilliant move on his part."

"Yes," replied Senator Axel, "but isn't that akin to merely 'buying' his votes? I have never paid anyone to vote for me."

"Senator Axel," a rather antagonistic Representative Holkom countered, "you've missed the point entirely. Dominus never said that if you vote for me I'll give you this ring. No, he said that any of his supporters could walk into one of his headquarters and be given the ring free, no strings attached."

"Vote buying!" Senator Axel yelled back, interrupting Holkom.

The pundits yelled back and forth for some time, before Senator Axel took a different approach. "Look, we all know that a convicted felon, and let's not forget that, Dominus *is* a convicted felon, is barred from ever holding public office. The moment he steps forward to claim the office, should he miraculously win, he will arrested and put back in prison. I also understand that the Department of Law wishes to prosecute him for additional crimes, including murder, the second they recapture him. So isn't this all just making a mockery of our time honored political elections?"

A half hour later, Lindsey was armed with what she felt was more than enough facts for her English informational paper. Her friends also felt the same way. For a moment, Lindsey felt a bit sorry for Professor Elaine, who would have to read all these papers on Dominus for President.

"Well, it looks like we have found out why Dominus needed to rob Fort Knox of the gold bars, and I bet those diamonds are the very ones he stole from Mr. van der Veer and Mr. van Ravinstijn," Pam declared.

"But how can that be proved?" asked Deiter, rather interested in this line of thought. "I mean, once the gold bars have been melted down, there's no way to trace them back to their source is there?" Pam had to agree with him.

Jeannette said softly, "Diamonds are marked."

"What?" asked Pam, now very interested in what Jeannette had to say.

"All cut diamonds have a microscopic serial number etched into their undersides," Jeannette replied. "Simply take the diamond out of its mounting and look for it. I hope someone does. If those are our grandparents' diamonds, he should be arrested and charged with grandpa's murder."

"Ja, he should!" Katja exclaimed.

Just then, Pam's computer dinged, announcing she had an incoming email of some importance. She had programmed her machine to make the faint noise when her father, among others, sent her an email. Hastily, she brought Agent to the foreground.

"Hey, dad is on it, Jeannette! He says that it has become top priority for the Departments of Law and Magical Misuse to get their hands on some of these rings. He wants them tested and knows about the diamond serial numbers. He has the list of those reported stolen from your grandparents. If the numbers match any on that list, we will know for sure where the diamonds came from!"

"Good!" Katja exclaimed vehemently. "Catch that bad man!"

"Yes, but so what if they find out those are the stolen gems," Ashley asked, "they still have to capture him. He could just claim that he bought them from a reputable dealer. It's not beyond him just to forge some documents claiming he bought them. So what? It's just one more crime pinned on him. He is still evading capture."

"Waarom doet hij dit?" Jeannette asked, lost in deep thought.

"She gets like this sometimes," whispered Katja. "She's thinking about something. She said, 'Why does he do this?' I think she means this Dominus."

Everyone stared as Jeannette, who seemed to be in a dreamlike trance. Certainly, she was oblivious to those around her. At last, her eyes blinked, and she looked at everyone looking at her. She blushed. "Ve need more data. Ve are missing someding very important." Rushing her words, her English slipped slightly.

She slowed down, "Dominus running for president—this is an unsolvable problem as it stands. Why, he should do this? Is as the man on TV says, if he is elected and shows up there, he's only going to be arrested. So I asks myself why he does this thing? Most interesting problem. Ve do not have enough facts yet. He cannot be wanting to be de President; I've ruled that out. If he is not running to win, like the other candidates, then why is he doing this? Why give out so many expensive presents? This man is not foolish or generous; he is a murderer, a thief; he takes what he wants; he cares nothing for others. He is a Black Hall graduate, personifying their traits to the extreme." Deiter and Peaches squirmed a bit, until she uttered the last qualifier. Yes, in their minds he had gone to the extreme of their Black Hall philosophy.

"Wat krijgen de verliezers? Oops," she blushed. "What do losers get? From the president race?"

"Nothing," Pam replied, "well, maybe a footnote in history books as the person who ran against whoever gets elected. Why?"

"Dis is very important, Pam, very." Jeannette gave her a serious look. "Wen the election is over, Dominus gets something dat is very, very, very important to hem. Probably bad for us."

Pam's sleuthing mind kicked into high gear. "Jeannette! You're right. We've all been thinking this is just some big joke of his. You are right, Dominus never does joke about anything. He is only running for president because he expects to gain something so critically important, so vital, so, well, everything to him. It can't be the actual Presidency. Look at the polls." She held up part of her current English paper, well, her computer screen, really.

President Lucius Dollington: 24%

Senator Missy Snow of Massachusetts: 60%

Dominus Malefic: 16%

"Missy Snow has a commanding lead over President Dollington, who has suffered enormous loss of public support since the hurricane disaster. He's on track to wind up with the worst public support of any president than that of President George Bush, back in 2007. Dominus is so far behind Missy Snow that it is hardly a race at all, though I can't say I like the philosophies of her any better than those of President Dollington. She's going around promising to dole out more free money, which only means everyone else's taxes will inevitably go even higher."

"He's not running to win, so why is he running in the first place? Giving out these expensive presents has to be a clue! After all, no one else has ever given out thousands of expensive rings to their supporters. Rather, they beg their supporters for campaign contributions and promise insider information or support for their underhanded key supporters."

Pam had a negative view of politics.

"Jeannette's right, we must ask ourselves what does Dominus get as a result of running for president? It must be something of monumental importance to him. After all, look at all the trouble, expense, and personal danger he is exposing himself to just by running! After escaping from prison, he could have just headed for Tahiti and hid out, living a life of luxury off his stolen money. Instead, every time he makes another public broadcast, he is running a serious risk of being caught again. What he expects to gain must be huge in his mind."

"Ja, you now see it as I see it," Jeannette replied, feeling pleased that, for once, someone else saw the point that she had discovered by her reasoning.

"Come on, gang; let's put on our thinking caps," Pam nudged them. "Let's make a list of everything that someone running for the president gets as a result of just running."

Deiter jumped in, "Fame, many more people know your name, kind of like a household word."

"Right, I'll write that one down." Pam began typing up their list.

"You get a lot of people who have put their money on you, kind of like betting on a horse," Emilio added.

"You get your picture all over the news media during the months of the race," Peaches pointed out.

"You get your whole life scrutinized with a microscope, by everyone looking for your fatal flaws," Kathy added.

"This is a good thing?" Lindsey asked; it seemed incongruous.

"I'll write it down, though I doubt that is what Dominus is after. Keep the ideas coming," Pam replied.

"You get to go on TV outlining your views about current issues facing the people," Andy added to the list.

"You get a whole lot of press coverage," Kathy suggested.

Soon, they ran out of ideas of benefits. Pam began to go down the list, one by one. "Fame, many people know your name. Dominus already is the most famous criminal in recent history. His name is already widely known, even among the norms. Scratch that one. He's giving away money; others are not giving it to him. Remember, he said he would reject any monetary political campaign contribution. Scratch that one. Picture in the news. He's always had his picture in the news, as a criminal mostly. Scratch that one. Outlining your views to the public, well that has some workability. After all, he did publish his Manifesto. This seems in line with that, but hardly worth the trouble of running for president. I mean he could vastly cheaper and much more safely put up a web site or run a blog. Still, I admit, his running for president is getting his views on things more widely known. I'll keep this one in there."

A bit later, that was the only item left that was not scratched out. "Now you see," Jeannette replied, looking at the frustrated face of Pam. "We don't have any idea of what his real purpose is. Dat's vat I been saying all along. Ve don't know, and it is important, very, very important, I feel."

The rest began to return to their homework, while Pam brought up her copy of his manifesto. She reread it in its entirety once more.

The Wizard Manifesto of Dominus Malefic

Whereas wizards and witches down through the long ages of history have been cursed, reviled, even burned at the stake, I, Dominus Malefic, am ushering in a New Golden Age for we users and controllers of magic on Earth—my Golden Path.

On Earth, man is at the top of the food chain. Consider the lowly sheep that lives its life to eat grass. Along comes mother wolf searching for dinner for her cubs, thus the sheep has purpose. In parallel, long has man, by virtue of his superior mind, been at the very top, dominating, controlling, ruling all other life forms on Earth. This is how it should be.

Yet, there are two forms of man! All throughout recorded history, man has known that there are two forms: the normal man and the wizard man. Yet during this enormous time period, man still believes in the Big Lie, that all men are created with equal rights. Why has man fallen victim to the Big Lie?

We have all told small lies at one time or other in our lives. Yet, we balk at telling a really big lie because we cannot believe that anyone would have the impudence to fabricate such a huge lie. Therefore, we don't, and yet those of feebler minds then believe the Big Lie.

Just like there is an enormous gulf between the sheep and the wolf, a similar intellectual, spiritual, and physical gulf exists between the norms and us wizards. If you do not see the truth, I invite you to lay aside your wand and take a normal job as a garbage man for one day. This gap between the two, in my opinion, is sufficient to divide man into two separate species!

Call them sub-man and man, or man and superman; it matters not, save that this enormous gulf in abilities is in fact very real and cannot be hidden. This is not to say that sub-man has not evolved. He certainly has. For example, it has only taken him ten thousand years of recorded history to realize finally that some prefer gay or lesbian relationships and to allow them to choose the partners of their choice without prejudice!

We are the superman species. Yet for ten thousand years, we have had to hide our abilities from sub-man. Do you really wish to wait another ten thousand years for sub-man to finally realize and allow us supermen our rightful position on Earth?

I say no! It is time for Truth to prevail. Time to cast aside the Big Lie.

It is time for us supermen to step out of the closet in which we have been hiding for ten thousand years. Step out into the sunshine, the warm light of day. Cast off our darkness and embrace who and what we are, the true supermen of Earth!

No longer will we be content to be second-class citizens. No longer will we be satisfied to live by the rules of the majority because the majority is but sub-man on this planet. Lacking the tiniest fragment of magical abilities, these norms will finally be forced to see the Truth and recognize the true rulers of Earth.

Consider the historical and long-standing relationship between man and horse. The horse depends upon man for its food, shelter, and veterinarian care when needed. In turn, the horse transports man, plows his fields, and otherwise works for man, obeys man.

What of the true relationship between norm and wizard, between sub-man and superman? Obviously, sub-man, lacking the superior skills, abilities, and magical knowledge of superman, should be his servant in all ways, as the horse is to man. That is the Truth of the matter, not the Big Lie. All men are not created equal. All supermen are born with equal rights, just as all sub-men are born with equal rights. The two species of man are not equal in any sense of the word, just as a horse and man are not equals. Just as saying all horses and all men are born with the same equal rights is the height of folly, so saying the blanket Big Lie is folly.

Sub-man is but a horse to us supermen. Now is the time in history when supermen take over the rulership of Earth. I do hereby cast off the Big Lie forever and don the mantle of rightful ruler of Earth. I invite those of you who have been living in the closet to step out into the warm light of day and assume your rightful place.

Worry not about harming sub-man, for would you not slap a horse that was disobeying your orders? Slap them as needed to achieve your superior needs.

At this time, I call upon all of you who can see the Truth to step out of your closet and lend me a hand in setting things on the correct path, this righteous path of Truth.

To quote another who said it best, "Those who do not realize the truth or do not wish to believe it will never be able to lend a hand in helping Truth to prevail."

Your help is needed.

Respectively yours,

Dominus Malefic, Wizard Supreme

Pam finished reading it and sat back, deep in thought. There was something in this manifesto, something that directly tied to what she had seen today. She was sure of it, but she could not place it. It was right there before her eyes, but she was not seeing it—well that's how she felt about it. Pam knew she couldn't rest until she identified it. The more she tried to find the connection with today's news, the more it seemed to elude her.

Around nine, Monique, desperate for a study break herself, came over to chat with Pam. Seeing her in this peckish mood, Monique pulled Pam outside in the cool September evening for a stroll in the gardens. Arm in arm, they walked slowly, inhaling the fragrances of the many varieties of flowers that still bloomed this late in the year. At last Pam spoke, "Dominus is giving out golden rings and some with two-caret diamonds on them, probably made from the gold he stole and the diamonds he likely stole when he killed the Dutch jewelers."

"Yes, we saw that too. Crazy, no one gives away three hundred dollar rings or three thousand dollar rings. What's he up to anyway?" Monique asked.

"Dunno yet. Jeannette thinks that Dominus is after something vitally important to himself by running for president. None of us can fathom anything that he could possibly gain by doing so. It defies all logic. Golden path, now golden rings. What's next, golden doves?"

Suddenly, a light flashed in Pam's mind. "Golden path—gold rings! That's it Monique! Those two must be somehow linked together. Somehow all these golden rings are somehow part of his golden path!"

"Cool, they must be magical somehow," Monique replied, trying to keep up with her girlfriend's lightning mind.

"I will email dad. He said it's their top priority to get their hands on some sample rings. I suppose he's already planning to check them for magical enchantments, but I will suggest it to him, just in case he hasn't thought of it. Thanks, Monique, you are super as always." The two hugged each other tightly, which soon turned into a romantic encounter. Pam wandered back into the study hall sometime later, a bit of red lipstick still on her lips. She sent another email to her father. She would have to wait for the results, and she hated waiting.

Chapter 11—Hard Work

Tuesday became Solo Day, as the students of the Teleport spell began to call it. On Monday, they began arriving precisely on top of the three-foot in diameter column, and Professor Arthur congratulated them. "Tomorrow you solo."

Lindsey realized that it was one thing to cast this spell, knowing that Professor Arthur was right there with you monitoring it, and quite another to do it solo. If something went wrong, he would step in, as they had seen happen with Lyle. Lindsey stepped up to the starting line and stared out onto the green lawn at the large white 'X' marking the destination point. "Anytime you are ready, Miss Barron," Professor Arthur said encouragingly.

Lindsey cleared her mind of stray thoughts, focused on the spot, waved her wand, and spoke the command words. The next moment, she saw the ground moving up towards her, and she landed on the 'X' but fell over. She was so surprised that she had done it that she lost her balance on the landing. Nevertheless, the fall did nothing to erase her excitement. "I did it!" she yelled to the others, who gave her a cheer. The whole class was watching her, so she really didn't need to tell them that she had soloed.

One by one, the others in her class took their turn, teleporting to the white 'X' spot. By the time that the class was over, everyone was racing to the starting line, casting their spell, and running back up the hill to the starting line to get another chance at it. Each person was taking only thirty seconds now to cast the spell. Just before the class ended for supper, Professor Arthur announced, "Tomorrow we will practice teleporting to your homes."

"Way cool!" Lindsey exclaimed.

"We should practice that," Pam commented, "after all, that will be our most frequent destination."

The next day, inside the Compton ranch, the monotone voice announced, "Lindsey Barron is arriving with a guest." This took everyone by surprise. Lena, holding Jonathon, rushed outside to see.

"Hi mom. This is my teacher, Professor Arthur. I've just learned how to Teleport and I brought him here, part of our class exercise. Stay there, mom, Ashley, Pam, and Audrey will be along when it's their turn in a couple minutes." She couldn't resist the temptation to give her mom a hug and plant a kiss on her little brother's forehead. Lena watched as Lindsey waved her wand and said, "Teleport:" The rest of her words were not heard, however. Lindsey landed in the parking lot of Bradbury's.

The rest of the week in spell casting, the students walked off the grounds to the mountainside. Here they worked on two spells: Convert Stone to Mud and back again. Obviously, this isolated spot of granite had been the recipient of each fourth year's spells for many, many years. This time, two were allowed to attempt to cast the spell simultaneously, for there was little trouble one could get into with this spell.

The third week was spent on another difficult spell, Mold Stone, the ability to take stone and mold it into some desired shape. Lindsey now realized that it was this spell that had been used to make the stone wall around the entire campus. The spell required a great deal of concentration and focusing upon the desired shape and dimensions. More than once, the outcome was far less than what the caster had desired.

"As you know, next week our foreign exchange students are off on a week-long sightseeing trip. Their mentors will be traveling with them, as well as selected faculty. Hence, all next week in spell casting you will be reviewing these first spells. The following Monday I will begin giving you your passes on these spells. You see, these Grade 5 spells are so complex that we dare not make you cast them in rapid fire as you did with your Grade 1 spells," Professor Arthur announced. Pam found this very encouraging, especially if this pattern held true for all the other spells. She would be facing one less comprehensive final exam, come next May.

On Saturday morning, while the fifth year students prepared for their mock combats, Lindsey packed for her first field trip with her Dutch friends. She had gone over the itinerary with Ashley, Jeannette, and Katja. This was going to be a National Parks sightseeing trip, and they were to take warm clothing. Shortly after ten, the twenty foreign exchange students and their mentors climbed on board the bus. Jimmy was their driver, once more. Professors Delius and Cho Lin were leading this trip, and four Security men rode along with them in case of trouble.

"May I have your attention," Professor Delius spoke, as the bus began to roll out of the parking lot. The excited teens hushed. "We are going to visit the more famous National Parks here out west this trip. As you know, precisely which parks and when and where has been withheld from you. This is for your safety. As you are probably aware, Dominus and his gang are after Miss Barron and Miss Stokes-Compton, having made attempts on their lives before. We thought it prudent then not to make our destinations and travel arrangements known beforehand."

"In fact, my clever scheme will certainly not give them a clue, because even I don't know where we are going first. You will notice that Cho Lin has given you each a paper with the parks and places to visit. I want each of you to take out a pen and rank them in the order that you would like to visit them. Mind you, there is no correct answer. Hand them to her when you are done and be quick about it. I will tally the votes, and we will go to the site with the most votes first. This way, no one will know where we are headed. We will vote each time we finish at a stop."

"Hey, Professor, that is really ingenious!" Deiter called out. He smiled and nodded to his Black Hall student.

"Way cool! We get to pick," Ashley whispered. A few minutes later as the bus reached the major state road, the ballots were given to Professor Delius. Lindsey noted that he used the Grade Test spell to count the votes quickly.

"Jimmy, we head for the Grand Canyon first." Students cheered as a Security man entered the coordinates into the GPS driving console, and Jimmy punched the bus into high gear. Later, Professor Delius explained that since they were "bouncing" all over the west, he had the bus driver use ninth gear for good speed, reducing the traveling time.

Deiter had been to several of the parks; Peaches, a slightly different set. For Lindsey and Ashley, all the parks were new, as they were for their Dutch friends. Lindsey and Ashley finally relaxed and began to enjoy themselves, confident that by using the random system, Dominus would never be lying in wait for them around the next bend. Lindsey had been very worried about this, but had not said anything to the others, primarily because Ashley had not had any dire premonitions about the trip.

They visited the Grand Canyon, Yellowstone, and Glacier National Park. At this last one, they hiked up the trail to Big Bear Lake, where the mountains came down to touch the lake. Lindsey took a fabulous photograph of the mountains reflecting off the nearly still waters. From there, they visited Yosemite and the redwoods. They drove through the Canyon Lands and did a day hike there.

On the last leg, they drove along Pacific Coast Highway for a time and then visited San Francisco's Fisherman's Wharf. Each evening, they stayed in a block of motel rooms, carefully protected with numerous spells. Lindsey saw that at these times, their Security men were on their highest alert and seemed slightly stressed.

The last night, Saturday night, they finally were allowed to go to one of the hot nightclubs for teens in San Francisco, the Delcotto Club. "Oh, it's just like all the pictures on the TV!" exclaimed Jeannette. The upscale club featured dancing, the latest hot bands, and plenty of fun for all, well except for the professors and the Security men, who had a nightmare keeping track of the many students.

When the bus rolled into the Bradbury parking lot midmorning on Sunday, all the students were still bleary-eyed, rock music running through their heads. All had the best time of their life at the nightclub. "How did it go? Tell us all about it!" pleaded Kathy, as the tired girls floated into their room.

"We got to see the Sick Dogs playing live at the Delcotto Club in San Francisco!" Ashley blurted out. Kathy shrieked. Pam opened her eyes wide, and Kathy forced the four to tell her everything about it.

Later, while the four began furiously to catch up on

their homework, Pam realized what was going on with their schoolwork. Whenever the exchange students were off on a trip, no new homework was assigned. The professors conducted review sessions or allowed them to work on their own. Hence, Pam quickly discovered that she had gotten totally caught up and had some spare time. This she used to good advantage, continuing her research in the library. Finally, she had something to report for Deiter.

"Deiter, how much do you know about the Beyond?" Pam asked him. It was Sunday night, around nine; he had followed her outside for a stroll the instant she suggested that she had something for him.

"That's what they call it, the whatever. It is what we pass through while teleporting," he replied. "They say that you go insane if you look at the Beyond as you Teleport. Some report that there are wild beasts there that will tear your body to bits. Some say the creatures look hideous, far worse than the Grade D horror flick."

"Well, that about sums it up," Pam stated. "No one has gone to the Beyond and returned alive and sane. Supposedly, it doesn't exist; at least one camp proposes that. The other camp says that it is full of terrible monsters that eat your mind or brain. I can't tell which for sure."

Deiter's face fell. He was so sure that he had seen something, something really important. "Is that all, silly scary stories?" his voice dropped into a bit of antagonism, though not directed at Pam.

"Until two days ago. Monique has been helping me, and we had just about given up completely. This whole Beyond thing is a subject filled with mere wild speculation, nothing based on any solid evidence, just designed to scare us all, we thought. Then, while you were gone, I came across an obscure paper in Nature magazine."

Deiter suddenly perked up, "Cool! What did it have to say?" Pam smiled. She loved watching him doing a roller coaster of emotions. Served him right for all he had done to Lindsey during their first year here.

"The article is now thirty-five years old, written by one Wizard Greeley Longsteen. What I find fascinating is that in the very next issue of the magazine, they totally retracted the article, claiming it was written by a quack. A large number of letters to the editor demonstrated that Greeley was a bumbling idiot, always messed up his spells, was a moron, and had such bad eyes that he couldn't see a thing without very, very thick glasses. Pretty scathing attack on the man."

"Nevertheless, Deiter, the paper was very well written, scholarly in fact, but altogether far too short. He reportedly discovered that when we Teleport, we are moving out of this universe, passing through a bit of space of another universe, which has been called the Beyond by the noted Wizard scholars since spells were first recorded, and then re-appearing back in our universe. He claims that this Beyond has inhabitants in it, which he calls goggles. As far as I can tell from his description, they sound sort of like pet dogs, only they look ghastly. He included a sketch of one. I printed out a copy of it for you. Here," she handed it to him. "Light." She illuminated the page.

Deiter's face turned white. Pam was watching his reactions intently. She'd spent hours working out this encounter and how she wanted it to transpire. "That's—that's what I saw," he nearly choked. "They are real then! I wasn't imaging them! I wasn't going mad or insane! I knew it! We are on to something, Pam! God, thank you! Thank you!" In his excitement, he gave her a big hug, which was not what she was expecting at all, and her face grew red. However, she canceled her Light spell so he couldn't see her face.

"We need to contact this Greeley fellow, find out all that he knows!" Deiter raced on enthusiastically. "How do we get a hold of him?"

"That's the really, really strange part of it Deiter. I searched everywhere; he does not have an email address."

"What? Everyone *has* an email address these days! Who could *not* possibly not have one?" Deiter exclaimed, slightly befuddled over this setback. "There is always MagGoogle or Hotmail free email addresses."

"He doesn't have a telephone either, Deiter," Pam only added to the mystery she had found surrounding this man.

"What? Everyone has a phone, I mean adults, that is.

You sure you looked him up right?"

"Monique double-checked me. We searched the International Phone Number Database as well, the IPND. As you know, that database has all phone numbers in it, including the secret and unlisted ones, though it merely says 'unlisted' or 'private' after the names. No, there is no one listed anywhere in the entire world by that name."

"Creepy. Maybe he is dead," Deiter's heart sank. He was so hoping to talk with this Greeley fellow, find out more real facts.

"I thought so too. I looked up his birth certificate. He was born in Yorkshire, England, went to Oxford School of Magic, attended Oxford University, and graduated with a degree in physics. According to the school records, he moved to New York after graduation, taking a research position at a secret laboratory outside the city. The place is blacked out on the forms. After this paper was published, he left the Big Apple and moved to Chicago. He was there only a few months before he was either run out of town by all the heckling he received from his paper or he left because of it."

"Guess where he went then?"

"I have no idea, someplace out of the way, where he could pass for normal?" Deiter suggested. Pam realized that Deiter was no dummy himself.

"Right, he moved to Leadville, Colorado, where he bought a home there. I'll email you his mailing address. However, there is more. There have been a couple local articles in the Leadville Courier about him over the years. Seems he is something of a recluse, which only makes sense, since he was ostracized so badly over his article. No one has really seen him for years, but he pays the neighbor boys to tend his lawn. Some say his house is haunted. Several spooky things have been reported by those brave enough to go inside. Yet, his property tax is paid, so he must still be alive."

"So now what?" Pam finished her report.

"I suppose that we should try to write him a normal letter," Deiter thought, rubbing his hands through his hair. "I can't thank you enough for doing this for me, Pam. I owe you a big one. I'd never have found all this out. I'll write him a letter tonight. I promise to let you know what he says back. We may be on to something very significant here." Deiter surprised Pam by shaking her hand in thanks. They went back to their studies. Pam crossed off one Sleuthing project from her list.

"Ja, dit is hard!" Lindsey bungled in Dutch. They were supposed to be practicing their foreign language.

Katja giggled, "No, it is English dat is hard, Lindsey! Let's try it again. Hoe u bent?"

Lindsey spoke very slowly, "Ik ben fijn, goed doend." Work, work, work. Lindsey really had more trouble trying to learn Dutch than she had with any other subject in all these years. Why was language so difficult, so strange? She longed, as did all the students, just to cast their Understand Language spell.

They all had a persuasion paper due on Friday, and Lindsey still had not picked a topic. Twenty trig problems lay beckoning for her attention, to say nothing of the two physics lab experiments that she needed to get formally written up.

All the students were struggling with the course load. The only bright spot was Andy, who had a keen knack for all the World Culture assignments. He claimed they were just an exercise in applied anthropology, and he helped everyone get those done rapidly, so they could concentrate on these more difficult assignments.

Then, there was Potion Making I. At first, Lindsey thought this would be an easy class. It was for the first few weeks. Just follow the recipes slavishly and a workable potion resulted. Now, however, Professor Delius wanted them to begin to memorize the potion aspects of plants and animal parts. Lindsey didn't mind adding a pinch of this and that to the brews she made. The pinch didn't really look like a bat's wing or a fungus or the tail of a newt. Reading over the lists, she pictured the plants and especially the animals, and her mind refused to memorize.

Their new spells were incredibly challenging. She was used to learning how to cast them in a day or two at the most. This whole week, they continually studied how to cast the Manufacture Object spell. Their passing standard was to turn the copse of dead tree branches on the southwestern corner of the campus into a bridge! Of course, once they had this spell down pat, they could manufacture nearly any non-living object from something that was similar in nature. Tough spell.

Already, they had spent a week just learning how to Enlarge and Shrink Animals. After three challenging days, Lindsey managed to turn the miniature poodle into a great mastiff, though it still looked like a poodle. She saw some applications of this though. While the spell lasted only a short time, she could shrink an attacking wolf or mountain lion into a tiny, miniature sized version, greatly lessening their threats. Deiter saw it the other way around, summoning a wolf to his defense and then making it the size of a grizzly bear to defend him better.

The spells got a little easier to grasp the following week. Pam thought the Magnetism spell would be very useful. Cast upon an object, in either attraction or opposition mode, anyone other than the caster would be automatically drawn to the object or repulsed from it. Deiter saw other uses for it. "Watch this, gang! Magnetize Rock to Andy." A heavy rock began slowly sliding across the grounds towards Andy. He backed up but it continued to slide relentlessly towards him until it made contact with his body, whereon it stuck to him leg.

"Get it off of me!" Andy shouted, and he struggled to get free from the rock. Everyone roared with laughter.

Deiter cancelled his spell. "See, we can magnetize rocks and slow down the Death Stalkers with this one."

Pam stuck up her nose at Deiter and cast her version of the spell. "Deiter, bet you a dollar you cannot get my wand from me." She held it up, as if she would let him grab it. Deiter moved towards it only to find his feet slipping away from it. Again, everyone roared at his futile attempts to take it from her hand.

The next class period, Professor Arthur was in a good humor. "Today, we are going to learn one of the historically important spells, which these days has little use. Back in the Middle Ages, in the era of knights in armor and stone castles, besieging an enemy castle was a costly affair. For months, the attackers would have to garrison the site, keeping those inside from breaking out. When the time was right, they would storm the castle, usually with a large loss of life. Now there were a few castles that were taken without the usual smashing of the walls, tunneling beneath them, that sort of thing. A few wizards made a deal with the Templars, by use of this spell, the Templars could pass through the stone walls of a castle. We are learning Walk Through Walls today."

"We have temporarily lowered the protections on this section of our walls for you to practice the spell. You can pass through stone or wooden walls, not steel, sorry. In today's world, this spell has relatively little use. However, you are still learning because of its historical importance."

A day later, Pam commented, "This is spooky!" She had successfully cast the spell and was walking through the outer wall surrounding the campus. By the end of the hour, all had successfully cast it as well. Spooky was the mildest expression. However, on the bright side, they had finally completed all their Grade 5 alteration based spells, just in time for Halloween. Next week, Professor Huan Su would be teaching them more attacking spells based upon evocation magic.

Chapter 12—Battles, Sports, and Dominus

The first weekend in October promised to be a busy one for Lindsey. On Saturday, they had their first soccer game, and on Sunday morning, they had their first mock combat session. At least their first track meet would not be until the following weekend.

Lil Ames, one of their new team members, her long hair tied back in a ponytail, bend down to tie her shoelaces for the fifth time. Lindsey guessed that she was a bit nervous. "All set, Lil?" she asked.

Meekly, Lil replied, "Well, not really. I'm so nervous! My first game. I never thought—well you know, that you'd let me be on the team. You are all so good, really. Say can I ask you something?"

"Sure, Lil, what?" Lindsey supposed that it would be something about their soccer match against Blue Hall, which was about to start.

"It's about the mock combats. I mean, well, I went and signed up for it. I, well, we all saw what happened to Monique Blackburn, Red Hall. I, I couldn't stand that happening to me, I just couldn't! I'm not a fighter, and I got to thinking that maybe I shouldn't have signed up for it."

"Don't worry, Lil. It's just a good practice session to help us all become able to put our spells to good use when we need them. You'll do fine, I'm sure," Lindsey tried to encourage her. "It's one thing to take your time and cast a spell in class and quite another to do it when someone is after you. I mean, I learned a lot when we had that first one last year. However, I wouldn't worry too much about being attacked like Monique, Lil. Monique knew where Pam was staying, and the Death Stalker tried to beat it out of her. So you see, you are not likely in any real danger."

Instead of seeing relief on the young girl's face, tears began forming, though Lindsey saw that Lil was trying hard to hold them back. Just then, the booming, amplified voice of Professor Blake began announcing the start of the game. Lindsey made a snap decision, "Jake, start Dirk in my place. I need to talk with Lil right now, please?"

Jake gave her a wondering look, but called out to Dirk, "Dirk, you are up. You are playing forward, roam the whole area, get open, and we'll pass to you."

Dirk, figuring he would be relegated to the bench for most of the game, looked startled, but he jumped up and raced to join the group as they headed onto the field. Amanda and Ashley shot a worried glance back at Lindsey, who gave them a thumbs up sign, not to worry.

"Okay, Lil, it's just you and me here on the bench. Can you tell me about it?" Lindsey suggested, wondering if she was asking the right thing. She barely knew Lil.

"I'm scared, Lindsey. I may be next." Lil tried to reply, before she lost control and began crying. Lindsey allowed her time to regain her composure, just putting a reassuring arm over Lil's shoulders.

"They are going to get me next," she finally added a bit later. Confused, Lindsey asked her to tell her all about it. Who was going to get her next?

Lil sighed and finally began trying to make sense for Lindsey. "I've got an older sister, Peg, Peg Ames, well maybe I had an older sister." She began really crying now. Again, Lindsey allowed her time to grieve. Finally, Lil recovered enough to go on, just saying this much had released a lot of her grief and worry. "Peg is or was nineteen. She's a norm—I mean, not a witch like me. Peg is beautiful, long, curly black hair, light blue eyes, and her smile—when Peg smiles, the whole room lights up. I guess that's why she was doing so well for the bar. She was working at the Holiday Inn Bar as their bar tender. She loved the job and was making loads of money, honestly she was."

"What town?"

"Oh, in Denver. We live in the suburbs. She still lives or did live at home with us. She was even helping me with my school tuition. Peg is so pretty! Boys were always fawning over her, so I think that helped her sell more drinks where she worked. Anyway, on July 25, she didn't come home after work. She has her own car even—one of those Toyota Eco cars, environmentally friendly cars. She was always worried about what we were doing to our world. Anyway, they found her car still where she always parked it, there at the inn. She went off duty at midnight, and a guard walked her to her car. The police have that on surveillance cameras. The guard went back inside."

"She never came home, and her car is still there. The police think that she was abducted! Even the FBI investigated it as a kidnaping case. We all kept hoping that she would come home any hour, but after days and then weeks, we began to lose hope. We never got any ransom note either, just nothing. Then just before I had to return here to school, we got the most horrible news. I vomited when I saw them. The crime lab identified her arms—what was left of them. Someone found them in a dumpster and reported it to the police. DNA proved those were Peg's arms, what was left of them. Something just awful happened to her! She must have been beaten so badly, and now the police think that her body was likely then dismembered!"

"Mom and dad—we just don't know whether to hold a funeral for Peg, burying what little we have left of her or not. Dad thinks that we should wait a little longer in case the rest of her appears somewhere. So we are, waiting, that is. Mom's been sick at her stomach every day since Peg's remains were found. Dad can hardly work any longer. Everyone says that I look really pretty, just like Peg, so I'm terrified that I will be next. So when I saw the announcement about the mock battles, I signed up, but now I'm not so sure that I can do it, fight I mean."

"Who would do that?" she asked. "Here. I always keep Peg's picture with me, just in case I need it to identify the rest of her body." She showed Lindsey a small wallet sized photo of Peg.

"Gosh, she is really pretty," Lindsey stated the obvious. "Who would want to hurt her? Did she have any enemies?"

"Oh no, everyone likes her. I mean liked her," correcting herself brought on more tears.

"Well, I think Pam Betts ought to look into this a bit; maybe she can find out something more. She's studying to be a Sleuth, you know. I'll talk to her about it after the game. I wouldn't give up hope just yet."

"Thanks," she sniffled, wiping her eyes on her shirt. "The ME said that cutting off someone's arms a few inches above the elbow would result in massive bleeding, so probably she bled to death. That's why everyone thinks that she is very likely dead, only we haven't found her body yet. Thanks for listening to me, Lindsey. I do feel better now. I've really not had the guts to tell anyone else about it."

"Well, that's what friends are for, Lil. Come on; we'd better put our attention onto the game. I wanted you to get some playing time on the field too."

"But what about you? Dirk's taking your spot," she asked timidly.

At half time, Jake replaced Hans and Dirk with Lil and Lindsey. Hans and Dirk had one goal each, but Hans was tiring. Amanda had their third goal, and the game was tied. Lindsey found that playing soccer was just what the doctor ordered for Lil. By the end of the game, Lil was physically pooped, but her spirits soared, since she had scored a goal as well. Lindsey had two. Yellow Hall beat Blue Hall seven to five with Amanda scoring another during the second half.

After the game and they had all showered, Lindsey had Lil come to their room to talk with Pam, who was eager for another Sleuthing job. Pam jotted down all the scanty information that Lil actually had and promised her that she would look into it right away.

Sometime later, a dejected looking Ashley joined them. "Arms, sometimes I wish I didn't have them," she declared.

"What?" exclaimed Jeannette and Lindsey in unison.

"Oh pool. We all played pool again with Professor Jasper. I can take everyone except the professor when I use my feet. Now that I have arms, they won't let me use my feet," she declared insolently, as if this was something horrible. "I'm just not very good at all with my arms, even Deiter beat me today."

"You just need more practice," Pam declared flatly, "that's all. You cannot expect to suddenly have arms and then have magically the same skill with them that you spent years and years perfecting with your feet, now can you?"

"Well, no," Ashley admitted, though she wished she didn't have to.

"There you have it, more practice," Pam stated as if this was totally obvious, and she returned to her new sleuthing assignment.

Sunday morning, twenty-four students showed up for their first fourth year mock combat exercises. Professor Delius was rather surprised at the large turnout. "Good, good, so glad to see so many of you are interested," he began enthused with the turnout. "We will run two sessions today. First, I want Lindsey to have to deal with protecting a large group from attackers. She has not had that experience. So, Deiter, Ashley, Pam, Kathy, Emilio, Katja, Jeanette, Hans, Klaas, Peaches, and Amanda, you are with Lindsey. The rest of you are under the control of Audrey. Audrey, your team's task is to see how many of Lindsey's team you can either subdue, eliminate, or take out of the battle. Lindsey, your task is to keep as many of your team members intact, and capture, subdue, or eliminate as many of Audrey's team as you can. Here's how the scoring will go. For each one of Lindsey's team that Audrey's team somehow eliminates, you get one point. Ten points if you get Lindsey herself. Lindsey, for each one of Audrey's team members you capture, you get two points, but if they are killed, you only get one point. The objective is to capture them so that they can stand trial, if possible, you see."

"Whoa, ten points for Lindsey! Gun for Lindsey, everyone," Audrey exclaimed and laughed. Lindsey thought, "Oh brother," but didn't say anything. She realized that if she were facing Death Stalkers, they most certainly would be gunning for her, the Dispeller. She wondered if her dad also felt this way—that the enemy was always after him.

"Now then, I've really gotten the battlefield vastly improved from last year. When you go invisible, I, as referee, will make you actually invisible. If darkness is cast, I will actually make that section, that area, dark. When magic is successfully dispelled, I will handle it. Do not, I repeat, do not actually cast any spell! I will be handling all the successfully cast spell effects. This new setup we've built is fabulous for this. Just call out the spell and it will be adjudicated and implemented. Remember, the whole event is being recorded, and we will all sit down and watch it after the battle is over. You have two minutes to prepare and then the battle begins. It will last five minutes only. As several of you can vouch, a spell combat rarely lasts longer than that. Questions?" He spent another two minutes answering them.

"Yes, I know that for most of you, this is a totally new experience. Don't worry about being unused to it and feeling foolish and all that. The whole purpose of these exercises is to help you prepare for the real thing, but let's all hope and pray that you never need it," he added, though not one of the twenty-four believed him, that they wouldn't need it one day. The troubles in the world beyond the walls of the school were growing daily. Crime rates were soaring.

Lindsey, Ashley, Pam, and Amanda cast their protective spells on themselves and their companions. Deiter took charge of their attack. "Peaches, Emilio, Hans, and I will go after the enemy. The rest of you look after Lindsey and keep yourselves safe." Lindsey smiled; Deiter was wise in his new role as leader.

Wild. That was the most frequent comment as the group finally halted five minutes later. Imagine two dozen wizards and witches casting all manner of spells as fast as they could manage during the hectic five minutes. Lindsey discovered that she had a keen advantage in that she could rapidly detect what spell any person was about to cast. This time, she concentrated on only absorbing those spells that would prove troublesome to her group. Indeed, many of Audrey's team kept attempting to dispel Lindsey's protective spells, keeping Ashley, Amanda, and Pam busy recasting the key protective spells back onto Lindsey, freeing her to continue to absorb what she needed to do, casting a few only to discharge her staff.

The challenge was keeping together. Often Lindsey's group would find themselves under a darkness spell, during which time, some of Audrey's team would attempt to move in for a surprise attack when the darkness had been dispelled.

Unused to such battles, Katja, Jeannette, and Kathy ended up being captured, well more specifically, entangled in webs or vines. Emilio goofed up and was eliminated; Lil had taken him by surprise and hit him with a Terror Mind spell when he wasn't looking. She pretended then to hit him over the head with a rock. Hans also ran into trouble and was captured as well. Audrey's team ended up with five points.

Deiter and Peaches each knocked out two of Audrey's team. He'd developed a surprise plan of attack, teleporting to behind one of those in the rear and then webbing or holding them via a surprise rear attack. Audrey soon got wise to this tactic, and at the last minute, nearly did the same to Deiter himself, appearing at his rear. However, Lindsey saw this and followed suit, landing behind Audrey, taking her out, just as she was about to take out Deiter.

"Hey, are we supposed to follow you?" called out Amanda, when she spotted where Lindsey had reappeared. The alarm sounded the end of the session.

"No, I was going to come right back to you as fast as I could," Lindsey called out from across the huge room.

"Thanks, you saved my butt there," Deiter grinned, putting his arm around Lindsey, as they and Peaches walked back to their team members. "Guess you can't use the same trick several times," he added.

"Right buster, I caught on to it and almost had you," Audrey giggled.

"Sorry I goofed up again," Emilio said morosely.

"Hey, so did I," Kathy replied, holding on to Emilio, cheering him up. "I never realized how hard this is—I mean trying to stay alive if Death Stalkers are after you."

"Well, it's even harder to try to think of some way to stop them in a hurry," Lil added, but she'd managed to capture Emilio. "Like this is really, really hard!"

"What must be really hard," Peaches begged to differ, "is going against wizards who are going to be using higher Grade spells than we know! I cannot even imagine trying to face off against Dominus. I don't know how you did it, DK!"

Ashley flushed; she'd earned that kick name, DK for Dominus Kicker, when she had kicked him hard in his privates when the big battle started, allowing Lindsey to get the Crown of Moses off his head and stop Hurricane Emily. "I certainly couldn't outdo him with magic," Ashley admitted.

"Okay, kids, let's take a seat on the floor and watch the playback," Professor Delius called out. Now everyone could see the whole view of the battle, not just their own frantic attempts. What surprised Professor Delius, who took note of it, were their requests to see it five more times.

"Honestly, Professor, I seem to be seeing things I never saw each time I watch it," Peaches explained, after asking to see it the fifth time.

"I'm pathetic with my staff," Deiter announced when they were finally done watching it. "I really don't know how to use this incredibly expensive, powerful toy."

"Precisely so," Professor Delius commented, "excellent observation, Mr. Cross. That brings us to the last battle for today. This time, Audrey, you get reinforcements. Lindsey, your team this time is composed only of those of you who have a Staff of Power. Everyone else, you are on Audrey's team this time. The objective is to give these staff wielders some practice in using them. Two points for each of Lindsey's team that you capture, ten for Lindsey, of course. Lindsey, your team gets two points for each of Audrey's team that you can get. You also get a point for each of your team members who remain un-captured at the end, but only if they are still on the battlefield."

"We're doomed!" Pam wailed. She saw no way that she could survive, not with nineteen opponents.

Deiter, Amanda, Pam, Lindsey, and Ashley looked at each other. "Don't try to protect me," Lindsey said. "Keep yourselves alive somehow."

"You sure?" Ashley asked, concerned for her sister. She didn't like the thought of ignoring Lindsey.

"Go!" barked Professor Delius. Instantly, all five cast Darkness on themselves and their surrounding area. Lindsey cast her best Invisibility spell and hastily vacated her location, feeling her way to the back wall.

Nineteen spells flew at their original positions, and the lights came back on once more, revealing Deiter to the enemy. He chose to try to take as many of the enemy with him, and after capturing Kathy, he was himself summarily overwhelmed by seven nearly simultaneous spells. He ended up being trapped in webs, while being held from moving, while being bombarded with Magical Missiles and one Acid Missile.

Now Audrey's team began to search for the other four. Amanda's cover of Invisibility was dispelled, and she quickly was overcome as well. Now she and Deiter could only sit still and watch. Audrey had a guess where Ashley was hiding and her Dispel Magic revealed her crouching in a corner. At once, Ashley grew angry and began a whirlwind of action. Unfettered as the others were, who had to hold on to their tall staves, Zappo was affixed to her back, giving her complete freedom of movement.

Ashley sprang into action, launching attack spells, while ducking and dodging. She flew through the air, blasting away as she went. Using the entire room as her playground, Ashley was a whirlwind of action. Down went Kathy, then Hans, then Katja. Finally, as the time nearly expired, Audrey, sensing her next location, shot a Hold spell, and Ashley accidentally flew right into it. Professor Delius actually cast the Hold spell on her, but lowered her gently to the ground, before releasing her from the spell. Ashley glared at the enemy; Audrey giggled back at her.

The buzzer sounded the end of the battle, but neither Pam nor Lindsey was anywhere to be seen. "Lindsey, Pam, will you please reveal yourselves now?" called out Professor Delius. Lindsey appeared, standing quietly against the back wall, where no one had thought to look. However, everyone in the room roared with laughter. Pam's head, upside down, appeared from her extra-dimensional room six feet above the floor. She'd cast the only spell that she could think of to save herself, conjuring a rope to climb up into this safe haven. Now she looked down from above before having her rope appear and sliding down to the ground. She looked a bit sheepishly at the others.

"Well, I was safe," Pam stated flatly, defending her action.

"Quite right, Miss Betts," Professor Delius replied. "Let's see, Miss Stokes-Compton got three, so that's six. Two remained, making Lindsey's team score of eight. Add one for Deiter, and you have a total of nine points. Audrey, your side captured three of them, making a total of six points. Let's review the video. Miss Betts was quite right. When you are facing overwhelming odds, stay alive is the motto. Granted, all five could have just teleported away at the sound of the starting buzzer, which is what I would have recommended if this had been a real battle."

As they watched, Audrey explained, "You know, I could somehow sense just where I needed to be to be safe and to get Ashley. I need to work on using this sense more."

"DK was awesome!" Deiter complimented Ashley. "You made me look like an idiot out there. You got three of them."

"Yes, but they got me," Ashley countered. "I lost my temper and got angry."

"Good observation, Miss Stokes-Compton. When you get angry, you lose your focus, which invariably leads to your demise," Professor Delius complimented her on her observation.

Again, they watched the video several times, before their allotted hour was up. All chatted together as they walked back to their dorms. Lil's comment spoke volumes, "Lindsey, I'm glad I came today. I really did learn a whole lot. I can see just how much more I have to learn."

"I agree," Deiter added, "here I had the staff and thought I was invulnerable. You all got me before any of the others. Humiliating. I have so much to learn it's not funny."

"So do we all, Deiter, so do we all," Lindsey said what she was thinking.

Their track meet the following weekend went well. Ashley proved that she could do the long twenty-mile relay race, though her overall time was more than a minute slower than the others. Andy beat out his Black Hall sprinter, and the mile relay racers won their heat as well. For the first time, Yellow Hall completely skunked Black Hall!

Though for Yellow Hall, the track and soccer matches were over until spring, the group found that PE was not allowing them to rest. Having had six weeks to learn tennis,

Betsy created a mock tournament for the class. As the end of October drew close, Lindsey, Ashley, Pam, Kathy, and Amanda had been eliminated. Surprisingly, the top four who remained were Audrey, Katja, Jeannette, and Peaches. While they all watched the final competitions, Katja finally beat out Audrey, while Peaches finished off Jeannette, whose new arms still did not have the strength of those of athletic Peaches.

The girls yelled and cheered as Katja and Peaches battled it out for their class championship. Peaches took an early lead thirty-love, but Katja battled her way back. For nearly thirty minutes, these two battled it out. Peaches had a powerful forearm drive, but Katja had a mean backhand, which often took Peaches by surprise, forcing her out of position. Finally, Katja succeeded in scoring the winning point; she lobbed a soft shot just over the net, way out of the reach of Peaches, who had been expecting a strong smash.

Betsy made a surprise trophy presentation, giving each of the top four players a small, gold trophy to commemorate their games. This pleased the two Dutch girls, who would be taking them home to show their parents and classmates.

Near the end of October, Pam got back to Lindsey and Lil. "Not much to report, sadly. I've searched all the records and files, Lil. Don't ask me how I can do that, but I went through the FBI files myself. You can take small comfort, Lil, in knowing that they did indeed expend a good deal of resources trying to find your sister and what remains of her body. You are right; their last entry has pretty much written her off as now deceased."

Lil sighed; she had long ago guessed as much. "Thank you for trying, Pam. It is good to know that they did try to find her. That's something. I would have felt awful if they had just sat on their butts and done nothing about it. Peg is probably dead these many months. I just wish we could find her body and give her a proper burial. I know that mom and dad need that. Well, I do too," she admitted.

"You want to know what is really queer about this?" Pam added a bit mystified by what she had uncovered in the Interpol files, via the FBI cooperation files. Both gave Pam their complete attention.

"Interpol now thinks that they are after a serial killer. Based on what they said—I had to translate from the French—I redid their searching and added a bit more. The key words for the search are 'missing' and 'found only arms'—just those. Your sister, Peg, was the most recent of the victims; she was a brunette. However, one Rika Gerolt, blonde and twenty-one, from Amsterdam went missing a month earlier, in June. Her arms were found a week later, again in a dumpster. Last December, one Pon Su, twenty with long straight black hair, went missing from LA. Her arms were found rotting in a field. A month earlier in November, Mimi Arsenne, nineteen year old from Paris went missing. She is blonde too. Her arms washed up on a riverbank a couple weeks after she disappeared. That October, a nineteen year old red head from Miami named Estelle Johnson disappeared, again on her way home. A fisherman found her arms later on."

"Even weirder, a month before that in September, Lynn Esterbrook, a blonde, twenty-three year old attorney for the Denver Department of Law went missing. It caused quite a stir in that department, especially when her left arm and legs turned up two weeks later in the grass near the large airport. They've spent nearly a million dollars on trying to track her down. Queer isn't it?" Pam pointed out, "Kind of fits the pattern, but not quite."

"Sure sounds like a serial killer," Lindsey said. "He just keeps on committing the same kind of crime, right?" She was not too familiar with that term, however. She couldn't imagine a woman committing this kind of a butchering crime.

"Yes, same MO, nearly so anyway." Pam replied. "But that's not all. I also found five more cases, women who were abducted months before that. However, their bodies have been found or rather what was left of them. The FBI conclusion is that these others have probably been murdered only their bodies have yet to be discovered."

"I guess I have always known that was likely what had happened to Peg," Lil said, letting her tears come again. "I hope they catch the bastard who is going around killing young women and then dismembering their bodies. It makes me sick to think that somewhere around Denver, Peg's mutilated body is just lying around. I wish we could find what's left of her so we could bury her properly."

Pam sighed, "I know, I wish I had better news for you, Lil. I just don't know of any way to go about finding her remains. However, I will continue to search for methods, if only we had some idea where her body might have been dumped."

During the last two weeks of October, the presidential race heated up. As usual, the candidates spent a fortune on TV advertising, infomercials appearing with the frequency of Wheaties ads. President Lucius Dollington's ratings slumped even further in the polls, 20%, while Dominus Malefic rose to 20%. Lucius placed ads highlighting his successes during his first term. They were not very significant to the average citizen, however. Missy Snow continued to promise a universal and better health care plan for the masses. She promised to raise taxes on the rich and large corporations, though she stood firm on lowering the official drinking age to eighteen. Colorado still stood alone in this arena.

Following the pattern of the others, Dominus also ran ads. His themes were to be expected: vote for change, vote for leaders who can lead in a crisis such as Hurricane Emily, vote for a strong, powerful leader. In a direct attack on Missy Snow, his ad called out, "When has anything good been free? Look at the Swedish Health Care debacle, the Canadian Health Care fiasco. Is this what you really want for our great country? If you have worked hard to earn your money, do you really want to give larger and larger portions of your dollars to the government? If you say no to these, vote for Dominus Malefic for President on November 7."

As the last week of October came, the balance of power began to shift. Missy's strong lead began to dwindle; many began throwing their support to Dominus, who now led President Lucius by a good ten points in the polls. Senator Missy Snow's ads now began to attack Dominus outright, stressing that he was a convicted criminal, a murderer, who by law could never be allowed into the office of the President.

Pam pointed out that Missy now seemed on the defensive, and Andy suggested that her campaign might be faltering, which was why she was now attacking Dominus.

On October 29, everyone on the Bradbury campus was glued to their big screen TVs in the commons. Hugo, face pale and somber, spoke, "A massive car bomb went off outside the parking deck of the Senate in Washington DC. The car carrying Senator Missy Snow and her running mate, Joules Cockney, was hit. KMAG is trying at this minute to get our cameras in close. As you can see, there is massive confusion. Secret Service personnel have taken total control of the area, sealing it off. However—here we go—our long-range telephoto cameras are picking up this horrid scene. Yes, that appears to be the Senator's vehicle—there in the center of the screen. How could something like this happen?"

Images of a blackened car filled the screen. Emilio yelled out, "Dominus at work! I bet anything!" A chorus of various agreements echoed his angered sentiments. A bit later, the cameras showed several bodies being removed; one was definitely that of Missy Snow. By the way that the rescue personnel reacted, Hugo suggested that she might still be alive, though he refused, for once, to speculate on her condition. As the stunned students watched, a Life-Flight helicopter lifted off, carrying three wounded with it.

An hour later that night, a subdued President Lucius appeared at a live news conference. "I have some good news in this time of terrible, unspeakable crimes of terrorism. Senator Missy Snow is alive. Her injuries are severe. Among other things, she has suffered the loss of both her eyes, and both of her eardrums have been ruptured. She has severe internal concussion injuries. I have ordered her to be attended by the very best healers of the Department of Magical Healing. I have taken this unusual step, even though she is not a user of magic. Without magical assistance, she will most certainly die. Hence, I have ordered her to receive the best care this country can provide. This is not about politics, but about common decency, humanity. Additionally, I have ordered the foremost facial reconstruction doctor in our country to come to the DC area and lend his expertise, once she is stabilized. Doctor Henry

Blackburn of Greeley General Hospital is already on his way here as I speak."

"On a sadder note, her running mate, Joules Cockney, passed away, along with two bodyguards. One guard remains in similar critical condition at the undisclosed hospital. The Secret Service has confirmed it was a car bomb. I have ordered every law enforcement agency in our country into action. We will spare no effort to find the terrorists responsible for such a heinous act of cowardice. In time, I'm sure that the terrorists responsible for this hideous act will be apprehended and stand trial for murder. I have sent a request to the Congress asking them that the death sentence be re-instated for those found guilty of this act of treason." He ended his short conference, but was besieged with questions from the media. As he left the Oval Office, he did reply to one. "No, we do not have any suspects at this time."

What happened next, none could have predicted. The satellite feed was interrupted, and Dominus Malefic appeared on the screen, dressed in morning black. His face was somber. "Greetings my fellow Americans. Dominus Malefic here. I wish to take this opportunity to express my personal outrage at the heinous and unprovoked attack on my rival, Senator Missy Snow. In light of this terrorist attack, I have ordered all of my campaign ads attacking her platform be removed. I have sent a quarter of a million dollars to the hospital where she is being treated to help cover the expense of her recovery. Personally, I hold President Lucius Dollington and his incompetent administration partially responsible for allowing this terrorist act to occur. You need to elect a president who is in control of the government, one who does not allow such acts of barbarism to occur on US soil. Please join me in a moment of silent prayer for Senator Snow and those who have been injured or died." The set went silent for a brief time, before the feed returned to a frantic Hugo at the KMAG studios.

"Oh, we're back. Oh, hi there. KMAG feed has once more been interrupted by this criminal. I don't know what to make of his statements, donating a quarter million dollars to Senator Snow's recovery? Let's go now to Fred Betts, our own Department of Magical Misuse, High Plains of Colorado."

"What?" exclaimed a very shocked Pam.

"Isn't that your father?" someone called out. Everyone stared at the screen.

Pam saw her dad on camera. He looked pale and tired. "Good evening Hugo. As you have heard, the Department of Law is all over this latest bombing. I have been asked to chat with you instead. Everyone is working overtime. How can I help you?"

Pam suspected her dad had been pressured into being the spokesperson by his superiors. She hoped that he did all right, knowing full well that he hated being interviewed.

Hugo said, "Good to have you here, Mr. Betts. What can you tell us about who is responsible for this wicked bombing?"

"Nothing at this time," he replied quietly.

"No suspect?" Hugo refused to let it go.

"Not at this time. The investigation is in its earliest stages. As you know, a proper investigation takes time."

"Surely someone or some group has come forward claiming responsibility?" Hugo continued to pressure Mr. Betts.

"Well of course they have. In nearly every major crime, someone steps forward claiming that they did it, mostly crack pots, insane people. One man claimed that he had done it, stating that he used a nuclear bomb to rid the world of Senator Snow. We all know that this was not a nuclear bomb." Fred replied in his usual manner, letting Hugo know that, while many claims of responsibility had been heard, none was seriously taken.

Hugo finally relented, picking up on the bomb instead. "Speaking of the bomb, you say it was not a nuclear device. Can you be more specific? What kind of a bomb was it?"

"Now that question I can answer. Plastic explosives were used, military grade C-4. The FBI lab has confirmed it and is searching for the manufacturer of the explosive. As you may know, each batch has a unique signature built into its chemical formulation. Samples were taken of the blast residue and are now being analyzed. In time, we will know where it was manufactured and can then proceed in a proper investigative manner. Eventually, the guilty party or parties will be uncovered."

"Military grade?" Hugo picked up on this tidbit. "Are you saying that someone in our armed forces is behind this terrorist attack?"

Unamused, Fred's face took on a stern look. "While no possibility can be ruled out, as you well know, Hugo, it is highly unlikely that is the case. Once the manufacturer is identified, we can then trace that entire batch of explosives. We will be looking for thefts and other possibilities. It is likely that the plastic explosives were stolen, but that is merely my personal opinion at this time. There is no factual basis for my speculation except that I have seen this before, stolen C-4 being used in terrorist attacks."

Hugo picked up on this. Hugo was a master interviewer. "Yes, that's right you have. Wasn't your own daughter attacked in a similar manner at Bradbury's School of Magic?"

"Correct. Old news. Ex-governor General of the US, Henry Albright is now serving a life sentence in the Denver Penitentiary. He hired several of Dominus Malefic's Death Stalkers to sneak into the school and set off explosions. Three cafeteria staff workers were killed. He provided the stolen C-4 explosives. My daughter played a pivotal role in obtaining the evidence of Albright's guilt."

"So you believe that Dominus Malefic is behind this attack on the presidential frontrunner, Senator Missy Snow?" Hugo asked the leading question that he had been waiting for all this time. Hugo grinned as the camera moved in for a close-up shot on Fred.

"Oh, so you wish me to speculate, Hugo? Propose possibilities not based upon the slightest shred of evidence? You wish me to propose that President Lucius ordered the hit because he's way behind in the polls, clever way to get rid of his true rival? Oh, that's not what you wanted me to propose, now is it?" Fred grinned back at a frustrated Hugo. "You'd rather me speculate that Dominus was behind the bombings, when we have not the slightest suggestion of his involvement? I'm sorry, Hugo. I don't speculate publically. I'd rather stick to the facts."

Fred continued, "Now take these thousands of rings

that Dominus has been doling out to his supporters. There's a fact. The latest estimates that the Department of Magical Misuse has places about ten thousand gold rings and another two thousand diamond rings have been given out."

"Ah, so the Department of Magical Misuse is involved in investigating these rings?" Hugo quickly recovered from his botched attempt to get speculation out of Fred Betts.

"Of course, the Department is always looking into misuses of magic. That is our function."

"And what have you discovered about these rings?" Hugo prominently displayed one of the rings with a two-caret diamond in it.

"If I were you, I wouldn't wear that ring, Hugo. The Department would like to go on public record at this time warning all those who have received such a ring perhaps not to wear them. We have discovered that they are magically enchanted, though as yet, we do not know the nature of that enchantment. Prudence suggests the use of extreme caution with these rings. The Department of Magical Misuse will issue a formal public notice just as soon as we are certain of the enchantment and what lies behind it. For now, we urge all those who have these rings to exercise extreme caution."

Hugo flushed slightly, perhaps the first time while in his studio chair, but the camera was still focused on the intense face of Fred Betts. "You are saying that there rings may be harmful?"

"I'm not saying any such thing at this time, only that they hold some, as yet unknown enchantment, in them. Considering that they are a relatively expensive gift from a convicted murderer, I leave you to draw your own conclusions," Fred hinted.

"Well, thank you Mr. Fred Betts of the High Plains Department of Magical Misuse for being with us at this time of disaster. After this brief word from our sponsor, we will be back with more live coverage of the bombing of Senator Missy Snow."

"Pam, your dad was really good," Katja exclaimed.

"Yes, he sure didn't give in to Hugo," Amanda added.

Pam wanted to become invisible; nearly everyone in

212

Yellow Hall began echoing their comments. Monique walked in just then, "Pam did you see your father?" She didn't get to finish her sentence—that she had was plainly obvious. Pam made a hasty exit with Monique, heading for the formal gardens and a bit of peace and quiet, though Monique was surprised and impressed that her father was leaving for DC soon.

Later in her room, Pam discovered that she had a high priority email from her father.

Dearest Pam,

A bit more on the rings. We have acquired one of each. Indeed, you were right about the diamonds. The serial number of the diamond was verified as belonging to those stolen from the Dutch firm. Please let your foreign exchange students know about this and that we are working on tracking down those responsible for the murder of their grandparents.

We have also detected a faint magical energy enchantment on each ring. You probably saw my TV interview. We know that it is an enchantment-charm magical energy, though no one has been able to identify the spell or spells involved. This is a particularly tough ID situation. Apparently, the spells have not yet been activated, but are somehow dormant. Most curious indeed. More later.

Love,

Dad

Pam did just that. Jeannette cried a little. "After fifteen years, the diamonds they stole have finally appeared. Dominus is using them. I bet anything that he was the thief and murderer."

"Well, if he was, you can be certain that my dad will eventually get the goods on him," Pam consoled her.

"Golden rings and golden paths," Ashley mused. "He sure has gold on his mind."

"What did you just say?" Pam suddenly sat up and started at Ashley. "That's it! There must be a connection between his manifesto and its promised 'Golden Path' and these gold rings! Somehow, these rings are connected to his Golden Path, one that puts him as the supreme leader. I better email that to my dad right now!"

Chapter 13—Halloween

Lindsey asked Katja, "Do you all celebrate Halloween in your country?" They were eating their supper. It was the night of October 30.

"Ja, sure ve do. It is the only time Jeannette could go out onto the streets and not be so embarrassed. Ve paint her up to look like someone just pulled out her arms, and den ve go to houses and get candy. Spooked many peoples." Jeannette just looked embarrassedly at her food, but that was the truth. Only on Halloween did she feel brave enough to go to a total stranger's house.

"Tomorrow, we get to go into Telluride and spend the day in town. Then, we come back to a festive supper and the costume dance. I keep going as a fairy," Lindsey admitted. "Never had the time to make any other costume. Jim keeps going as a pirate. Don't worry; Amanda is really good at figuring out costumes for us." The Dutch teens didn't have any costumes.

"May I have your attention?" Governor Alister called out over the hustle and bustle of the evening meal. At once, a quiet fell in the dining room. "Thank you. As you know, tomorrow is Halloween. Traditionally, on this day, third years and above are allowed to go into Telluride for the day. Last year, Dominus and his gang of Death Stalkers kidnaped some of our students. Although I was inclined to cancel all further trips into the town, the Department of Security has assured me that they will have two dozen men on patrol."

"So tomorrow at nine a.m., please gather here in the dining room for last minute instructions. However, I cannot stress too strongly the new rule that I wish to be followed. Please, stick together. Divide yourselves into smaller groups. Under no circumstances are one or two of you to go off on your own. Always travel in bunches. This is for your own safety. Now let's continue with this fine meal."

"Well, I'm glad that he didn't cancel it," Jim said to Ashley. "I want to take my princess into town."

"Yes, but we all need to stick together, Jim," Amanda cautioned her older brother.

"Let's figure out who is all going with us?" Lindsey suggested.

"I am!" Fern nearly yelled it out. She was finally old enough for her first visit to town. Amanda grinned, knowing how much her little sister had been waiting for this day. A few minutes later, Lindsey had a huge group going together. Deiter and Peaches wanted to join them, along with their Dutch student. Monique was with Pam, and Audrey came with them as well.

Pam then said, "We should make an itinerary of places to go so that no one gets left out."

"I want to go to Dominos and have Deiter feed me like we did last year, Ashley. That was so romantic!" Peaches exclaimed. Everyone vetoed going to an afternoon movie, for which Lindsey was grateful.

"Er, gang, Monique and I want to check out one old building. Probably won't amount to much, but we want to check it. Also, can we go past that house where we were held captive? I want to see if it is being repaired yet. It hadn't been this spring."

"What building?" asked Lindsey, suddenly curious about what Pam and Monique were investigating.

"We have been researching this Mac Fluide Enterprises company. They own that house where we were held captive, Lindsey. Anyhow, we've found one other home in Telluride that this corporation owns, and we want to go inspect it. It's probably just another rundown house, but maybe the Death Stalkers have been using this as a hideout as well. We want to have a look see," Pam explained.

Lindsey was given the thankless task of trying to organize everyone's suggestions on what to visit, where to go, and when. She certainly wanted to show her Dutch girlfriends the various quaint shops, where they could buy some souvenirs for their relatives, and she wanted to show them all the sights. Jim and Deiter protested that they couldn't spend a couple of hours in the pool hall, though Ashley was very relieved to hear that the group would not be going there this

216

trip, because her skills at pool using her hands still left her wanting.

At nine the next morning, over four hundred students, dressed for a chilly visit into town, congregated in the dining room. At last, Governor Alister arrived and gave them the password: elephants. This allowed them access into the secret doorway that led to the kitchen and dishwashing area underneath the dining room. From there, a long tunnel led into Telluride. Again, the password was needed to exit the tunnel in a friendly wizard's store. The hundreds piled out onto the streets of Telluride, where a light dusting of snow had fallen over night.

As expected, the twenty Dutch students gaped and stared at the mountains. They looked so close, so huge, and so impressive to them. Presently, Jim and Monique, the two older students, led the pack around the town, showing them the sights. Soon, the girls began disappearing into the many shops. "You stand guard over me, Deiter," Peaches teased him.

"Got my trusty staff," Deiter teased back. Indeed all had brought along their Staves of Power, just in case of trouble, though Lindsey didn't believe any would come this time. The town was too heavily guarded. Already, she had seen seven Security men watching them from the tops of buildings and even two homes. Today promised to be a relaxing, carefree day in town, a respite from their heavy schoolwork load.

Shopping done, packages magically shrunk in size and fitted into pockets, the group headed to Dominos for a pizza lunch. As usual, the place was packed with students, so much so, that it was elbow to elbow and standing room only. Peaches had to give up her idea of a romantic meal; it was just too crowded. Nevertheless, the Dutch students enjoyed it immensely.

"Ja, it is just like home!" Katja exclaimed enthusiastically.

"Vell, not exactly, everything is in English," Jeannette teased her dearest friend. They giggled.

"Next time, ve go to the Arches," Hans declared, he preferred burgers to pizza.

Around one and with full bellies, the large group again

took to the streets. This time, they headed to the old abandoned house where they had been held captive when Dominus was using the Crown of Moses to control Hurricane Emily. "Doesn't look any different," Monique whispered, as they stood a few feet from the gaping hole in the front room wall where the four Disintegrate spells had been cast.

"I think it is really weird that they still haven't repaired it," Pam declared.

"Hey, look there is a sign posted on the door," Deiter pointed out. "Condemned, they are going to tear it down in the spring."

"Well, I shouldn't like such an eyesore as this if I lived around here either," Kathy pronounced. "Where's this other house we have to see?"

"One block down and over two," Pam called out. Once more, the troupe marched along the sidewalks admiring the homes and the spectacular view of the mountains, like white teeth chewing at the blue sky.

"Next time we come, let's all go skiing," Jim declared. As they walked, skiing became *the* topic of conversation. Ashley was willing to try it again; with arms, she might do better at it. A few minutes later, Jim asked, "Say, Pam, where did you say this house was at?" They'd reached a dead end street.

"What? Where? How? Darn, we passed it!" Pam declared, very annoyed with herself for having not paid attention. "Follow me," she declared, very determinedly. The group did an about face and began walking back down the street.

A bit later, Andy, who was now at the lead with Jim bringing up the rear, called out, "Pam? Which way did you say we had to go?"

"What? How did we—we passed it again!" Pam felt her face heat up; never had she been so embarrassed and with so many of her close friends here to witness this mix-up. "Back there, next block, brown clapboard house. Sorry, I don't know what's come over me." She apologized profusely, as the large troupe turned around once more and headed down the street.

A minute later, Jim called out, "Pam, which one was it

again?" Pam turned around; there was the house behind them. For the third time, they had just walked past it!

"Wait a dog gone minute! Something is not right here. We've gone by that stupid house three times now. Come on gang; follow me. I'm walking directly to its front door!" Pam angrily called out. Shortly, she neared the house and found her mind drifting to thoughts of her father's TV interview. She forced them out of her mind. "Dispel Magic!" Pam called out, pointing her staff to the house.

"Whoa, Pam, what are you—well, I'll be!" Jim called out. He, too, just realized that they had all been subjected three times to the magic enchantment placed on this house. Many had just learned this spell too. "Wow, it really does work. We've totally avoided this particular house and barely even noticed that we were missing it. Cool move, Pam." The others joined him in praising her cleverness at recognizing what they had not.

As they walked up to the front door of the otherwise non-descript house, Audrey complained, "I should not be here. I don't think we should be here."

Ashley immediately attempted to put her diviner skills to work. True, she and Professor Mary Ann were still working on her gaining control over her premonitions, but she tried. "Lindsey, there are people in there in dire peril, I think. Several of them. They need help, but it's dangerous."

Pam at once backed away from the door that she was about to knock on to see who lived here. Now she had second thoughts about being so bold. Deiter took charge, "Say, why don't I use my spying eye and have a peek through the keyhole—you know, see who's inside, what we might be facing?"

"Good idea, Deiter. The rest of us, let's stand guard in case of trouble. Deiter, I will be protecting you while you are tied up trying to spy on the insides," Lindsey suggested.

"Jim, you and I ought to put a full Invulnerability spell on everyone, especially Fern," Monique added. Hastily, she and Jim cast their Grade 6 spell on each member of the group. "There, Fern, now no spell of Grade 4 or lower will have any effect on you."

"Wow, way super cool! I can't wait to learn that one!" Fern bubbled enthusiasm, her wand at the ready. She felt incredibly powerful, just now, here with her older brother and sister and Lindsey's whole group.

When everyone was protected, Deiter cast his spell. They watched as a disembodied eye moved out from Deiter's head, shrinking down in size and slipping through the key hole. "What do you see?" asked an impatient Pam.

"Cool insides. Everything is red; whoever lives here likes red. Plush velvet chairs even. Ritzy. Wait a second, I'm seeing some man; he's got a wand and is pacing the front room, just inside the door."

"Who is he? Do you recognize him?" Lindsey asked, though as soon as she asked she realized this was a silly question. Deiter probably had not studied all the known photos of the Death Stalkers.

After a bit, Deiter said, "He's a Death Stalker all right. He's wearing a short sleeve shirt, but I can see his mark on his shoulder, skull and crossbones. Wait a second. I think he knows that we are out here. He's—ouch!" Deiter held onto his eye. "He Dispelled my scrying eye. He's on to us."

"I told you we are in danger," Audrey whispered, though no one paid her any attention.

"How many are in there?" Jim asked.

"I only saw the one man. Surely, we can take one Death Stalker," Deiter suggested.

"Sure we can," replied Peaches, eager for a fight.

"Okay, I'm going to knock on the door and see if he will talk with us," Lindsey decided. Her friends protested; she added, "Look, I can detect whatever spells he might choose to shoot at me or us faster than the rest of you. It has to be me. You all guard my back." Jim saw her reasoning and ordered everyone to take up battle positions. Audrey and Pam moved to the very back of the group, along with the four Dutch students. Amanda ordered Fern to the rear as well, though Fern protested a little.

Lindsey knocked politely on the door and waited, her staff at the ready. She had butterflies in her stomach, though she dare not say anything to the others. Besides, they probably did too. She knocked a second time. Perhaps he won't answer the door, she thought to herself. If she had seen who was outside, she wouldn't answer the door.

Just as she was about to knock for a third time, the door opened a crack, enough for her to see a young man, perhaps in his mid-twenties, clean shaven with short black hair looking out at her. He held his wand at the ready. "Go away."

"Sir, we believe that there are several people inside this house that are in dire need of help," Lindsey said, quite unsure of what to say to the man. She decided to bluff. "If you don't let us in so we can see for ourselves, then we'll return shortly with the thirty Security men who are watching over us this Telluride visiting day."

The man's eyes moved from person to person. He saw five Staves of Power pointed his way to say nothing of the large group of wands similarly pointed at him. Lindsey added, "Don't try anything either. There are an awful lot of us here, and five Staves of Power, if you hadn't noticed. We just want to come inside and see for ourselves if anyone in here is in trouble."

"There's no one here but me," the man ventured. Lindsey suspected that he was lying; his eyes avoided hers.

"Well, we won't be but a minute checking on that, so let us in, please." Lindsey continued her bluff. "We know that you are a Death Stalker, and none of us will hesitate to spell to kill, that being the new philosophy that Bill West has been teaching us."

The mere mention of Bill's name caused the man's face to whiten noticeably. Lindsey felt even more confident now. "I guess it won't hurt to let you look around. No one is here." He opened the door and stepped back into the front room. One by one, everyone followed Lindsey inside.

At first, Lindsey did not know what to make of the room. All the blinds were drawn; elegant lamps provided soft illumination. The furniture was plush red velvet, as was the thick pile carpet. The wallpaper blended nicely, Lindsey detected a faint odor of perfume. What was this place anyway?

"Looks like a brothel," Pam said flatly, and then her face turned nearly as red as the room.

Monique came to her rescue. "We've seen lots of pictures of brothels in the movies and magazines. This certainly looks like one. See, the man's been reading Playboy." Indeed, all eyes glanced at the half-opened page lying on the table. Giggles were common, though Jim and Deiter could hardly keep from staring at the partial images.

"Okay, we should search this place," Lindsey suggested. You all fan out; we will keep the Death Stalker covered with our staves."

Peaches began heading for the wooden stairway leading upstairs, while others headed into the other rooms. "Wait! Please, don't go up there, please, I beg you," the man unexpectedly interrupted them.

Lindsey suspected something was up from the tone of genuine concern in the man's voice. She decided to follow her instinct. He may be a Death Stalker, but he didn't seem as hardcore as Rubius, the man who held her prisoner during her first year at Bradbury's. She also remembered how the Death Stalker, Allen Hall, had been when he was assigned to guard them after Dominus had cut off her arms last year when they were kidnaped. "Hold on a second everyone. What is your name?"

"Jack Benson. I know you. You are that Barron girl aren't you?"

"Yes, I'm Lindsey Barron, daughter of Sam Barron, the Rat Pack Dispeller. Something is going on in this house, something awful isn't it, Jack, something that bothers you?" She watched his surprised reaction; his face flushed ever so slightly. He nodded. Encouraged that her intuition was spot on, she added, "Jack, this is your chance, probably the only one you are going to get. Surrender to us. Tell us what is going on in this house. Help us put things right. That will go a long way for you."

Deiter's mouth fell open as he watched. Jack handed his wand over to Lindsey! "This probably means I am a dead man, but I just can't take this sadism any longer. The man's a sadistic beast. If I had known that, I would never have joined him."

"Who?"

"Dominus. This is his private whorehouse. You young girls shouldn't be here. I mean, it's horrible enough for me, a grown man of the world, but what is upstairs—well that isn't fit for anyone to see, let alone young teens. Probably nothing can be done for them now, but make them as comfortable as possible."

Wisely, Jim spoke up, "Lindsey, ask him if any others are due to arrive here in the next little while." He was getting a bit nervous about being inside one of Dominus Malefic's known homes!

"No one is likely to come today, probably not until next weekend," Jack replied, not waiting for Lindsey to repeat it. "However, others do come here unexpectedly from time to time. I'm not expecting anyone, though. You understand me?"

"Okay, Jim, some of us should stand guard down here while the rest of us go upstairs and see what we are dealing with up there," Lindsey decided.

"Please, you shouldn't see them, the women. He's a sadist, pure and simple. Their condition is just too shockingly horrible. Please don't go up there," Jack sounded very sincere, but Lindsey knew that she really had to see for herself.

"How many are up there? What is their condition? Are they in immediate danger of dying?" Pam spoke up, asking what she felt were the key questions that she needed to know. "What has he done to them?" she added.

Jack slumped onto the soft sofa, wiping his head with his hands. After a moment, he spoke so softly that they had to strain to hear him. "Dominus's private toys—that's what he calls them. He'd got five young women captive up there. You can't do anything for them. He's mutilated them something horrible and has forced them to wear erotic clothing, what little there is of it. Please don't go up there. If I had a daughter, I'd never want her to see them like this, please, miss."

Pam made a quick leap of logic. "Has Dominus cut off their arms? Is that what you mean?" Suddenly, everyone made the connection, especially Lil, who began to wonder if perhaps her sister might be being held captive here.

"How did you—oh, I've seen your picture before. You are that Betts' girl, the would-be Sleuth. Yes, four are like that, but he's also blinded them. The fifth has given him lots of trouble, and she is in even worse condition. He cut off both her legs, cut off one arm, cut out her tongue, and blinded her in one eye. Now he makes her look after the needs of the other four who are helpless. I'm their cook. I make them their meals and keep them from trying to escape, though there is no way that they could. It made me sick, but I've been trying to look after them. Please, it is the worst thing I have ever seen. Don't go up there, I beg you."

Lindsey replied, "Well, if we don't, then who's going to rescue these poor women, eh? Jim, you and the fellows better stand guard down here. If they are in such bad shape, it's probably better if they're not around men," she added growing more worried about the women's well-being.

Lil wanted to rush the stairs, fearing that her sister, Peg, might just be here, but Ashley caught her arm, motioning her to wait a moment. "Okay, Ashley, Jeannette, Lil, Pam, Amanda, Monique, you are with me. We will check on the women. Everyone else, stay very alert; who knows if other Death Stalkers might come. Jim, watch Jack like a hawk. Okay, wands at the ready. He might not be telling the whole truth," Lindsey ordered.

She took a deep breath and headed determinedly for the wooden staircase leading to the second floor. In their favor, this was not a large house. At the top of the stairs, they peered into the first room. Another plush room with satin sheets and covers greeted their curious eyes. Monique whispered, "Probably this is the room where Dominus sleeps with the poor women."

Lindsey agreed they moved on down the hallway. A tall guardrail blocked any accidental falling down the stairs. They passed a large bathroom, equally plush, perhaps the most elegant bathroom Lindsey had seen. Ahead lay two more rooms. The door to the next was open; stealthily they peered in to see a low table. Evidently, this was where the women were fed. Some dirty dishes lay stacked on the table along with some cups. Only one more room to go, but its door was closed. They gathered around it.

Lindsey imagined how she had felt when Dominus had

mutilated her body, similar to what Jack had said the evil wizard had done to these women. Blind and helpless, these women would be easily frightened. "Stay calm, no matter what we see," she whispered. Gently she knocked on the door. She heard some movement inside, knocked as softly as she could a second time, and then opened it. In spite of her own life situations, Lindsey was woefully unprepared for what she and the others saw inside the room.

Five beds lined two walls, along with a low mattress on the floor. The room decor was the same velvet red. A sofa and chairs lined the third wall; six women sat on the chairs. Five had very short arms left, only about two inches from their shoulders. These five wore various colored wasp waist corsets, tightly laced; they could barely breathe, Lindsey soon discovered. Garters held up silky black seamed hose. Black patent ankle boots covered their feet. Each boot had some kind of lock on it, but the spiked heels were nothing like any of the girls had seen, rising to at least six inches, making walking treacherous, though possible. None wore any panties, which Lindsey later learned was so that their nursemaid could manage to help them use the restroom. All five girls had grey eyes, blinded just as Lindsey had been.

However, what shocked the girls the most were the five's breasts. Dominus had used some form of Enlarge spell on them. Their breasts were as large as their heads. This datum made a lasting impression on Lindsey, who had never seen such before. In the back of her mind, she filed this under "Ways to Attract Dominus so We Can Capture Him."

The sixth woman, or rather what was left of her, sat staring at them from a lower chair. She too was tightly encased in a corset and had the same exaggerated breasts. However, her legs were only six inches long, her right arm barely two inches. Her left eye socket was empty, making a gruesome sight. From the noises she made, Lindsey could tell the woman had no tongue any more. She was obviously the nursemaid for the other five, who were completely helpless, unable to see, and barely able to walk in those spiked boots.

Lindsey was standing in the doorway, and she recovered enough to say, "Hi, I'm Lindsey Barron. We are all from Bradbury's School of Magic. We are here to rescue you and get you out of this vile place." The nursemaid woman made gestures with her hand and tried to speak, but Lindsey couldn't make any sense of her words. All the women looked terrified.

As Lindsey stepped into the room, Lil rushed past her. "Peg! Oh dear god, Peg! What has he done to you? It's me, Lil. We've come to rescue you from Dominus." She rushed over to the tall brunette, whose shoulder length hair covered what remained of her arms. Lil threw her arms around Peg, who staggered to keep her balance.

"Lil? My little sister?" Peg exclaimed. "Is it really you or is this some trick you are playing on us all?"

"It's really me, Peg. We used to play pirates before you left to take the bartender job. It's me, Lil." She frantically tried to convince her blind sister that she was indeed her sister. She held on tightly to Peg, however, for which Peg was grateful; it kept her from falling.

"Lil, if it is really you, please, I beg you, please just kill me right now! Kill all of us! Right now! Please, we are begging you! We can't live like this. We all would rather be dead than suffer more of this horrible misery. Promise me you will kill me right now, promise me Lil. You have to. None of us can do it, though we have tried. Please, Lil, stab me or something. Just kill us all right now, before Dominus comes back. Please Lil, please, have mercy on us. Don't make us live like this anymore."

Lil began bawling, emotionally out of control. The other women added their pleas to hers, begging to be put out of their horrible torture. Only the nursemaid could not express her views, but nodded, which Lindsey took to mean she agreed with Peg.

Lindsey understood just how Peg and the others felt. She took action, "Look, we are not going to kill you. I give you my solemn promise that the very first thing we are going to do the second we get you to safety is to heal you fully. Listen to me. Last year, Dominus cut off my arms just like yours and blinded me. He even sewed my lips together, but I'm fully healed. My sister Ashley here—she lost all of her arms in a traffic accident when she was two and now she has new arms. Jeannette, our foreign exchange student from the Netherlands—she was born without arms, and now she has perfect arms. I promise all of you that I will do whatever it takes to get your bodies fully healed, your arms back, and good as new. I promise you I will do this, but first we have to get you out of this house and to safety. The world's evilist wizard did this to you, but the rest of us wizards and witches will do everything to get you six fully healed. It is the very least we can do for you."

"Now we have to get you out of here. Do you have any real clothes around here?" The nursemaid shook her head no.

Lil suggested, "Lindsey, we have to get them out of these, these things! Peg can barely breathe, and she can just barely stand in those boots!"

"Wait, Lil. I can see that, but they could well be booby trapped. If we attempt to remove them, some awful trap might trigger. I wouldn't put anything past Dominus." The nursemaid made gurgling noises. Lindsey turned to look at her; she nodded her head up and down, suggesting Lindsey may be right. The clothes might be trapped.

Lindsey thought fast. "See if you can get their bed sheets around them as a cloak, anything to keep them covered and warm. It's way to chilly outside for them to go this way. I'll Message Governor Alister for help. Pam, Message your father. We should get him here to search this house for other evidence. Let's hurry up. I want to get them out of here ASAP!"

A moment later, a paper flashed before Lindsey's eyes, vanishing as she read it. Likewise, with Pam. "Dad's on his way. He will need directions once he gets to Telluride so he can find this house quickly."

Monique, Lil, Amanda, Ashley, and Jeannette decided to use a soft, velvet-feeling blanket as a cloak; the women would be warmer. One by one, they draped the blankets over the five girls. Lindsey yelled down to the others. "Fern, go outside and wait for Mr. Betts. He's on his way with others to take over here. Alister wants us to get these six women into our Infirmary as fast as we can. Let us know the second that Fred gets here, please, and we will take the women out of here pronto."

"You got it!" Fern yelled back. Lindsey heard the door bang shut.

"Are they alive?" called Jim.

"Need any help?" Deiter added.

"We've got everything under control down here," Emilio put in his comments, not wanting to be left out.

"We've got them. They are alive and as well as can be expected. You can stick around and help Mr. Betts if you like. We make a good team, gang. Thanks!" Lindsey validated them. She knew that they all wanted to see the captive women that they were rescuing. However, Lindsey knew what these women were feeling and wanted to keep outside contact to a minimum. They were terrified enough just now. Worse, they were soon going to have to do some walking.

"So what's the plan?" asked Ashley, who finished covering the nursemaid as best she could.

"Alister wants us to get them to the Infirmary as fast as we safely can. However, as we all know, we can't teleport into the campus nor can we teleport into the mile long tunnel, but we can teleport to the entrance. Once we get them inside, we'll have to walk them down the tunnel. Once we are outside the kitchen area, we can then use our Magical Door spell to step them directly into the Infirmary, where Alister will be waiting for us, along with Doctor Caterwall. He said under no circumstance are we to try to remove any of their clothing. He thinks there is a good likelihood they might be trapped. If we can't manage the tunnel, we're to let him know. We can each take one woman with us."

"I'll carry the nursemaid, Lindsey," Monique volunteered. "I'm the strongest here. She certainly can't walk. Pam, can you help lift her up? See if she can put her arm around my neck to help hold on." Both Pam and Amanda gently lifted the poor woman up and got her into a good position for Monique. Pam then adjusted the blanket to keep her warm and covered. "Thanks, she is pretty light." The woman began crying, however.

Lil put her arm around her sister's thin waist and held on to her. "I've got you, Peg. I won't let you fall."

"If, if this doesn't work, promise me you will end my misery, please, Lil!"

"Don't be silly, Peg. Lindsey knows what she is doing. You are going to be just fine in a while."

"The others, they don't' speak English," Peg finally volunteered a useful datum. Indeed, the others merely sat like rigid statues, only agreeing with Peg that they wished to be put out of their misery as well.

"I speak English. I am Pong Su from LA," the twenty year old woman of Asian descent finally spoke up, her voice trembling. She was still very confused about what was happening and just who the voices she was hearing actually were. Like Peg, she figured it was just another one of Dominus's nasty tricks he was playing on them. "I like your really long hair, Pong," Lindsey whispered an encouraging word to the woman.

"I, I am Estelle Johnson from Miami," the nineteen year old redhead volunteered.

Hearing the others speaking, the twenty-one year old blonde ventured, "Ik ben Rika, Rika Gerolt van Dordrecht."

Jeannette gasped and hastily replied, "Ik ben Jeannette van Utrecht. Ik bezoek de USA. Wij gaan u redden en volledig u helen." She looked at Ashley and added, "I told her we are rescuing her and going to heal her."

Hearing the other women around her speaking, the fifth armless woman spoke up with a decidedly French accent. "Mimi Arsenne, Paris. No say Englishs." She had gorgeous, long, slightly curly brown hair.

Pam quickly cast her Understand Language spell and replied, "Nous allons vous sauver et vous guérir entièrement."

Jeannette put her arm around Rika, preparing to teleport her. Ashley did the same with Estelle. Lindsey moved to the side of Pong, steading her with her arm around her waist, underneath the woman's long, thick hair. Amanda did the same with Mimi, so that Pam was free to brief her father. Amanda cast her language spell as well, so that she could speak with Mimi when the time came.

"Mr. Betts is here," Fern called up. "He said hold on one minute. He wishes to see the women before you take them. He has ten men with him. Wow."

A moment later, Fred dashed up the stairs, where Pam met him. "Dad, we've got them covered up. They are nearly naked and horribly scared. Be soft and gentle, please."

"You have done fantastically well, Pam, Lindsey, all of you. I just want a peek at their faces for now. Oh god! I recognize the one you are holding, Monique! That the missing Department of Law attorney, Miss Lynn Esterbrook! Okay, what's the plan?"

"Teleport to the tunnel and walk down the tunnel until we get close enough to use our Magical Door spells to get them to the Infirmary, dad," Pam explained.

"Okay, kids, best get to it. Message me if you need anything. Our men will secure this place and gather evidence. Again, I thank you all; there are just no words to thank you enough. Now get to it."

Pam and her father watched as the six waved their wands and spoke clearly, "Teleport: Blackbury's Telluride Tunnel Entrance." However, neither heard any words but "Teleport." All vanished.

"Come. We need to search this place, Pam. I assume that you and your friends below want to lend a hand?" he grinned.

"You bet, dad!" Indeed, they all really enjoyed being officially deputized and instructed on how to search. Five of his men remained on top alert, just in case a Death Stalker should choose to appear unexpectedly. One tied up Jack and stood guard over him.

"Here we are, Pong Su. We are in a long tunnel, smooth stone flooring, with no bumps, ridges, or obstructions. We need to walk down here a ways before we get close enough to get you into our Infirmary. Can you walk?" Lindsey asked. Behind her, she heard the others explaining the same thing to the others.

"Yes, but only very slowly. I can't breathe much either." Bravely, the blind woman attempted to take a step. Lindsey saw instantly that she would need to support the woman; her balance was most precarious. The women could only take very tiny steps and required a continuous hold around their waists

230

to keep them from falling. Progress was excruciatingly slow, Lindsey thought. Frequently, they had to stop to allow the women to catch their breaths. No good having them faint here in the tunnel. Earlier this morning, they had all rushed down the tunnel at a good clip, taking about fifteen minutes to reach Telluride. Now an hour passed as the nearly helpless women struggled down the stone, underground tunnel. Their steel tipped heels clicked along, marking their progress.

At last, Lindsey saw the kitchen ahead. "Just a little ways more, Pong. You can do it." Finally, she saw Professor Cho Lin waiting for them. The professor cast a Magical Door and opened it. Cho Lin held her hands across her mouth to keep from emitting shocked gasps at the sight she was seeing. Tears trickled down her cheeks as well. Lindsey stepped Pong through the doorway and set foot in the Infirmary's emergency room.

Lindsey had silently cast and exchanged several Message spells with Governor Alister. He now knew the names of the women as they arrived. "Welcome, Miss Pong Su. I am Governor Alister, and this is our esteemed Doctor Caterwall. You are totally safe and free from the likes of Dominus. You are in our hospital's emergency room where we are going to first examine you, safely remove your constraints, and then set about fully healing you up. Is this okay with you?"

"Yes, but if you cannot, please, please, we all beg of you, kill us. None of us want to have to live like this. Promise me you will do this, if you can't heal us," she begged him.

"Oh, I'm sure that we can get you fixed up, Miss Su. Now Lindsey is going to lead you to the exam table and help you get up on it." Alister didn't answer her question, but was very gentle with her. Lindsey followed the directions Doctor Caterwall indicated and soon had Pong Su beside the table. At last, Lindsey had to remove the warm blanket, and hoped that no one would say anything to upset Pong Su or the others. Doctor Caterwall's eyes nearly popped out of his head, but he was professional enough not to make a sound that might alarm his patient. Together, they Levitated her up and onto the table. Lindsey stepped back, ready to assist in any way possible.

One by one, the others arrived and were likewise placed

on one of the seven tables. As Doctor Caterwall took a cursory observation of each patient, he then covered them back up with the blankets. Now came the hard work.

"Kids, this may prove educational for you," Governor Alister spoke softly. "Dominus has a nasty habit of installing booby traps for the unwary. Before I allow Doctor Caterwall to proceed with the healings, we must discover any and all traps and disarm them, before we can safely remove their constraining clothing, such as it is. Now then, are you ready to learn a new spell?" Lindsey was all ears, though she wished Pam were here to learn it as well.

"This spell is not in the official Grade spell books, it is called Detect Traps, one of my own little contributions." He spent the next ten minutes going over its casting. Then, he had them cast it on the first patient, Pong Su. He cast his spell on her as well. "Now we look closely for signs of magical enchantments. This is slow and methodical work, kids. If we goof and miss one, Miss Pong Su may be harmed further." Carefully, they all looked over her shoes, especially the two padlocks. Lindsey clearly saw the shimmering energy around each.

Amanda, already keenly attuned to magical energy traces, saw them first, however, pointing them out to the others. "Excellent Amanda. Yes, there is some kind of trap on each padlock. Now we must determine what kind of trap and how to disarm it."

"I think it is a simple Ball of Fire spell, sir," Ashley decided to speak what she had been sensing.

"I concur, Ashley. Well done. How about the rest of you? Can you sense that is the spell that will detonate should we attempt to unlock these boots?" Slowly, they all saw that this was indeed the spell in effect. "How should this one be defused?" he asked.

"Dispel Magic ought to do it," Lindsey replied.

"Right. Remember that it was probably Dominus himself who cast it, so it may take us a fair number of tries to disarm it. Let's all have a shot at it." For three minutes, they continued to fire off Dispel Magic spells on the two padlocks.

At last, Amanda announced, "That did it. It's gone."

"Ah good, but let's not be hasty. Let's all check once more. There may well be another here as well. After a couple more minutes, they all agreed there were no more surprises. Lindsey did the honors of unlocking the two padlocks, removing her boots. Lindsey placed them in one corner of the room, starting a pile.

"Let's check on the other boots, shall we," Alister suggested. This way, they would be likely looking for the same trap. Fifteen minutes later, Lindsey placed the fifth pair of boots into the pile, along with the five sets of fine silk hose.

"Now for the harder part, we must examine the corset from all angles. A trap may be placed on the front busk, but more than likely on the drawstrings or padlocks on the back side. Let's be thorough." Again, they cast their new spell and began studying Pong's exotic corset.

Fifteen minutes later, they all agreed that undoing the backside padlock would unleash a cloud of poison gas. Again, a Dispel Magic spell would remove it. Several dozens of attempts later, it vanished. However, they searched for additional traps. Indeed, they found that loosening the strings could cause an explosion, very likely killing the person who undid the strings. Sometime later, Pong Su felt the long anticipated release of the intense pressure around her waist. She could breathe easily once more, a great relief. A while later, Lindsey placed the sixth corset onto the pile of items.

"Are they ready for their healing now?" asked Lindsey. All six women were now naked, lying on the exam tables.

"Prudence, I always believe in prudence. We have found three sets of traps on each of them, there may be more. Let's give them another close look before we start in on the healing, shall we?" Lindsey liked his attitude. He was taking no chances with these women's lives. She tucked this observation away for future reference. A half hour later, they finally decided that they had found them all.

"Okay, first we observe their eyes. I believe a simple Dispel Magic will cure their blindness, Alister," Doctor Caterwall announced. The eight of them stood over Pong Su and began casting their Dispel Magic spells. Considering just how powerful Dominus was, many attempts were unsuccessful. At last, Alister's did the job, and the grey orbs began changing taking on a bluish hue. Soon Pong said that she could see light. Before long, her vision was back to normal.

She looked at herself and especially her enormous breasts and gasped. "What has he done to me?"

"He has used magic to permanently enlarge them," Doctor Caterwall explained very professionally. "While it will not be a problem to re-grow your arms, Pong Su, with your breasts, well, we don't know what they were like before. Some women prefer to have larger breasts, so we will be diminishing them bit by bit. You need to tell us when to stop. This is your opportunity to have them the exact size that you wish them to be." She began to understand, because he was speaking slowly, allowing her time to absorb what he was saying. At last, she grinned, and he began casting Diminish spells.

Sometime later, she flushed and said, "You can stop now; they look perfect. Thanks." Lindsey suspected that they were larger than what she had before, but no one said a word. If she now had the breasts she had always wanted, this was a small benefit of her long torture.

"Excellent. Lindsey, Cho Lin, if you would be so kind as to dress her and put this hospital gown on her? Then, take her into the next room. I'll be along shortly to begin the arm regrowth process. Pong Su, the worst is now over. It is a simple matter of time, and you will be as good as you were." She smiled, though she didn't believe him.

An hour later and all five women were dressed and lying on soft beds. Each had been given a strong potion and was now sleeping. Before he administered the first dose, he explained that for the next couple of days, they would be tied to the bed so that they could not move or injure their growing arms. They were also under orders to drink as much of his special milk as they possibly could. Lil stayed by the side of her sister, even after she fell into a deep sleep.

Finally, Lynn remained. Doctor Caterwall intentionally left her for last. Something about her behavior bothered him. As the group approached her, he finally said what he had been feeling, "Something's not quite right about Lynn here. I don't know what. Before I start in on her healing potions, we ought to figure out what else may be wrong with her."

"The others were normals, Doctor Caterwall," Lindsey said. "Lynn is a witch. Could that have something to do with it?"

"You are quite an observant young lady. Yes, the others are normals. They had no idea of the nature of the spell or quite what we were doing to them, just accepting it as they could observe for themselves. Now, Lynn is a competent witch. Yet, she has been acting strangely, which is why I have left her until last. I think that I know what is going on, but since she cannot speak, I have to become cleverer than normal. Please watch her reactions closely, in case I miss something."

He then stood before Lynn, who looked up at him with her one eye. "Now then, Lynn, the first spell that we wish to cast on you to repair your vision is the Ball of Fire spell. Does that meet with your approval?"

Lindsey and the others watched. To her utter amazement, Lynn nodded affirmative. "Good, good. Now once that is done, we should use the Disintegrate spell to fix up your good eye. Is that a good plan of action for us to follow? Just nod yes or no, please." Again, Lynn nodded that is was.

Doctor Caterwall backed away and the others followed him. "See what I mean?"

"She said yes to both, but that doesn't make any sense at all. Even a first year student would have answered no to both," declared a confused Ashley. The others agreed with her.

"Precisely so, something else is wrong with her."

At nearly the same moment, Lindsey and Ashley called out, "Idiot Mind!" Alister and Doctor Caterwall grinned.

"That would explain it. The real question is how do we prove it? If we treat her for that and it is something else that is wrong, we run the risk of creating complications."

"Say, Pam couldn't even count to two," Lindsey suggested, "Maybe we could test her arithmetic."

"She's supposed to be an attorney. Maybe we could ask her something about that and see if she knows," Ashley suggested. A bit later, Lynn responded by putting up two fingers when asked how much was three plus two. She nodded yes, when asked if Dominus went to prison because he was innocent. The diagnosis was confirmed. Doctor Caterwall then set to work healing both the effects of the Idiot Mind spell and her grievous mutilations. She would need several weeks of bed rest healing; the others, he expected would only need a week for their arms to be re-grown.

With all patients now sleeping, their bodies hard at work recovering, the group met in the emergency room once more. Ashley asked the question that she'd been stewing over in her mind ever since they found the women. "I know that their bodies will be fine and back to normal in a few days. But what about their emotional trauma? I mean they must have been raped, tortured, humiliated, and who knows what all by Dominus. Won't they have deep emotional scars forever? How can Peg ever go back to work at her job as a bartender? I mean she will likely be spooked by every man she sees?"

Governor Alister replied, "In the most drastic cases, a Mind Wipe could be used to erase all memories of the time they were imprisoned and tortured. However, I find permanently erasing someone's memories terribly offensive. This, I fear, may be a wound that we cannot heal."

"Alister, I have an idea. I know a colleague who may be able to help," Doctor Caterwall scratched his head. "I believe he would be willing to lend us his expertise in this matter."

Just then, Pam, her father, and the others came walking in, "Hi Princess," called out Jim to Ashley, who blushed.

"How are they doing?" asked Fred, quite seriously.

"All will recover fully on the physical side," Doctor Caterwall replied. "Emotionally, that has yet to be determined. Dominus laid many traps for us to undo to free them, I will say that."

"Pam, we learned a new spell, Detect Traps!" Lindsey excitedly said to Pam, whose eyes opened wide.

"Coolest! So did we—learn new things. I got to do a thorough dusting for fingerprints! I picked up one hundred of them, and Kathy took twenty-five DNA samples, most from his bed. If Dominus was in that house and we find his and their DNA on that bed, we have him good this time!"

"Hey, I got to search for secret doors," Deiter hastened to add. Peaches added her, "Me too."

"Seriously, Governor Alister, the Department of Magical Misuse extends a huge thank you for taking in these six women and healing them. I know it is a bit on the costly side. I will see what I can do to get you some compensation," Fred said.

"Don't bother, Fred. You need those funds elsewhere," Alister replied.

"But I said that I would pay for their healing," Lindsey protested.

"Indeed you did, Miss Barron. Seldom have I ever seen such a generous heart. However, I do believe that the school has a little excess funds that can be used. If we are short, I will accept your offer, Lindsey."

"Wow, you offered to pay for their healing?" Deiter exclaimed. "That's a small fortune! Why? You could have sent them to the Department of Magical Healing."

"Yes, perhaps we could have, Deiter, but a wizard did this to them, and I wanted to show them that not all wizards and witches are bad. Healing them is the very least thing that we can do for them. Besides, if we sent them there, they or their families might have to pay, and they might not be able to afford it," Lindsey explained.

"You ought to be in Black Hall, Lindsey, that's all I got to say," Deiter replied, Lindsey saw that he was serious, though.

"Well, look at the time!" Alister interrupted. "If you hurry, you all have time to change and join everyone for the Halloween Dinner and then the dance. I assume that you all wish to dance?" He teased them, of course.

"Shouldn't we sit around here to help them?" Monique asked.

"Tonight, they will sleep soundly. Tomorrow morning, I expect they can use some morale boosting," Doctor Caterwall. "Go enjoy yourselves. I'm very pleased with your actions today, all of you. You're a credit to our fine school and yourselves." He gave Lindsey a pat on her butt. They needed no further encouragement.

"Wait until I email my folks about this!" exclaimed Jeannette.

"Ja, me too," echoed Katja.

As Lindsey passed the pile of discarded clothes and boots, she cast a shrink spell on them and threw them into a small sack. Instinctively, she took them with her. Perhaps there might be another clue in them. She threw the sack in her bottom drawer, and they all headed down to the fancy Halloween dinner.

When everyone took their seats, Governor Alister got their attention and explained what Lindsey and her group had done today in Telluride. He gave each person credit and had each one stand to receive a round of applause from their fellow students. "Once more, it proves that if we all stick together and work as a team, we are stronger then the forces of evil out there. Now, enough of this; as you kids say, it's party time. No, I'm sorry. I have it wrong. Party on!" Everyone roared and dove into the fancy food especially prepared for this evening.

The chicken was cut into the shapes of bats and goblins. Potatoes looked more like skeletons. Their punch took on the look of blood. Even the peas were doctored to look like the brains of a ghoul. With the meal out of the way, everyone headed up to change into their costumes. Now came the scramble to invent a costume at the last minute.

Amanda dressed Jeannette up in the Indian maiden costume that Ashley wore last year. Then, she cast an illusion spell and made Katja also look like one as well. Never much on costumes, Lindsey donned her fairy costume, which needed some last minute major surgery. She'd really been growing since last Halloween. At last dolled up, they headed down to the dance.

"Ah there you are," Henry Waldorf called out to Amanda. "I heard about what you did this afternoon. We all went to the movie, I think from now on I ought to go with you, you know, to lend you my strong arm." He was teasing, of course. Amanda was definitely the physically stronger of the two. "I bought you a little something for tonight." He pinned a small golden spider onto her dress.

"Cool, Henry, it's beautiful! Thanks, let's dance," Amanda said, whipping him out onto the dance floor. He was an accountant by heart, but held her in the highest regard.

Once more, Lindsey just could not figure out how it came to be ten so darn quickly! Dancing with Andy had only begun when it was over. However, this time, Lindsey was jerked off her cloud by Governor Alister. "May I have a word with you?" She saw that he had already pulled Pam over to the side of the dining hall. She was standing with her father. Lindsey had thought that he had returned to Sterling or her ranch.

Alister created a Magical Door to his office and the four stepped through it. "Have a seat, please. It seems that we have a slight problem, and we wanted to clear it with you two. The Death Stalker, Jack Benson. Fred has checked, and there are no crimes attributed to him, excepting helping keep those women imprisoned at that home. He was recruited this year and really has nearly nothing of value to tell us. Pam has put in a good word for him, telling how he was sympathetic towards the women and did all that he could to make them as comfortable as possible, under the circumstances. Admittedly, he ought to have rescued them and turned himself in to the authorities."

"The problem that we face is this. If we throw him in jail, Dominus most certainly will attempt to free him and then kill him for allowing you kids to raid his home and free his prisoners. He is a walking deadman, if we do that. However, there may be two other possibilities. One, we could fake his escape from custody, allowing him to return to Dominus and make his case that he was overpowered, but eventually was able to escape. If Dominus buys it, Jack will act as a spy for us in return for complete immunity from his prior actions and any that he may be forced into doing for Dominus in the future. Two, we could turn him loose and let him do his best to go into hiding until Dominus and his men are finally apprehended."

Lindsey thought a moment before replying, "Sir, I don't think that Dominus is going to be that stupid. I mean he's likely to torture Jack into telling him the truth or used truth potions on him. I know that I would do that if I could before I would trust him again. Can he actually find a way to hide out from Dominus, somewhere he cannot be found? Is that realistic?"

Fred answered that one. "We have some secret federal locations where he could stay. None has yet been breached. Personally, I think that is his best chance to stay alive, but that means not trying him for what he's done."

"I think that he deserves another chance," Lindsey replied. "After all, he made sure that we all didn't go up there, tried his best to warn us of their condition, and cooked for them. I say give him another chance." Pam smiled; evidently, she thought the same way.

"Good. Then I will make the arrangements. On tomorrow's news, you will hear that he was killed making his escape. We will be burying a recent person whose build is similar and who was terribly burned in a car accident. If Dominus should exhume the grave, the body will not be readily identifiable. Again, Pam, Lindsey, I cannot thank you enough for what you have done today. I'd best get the wheels in motion; time is of the essence. This has not yet hit the news, but it will soon. Night Alister." He gave Pam a long hug, shook Lindsey's hand, and left.

The two girls walked back to their dorm room. "Pam, you and Monique were terrific today. I don't know how you did it, but good going, Madam Sleuth," Lindsey complimented her friend.

"All in a day's work," Pam teased her.

Chapter 14—Recoveries

After breakfast on Sunday morning, Lindsey, Pam, Ashley, Lil, and Jeannette headed down to see how the women were faring. With the exception of Lil, they all knew the immediate needs these women would have. Lindsey herself had already faced being strapped down for several days while her arms were regrown. She had to depend utterly on her friends for everything, especially eating.

They found all six women awake, though Lynn was too groggy to pay them much attention. Already, Lindsey could see the ghostly outlines of their arms as they were slowly materializing. "Hi all. Looks like it is working," Lindsey said cheerily, as they pulled up chairs beside the five women.

"You look a whole lot better today, Peg, honest you do. I can see your arms regrowing," Lil tried to be as cheerful as Lindsey, though she found it very difficult to do so.

"The nurse—she held up a mirror so I could see them," Peg admitted. "They look so thin."

"The process takes several days," Pam declared, "so this is to be expected. When Lindsey's arms were regrowing, they first looked like this too. You will see."

"I don't know how to ever thank you," Peg began bawling like a baby. It was catching. The other four also began to cry, so overcome with emotion with no real outlet.

"Just recover and get on with your lives and do good," Lindsey jested. She allowed them to finish crying.

Peg finally recovered, "Lil, it was so horrible! I was walking to my car and my body just froze stiff! I couldn't move a muscle. Then, I saw him, you know that evil wizard. He toyed with me, said I'd do fine. Two men held out my arms, and he did something with his wand. God, the pain. I couldn't move, not even scream out! Then he did something else, and everything went totally black, and I couldn't see ever again! I passed out, I'm sure of that. When I woke up, I must have been in that house. They never moved me from there after that. But I couldn't breathe! I know I must have screamed when I tried to move my arms, and they weren't there, but I passed out again. When I woke, I had to pee. That's when I tried to get up and walk, though I don't have any idea where I was going to walk. I fell over. God, those boots made walking almost impossible for us all. That's when Pong began talking to me, asking what I needed. She told me that Lynn would help me to get to the bathroom."

"Lil, you have no idea what tortures we all had to endure, just trying to live. Every now and then that same evil man, I think it was him, would come and use me as a plaything. It was awful, but the strangest thing, just trying to live was far worse, far, far worse than the few minutes he spent with me. We could only sit there and do nothing. It was a major ordeal just to get to the bathroom! Poor Lynn, she had to feed us, but it took us a while to figure out that she only had the one arm left and no legs. She was far worse off than we were."

Lindsey felt a tremendous sympathy for these women. "I know, he did that to me last year, stunned me, cut off my arms, much like yours, and blinded me, even sewed my mouth shut. I don't know what I would have done if I didn't have such good friends to look after me while I was healed. So Peg, Pong, Estelle, Rika, and Mimi, you can count on us. Some of us will be here with you all the day long, until you go to sleep at night. Say, have you been drinking your special milk? Growing bones need lots of it." The five helped the women down another large glass.

Estelle then asked a key question, "Whatever are we going to do when we are healed? I mean if I go back to my job, he'll know where to find me again. What's to keep him from kidnaping me again a month from now? I'll be living in total fear every second of every day!"

Lindsey had no answer. Pam did. "I've been thinking about that. I figured you would think of this. I know I would. I've got some ideas I'm going to investigate. When I have some answers, I'll let you know. You have every right to be worried. After all, he could just kidnap another Diviner, find out where you are at, and come get you again, that is, if he wants you back as his play toys." Poor Pam couldn't think of any better way to disguise what they had been to Dominus. Even so, all five began to cry again.

Rika begged Jeannette not to leave her; she couldn't understand much English and was very scared. Jeannette explained that there were twenty Dutch students here from Utrecht and that one of them would be with her all the time, taking turns sitting beside her bed. The relief on the young woman's face was very apparent to Lindsey and Ashley.

"How did you ever find us? We had long ago given up all hope of ever being rescued, we just kept praying to somehow die and be done with it," Pong asked.

"Pam and Monique's doing," Lindsey explained. "Pam's a beginning Sleuth, a detective." She nudged Pam to continue.

"Well, Lindsey, Ashley, and I were kidnaped last year. They kept us in a house in Telluride, just as you were kept, only this one was mostly abandoned. Anyway, I found out who owned the house, the Mac Fluide Enterprises. When we were rescued, they smashed down the front wall the house to get to us, you see. Monique and I kept checking back on that house to see if it was being repaired. After all, if we owned a house that had been damaged, we'd have gotten it fixed up quickly. However, it just sat there, a derelict. Now it has been condemned and will be torn down next spring if it is not repaired by then. I got curious and checked the registry to see if this company owned anything else in Telluride. Sure enough, only one other home, the one you were being held inside."

"This was our first trip into town from school; we only get four visits each year, you see. So Monique and I just had to see what or who lived in this company-owned house. We did not expect to find you all, though. We did know about you, however. Lil had me searching for Peg here, trying to find out what had happened to her. So we were just very lucky to find you."

"Thank you little sister," Peg managed to grin towards Lil.

"Anything for my pretty big sister," she replied.

"They asked us about our family, Lil. Our folks want to come to see us, all of ours," she rolled her head toward the others. "I didn't want mom and dad seeing me like this. Neither did the others. We've asked them to come next Saturday; we are supposed to be healed by then. It won't be so shocking to our parents or so humiliating for us," Peg explained.

Just then, Deiter, Peaches, and several others came to relieve Lindsey. To Lindsey and Jeannette's surprise, Deiter spoke in Dutch to Rika, "Hi, I'm Deiter Cross. It was my high honor to assist in your rescue yesterday." She smiled, thinking this was a bit much, but Rika enjoyed his attention and seemed pleased that he spoke her language somewhat. Deiter gave Lindsey a satisfied look as she left.

"Tons to do now," Pam exclaimed. "Check on the DNA results; check on the fingerprint matches." She began a litany of test results she needed to examine. Lindsey smiled. Pam was in seventh heaven, if only for a few days at least.

Looking up from her laptop in the study hall, Pam declared to her group, "Proof positive! Dominus left his DNA on the bed sheets, along with the six women. We have him for rape and false imprisonment, if we cannot prove he did the mutilations. We've identified six other Death Stalkers who were in that house, including Nadia van Nye. This sadistic, evil man is going to go away for life, once he is caught!"

"Yes, but how did he know that these homes owned by that company were abandoned?" asked Lindsey. "I mean, he was running the risk that someone from the company might have dropped by to check on the house at any time, to say nothing of keeping the grass mowed and all that."

"I know, Lindsey. I've been thinking about that very thing. With the other house, they seem to have just abandoned it. Yet its lawn was tended, leaves raked in the fall. Deiter checked with the neighbors of their house yesterday. One of the neighbor boys has a yearly contract to mow the lawn and rake the leaves, but none of the neighbors has ever seen anyone coming to the house, though many saw lights on at night. Some even knocked, but no one ever answered. Strange isn't it? I guess the company has little interest in these houses, so why haven't they sold them long ago? I have too many questions," she stated flatly.

On Wednesday, the five women were allowed freedom of motion, though Lynn was still pretty much out of it. Their arms were very solid now, and they no longer needed to be kept motionless. Curiously, Deiter's mother had taken it upon herself to purchase a complete set of clothes for all six women. Deiter had the honor of presenting her gift to the women, which he did in a grand manner, Lindsey thought. However, all five now looked very healthy and well dressed, which did much to restore their self-respect.

Doctor Verner arrived that evening, while Lindsey and her crew were sitting with the women, chatting and attempting to do a little of their homework. Jeannette was having Rika give them all practice in speaking Dutch, which brought a real smile to her countrywoman.

"Ve are now going to discharge the pent up emotional trauma that you have suffered," Doctor Verner spoke with a German accent. "We do not want to erase your memories, only remove the harmfulness of them on your psyche. This way, you will be able to remember all that you have experienced, but you will not be troubled by them. Is this acceptable to you?" He addressed Peg first. She nodded.

"When I cast my spell, you will be remembering all the trauma that you have experienced recently. It will be playing back in your mind, and the harmful energies will be being discharged. It is expected that you will be flooded with all sorts of emotions. This is to be expected; cry, scream, shake, whatever it is, just let it go by you. I promise you that this will be the last time these memories will ever bother you. All set?" She nodded. "Okay, I want you to focus on the moment when you were first abducted." She closed her eyes and that terrible night appeared in her mind. Doctor Verner waved his wand in a most peculiar manner, Lindsey thought. "Memories: Discharge!" he commanded.

Neither Lindsey nor any of the others were prepared for what happened next. Peg began shaking, screaming at the top of her lungs, and crying at the same time. Doctor Verner cast a diminution sound spell so her noise didn't carry so much. Lindsey could see her going through all manner of traumas. In five minutes, it was all over. She ceased crying, shaking, and all of her worries, fears, and terrors were gone. She gave a little chuckle and smiled. "I feel so light I might float away, Doctor."

"Ah, that is normal, Miss Ames. Later on, if you discover more traumas that we did not reach today, please let me know, and we can have another go at it." She thanked him profusely, and he went on to the next patient. An hour later, he finally finished up with Lynn, who was still mostly out of it, though she was clearly eating and drinking now. She slept most of the day as her body was regenerating nearly a third of its total mass.

When he was done, he then spoke to Lindsey. "I am told that you have experienced a good deal of similar traumas in the past, Miss Barron, is it?"

"Well, yes, Lindsey Barron. I'm fine," she replied.

"Shall we see about that?" he smiled and cast his spell on her. Lindsey found herself re-living first her first year fall that had broken her arms in three places, then the attack by Dominus, cutting off her newly grown hands, and then again the losing of her arms last year. She shrieked in pain, cried, and shook, though she had no recollection of having done so; Pam and Ashley told her about it later. When the spell ended, she too felt really light and cheerful, and thanked him.

Doctor Verner also cast the spell on Ashley, who re-lived the car crash when she was two and lost her arms. Her reactions were vastly more subdued than the others had been. Her trauma had been smallest of them all.

"Well, now I am off again. More patients to see. Dominus and his cutthroats are keeping me busier than normal. It's been a pleasure, Miss Barron, Miss Stokes-Compton." He shook their hands and left. As he did so, Lindsey spied a smiling Governor Alister standing beside the door. He winked at the two girls. Lindsey realized that he had been behind having Doctor Verner aid them as well. She smiled back.

By Saturday, Lynn could finally speak again, but she was only allowed to sit up in bed. One of the Bradbury school buses brought their families from the Denver airport for a loving, welcome reunion. Because it was such a large group, they met in the dining room, and Lynn's bed was temporarily moved there as well. Governor Alister had all the students who participated in the rescue operation meet with the women's families as well. After nearly an hour of being thanked repeatedly, Lindsey was grateful for the respite when Alister began speaking once more.

"Miss Betts and I have taken your fears that Dominus will try to abduct you again seriously. Hence, we have arranged for your security once you return to your normal lives. Via the various Departments of Security, a Security man will be assigned to each of you. For example, Miss Ames, if you return to your bartending job, he or she will appear to be your co-worker, but accompany you either openly or discretely. None of you needs fear that Dominus Malefic will abduct you again. They will provide for your security until this sadistic, evil man is once again captured. This protection will cost you nothing. It is the very least we wizards and witches can do for you, who have suffered so much at the hands of this wicked man."

Of course, this appealed to everyone, particularly the relatives, who greatly feared for their daughter's safety. He got a loud round of applause. During a lull, Deiter whispered to Lindsey, "I've never felt so great, so powerful. We sure did a good deed, didn't we? We all make one terrific team!"

Lindsey didn't quite know what to make of this, she replied, "We do. It is a good feeling to be able to help someone. Please thank your mother for getting those clothes for them. I was thinking that we could perhaps order them online. They look really nice, don't they—the women we've rescued."

"I'll tell mom. Yes, we've given them their lives back. Say, the clothes they were wearing, those are called fetish clothes. I looked it up. Guys find it a real romantic turn on to have their wives and girlfriends dressed up fancy like that," he flushed and added really quickly, "or so I have been told."

Lindsey, who had never seen such before, had no idea how to respond. Pam, however, did. She had overheard them and whispered to them, "There is nothing wrong with dressing fetish for your marital partner. It adds to the relationship, but it most definitely belongs in the bedroom, not on public display."

"You know about this stuff?" asked an incredulous Deiter.

"Well not directly. After all, none of that getup would make me any less homely, now would it?" Pam stated flatly, promptly ending the conversation.

Sunday night, speculation began running wild. The Presidential Election was two days away. All the candidates were airing last minute predictions and ads, naturally. Five times this evening Dominus interrupted the regular telecasting to deliver his last minute pitches. Hugo insisted on updating his polls every hour Sunday night. President Lucius continued to lose ground, while Dominus continued to gain. Senator Snow, still hospitalized, also lost ground to Dominus.

"Why do people vote for that rotten criminal?" Emilio angrily yelled. He was losing patience with the whole campaign news. "Let him get elected and then thrown into jail where he belongs!"

"I've had enough of this," Pam declared and went in search of Monique.

Ashley decided to see if she could divine the outcome of the election. She sat back and quietly concentrated. After a while, she grinned. "Hey sis. I know who is going to win the election!"

Lindsey stopped watching the news and gave her sister her complete attention. "Senator Snow will win with 51% of the vote. Dominus will get 39% of the vote. President Lucius will get only 10%. He's going to suffer the worst defeat of any first term president in history. Now let's all forget this stuff and work on our homework." Lindsey grinned; soon all Yellow Hall knew of her prediction. Many wrote down the percentages, intending to check how accurate Ashley was with her prediction. By Monday supper, everyone in the school knew about Ashley's presidential predictions.

Indeed, on Monday, all the professors seemed to be oblivious of the exciting presidential race, which was about to culminate on Tuesday. All assigned mountains of homework, at least that was Lindsey's viewpoint. That didn't stop anyone from paying some attention to the news either Monday night or during the daytime on Tuesday afternoon. Several professors had to order students to stop watching the polling place results on their laptops and pay attention to class.

After supper that night, everyone gathered around the big screen to watch the results as they came in, all the while making a halfhearted attempt to do homework. Lindsey, Ashley, and their Dutch friends went into the study hall instead. Pam soon joined them. "With the computerized voting machines, the final results will be in by ten tonight," Pam announced. "Then, we can put all of this nonsense behind us. I'll be darned if I am going to do Emilio and Kathy's homework for them while they sit there watching the dumb TV!"

Sure enough, around ten, the rest of Lindsey's gang returned to the study hall room. Amanda called out, "Ashley! You are incredible. You got the winning percentages correct! Senator Missy Snow is our next president. How about that! Dominus lost. I bet that will put him in his place. Honestly, the nerve of that criminal! Now I bet he is broke. Hugo said that he has spent at least twenty million dollars on the race. Well, that is his guess, mind you. No one knows for sure, except Dominus."

"Yes, but that means there are something like ten million voters in our country who supported him. Now that *is* scary," Pam declared in her usual flat tone of voice.

Chapter 15—Victory Celebrations

Late Tuesday night, Hugo showed a cameo appearance of President Lucius visiting President-elect Missy Snow in her hospital bed. He gave her a warm congratulation and offered her full access to his office so that the transition of power would be a smooth one. She had yet to name a vice-president, however. From their US history class, Lindsey and her friends knew roughly how much work Missy now faced, choosing her cabinet members and so on.

Lying on his plush divan in his secret office in the now deserted manufacturing plant in Montrose, Dominus watched the election results come in. Nadia's body was draped over his, feeding him caviar and crackers, occasionally stealing a kiss as well. Around ten, his top two dozen Death Stalkers arrived, teleporting to the main factory floor, before climbing the stairs to his office.

"Come in, come in. Caviar and the finest wine; help yourselves. Tonight we have everything to celebrate, smashing success." Dominus was in the best humor that anyone had seen for days now. A bit later, Chief Engineer Smythe St. Johns arrived, carrying a briefcase, triply locked and with appropriate spells cast on it as well.

"Come, come in Doctor Smythe! I owe you everything. Smashing success, beyond my wildest predictions," Dominus greeted his man. Even Nadia got up and put her long arms around him, flirtingly leading him over to her master's divan.

The old engineer smiled; his long unused talents had been recognized many years ago by the then young Dominus. He had nurtured this engineer carefully, finding that money was what Smythe greatly desired. Already, he had funneled over ten million dollars into Smythe's offshore bank accounts.

The bespectacled older man, grey hair now prominently replacing his brown, carefully unlocked his briefcase. "Sir, I have the final production statistics. One million three hundred fifty-five rings are in the hands of your supporters with an additional two thousand more in possession of those with the diamonds. My batch enchantment process has worked to perfection, Dominus. Thank you for having faith in my research. This is indeed a glorious day for us powerful wizards! Here are the final lists, which indicate who is in possession of the more critical diamond rings. This incredibly lengthy list contains those with the lesser rings. Mind you, a few are in the hands of the authorities, but that couldn't be helped. However, those idiots still haven't got a clue about my work."

"Here is the small laptop, which contains the electronic version of these data. All the factory workers have been dismissed. A few who you didn't trust have been given rings. When you are ready for activation, let me know, and I will power up the machine for the last time." Having finished his rehearsed speech, he complimented Nadia, "My you look ravishing this evening, Nadia." She beamed, having purchased this elegant, but expensive, red velvet gown especially for this occasion.

To the old man's surprise, Dominus got up from the divan, came over to him, and shook his hand, while warmly patting his back. "Well done, my old friend. I couldn't have done this without you. One day in the not too distant future, you shall take your rightful place at my side as the world's foremost magical research engineer. Well done, Doctor Smythe, well done indeed. Come, celebrate with Nadia and me." He helped himself to some of the caviar and a large cup of wine.

"Boss," Ben Johnson spoke up, a note of concern in his voice. Dominus gave him a sign to continue speaking. "I don't understand. We've lost the election by a large margin. I don't understand what we are celebrating. I speak for many of the others here too; we don't get it."

"Come, come, my top Death Stalkers. Gather around, help yourselves to some wine; it is a hundred dollars a bottle. I prefer wine to champagne. Let me explain our incredible victory." As the twenty-four helped themselves, Dominus went on with his explanation.

"Gentlemen, this race was never about my being elected to the presidency. That's pure folly. We all know the instant I set foot in public, the Department of Law will be all over me and thee. They would never allow one as powerful as me ever to ascend to their President post, what with their silly concept that a criminal can't hold office. That is not the Golden Path that we are following. Look at how ineffective the office of the President actually is. Congress can override him, and the Justice system can do so too. No, that is a dead-end position from which feeble attempts to rule are done at this time. No, one day now soon, I will ascend to the throne of the United States as their king, with sole and total power over everyone! That lies at the very end of the Golden Path."

"Tonight, we celebrate because we have just taken one huge step towards that end. Never in my wildest speculations did I believe we would make such a giant step on our first try. Gentlemen, ten million voters supported us! Ten million! I had anticipated about one million, thus my engineering endeavors have barely captured a tenth of our supporters. Yet, I had planned for only five hundred thousand, figuring that would be a staggering sum, a whopping victory. We have doubled that and then some, beyond my wildest imagination!"

"Gentlemen, at midnight tonight, our chores in this country will become vastly, vastly easier for us to accomplish! At midnight, I will activate the rings. From now on, my top Death Stalkers, you will have abundant people to help you! More than abundant—we will be swimming in them!" Dominus gave a long, hearty laugh. Though his men chuckled along with him, none knew what he was laughing at or about, save Doctor Smythe, who grinned, knowing that his lifelong work was coming to fruition in mere hours.

"Now then, it is time I called President-elect Missy Snow to congratulate her and suggest that she can call on me for help when she needs it. Gentlemen, she will need it." A bit later, using a disposable cell phone, Dominus called Missy Snow and wished her the best. "Again, if you need my help with something, please don't hesitate to contact me. Unlike your predecessor, you are smarter than he is. I can be very helpful in the right situations. Goodbye for now, President Snow." He hung up and disintegrated the cell phone.

Around midnight, Dominus had the six workers who he did not trust brought in allegedly to watch the Grand Golden

Activation Ceremony. Doctor Smythe started up the energy generator. Dominus sat in the main seat, while Smythe adjusted the electrodes to his head. When all was ready, he threw the master switch, and a loud electrical hum echoed in the vast, now empty factory. Nadia watched fascinated, as Dominus seemed to be surrounded by a glow of golden energy. He waved his wand while speaking activation words. Then, he did it a second time, but no one knew what he was casting, save Doctor Smythe.

Shortly, the six men cried out in pain, staring at their ring fingers. Then Doctor Smythe shut off the machine, powering it down completely. He gave a small handheld device to Dominus and bowed respectfully to him. Dominus accepted the device as if it was a gift from god.

"Now behold, my trusted men, see what has become of my rings." Everyone stared at the ring fingers of the six men. To their utter amazement, the rings had somehow merged into their flesh. More precisely, the rings had become sub-dermal, that is, the rings had physically moved underneath their flesh. A thick layer of skin covered the rings, making them impossible to remove. However, their shape was visible clearly as a raised bump on their finger. "Over a million rings have become permanently implanted on our supporter's fingers, all thanks to your Herculean efforts at mass distribution."

"Now watch this." He scrolled to the name of one of those who he didn't trust and selected that man on the device. He spoke into the device, "Bob, I want you to smash in the face of Bill next to you for me. Thank you Bob." At once, Bob began throwing solid punches at Bill who backed away to keep from being killed. Satisfied, Dominus asked Bob to stop, quite pleased.

"You see men, from now on, whenever we need a little assistance, I merely dial up the appropriate supporter and politely ask him to do whatever is needed. I control absolutely over one million people at this moment and several thousand relatively important people as well. Our task of walking the Golden Path has just become a cakewalk!"

At last, the men understood fully what they had been working diligently on for the last many months, some over a year. They gave Dominus a loud and boisterous round of applause. However, it did not escape their attention that they alone did not wear these controlling rings. That their master trusted them implicitly only added to their adoration and devotion to Dominus. He had calculated this effect very carefully, however, using it to his advantage. Yes, Dominus now had a veritable army of both normals and wizards and witches spanning all corners of the United States.

Sometime later, everyone left, leaving Dominus and Nadia some personal time. Dominus sighed, "Nadia, I have been putting this off for far too long. It is long past time that I took a wife. Not having a wife during the election process may well have cost me further votes, though I hardly needed more. We ran totally out of rings by a factor of ten! What would you say to becoming my wife and being officially at my side, Nadia? How badly do you wish it?"

Nadia finally heard the words that her heart had longed to hear! "Yes, I would love to marry you and be your faithful wife. I know your fondest desires, Domi. If you would marry me, to show you my utter devotion to you and to show you how much it means to me, I want you to fetish my body as you did for your toys. Those silly women had no idea of your undying love and devotion to them, but I do. Let me do this for you, Domi. Besides, whenever you need me to be a witch, you can simply use a Morph spell on me, and then I can be back to my normal self and fight on your behalf. Unlike those silly norms, I can be both for you. I can give you what they could not."

"Nadia, you are indeed the woman of my dreams. I accept your gift with the love and devotion intended. Yes, you are right. I can use Morph spells when we need you. Shall we tie the knot tomorrow, my love?"

"Yes, Dominus, yes, but let's transform me to your ideal form tonight so tomorrow we can get married looking as we both desire. I love you like I've never loved anyone before!" They embraced long. Nadia's dreams of becoming the Fetish Queen were about to become real. It didn't matter that she really didn't love him or that he never confided his plans in her. This was her opportunity, and she seized the moment.

A bit later, an undressed Nadia stood proudly before him. He cast a number of spells on her body, beginning with his usual Stun spell so she couldn't move and possibly become harmed by his subsequent spells. Two precise cuts and Nadia's arms only extended two inches below her shoulders, a perfectly exquisite cut, Dominus thought. A series of Enlarge spells later and Dominus gazed upon the bosom of his dreams. Next, he brought out one of the finest corsets money could buy, along with properly elegant hose and very high heels. Once he finished dressing her properly, he stood back and made triply sure Nadia looked perfect. Satisfied at last, he cast his newest spell. "Meld: Corset," he commanded with a wave of his wand. It melted into her flesh, becoming an integral part of her anatomy. He cancelled his Stun spell and held on to her as she gasped, recovering from her ordeal on his behalf. He led her to their plush bedroom; both were elated over the transformation.

The next day, a fellow young woman and friend of Nadia's from the Netherlands, Jolina Wessel, became Nadia's handmaiden, dressing her for her formal wedding. She wore a strapless, white satin, full wedding gown. In the eyes of Dominus Malefic, she looked the perfect queen. On November 8, Nadia and Dominus were officially married.

Should someone better come along, he could always dispose of Nadia. For now, he did have strong feelings for her, but with a former Black Hall student, feelings never ruled the mind. Besides, without arms, he didn't have to worry about her experimenting with his handheld device.

As they enjoyed their hastily arranged reception, Nadia commented, "Dominus, I'm going to need a new wardrobe. Nothing fits; between the ideal waist and the full bosom, dear, nothing fits properly."

"Of course, we should see to it at once. Say, is not a honeymoon in order, my love?"

"Oh, yes, yes, indeed. Where would you like to go? Anywhere warm is fine with me. I'll have some difficulty in the snow with these heels."

"How about Tahiti? Fancy yourself at my side on the sandy, warm beaches?" She leaned over. Pressing her bosom onto his shoulder, she finally reached him and gave him a loving kiss. Mid-November, the happy couple spent two weeks in the sun, before returning to the States to set up housekeeping and get down to the business of the Golden Path.

In Nadia's mind, she was paying an almost trivial price to become the wife of the most powerful wizard in the world and his eventual Queen. Fetish Queen Nadia, now that appealed to her more than anything else ever had.

Around two in the morning, Ashley woke everyone in her bedroom up with her nightmarish scream. Lindsey got her calmed down with a quick Emotion: Calm spell. Still Ashley looked terribly frightened. "I, I just had a horrible premonition. Something horrid, really, really horrible has happened tonight and to a whole lot of people! I just know it! It's like the end of the world or something!"

Pam was all ears. She tried to get Ashley to relate more details of what happened. Unfortunately, it had occurred while she was in a deep sleep, and awake, she could not remember much of anything. "Rings, that's all I can remember, just rings, Pam. I'm sorry."

The next day, Professor Mary Ann, her Divination teacher looked just awful, far worse than normal, when Ashley showed up for her special Divination Theory II class after supper. "Did—did—did you sense it last night too, Ashley?" she asked, her voice full of real fear. Ashley related her nightmare. The two Diviners took comfort in each other; both knew that the other also knew. Something horrid had happened last night, something with wide-ranging, far-reaching consequences. Nothing, however, was reported on the news that day. Still, these two Diviners knew, just not the details.

Chapter 16—Thanksgiving and the Rodents

Lindsey and crew worked feverously to keep up with their homework load. Pam suggested that the professors had to load it on so that they could have the spare weeks in the fall and spring to take the foreign exchange students on their field trips. Lindsey thought that Pam was probably right with her suggestion.

Pam did share an email from her father with everyone. It seems that the gift rings of Dominus had either disappeared or merged into their owner's bodies. No one was quite sure just yet. Inquiries to those who had been known to have gotten one of those rings went unanswered. No one was talking about the rings anymore—not until Saturday, when Deiter came to find Lindsey and Pam. "Can I talk with you all in private?" he asked very subdued and mysteriously, totally out of character for him. The three went outside, where it was quite chilly.

"It's those cursed rings that Dominus was giving away. Henry Fielding was stupid enough to get one of the plain gold ones. Now he is in big, big trouble, and I really need your help and advice. He asked me to beg you to come, that's how scared he is," Deiter explained.

"Well, everyone was warned not to wear them," Pam declared flatly, but relented. "Let's go see him." That she might just find out some useful, key information totally overrode her concerns that she would be helping a Black Hall student. Deiter led them to the Formal Gardens, where only rotting pumpkins remained. It was deserted except for a shivering Henry Fielding, who got up from the stone bench the second he saw the trio coming his way.

"Thanks for coming! I didn't think you would come. I—I've been very stupid. I ought to have listened, but, well, I didn't. Please, you've got to help me."

Pam stated didactically, "Well, please start at the beginning and tell us what this is about; don't hold anything back or we may not be able to help at all." She didn't like Henry much.

"When I was in Telluride, I accepted one of those rings Dominus was giving out to his supporters. I thought it was cool, you know, to have one of those. Maybe they will become very valuable, maybe twenty years from now, and all that. Then during the night while I was sleeping, ah, Tuesday night, this happened!" He finally showed them his left hand ring finger.

The girls stared at it, and Pam began feeling it. Indeed, it looked as if the ring has somehow moved underneath his flesh! You could tell there was a ring there. The raised bump of flesh clearly marked where the ring now resided. "Does it hurt?" Lindsey asked, feeling the raised bump.

"No, it doesn't hurt; finger is kind of stiff, doesn't bend properly anymore."

"Well, I guess you have the ring permanently on now," Pam stated the plainly obvious.

The look of fear that came over Henry's face bespoke of something far more sinister. "It—it—it controls me! Dominus controls me now! He can make me do anything that he wants! I can't resist it! It's too powerful! Please, please, you must help me, before he makes me do horrible things against my will. Please, you are the smartest students on campus. You've got to help me."

"We most certainly do not have to help you, Henry," Pam declared. "However, we may wish to help you, if we can. There is a big difference there, Henry. Now what all have you tried to get it off of your finger?"

That didn't take long to answer. Henry had tried every spell he knew, but nothing had worked. Pam knew that as a sixth year, Henry knew many more spells than she did. Thus, if it had not responded to those he knew, it certainly would not respond to those that she knew. "Henry, I'm going to have to have you trust me fully and completely. Can you do that?"

In his current position, Henry wailed that he would do anything to be rid of this ring. "Good, now follow me; we are going to the Infirmary. I want Doctor Caterwall and Governor Alister to examine this magic. After all, you are not alone. They gave out thousands of those rings. Come on." She led the way, while Messaging both men, who were there to meet them.

"Morning Miss Betts, what have you brought me today?" asked Doctor Caterwall.

"A real challenge, I'm afraid. Henry, here, was foolish enough to accept one of those free gift rings of Dominus. Now look what has happened to it." She held Henry's hand so that both men could see.

"Now this is totally unique, Alister! I've never seen anything like it before, have you?"

"No, nothing like it. I was wondering when we would be seeing the mischief behind those rings." Alister had Henry relate what had happened. Slowly, it all began to make sense to Governor Alister, although he had no idea of the actual magical spells that lay behind the phenomenon. He decided to cast an Identification spell on the ring, and Lindsey, Pam, and Deiter follow suit, along with Doctor Caterwall.

"Powerful charm energies are now radiating from the ring as well as a low level alteration magical effect," Alister mused. Pam quickly saw what he meant, though Deiter and Lindsey did not for several more minutes.

"In some ways, it looks like a simple Grade 1 Charm spell," Pam observed, "but there is more to it than just that. I suspect it activated when they were sleeping so that they had no chance at all of avoiding or deflecting the Charm spell."

"I agree; it has the look of a Charm, astute observation about the time, Miss Betts. Yet, it is a deeper spell than mere charm. It feels almost like he could become an automaton. From the energies radiating from the ring, Miss Betts, any guess as to the Grade of spell?" he asked.

"Mind you, we are only studying Grade 5 spells at the moment, so I can only hazard a guess," Pam hedged her bets. "Considering it may well turn Henry into a zombie following the orders given to him by Dominus, this has to be very powerful to exert that kind of control over him. Grade 8 or 9 would be my guess." Deiter looked at Pam, completely amazed that she could even answer that question! He had not the slightest idea and could only make a random guess. "This kind of spell would be way beyond what the usual Magic School graduate could cast, otherwise the world would already be besieged with automatons running around," Pam explained her reasoning. Now that she had, Deiter saw that she was probably right; it was so simple when she explained it.

"But can you stop it?" Henry asked, his stomach began tying itself into hard knots. He felt his legs go weak. Lindsey spotted this and lent him her arm for support.

"It is a spell property of the ring, Henry. It cannot be dispelled, though if it suddenly activates and if one were successful in casting a Dispel Magic countering Dominus, then for a time it would not affect you. Only the destruction of the ring can undo the enchantments placed into it." Alister spoke softly the news that he knew that Henry didn't want to hear.

"More to the point is can the ring be somehow removed? That is your province Doctor," he added.

"Been studying that, Alister. Leave the 'what's it' to you. This is the most ingenious work that I have ever laid eyes upon. It is almost as if the ring has become a living part of his body. Look—oh, Henry, I am going to poke a needle into your finger; try not to flinch. Look at what this needle does." He used a sterile needle and gently, but slowly, pushed it into the raised bump that outlined the ring's location underneath the skin of his finger. "Notice anything unusual?"

Lindsey wanted to ask him to do it again, but thought better of it. Pam replied, "It seemed to go right through the bump, which ought to be the solid gold ring. Has the ring dissolved or something? That's not possible, gold is inert."

"You have the eyes of a doctor, Miss Betts. Precisely so. Henry, I want to take an x-ray immediately. What has me terribly worried is has the ring's substance has spread throughout his whole body?" Hearing that, Henry upped his breakfast. Pam cast a Clean spell, without thinking about it. Her mind was on what might be the ramifications of the ring's spreading throughout the entire human body.

A couple of minutes later, Doctor Caterwall returned with the developed x-ray, placing it on the lighted display box so that all could see. "Here is the definite outline of the ring showing up very bright. I've been looking but thankfully, I do not see any tendrils extending out from that ring mass. How about the rest of you? Take a good look. This is a very critical and vital observation that must be made, for Henry's sake."

Lindsey had no idea what to look for, though, neither did Deiter or Pam. Doctor Caterwall was careful to explain what they should see if the ring had embedded itself in, say, his nervous system. A bit later, all concurred. The ring was isolated to the ring finger, but was fused to the bone.

"Well, I can see only one avenue of approach at this time," the doctor continued. "The finger will have to come off and a new one regrown. I can see no other way, unless someone can figure out how to undo this diabolical spell."

"Pam, please relay all of this information to your father. I will relay it to my peers. Doctor, can I rely on you to document this fully to the others in the medical profession?"

"Yes, of course. Now we best get this going immediately. No telling when Dominus might chose to active Henry here."

An hour later, Henry was in recovery, and a new finger was beginning to form. The others gathered around the operating table as Doctor Caterwall began dissecting the finger and ring. Pam ran his video camera for him, taping the finger autopsy, as she called it. He provided the dialog as he worked.

"It's a soft, golden, spongy mass attached solidly to the bone of the finger. Rather the consistency of Jell-O." He made additional observations for several minutes, before Lindsey made a startling comment.

"Doctor, that ring massy thing—it looks shinier than it did. I think it is somehow changing."

"This is incredible. The finger has been dead now for about two hours. The ring mass is starting to change form, becoming more solid, more metal-like." Ten minutes later, they were looking at the original ring, which Henry had been given. It had completely returned to its original form of a golden ring!

Alister then checked for magic and found that the active energies were gone, replaced by the low, tiny trace amounts that the rings had originally had before Dominus activated them. All this was dutifully documented. "Alister, take the ring with you, and lock it up somewhere safe. I don't want to have to cut it off of some other student."

As they all prepared to return to their respective rooms, Henry called out, "Thank you, Pam, Lindsey, Deiter. I owe you a very big one! I won't forget this."

On their way back, Deiter decided to write up the findings and submit it to Ashley for inclusion in their next school newspaper. Pam promised tell her father about it. Lindsey felt a little funny in that she had no one to tell. Then, she remembered Wilma and Monane and promptly wrote them, the Whitewaters, and her own parents, telling them all about it.

Henry showed up at suppertime. Doctor Caterwall had made a protective box over his left hand so that he could go about his daily routine. He obviously had a lot of embarrassing questions put to him by his fellow classmates.

Things then settled down. Professor Huan Su taught them a most useful spell, particularly so for the girls, Blocking Hand. When they cast this spell, a large three-foot in size hand appeared and could be used to block someone from getting close to them. Lindsey thought of many uses for this spell; Pam, likewise.

The next two weeks, they struggled to learn three interrelated spells of tedious complexity. The first Lindsey had seen cast on several occasions, the Force Wall, which created an invisible force field that could be used to protect them. Closely allied was the Iron Wall and the Stone Wall, the latter Pam decided had been used quite a lot in the construction of this school. After two arduous weeks, the entire class had these three down pat.

He then moved on to the power evocation spells of Cold Blast and Killing Gas Cloud. Both were done under tight supervision and out of doors. Lyle, the friend of Deiter, excelled with the Cold Blast spell, being the first to master it. His blasts always seemed to be more powerful than those cast by the others. Everyone paid special attention to Huan Su's caution. "The Killing Gas Cloud spell is particularly lethal. If cast on normals, it will kill them outright. Even second year students haven't the slightest chance of surviving it, if they breathe much of its toxic fumes." Lindsey realized that she ought to be on the alert for this particular spell and always absorb it, taking no chances with its deadly effects.

"Your last week of November will be spent with Professor Mary Ann, who will be teaching you the two divination based Grade 5 spells," Professor Huan Su announced on Friday.

It was overly warm in Professor Mary Ann's classroom, far warmer than normal. Yet she wore several layers of clothing and was still shivering. Lindsey noted that she had markedly changed since the night Dominus activated his rings. "Today we will try to learn a counterstrike you can deliver when you detect that someone is attempting to scry on your thoughts. It is called Counter-scry. After that, we will attempt to use those intuitive powers, which lie within ourselves, to obtain answers to questions and problems and situations that we normally consider that we do not know. For example, what do I have in this box up front? None of you can see what is in there directly, and yet, with the added thrust of the Know Answer spell, you may be able to tap into your often hidden intuition powers and tell me. We have much work to do this week. Both of these are very tough spells to learn to cast well, so let's get to work. From now on, Counter-scry may be a most powerful weapon for many, many of us. Times have changed for the worst, I'm afraid, very much for the worst."

Deiter didn't like her doomsday attitude, but began struggling with the spells. He quickly found that he was not good with either spell. At the end of the week, he still was unable to cast both. More than a few had difficulty with these. Lindsey and Ashley, however, picked up these two rapidly, especially Ashley. Emilio failed utterly at Know Answer, but managed to grasp the Counter-scry spell. Pam was the only one in the class who excelled at Know Answer.

During these weeks, Fred Betts was busy. After the startling discovery about the true nature of these rings, the Department of Magical Misuse began a coordinated effort with the Department of Law. It was code-named: Identify. Essentially, the goal was to create a database of all people known to have received one of these rings.

On the evening of the school's Thanksgiving feast, Fred Betts came to Bradbury's under a cloak of invisibility. He'd cast several versions of the spell, along with several anti-scrying spells as well. He purposely teleported to five locations before arriving at the school, where Alister opened the door and let the invisible man inside. Fred canceled his many spells and followed Alister to his office for a brief meeting. He then joined him for the feast.

He waved and smiled to his daughter, as he walked to a guest seat beside the Governor. "What's your dad doing here?" Lindsey asked Pam.

"I have no idea, but he's never done this before; something must be very wrong," Pam conjectured. While they enjoyed their feast, a Message appeared before Pam's eyes followed by one in front of Lindsey's as well. Fred wanted to meet with them after the meal.

An hour later, Governor Alister whispered, "My office, directly." A few minutes later, the four entered his office. Alister put his finger to his lips, indicating silence. He then cast a spell before he relaxed and offered them a seat. "Never can be too careful. It's safe. My protections are still in place. Pam, Lindsey, Fred has some bad news for you to hear. No, none of your family is in trouble. Fred."

"Based on the data you obtained here about the real purpose of those rings, I informed my superiors and for the first time in a long time, the Departments of Law and Magical Misuse launched a joint cooperative operation known as Identify. Our purpose was to build a database of all the people known to have received one of those rings from Dominus. Two weeks into the project, today, this morning in fact, we received an official order to disband the operation. The accumulated database we had been building was wiped clean, totally erased. Backup copies gone. I'm not privy to who issued the order, but I can say that it had to have come from the Oval Office, the President or one of her staff. This means the Department of Law and the Department of Magical Misuse have been compromised. Dominus can now 'pull our strings,' stopping anything he finds objectionable"

"I can't tell you how serious this is, but I believe that it is just the tip of the iceberg. Hence, I came here tonight, in total secrecy. No one knows that I have come or why, excepting Alister, of course and you two."

"Pam, take this. It's a new bypass, top security clearance password. I've installed a special backdoor for you into our systems, known only to you and me. I admit I was very excited about this special database project, because with that knowledge, we can know who may be trusted and who may be at any moment under the direct control of Dominus. I guess some of you, Pam, is rubbing off on me. Each night for the last two weeks, after the close of the day, I shunted a current copy of our ever-growing database over to your triply secure server. The file is called Identify, nothing more. Officially, I'm no longer allowed to collect such information; I could be fired if I'm caught doing such."

"However, Deputy Pam, you are under no such obligation. I can't order you to do this, but I can only say how vitally important this bit of research may become in the chaotic days we all face ahead of us. Governor Alister backs me up on this all the way. Alister?"

He cleared his throat, "Yes, knowing who can be trusted and who cannot is going to be perhaps the single most important item, if we are to stand against Dominus. Pam, Lindsey, if you are to continue this project in secret, of course, I will see to it that you are given less homework and the full cooperation of our staff here. If you need something, ask."

"Of course we will do it, dad! I'll need lots of help," Pam answered without hesitation. "However, it must seem like something we kids have decided to do on our own. What I mean is that it'll not be connected in any way with any other organization or group, just a student informational kind of thing. That way, no one can get into trouble, unless they get to the Board of Governors who come down upon Governor Alister." Pam continued to speculate and think fast.

"We should give our group a name. How about the 'Rodents?' Yes, the Rodents Research project; after all, they are the rodents now, aren't they? Dad, I'll reorganize the existing database so that the names there can't be traced back to your original list. That way, if it is hacked, then no one can trace it back to your operation. We need a cover for it too, because we'll want to review nearly all the press coverage since the rings first began appearing. How about having one of our professors assign us a political science research project? That way everyone is covered."

Lindsey just sat there admiring just how fantastic Pam actually was. Here was a crisis thrown in their laps, and instantly Pam was all action. Each step was positively brilliant, as though Pam had spent weeks planning it out to the last detail. Finally, Lindsey thought of some tiny contribution she could make and interjected the moment Pam stopped for breath. "We ought to first identify any other students at Bradbury's who has a ring. After all, Henry might not be the only foolish student."

"Excellent, we don't want to leak what we are doing to one of them. Good thinking Lindsey," Pam rattled on. Alister raised his hand, causing Pam to falter a second.

"Excellent, Pam, excellent. While you are working on the identification of those who received the rings, I will work on some way we can detect their presence. Right now, only a close inspection of their ring fingers for the telltale bump can be used, hardly a quick and easy way. We need an easy way to tell who in a group of people bear these rings. I will see what I can do. R. B. is also working on it. I believe that Monane and Wilma will be lending you a hand from time to time as well. However, at the moment, Fred and I have them working on a related matter."

Pam and Lindsey were all ears. "We really need to know just how many of these rings Dominus made and how many are in circulation. If we know that number, then we can correlate that with the number in the rodent's research listing. We'll have a better idea where we stand." That made perfect sense, except Pam had no idea how the two women could possibly learn that datum.

"Say, I have an idea," Lindsey just had her second thought, a far cry from the machine gun of ideas from Pam. "When I was in grade school, one time someone came in with head lice. The school nurse had all of us line up, and she inspected each one of us. I was thinking maybe Doctor

Carterwall could 'find' some contagious disease or something, and one by one, examine every student, but he would really be looking for signs of the rings. We'd know real fast if there are more students like Henry."

Fred grinned, "Alister, I like that one. I told you bringing the girls into our confidence was a great plan."

He chuckled, "Yes, Lindsey, that is a good idea. Kind of wish I had thought of that one myself. I'll see to it. Now Fred should get home before he is missed, and I believe you two have a lot of planning to do. Good luck and thank you both for accepting this mission."

On their way back to their dorm, Lindsey said, "Pam, you were just super back there! I don't know how you do it! I only could think of two ideas in that whole time."

Pam blushed, but replied, "You realize just how serious this has become? Both departments are now going to be powerless to stop Dominus! As soon as anyone in either department does something he doesn't like, he will use his newly made rodents to put a stop to it. Imagine, coming from the Oval Office! Incredible."

The next day, an official announcement was plastered all over the dorms. During the next week of school, all students had to report to the Infirmary to take the Colorado State Board of Health Physical Exam. The exam would take approximately five minutes, unless the person had a history of physical problems. This became the talk of the students as they headed off for their eight o'clock classes. Lindsey smiled; one week from now, they'd know how many more Henry's were among them.

Pam and Lindsey took both Monique and Ashley into their immediate confidence and all four set to work. Pam assigned Monique to acquire and review all videos that she could find, looking for more rodents. Ashley was given the newspapers to scrutinize. Lindsey took online web sites, particularly the blogs, and the "personal friends" types of sites, such as MySpace2200. Meantime, Pam decided to review the original database her father had stolen, re-organize it, and to come up with some form of estimate of the sheer number of rings that might be in distribution.

Pam's reasoning went thusly: measure the weight of one ring. Take the known quantity of gold that was stolen from Fort Knox and divide by that one weight. This assumed that all the gold went into the rings with no waste and that it was all turned into rings. This yielded one hundred twenty-eight thousand rings. However, as she reviewed her dad's file, she also noticed a notation about other gold robberies that had occurred in South Africa.

Immediately, she decided to investigate this tip. A while later, she exclaimed in awe, "My god! If I add in the South African gold, we are dealing with at least one million rings!"

Monique, sitting beside her, gaped, her eyes opened wide, but she couldn't speak! The number was staggering. Lindsey and Ashley swallowed and looked at each other. "Told you so. This is really bad," Ashley finally managed to say. Her premonition had been particularly strong, though vague in details.

"We've got only about ten thousand names so far," Pam's voice only came out as a whisper. She, too, was flabbergasted at the revelation. She recovered and fired off two emails, one to her father, and one to Alister. The message just said, "Estimated rodents: one million plus."

December 1 brought their second day in Telluride. Once more, Governor Alister urged everyone to travel in packs and to keep in contact with each other. Lindsey explained to the foreign students, "We usually spend a good part of the day shopping for Christmas presents for our friends and families. Jim says that there is enough snow that we can go skiing in the afternoon as well."

They divided into two smaller groups, the boys and the girls. They spent the morning doing their shopping. At noon, laden with packages, though you would never have guessed since they used their spells to shrink everything down to a tiny size and weight, they all met at the Arches for lunch. This pleased the Dutch students, who had a project from their friends back home: compare the food at the US Arches and see if it was the same as theirs. It was.

In the afternoon, they went skiing. This year, Lindsey

and Ashley finally caught on and managed to handle the beginning slope well. However, the Dutch students were on familiar ground, so to speak. All were excellent cross-country skiers. Unfortunately, Jim had no idea where they could cross-country ski. Lindsey promised to check with Governor Alister about this when they returned. Indeed, Katja begged her to do it. She loved the freedom of quietly sliding across the white, snow covered lands. Of course, Jeannette had always had a difficult time of it, but now with her new arms, she was nearly as enthused as Katja about taking a long hike on skis.

Unlike their previous day in Telluride, this one was enjoyable and profitable. All returned tired but happy.

Normally, the last few weeks before Christmas had been filled with reviews and tests, with a lot of time off available for cramming and catch up work. Not this year. Perhaps it was the unexpectedly shorter year due to hosting the Dutch students. Perhaps it was just the usual fourth year; Lindsey couldn't tell which.

Doctor Caterwall sent Pam a Message, announcing that all staff and students had completed their physical exams. "Five rodents found and eliminated." This was his way of telling her that five additional students had had Dominus rings. Later, she learned from Deiter that all had been sixth year Black Hall students. Everyone had been too afraid to come forward and seek help, not until Doctor Caterwall's examination.

At last, Pam brought the others onboard the Rodents Research Project. "Way super cool, Pam!" exclaimed Deiter, after he heard the news and all about this special project. Both he and Peaches set to work, helping Monique and Lindsey, who were swamped with videos and online sites to check out.

Deiter soon named their growing group, which now numbered twenty conspirators, including Alister and Fred Betts, the Rodents Pack. Everyone had a good laugh over his choice of group name. In part, it was a take-off on the famous Rat Pack. They were still teens, not adults, hence rodents. Also, those that they were searching were real rodents to the general society at large. Twenty students spent all their spare time searching for names until the Christmas break came. Pam felt only a little better about it when they were heading home for vacation. She had doubled the size of the database. Still twenty thousand names out of a million was only a drop in the proverbial bucket, as she constantly hounded everyone.

The first week of December in Spell Casting class, Professor Jerry Thalmus had but one spell to teach them. The abjuration magic, Go Home spell, when properly cast would force any person to immediately be relocated to the place they called home. Rather akin to Teleport, this spell transported the person home, whether or not they so desired. Of course, if they didn't desire to be so transported, they could attempt to resist. If they were successful, the spell had no effect on them.

For the first few days, frustrations rose, no one got the spell to activate. It was a tough one. Then, one by one, the students began forcing their friends to return home. "Hi mom. Working on a spell again. Ashley sent me home. Gotta get back and send her home, bye," Lindsey hastily said to her surprised mother when Lindsey suddenly appeared in their front room. Not long after, Ashley appeared briefly, and then Audrey, Pam, Katja, and Jeannette made similar appearances.

By Friday, over half of the class was able to fight off such a dismissal, and the spell had no effect on them. Deiter was one of the first to be able to resist this spell's effect. Emilio and Kathy continued to be sent home by the spell. After Friday, they resigned themselves to the fact that they just couldn't resist this one.

Final term exams followed the second week in December. Fortunately, everyone had the last period of the day free now, since spell casting was finished until they came back from Christmas break. All were facing big tests in English, trig, physics, world cultures, abjuration theory, and potion making. Lindsey felt comfortable with English and world cultures, and everyone thought that the abjuration theory class was the easiest class they'd had yet. Hence, she concentrated on trig and physics. She found potion making incredibly boring, but dutifully followed the recipes. She decided to leave the potion making test to fate. Either she would be able to make what was assigned or she wouldn't. Lindsey didn't see how she could study for that test. After all, they didn't need to memorize anything.

On Monday afternoon, while Lindsey was getting ready to cram on physics during this free last hour of the day, Deiter Cross came into the nearly deserted Yellow Hall study hall. "Lindsey, can I interrupt you for a minute?" Lindsey noticed that he seemed very nervous. He kept fiddling with his hands, as if he didn't know what to do with them.

"Sure, Deiter," Lindsey looked up from the physics book.

"On Friday night is the Christmas party and dance. Would you go with me? I mean, I'd like to take you to the dance."

As far as she was concerned, this invitation came from left field. She'd never anticipated that Deiter Cross, of all people, would ever want to take her to the dance. She'd expected that Andy would take her, although he had not gotten around to asking her yet. Only Monique had already asked for Pam's hand. She started to reply, "Andy. . ."

"I know, I have already talked to Andy. He is willing to take Peaches to the dance if you go with me," Deiter quickly added, attempting to counter her resistance.

"You have? I mean he will? Er," Lindsey didn't quite know how to field this one. "Well, I suppose so, I mean if Andy isn't upset about it."

"No, he is fine with it. You can ask him if you want. Please say you will," Deiter started to plead, but thought better of it and stopped.

"Well, okay then. If Andy is okay with it, then it's okay with me, Deiter." Lindsey wondered why Deiter Cross would ever want to take her to the dance. Although he skipped out before she could change her mind, she found that she could not study her physics any longer. She kept thinking about Deiter. Only when Pam arrived and began chatting about the physics test was Lindsey finally able to get her mind back on track.

Over supper, she asked Andy about it. He seemed cheerful about taking Peaches, so she told Pam and the others about Deiter. Pam only commented, "Be careful; he's a Black Hall boy." Lindsey wondered what exactly she meant by that.

On Friday, the last day of the fall term, Kathy came bubbling out of Potion Making I, elated and wild with excitement. "I did it! I did it! I did it!"

"Did what?" Pam asked, a bit sour because she had missed one small step and her potion only rated a 90.

"Professor Delius said I set a new record on the test, the best made potion ever on the first term test, A++. Yes! Yes! Yes!" She pounded her fist in a victory celebration.

"Way to go, Kathy!" Lindsey cheered her on, very pleased that Kathy had found a class in which she excelled. Nearby, Deiter heard and came over to them.

"Nice going, Kathy," he said. "I don't know how you did it. Set a new record, according to Delius. Incredible."

"How'd you do?" she asked without thinking about it.

Sourly, he replied, "I only got a B. I botched the potion."

Lyle, standing behind him, muttered, "That's better than mine; I only got a C, probably because Delius likes me. My potion turned green! No way would I ever drink that one." Kathy wanted to say that's probably why he got a C, but thought better of it.

This being their last final, everyone headed to the dining room, where their grades were to be posted on the giant wallboard. Of course, Lindsey could only see her own grades. All the other student's grades were invisible to her. She'd gotten all A's except a B in Dutch, primarily because she just didn't practice it enough. Jeannette giggled when Lindsey told her what she had gotten.

The girls chatted about their grades, while they changed into their gowns for the fancy Christmas feast and dance. At five, they headed down to the dining room. As usual, Monique was dressed as a man, and she whisked Pam off the instant she spied Pam entering the room, the two giggling over some comment Monique had made.

Deiter entered shortly after that and came up to Lindsey, offering her a red rose for her dress. "Thanks, Deiter, it smells great."

"You look great," he replied, offering her his arm. As usual, Professors Janice and Blake had decorated the room for the holidays. A huge tree with silver icicles, fancy colored bulbs, and lots of blinking lights stood in one corner. The food was delicious.

Desert consisted of over a dozen different kinds of Christmas cookies. Emilio had to sample them all, while Kathy merely giggled at his boyish manners. "I'm still a growing boy," he said between mouthfuls.

Finally, tables were cleared, and the dance began. Deiter was slightly awkward around Lindsey. "I sort of know what Peaches likes," he admitted, "but you are really special." He felt a bit embarrassed saying this and decided to change the topic. "I was able to add over a hundred names to the Rodents List, but it's only a drop in the bucket."

"I know, he gave out so darn many. Honestly, can you believe that someone very high up ordered the Department of Law and Magical Misuse to stop gathering their names. That's scary," Lindsey replied.

"No kidding. Dominus is a disgrace to Black Hall. Dad is getting really worried. I can tell. He's been studying the news stories a lot lately. He never does that. Lindsey, I'm worried about this. What if someone high up orders everyone to ignore any and all crimes that Dominus and his men commit?"

"Is that likely?" Lindsey asked, though she herself had thought about this, since hearing someone stopped the two departments from investigating the rings.

"Dad has not come out and said so directly, but I think that's what he is thinking. Scary." They danced a while longer.

A bit later, Deiter said, "I've been doing a lot of thinking about those women that we rescued, you know, the ones that Dominus called his play toys." Lindsey, taken by surprise, didn't reply. "I mean, guys, well, we like to see, well, you know what I mean. Even I have fantasies like the pictures in the magazine that Jack was looking at when we raided the house. I think that is perfectly normal, I mean for guys to have fantasies about pretty women and all that. Peaches says that girls do to, I mean have fantasies about boys. Is she right?"

Lindsey flushed, and she had no idea where Deiter was heading with this conversation. "Well sure we do, but I don't think we have quite the same fantasies. I've no interest in looking at a magazine with, well you know, the opposite of what Jack was looking at." In fact, Lindsey didn't even know if such magazines even existed.

Deiter persisted, "Well, I've heard how those women were actually dressed. I've been giving this a whole lot of thought. Somehow, I think that this is very significant, with Dominus, I mean. He kept them there dressed the way he must fantasize about women. Is that a safe conclusion? Is that kind of what you think?"

"Well, sure, probably," Lindsey answered, "though maybe some of it was to keep them docile and unable to escape, but Dominus does seem to have this thing about cutting off people's appendages." As she recalled her first impression of the helpless women, what Deiter was saying did make a whole lot of sense: that he kept his toys the way he wished them to appear.

"Good. I keep thinking of them as kept toys. That's what got me thinking, Lindsey. Toys are objects, things, not people. I think of you as a real person. Dad looks at mom as if she were a person, not a toy. This has got to be a very significant difference between us and Dominus."

Finally, Lindsey grasped where he was heading. "Women are not objects of lust or whatever. We are people just as guys are people. Dominus probably cannot see any woman as a person, only as a potential object, another toy. Is that what you mean?"

"Yes, that's what I mean. Do you see what that means?"

"Er no," Lindsey certainly didn't.

"That means he does not really see women as people, only men. Mark my words: it will be a woman who finally takes him down, because he will never be able to see it coming, since he cannot see a real woman, only his potential toys."

"Deiter, that is profound! I never thought of it that way, but you are right. He doesn't see women as people. Wow."

He beamed and felt more confident. "We Black Halls know that self is what is vitally important. If you don't take care of number one, all else crumbles. That why self-strength and might are so important to us. If we let feelings run our lives, as those in Red Hall do, we believe that we are failing to be true to ourselves, letting down our power for a mere feeling, you see. This is where I think that Dominus has just gone off the track. He's having the whole world revolve around himself."

"But feelings are important too, Deiter. After all, your mother and father must love each other," Lindsey countered. "Of course, one must take care of oneself, but there is more to life than yourself. There is your family, your friends, the groups you belong to, animals, plants, a whole universe. You are not going to do well in life if you totally ignore everything but yourself."

"Of course, mom and dad love each other, but they don't let that get in their way. It was mom's idea to get these rescued women some descent clothes. Dad didn't even consider it was important. When Mom got the kudos for doing it, he was a bit miffed that he hadn't stepped in and done it. I sometimes think dad might be a bit too self-centered. He certainly had me being that way when I first came here."

"Perhaps he just doesn't understand the needs of women," Lindsey suggested.

"You are probably right, because when I started following mom's advice," Deiter started to say. Then his face went red, and he shut up.

"Yes?" Lindsey's curiosity rose. Just what happened when he followed his mother's advice?

"Well, er, things started working out better between us. You know giving you all flowers, roses." Lindsey suddenly realized what Deiter really meant was that he had now gotten her to dance with him. This meant that Deiter really did like her a lot, perhaps more than Peaches, which greatly surprised her. She didn't know how to react or what to say.

She filled the gap in their conversation with, "Well, your mom was right. We are getting along better than when we first met in our first year here."

"No kidding, sorry. I was being a self-centered pompous ass, Lindsey," he admitted.

"Self-centered, maybe, Deiter, but maybe you just didn't know how to act around someone who was so very physically different than you," Lindsey tried to smooth it over a bit. "I mean I didn't have any hands. To someone who believes that strength and power are vital, I probably seemed completely the opposite."

Deiter looked incredibly relieved. He brightened up. "Yes, that's really it! You seemed to be completely the opposite of me. That's exactly how I felt."

"See, you acted on your feelings, Deiter. You are human too, just like the rest of us."

"Darn it; that was bad feelings to act on then. Guess that's why Black Hall's are not supposed to put much stock in feelings, because, well I don't know."

"Look, if you always force your feelings to take a back seat, how will you ever know which feelings to pursue and which to ignore?" Lindsey asked. She was not about to let him off the hook this easily, by ignoring all feelings. "After all, what about love? If you ignore those feelings, how will you ever find anyone to marry? That might be what's wrong with Dominus. He has no idea of what feelings are good and to pursue and what feelings he should ignore."

"That's kind of what my mom told me, I mean about feelings. But you might be right; Dominus just indulges himself in whatever feeling he may have, as long as he feels mighty and strong doing it. Mutilating women's bodies must make him feel superior. Me, I find it revolting."

"I think any ordinary person would find it revolting."

After the next dance, Deiter admitted, "You know, I don't think that I understand girls very well. You seem so different than us."

Lindsey giggled. He piped up, "See, I don't get it. Why are you girls always giggling?"

"I don't understand you guys very well either. It goes both ways. I found it kind of funny. We *are* different from you boys, if you hadn't noticed. We have a different anatomy. Half of the time, I can't figure out why you guys do some of the things that you do. I think we are even in this department, but keep on following your mom's suggestions, Deiter. I like this new Deiter tons better than the old Deiter that first year," Lindsey admitted. This pleased him tremendously, more than Lindsey had guessed that it would have. Again, she had no idea why.

"Take Peaches, for example," he replied. "We've been good friends since we were kids, went to grade school together. Now she is wearing makeup, spends a lot of time fixing her hair in various ways, spends time looking at those teen fashion magazines. Why?"

Lindsey had a flash of understanding. Kathy had been doing this too. Suddenly, things began to fall into alignment in her mind. "I think that girls are trying to be attractive, to be pretty, to attract the attention of guys. It's as if we want to be wanted, as if we are trying to attract a mate, a partner. Our whole society is geared to run this way, though many don't play by those rules. I know my mom has never played that game at all, and she's had two great husbands. And you guys strut around trying to look important, to look powerful and desirable so as to attract our attention, like a flock of peacocks!"

Both laughed. "Wow, you are right. I can see it now. Incredible, why didn't I see it before? That's what so many of the fifth and sixth year guys are doing, strutting around, acting like they are big and powerful. They are trying to get the attention of the girls. Lindsey, I think this is rather silly, don't you?"

Lindsey laughed, "Absolutely. Kathy has been trying for a couple of years now to get me to do just that. I like to dress up because I feel good. I like the way I look when I wear this gown and heels. I like myself, so to speak. I am not doing it to attract anyone's attention but my own. Amanda's like this too; she despises putting on makeup, though Kathy has tried to get her and me to try it."

"Now that is cool indeed, Lindsey! I agree with you completely. We have a lot in common, I think."

"Well, I don't know about that. I like to run and ride horses," Lindsey replied.

"Oops," Deiter chuckled. "You know I don't like to run. I'm not good with sports. You ride horses? I thought they were only in zoos." He was teasing, of course. "Sorry, I'm a city boy."

Without thinking of what she was saying, Lindsey said, "Well, you will have to come by our ranch sometime, and I can show you how the other half lives."

"Okay, you're on! How about over Christmas break? We can Teleport now. Only I don't know where you live—where your ranch is at." Deiter looked incredibly pleased.

"Deiter, living on a ranch on the High Plains is vastly different than living in Colorado Springs," Lindsey tried to dissuade him.

"Hey, I know. When you are ready to have me come and visit, we can both Teleport to the parking lot here. Then, you can take us to your ranch. How's that?" Deiter looked pleased with his fast problem solving skills. Lindsey did admire this aspect of Deiter: his ability to resolve a problem rapidly.

"Well, okay then, but it will have to be after Christmas. What about your exchange student?"

"Maybe I can bring him along, and he can spend time with yours, that is if they don't object. If not, Peaches can entertain him for a day. She's been flirting with him some." Both chuckled.

Governor Alister announced, "Last dance." The lights dimmed.

"How on earth did it get to be ten!" exclaimed Lindsey.

"I protest; we have only just gotten started," Deiter protested, unable to fathom where the four hours had gone. "I feel cheated! It hasn't been four hours yet!"

"Actually, I guess it has," Lindsey pointed to the clock on the walk. Deiter pulled her in close to his body, and she rested her head on his shoulders. Together, they slow danced until the music stopped.

"Thank you Lindsey. I have really enjoyed being with you tonight. Don't forget to email me when it's a good time for me to come for a visit," Deiter said as they began to walk to the stairs.

At the door, Lindsey watched as Jeannette and Hans exchanged a loving, passionate farewell kiss. Not far away, Katja and Klaas were doing the same. Lindsey smiled, and then the two joined her heading to their room.

Chapter 17—Christmas Holidays

"Come on; we don't want to miss the bus," Lindsey called out to her gang. They all hastily headed down the stairs, using a Magical Door to get to the parking lot rapidly. Lindsey and Pam began moving all their students' many bags from their rooms to the bus loading area. Nearby, Deiter was doing the same thing as one of the Black Hall monitors. He spied Lindsey and flashed her a big smile. Lindsey's mind flickered on last night's dance, and she returned his smile.

Soon, they all piled onboard, and the bus left Bradbury's. Lindsey half hoped that Deiter would come back and sit with her Yellow Hall group, but he was kept busy with Floor Monitor duties. Before long, the bus arrived at Colorado Springs. He waved to her as he got off.

"I'd say Deiter has taken a fancy to you, Lindsey," Kathy giggled. "Imagine that!"

"Well, he has changed for the better," Lindsey stuck up for him. Most of her friends thought ill of him, ever since his relentless taunting and teasing of her that first year. "We had a nice time last night."

"Hey, so did I," Andy replied. "I would never have expected it, but Peaches is quite a gal. You know she is a really good diver?" They all chatted away and before long, the bus made its last stop outside the Compton ranch. All the Whitewater clan also exited here as well for safety concerns. Lloyd and Lena, holding little Jonathon, were there to greet them as well as Polly Betts, Lottie Blackburn, and Luci and R. B. Whitewater. Noticeably absent were Wilma Weltsi and Monane Tumble. It was a very happy reunion of parents, children, and friends.

Just as the Whitewater's were about to use the front room teleport pad to return to their ranch, Wilma and Monane arrived, looking drawn and haggard. Wilma commented, "God do I ever need a bath!"

"Filthy business," Monane added.

Seeing the confused faces of all the teens, Wilma

explained, "Been off doing Rodent Research. Been in filthy places as filthy men. Got more data for you, but let us take a bath first, please!"

It took the gang an hour to unpack and get settled in to home life once more. Over hot cocoa, Lindsey and Pam had to explain their Halloween mini-adventure. Lena just could not believe how horribly those six women had been treated. Pam, who had taken pictures to document the women's condition upon their arrival at the Infirmary, pictures she hoped would one day convict those responsible, namely Dominus, showed everyone just how they had looked. Gasps and vehement curses were the usual responses to the sight. "How could anyone do that to those poor women?" Lena asked rhetorically.

"We can add to that," Wilma took over from Lindsey. We have another photo to show you all. Surprise, surprise, here is the wedding photo of Dominus and Nadia. They got married shortly after the election was over. She showed them the official wedding photo submitted with their marriage license.

Lindsey gasped, "What happened to Nadia?"

Pam added staring hard at the photo, "I recognize her face, but what happened to her body? Did he?"

"Yes, the underground scuttle-butt has it that this is what he wanted her to look like if she were married to him. He turned her into this. Compare photos, and use your imagination; remove her strapless gown," Wilma added. Sure enough, the remaining length of her arms matched the five women; her tiny waist bespoke of a tight-laced corset, and her bosom was just as enormous as the five had been.

"I can see Dominus marrying her now, when she looks like his apparent fantasy woman," Lindsey said, "but why on earth would she want to be this way?"

"Honey, love makes some people do the strangest things," Lena suggested.

Once everyone finished gaping at the wedding photo, Wilma said, "We have been working underground for weeks, disguised as real lowlife characters. Picked up a whole lot of curious, but useful information. It seems that there are precisely two thousand diamond rings in circulation, but those went to men and women in high positions or who are significant opinion leaders in the US. We've heard several figures on the number of regular rings that are out. All are at least one million, though some suggest the figure is closer to one and a half million rings."

"I told you all that this was going to be really, really bad," Ashley spoke up.

"You can say that again!" Monane chimed in. "When Dominus was on the loose before, it was nowhere remotely this bad. He may well take over our whole country!"

Pam lamented, "Rodent List only has one thousand one hundred fifty-two diamond rings accounted for and a little over nineteen thousand regular rings. This may be a hopeless task. We may all be doomed."

"Where there is a will, there is a way—old proverb. Have faith, Pam," her Aunt Wilma said.

"Well, we've all had career counseling," Monique added. "I've made up my mind. I am going to college to become a Magic Medical Doctor. The world is going to have a dire need for medical help, that's for darn sure! After seeing how awful those women were treated, I knew that I just had to become a Magical Medical Doctor so I can help other poor victims."

"Good for you! Wonderful choice! I am so proud of you, Monique," Lottie exclaimed. She was taken by complete surprise by her eldest daughter's choice. She had expected that she might pursue a career in the computer field.

"Wow! Cool!" exclaimed her little sister, Ellie.

The teens spent the afternoon baking cookies and fancying up the house, decorating the same living tree as last year and in general thoroughly enjoying their respite from their studies. At suppertime, both Henry and Fred joined them. Fred, Pam noted, looked awfully exhausted and tired.

Henry was elated to hear Monique's career choice. He spent a good hour discussing various aspects with her, including the best college to attend. Pam eavesdropped on them, though she need not have. Monique wanted her to hear too. "Now one good thing you have going for you is the choice of Magical Medical Doctor. This means that you only need four years of training, though after the first year, you will be able to begin limited healings. Boston is probably the best Magical Medical School in the country."

"Yes, but dad, I want to be closer to Pam. How good is Denver Magical Medical School?"

"Well, they are fine too. I know many fine doctors who graduated from there. Denver it is then. When you submit your application, put me down as the person who is recommending you. I carry a lot of pull."

"Dad, I have found out about you!" Monique teased her father. "You are the world's foremost skilled facial reconstruction surgeon. You never told us that!"

Henry blushed. "Well, I just do my job, dear. I never pay much attention to those claims."

"Dad, my face is a testimony to your skills. I'm now fully healed. Hot and cold don't bother me anymore. Thank you very much!" She gave him a big hug and kiss. Pam smiled.

Fred pulled Pam's attention off the two. "Say, dear, how goes the Rodents List?"

Pam sighed before she explained that they had doubled the list, but that it seemed hopeless, in light of the sheer number of rings now being worn.

"I know dear, I know. It is most discouraging. We are in for some very terrible times ahead of us. However, we must continue to do all that we can." The two hugged each other for some time. Pam really needed the support from her father just now. Rodents seemed overwhelming.

The days leading up to Christmas were fun filled. The teens baked up large quantities of Christmas cookies, cakes, and breads. Many were traditional Dutch recipes, compliments of Katja and Jeannette. Afternoons were spent skiing around the Whitewater ranch or ice-skating on the frozen pond. Only the Dutch teens knew how to skate, but they patiently taught all the others. For a week, no one thought of schoolwork, of spells, or of the Rodent situation, just wholesome, winter fun.

Lena had a big surprise for her daughters. At an estate sale, she had come across an antique horse-drawn winter sleigh. Lloyd had made major repairs to it. The teens took daily sleigh rides across the winter wonderland of the two adjoining ranches, by hitching up Dusty, the large Percheron, to the sleigh. Lindsey even took little Jonathon for a ride as well, though she realized he was probably too young to appreciate it.

Late Christmas Eve, Pam and Monique held a private talk between themselves. For days, Pam was a little bit miffed with Monique. "Dear, what's wrong? I know you well enough to know that something is bothering you."

"You are going away to medical school," Pam finally let out her pent up feelings. "We aren't going to be with each other anymore. I don't want to go to med school, Monique. I know that you are going to graduate, and we've only got a few more months together, but, well, I love you. I need you."

"I know, Pam. I love you too. I've spent hours thinking about us, Pam, how we can be together, and all that. At first, I thought I could just get some job, maybe a shopkeeper in Telluride; that way we could see each other more often. Now, things are getting really bad in the world. I just have to do my part, Pam. Honestly, those poor normal women—treated so horribly. Pam, I have to do something to help others somehow. This is the strongest feeling that I have ever had, even stronger than the love I feel for you. I can't live if I don't follow that powerful emotion. I have to do this to help. I know you don't hold feelings as a driving force, a leading guideline for life, but try to understand me. I do. It's who and what I am, Pam. I've just got to do this."

Pam started crying. She knew that Monique was right; she had no right to try to stop her from doing what she needed to do. Monique began crying as well, and the two held each other tightly for some time. Finally, Monique said, "Pam, I've never loved anyone as I have you. You are the dearest thing in my life, well except for my family. I feel so badly that I'm hurting you so. Honestly, it's tearing me apart too. But then I see images in my mind of those poor women, and I know that I have the ability to do something to help, and I just have to try."

"I know you do, Monique. If you can become a Magical Medical doctor, that would be the absolute greatest thing for the world. I want to support you all the way on it. It's just that

I'm going to miss you horribly. We just should not make promises to each other that we might not be able to keep. A lot can happen in four years, when you graduate. I may be dead at the hands of Dominus by then. Who knows, just that we shouldn't make promises that we may not be able to keep," Pam admitted what she was feeling.

"Pam, you are the greatest person I know. You are right. I know that we shouldn't, but it is so hard not to, you know. Why don't we leave it as it is? Let's just see what happens, what develops. If we are meant to be together, we *will* somehow. If we aren't, well, you will always, *always* be my very best friend, ever!" They hugged again. Pam felt satisfied with this arrangement. She could live with this.

The day after Christmas, Lindsey emailed Deiter, suggesting that he could come for a visit tomorrow, that is, if he was still interested. The teens spent the day with their many presents and relaxing. Even Fred was more cheerful this day. In past years, some calamity had called him away to work on Christmas Day, but this year he'd been able to spend the whole day with his family. However, while he was relaxing in a sofa, Polly lying on his lap, he was again emergency-paged.

"Darn, I can't even have two days with my family," Fred grumbled.

"Do you have to go, dear? Can't someone else respond this time?" Polly pleaded.

"No, top secret. Got to go. I'll be back as soon as possible. Love you," he gave his wife a long kiss, before leaving.

Deiter replied almost at once. Lindsey wondered if he had been sitting in front of his computer just waiting for her email. "Isn't that the boy who was teasing you so badly your first year?" Lena asked, when Lindsey told everyone that Deiter was coming for a visit tomorrow.

"Yes, but he has grown up a lot since then. He was kind of persistent in wanting to come to visit me," Lindsey replied.

The others chatted about it quite a lot during the rest of the day. Opinions ranged from Amanda's suggestion that Deiter, too, had a crush on Lindsey to Pam's idea that he just wanted to become friendlier with her so he would be included in all their future adventures and not be left out.

Fred returned late that afternoon. He was livid with anger, summoning everyone on both ranches to their front room immediately. Polly had never seen her husband this upset, but she hastily headed to the kitchen to make a large pot of tea, commandeering Pam to help her so Pam would not further upset him by asking questions. Before long, R. B. and his family and the Blackburns stepped into the front room.

R. B.'s first action was a slight wave of his wand, "Emotion: Calm, Fred." For the first time, Fred seemed to relax slightly. The vivid redness of his cheeks turned to pink for a bit. Polly began serving up tea, while Pam, Lindsey, and Ashley passed around trays of cookies and treats.

Fred took a sip mechanically, not even realizing it was a bit hot. "Okay, you know that the new President is installed on December 28 now—that was changed from years past over a decade ago. The inaugural ball is held on New Year's Day. With that said, you are never, ever going to believe what I just found out!" His anger began rising again, in spite of R. B.'s spell. "President-elect Missy Snow has just issued her first formal proclamation, endorsed by outgoing President Lucius Dollington. She has just issued a full presidential pardon for Dominus Malefic and his Death Stalkers! The Department of Law and Magical Misuse have been ordered to stop all current investigations of their criminal activity! She and Lucius will be making a presidential news conference announcement of this at six tonight! Dominus has been invited to her inaugural ball!"

"Dear god! What has happened to our country!" exclaimed Wilma. Other curses echoed throughout the room. The anger level rose to unprecedented heights!

"It's almost like Dominus was elected, not Missy," Pam declared angrily.

"Ah, Pam, I believe that you can add another name to your Rodents List, Missy Snow," R. B. declared angrily. "It's obvious that she is wearing one of them. I don't even have to look at her fingers!"

"Why would she do this? He's a convicted murderer. He's done nothing but continue murdering and mutilating people since he escaped?" asked Lena, unable to grasp this shocking turn of events.

"I told you it was going to be really bad," Ashley muttered in the background; only Lindsey heard her though.

Everyone talked at once. It was impossible to follow the conversations, but all were highly upset. Lindsey tried to follow what Fred was saying, though, but over the din, she was unable. Later, she learned that Pam now had a new and huge set of files on her secret, triply secure server. Fred had saved a copy of all known data in all the many institution's databases. Pam now had total access to everything ever known about Dominus and his gang, everything. Fred had been a busy man before the files were removed and placed in offline, backup storage archives.

After supper, which no one was particularly interested in eating, except Jonathon, who was either hungry or sleeping, everyone in both households gathered around the big screen TV in the family room. Lloyd and Lena smiled at each other, as they gazed upon the large number of people gathered in their room. They had long ago decided to make a big family room, and ranch house, for that matter. Now it was coming in very handy indeed.

Precisely at 6 p.m., the Mag news cameras showed a haggard looking outgoing President Lucius Dollington and incoming President Missy Snow walking together up to the podium brimming with microphones. Missy, looking well after her recovery from the bombing, spoke first.

"Good evening, fellow Americans everywhere. This afternoon, I issued my first formal proclamation, a full and complete pardon for Dominus Malefic and his band, often called the Death Stalkers." As expected, the crowd who had gathered to hear this historic announcement reacted much as Fred had. She smiled and let them vent their protests, before she continued.

"These past years have been filled with internal bickering, strife, hostilities, and natural disaster unparalleled in the history of our great country. Wizard Dominus has on many occasions offered his assistance with everything from terrorist bombings to the Hurricane Emily disaster. Animosity levels on both sides have never been greater. This hatred does no one any good. Look, if Dominus can help forward the aims and goals of our great land, why should certain people in our government refuse his aid?"

"In these troubled times, we need all the help and support that we can get from all of our citizens, wizards, witches, and the rest of us. Now is not the time to be fighting among ourselves; power is fleeting. Our country has stood the test of centuries. We are great because all throughout recorded history, we have always made use of the wonderful skills and abilities of our citizens. From Benjamin Franklin, to Abe Lincoln, to Herman Melvin, to Janice Jones, great men and women of our country have stepped forward to lead, to help, to assist our people. Melvin finally brought wizards and witches out of hiding and into mainstream lives. Look at all the incredible benefits our people have had from those that are gifted with magical skills! Look at the magical healing that Doctor Jones established throughout the country. Why, there is not a big city anywhere in our land that does not have a Magical Healing Hospital in it."

"We are at a crossroads. These are troubled times. I feel badly for President Lucius here, for no sitting President has ever been held in such low popularity. Yet, he has worked hard to keep our country going in spite of unforeseen disasters. Now it is time for change. You, the voters of our great land, have elected me to be your next leader. I have promised reforms. Tonight I give you the first of many such reforms."

"We must put hatred, strife, and bickering among ourselves into the past. We must all put our shoulders to the wheel to strengthen and help our wonderful land. We must all learn to live together in peace and harmony. We must all learn to get along, in spite of our differences, our varying political philosophies, and religious beliefs. I know that if we all work towards this goal, we are powerful enough to achieve a unified harmony."

"Each of us has some skill that we can use to better our lives and the lives of others around us. We must, I repeat, we must use that skill to its utmost. Dominus Malefic is a powerful wizard. I've found no one who would counter that statement. I have met personally with him and his new beautiful wife, Nadia. Yes, I found him full of anger and disgust that his many offers of help and aid had been ignored over the years. Yet, I was able to get him to agree to put his many and powerful skills to work to help us all. I have his solemn pledge that he will continue to offer all aid that he can provide for our country and our people. I gave him my sworn word that I would not hesitate in the slightest to ask him for his help when situations arise."

"In light of that and of the enormous help that our country needs, I am making the full and formal pardon of Dominus and the men and women who are aligned with him. We cannot change the Constitution. I agree with so many of you that a convicted criminal cannot hold this high office. Yet, even so, Dominus spent a fortune of his own money, as you well know, on making a bid for the Presidency of our country. Why? I asked him that question. His gorgeous wife Nadia answered for him. She put it very nicely. 'Dominus ran for president to show all those in power that the average person in our great land is demanding a change in the way our government does its business.' Considering the results of the election last month, it is clear to me, as it should be to every American, that nearly half of our country is behind him. We need a change. Today, I'm making this pardon to show everyone in our wonderful country that change, positive change, has at last come. You may expect many more changes in the weeks and months to come."

"My administration will be sending dozens of new bills to Congress just as soon as we can get them formally written. I promise you that the very first bill we send to Congress will be our proposal for Total Health Coverage for every American! No longer will appropriate health care be available for only those who can afford to pay for it. This I promise you will happen. I encourage the Congress to take a cold, hard look at this election's results. See this as I do: a dramatic call for change. Let's give our voters a good, positive change. Let's all work together to make the United States of America the best country in the world."

"Thank you. President Lucius would like to say a brief

word as well, Lucius," she stepped back and a very sober looking Lucius stepped forward.

"Good evening, my fellow Americans. I would like to take this final opportunity of my presidency to say a few words to you. First, I would formally like to apologize to Mr. Dominus Malefic for refusing to seek his aid during the worst natural disaster we have ever faced. Second, you, the voters, have spoken. No one in government can ignore the incredible message that Mr. Malefic has sent to us in this past election."

He looked straight at the cameras, as if he were speaking to each viewer personally, "Let this be our *wake-up call*, our wake-up notice that things must change in our country, and change soon. I encourage every one of us law-abiding citizens to do our part to bring about the positive change that President Snow is asking for. Together, we can rise above these troubled times. Working together as one, we can make our country great once more."

"My final message to you, my fellow Americans, is do not give up hope. Band together; help each other. Use your skills and strengths to help make our land great once more. Put down your biases; forget your anger and hatreds. Ignore the color of skins. If we all work together, we can succeed in making the Unites States a great country once more. Even though my term is done, I, as just another ordinary citizen, will do my part as I know you will too. Thank you and good night."

Hugo appeared and began recapping the speeches. Fred turned the TV off. Pam spoke up first, breaking the stunned silence, "Snow's speech was just a bunch of pure psycho-babble! She's a complete idiot!"

"I do believe she is being very subtly influenced, mentally, that is," R. B. announced his opinion. "I think Dominus played to her goals. She seemed sincere, not under someone's charm spell. Poor Snow actually believes what she was saying, but, yes, Pam, it was mostly just the usual psycho-babble, utter nonsense, but very, very believable, mind you, and very hard to counter."

"Wilma," Fred asked, "what did you make of Lucius's final words? I thought that he was sending us, the good guys, so to speak, a clear message."

"I agree, his speech, which at first looks as if he is supporting all that Snow outlined, clearly did not. I think he was sending us a message to band together and that he will be on our side. Interesting political move on his part," Wilma replied.

Before anyone else could comment, the monotone voice announced, "Mag Post arriving." Lloyd went to the door and accepted the small package. "It's for you, Fred. Governmental seal on it. Must be important." He handed the package to Fred.

Fred opened the package and groaned. "It is from President Missy Snow. It seems that my attendance at her Inaugural Formal Ball is required. I'm to bring along a party of eight, including myself."

Polly spoke up, "Dear, think of the children, such an experience would be wonderful, even if these are hard times. It would be something to tell our grandchildren about, dear." Pam flushed.

The monotone voice spoke up once again, "Governor Alister Broadwell is arriving." Again, Lloyd headed for the front door, reappearing in the hall beside the family room with Alister.

"Good evening. I take it you have all heard the news?" Alister said, his voice was more subdued than normal. Everyone had, of course. "R. B., Wilma, Monane, Lloyd, Fred, Henry, can we have a private discussion immediately?" Lindsey had never seen him this sober, but she did notice that he had a small pouch attached to his belt. When he returned from their meeting in R. B.'s secure workshop, the pouch was absent.

The adults quickly left, using the teleport pad to go over to the Whitewater ranch and then into R. B.'s workshop. A few spells later, they could not be overheard or scryed upon. They were gone over an hour, leaving the others speculating furiously over what this was all about.

When the group finally returned, Lindsey was happy to see that they were a bit more cheerful than when they had left. Governor Alister seemed to be definitely more at ease. He sent the Dutch visitors over to the Whitewater ranch, their purpose was to "clean up the mess" that they had made. Lindsey suspected that he was just getting them out of the way. "May I have your attention?" he spoke, as if he were addressing the students in the dining room. Lindsey grinned.

"As you know, Fred has been invited to the Inaugural Formal Ball. He's decided to go and will be taking Polly, Pam, Lindsey, Ashley, Amanda, Wilma, and Monane with him. I, too, was sent an invitation, probably at Dominus's insistence. I'm to bring one guest, though he knows well enough that I'm not married. I will be bringing Mr. Deiter Cross with me. This is a very sophisticated affair, so I'm afraid you ladies will need to purchase some new gowns and such. Fred and I will need to rent tuxedos. Don't fret, ladies. I will defray the cost of your new gowns. Please pick out very elegant gowns. This is a most formal affair."

After the oh's and ah's and thank you's died down, Alister continued. "We have taken Lucius's words to heart. Obviously, the resistance movement against Dominus must now be both secret and underground. The Departments of Law and Magical Misuse will now be under his indirect control. It is imperative that our organization remain completely secret. We've chosen the name the Rodent Pack, which we feel is most appropriate on several levels." This brought many giggles from the girls, who saw many levels of references in the name, none the least being the old Rat Pack.

"I hereby appoint all of you here into the Rodent Pack. Our first mission is to attend this ball. Pam, please acquire a spy camera. Your task is to get good photos of everyone who is at the ball. We need finger shots, for obvious reasons. With luck, we can know far better who is under the control of Dominus. Ashley's mission is to stay alert and warn us of any impending calamity, since after all, Dominus and his men will be there. I wouldn't put it past him to attempt to harm us. The rest of us will mingle with those who are there, becoming friendly and making new acquaintances. Some will be under his control, but others will be looking for ways to fight Dominus. We need to gain knowledge of those who may be on our side and for them to at least know of us, though do not mention the Rodent Pack to anyone there."

"Additionally, Pam is hereby appointed our Keeper of Bumf, that is, our database of information. Like pack rats, we will be storing away volumes of things that may one day be useful to us all. R. B. will be our official Keeper of Admittance. All new inductees into our Rodent Pack will first have to meet his seal of approval. For your information, Professors Chi Lin and Huan Su Sung have been admitted, as has been Professor Delius Dogs and Professors Arthur and Mary Ann Thornby. The other professors I have not yet met with, so do not breathe a word to them for now. Questions fellow rodents?"

The girls giggled. "Well, I have to get going. I need to meet with the Cross family yet tonight. Arrangements to be made and all that." He left and the families chatted a bit, but had to stop when the Dutch teens returned. R. B. thanked them profusely for having cleaned up his mess. They seemed pleased.

Now the teens turned their attention onto ball gowns. None had the slightest idea of what was required of such dresses. In fact, none of the women did. Monique came to their rescue. She found a web site that had excerpts from the last Inaugural Formal Ball. Eagerly, all the women crowded around her laptop to peek.

"Gosh, those are some dresses!" exclaimed Lena. "I've never seen such elegant dresses in all my life!"

"We are not going to be able to make dresses like that," Polly added. "In fact, I have no idea where we can even buy such dresses!"

"I do," Monique replied, "I did a quick search, Jane's Gowns in Denver makes a lot of the gowns worn to these kinds of balls." Everyone stared at the website.

Ashley gasped, "My god! Four thousand dollars for one dress?"

"Good thing Alister is paying for these!" Polly added, greatly relieved. So were all the adults. None of them had that kind of money to spend on one dress!

"I've made an appointment for us to get fitted tomorrow morning at nine o'clock. On our way back we can stop and pick up Deiter," Monique added, taking charge of the dress situation.

Just before nine the next morning, all the women gathered together outside the ranch house. Wilma and Monane teleported the group of women to the dress making shop in a ritzy portion of downtown Denver. The excited women entered. Alister was kind enough to forward verification of their attendance at the Inaugural Formal Ball. Hence, the store was prepared to meet their needs.

"Welcome to Jane's. I'm Madam Philomena. I will be your hostess. Coffee, tea?" asked an elegantly dressed woman, who wore shiny, black patent pumps with rather high heels. All declined the beverages, however. They were too excited to drink just now.

"Very well, then let's get straight to business. You are all going to the foremost ball in our country. This means you must wear the very best gowns that money can buy, hence you are at Jane's. This is our specialty. Your first choice will be between the traditional long, billowing gowns on your left or the new fetish trends there on your right. Mrs. Nadia Malefic has chosen one of the new fetish gowns, but the President has chosen the more traditional gown."

They took one look at the slinky, tight fitting fetish gown and all opted at once for the traditional style. Next, Philomena led them down the traditional gown isle, asking each woman to pick the dress that she desired. In fact, they were all pretty much the same, with minor variations. All were very billowing at the feet, stretching out for several feet. The tops varied depending upon how much of the chest one wished exposed and the style of the short sleeves. One by one, each picked theirs out. Color choices came next; however, all color choices were pale and subdued. They went with Philomena's suggestion of off-white, that being the usual color, unless one wished to make a statement, which none of these did.

"Now, with each dress, the proper undergarments are required as well as the proper shoes. This year, the pump oxfords are the latest in style and fashion. Since you are all going traditional, you should continue that look by wearing the accepted heels." She showed them an example pair of oxford pumps, with tie strings. Lindsey gasped at the heel height, though. Philomena noticed, "Yes, these are a full five inches, to date, one hundred-five women will be wearing these. However, the President has chosen a lower height, but then she is the President. If you are not experienced in wearing such heels, I would suggest that you wear them around the house for the next few days to get used to them. The secret is to take much smaller steps." They again decided to go with what the majority of women would be wearing; none wanted to look out of place.

"Well, then, we are just about finished. If each of you will step into the booths and undress fully, one of our attendants will join you and begin your transformation. Once you are fitted and wearing the proper undergarments, the dress of your choice will be fitted and tried on for fit. If any adjustments are needed, they will be made on the spot. An hour from now, you will be leaving with your new outfits in hand, compliments of Jane's, where we use magical sewing to meet your most elegant needs."

Indeed, an hour later, each now carried a small sack, which contained everything. Of course, the saleswoman had magically shrunk each item and carefully packed the sacks for them. The total bill was a staggering thirty-two thousand dollars! All the women sent Alister an email thanking him profusely for his incredibly generous gift.

A minute later, they all appeared in the parking lot of Bradbury's School of Magic. Sure enough, there stood Deiter Cross bundled up against the chilly weather. It had started to snow.

"Wow, what a reception," he teased when they all arrived. Then, his face turned very serious. "Have you heard about what Snow did?" They had.

"Pay attention. Here we go to our ranch," Lindsey interrupted him. A second later they all arrived outside their front door. A few inches of snow covered the ground. "Welcome to my house, Deiter," Lindsey said formally and led him and the others inside.

While the girls wanted to put on their fancy new gowns to show everyone, they didn't because Deiter was here.

Chapter 18—Deiter Gets an Education

"Everyone, this is Deiter Cross. My mom, Lena, little brother Jonathon. Polly Betts, Pam's mother," Lindsey began the lengthy introductions. Then, she took him on a quick tour of their house. He was amazed with its size. From the outside, it looked to be a small house, twenty by forty feet. Inside, it was more like a football stadium, his words. It expanded five-fold, being one hundred by two hundred feet.

He was amazed with all the bathrooms and the size of their bedrooms. The workrooms were enormous, but the family room was three times the size of his folk's, to say nothing of the living room. One of the workrooms was Audrey's, and she and Fern were carving away. Deiter complimented them on their fantastic carvings. They had three finished ones, and the tongue oil was still drying. "Sold already. Fifteen hundred dollars for the three," Audrey said quietly.

"Wow! I never knew about these. Can I order one for my folks?" Deiter asked.

"Sure, just fill out an order on my website, AudreysCarvings.bus. I have ten more orders to fill right now." Indeed, Deiter suddenly realized that Audrey was making a considerable amount of money with her artwork and was most impressed.

"Come on. I'll show you the barn, our horses, cows and chickens," Lindsey said, leaving the others to unpack and un-shrink their fantastic new ball gowns. While she wanted to try hers on, she felt obligated to Deiter. Outside, she pointed out, "Those darker circular areas are our three one-mile in diameter irrigated fields. Our ranch is small, five miles on a side, a square. Down that way into the arroyo and then to the right is the Whitewater ranch. This is our barn."

"Wow, an old fashioned, antique buggy," he exclaimed.

"Yes, mom just found it. We've been going for a sleigh

ride nearly every day. If you want, we can go for one later one today. Here are all our horses. The draft horses, those big ones, we use for our farming. This is mine, Betsy. This one is Audrey's, this one is Pam's, this one is Ashley's."

"How many horses do you have anyway?" he asked, never having seen so many horses in one spot before.

"We own a dozen, but mom's a breeder. She has two mares that she's trying to impregnate with Jack, our newest Percheron. Now here are our four cows. We milk them every morning. That's how we get our milk. It's free. This is the chicken coop. Pam fetches the eggs each morning. We have so many eggs that we give a bunch to the Whitewater's every couple of days. We've three water wells, so we never run out of water. The house almost never needs heating or cooling, since it is R. B.'s cool design. Dad has solar cells on the roof, so we don't need any electricity either. Mom and Audrey have been growing our own vegetables, and one patch is in wheat, so we grind our own flower. About all we need from the outside world is meat, sodas, and of course, Domino's pizzas."

"Incredible, Lindsey, I had no idea. This is really cool. Do you realize that with all the trouble we are going to be having that you can live here and get by really well?"

"That was the plan, Deiter. The Whitewater's are also independent. R. B. says he can provide fresh game if we run into problems getting meat. Plus dad and R. B. have all sorts of magical protections on both ranches. We are pretty safe from Dominus here; we have to be; he's been after us."

"Hey, there you are," Jim called out. He, Hans, and Andy came over to see what was happening. "Amanda's trying on her new gown. Got mom all in a dither, so we left them alone. Hi, Deiter. You want to see our ranch too?"

"Hi Jim. Sure, Lindsey's been showing me hers. So many horses!"

"Well, we have two ways to get to our place: the front room teleport pad that dad made or the old fashioned way, buggy ride. You two up for a buggy ride?"

"Let's!" Lindsey decided. "You guys bring out the harness, and I'll fetch Dusty. We can take a sleigh ride over to your place and back." Deiter stood back out of the way. Dusty towered over him, and yet Lindsey pulled him around as if he was a docile pussycat. "He's fun to ride in the summer; you sit way high up!"

A few minutes later, they climbed in and argued over who got to drive. "It's my turn, Andy," Jim declared. "Remember, you drove it yesterday." Jim gave Dusty the go ahead, and the giant horse easily pulled the sleigh through the snow.

"Let's kind of go around our ranch a bit, so Deiter can get an idea of how small it is, and then cut down the arroyo to your place," Lindsey suggested. A half hour later, they pulled in at the Whitewater ranch.

"You have two houses?" Deiter asked.

"Yes and a pond. We've been ice-skating every day. The Dutch teens are amazingly good at it," Jim explained. "The Blackburn's are staying in our spare house—that's the new one over there. Come on; let's show you around. You probably want to see dad's workshop. Everyone does. Just ignore all the junk that you see around here. Most all of it is not junk, but magical inventions of dad's. See that rusty milk can? It announced to everyone in the house that we arrived. Pretty cool."

"Hey, you boys stay out of the back. We are working with Amanda and her new gown. Go see R. B. Why don't you," Luci called out. "Oh, you must be Deiter Cross. I'm Lucinda Morning Dove, Luci for short. Bye." She ducked back into Amanda's room.

"Hey, I like your house. It's cozier," Deiter said.

"You mean messier," Lindsey teased.

"Yes, well that too; it makes it more livable," Deiter replied.

"Hey, a guy after me own heart," Jim teased. He led the way into R. B.'s shop, while Hans and Andy headed to the kitchen to grab a snack.

"Dad, Deiter Cross," Jim announced. R. B. looked up from his workbench. Lindsey spied five of those Dominus rings on his table. Evidently, he, too, was working on them.

R. B. said, "Good, just you folks. Hello Deiter. Welcome to the Rodent Pack. Been working on these infernal rings of

Dominus. Hear Alister is taking you to the Inaugural Formal Ball."

"Yes, incredible experience. He's already gotten me all fixed up with a black tuxedo. Darn complicated to get on, though. I'm supposed to be escorting the girls and providing back up protection, if there's a fight. There isn't likely to be a fight with Dominus there, I mean at the ball, is there?"

"No, that would be the stupidest thing imaginable. No, I expect that he will be cordial to everyone. Stay alert, Deiter; memorize the names and faces there. You will be meeting some very important men and women. However, secrecy is now the name of our game."

"No kidding," Deiter replied. "I just can't believe that the President did that. Dad about blew a gasket when he heard the news. Mom, she broke down and cried. I'm glad that they're not going. I think that dad might just try to kill Dominus outright there at the ball."

"I doubt that he would be successful. Dominus will have many protections on his person, expecting just that. No stay alert; meet the important people; remember their names and faces. Now, I need to get back to work on these rings." The three left and Hans handed Deiter a plate of cookies and a soda. Andy handed Lindsey a soda as well. A bit later, they rode the sleigh back to the Compton's barn.

At lunch, all the teens gathered around the large Compton dining table for soup and sandwiches. As they ate, they tried to decide what to do after lunch. After taking several votes, they agreed to go ice-skating first and then go cross-country skiing. By the time that Deiter had to go home, around four, he was totally pooped out. He'd had more exercise than a week at his house in Colorado Springs. Lindsey walked him to their front door and stepped outside to see him off.

"Thanks for having me today, Lindsey. I have really had a whole lot of fun. Your place is incredible to say the very least. Thanks for inviting me. I'd like to come again, that is, if you don't mind."

Lindsey was surprised with this, "Ah sure. I suppose you can pop by whenever. There is always a lot going on, so I suppose you ought to Message me first. We might have to go to town to get more things for this ball."

"Great! Will do. Guess I had better be going now," he said, though he made no real actions to do so. Lindsey didn't know why she did what she did next. She leaned forward and gave Deiter a loving hug. His arms hugged her back. Then, he finally got out his wand and cast his spell. She saw a big smile on his face as he vanished.

"He seems like a nice boy," Lena commented when Lindsey came back inside. "It's hard to believe that he was the one who caused you so much grief your first year. Anyway, after supper, you girls ought to put on your new gowns. We all want to see these four thousand dollar gowns. Besides, according to Polly, you are all going to need to practice walking in your new heels. They are awfully high, but Polly says that is what the women there will all be wearing."

Just after supper, Amanda and Monique came over carrying their sacks with their new gowns. They had spent the morning trying theirs on and were now at least familiar with what went where. Lindsey finally had the time to unpack hers. The five girls then stripped and began to get dressed up.

"Golly, what goes on first? There are so many parts," Lindsey exclaimed.

"We can't decide whether the lace panties go on first or over the garter belt," Amanda declared. "If it is over the garter belt, then we can more readily go to the bathroom. Monique claims it is supposed to go under. When we get everything on, it will be really tough to go to the bathroom, so I'm going to put mine over the garter belt."

Slowly, item by item, the girls helped each other into their outfits. They left their heels for last, only to discover that they could not easily put their own on by themselves. Each helped the other, tying the laces in a nice bow. "Gosh, these are really high!" exclaimed Lindsey.

"Remember, she said take small steps," Monique reminded the other four. Still, they all found it a bit daunting. "Gosh, we can't see where we are stepping in these full dresses!"

"I think you have to pay attention to what is just ahead of you and remember it as you get to it," Pam suggested. "How do I look?"

"Like the most beautiful woman at the ball," Monique replied.

"Don't be silly," Pam replied, "that would be Ashley." Indeed, dressed up as she was, Ashley did look every bit the teen fashion model. She blushed. Holding on to each other for support, the five walked slowly out to face the gathered audience. Everyone was sitting in the living room awaiting the girls to make their grand appearance.

"Oh my!" exclaimed Lena, when she saw Lindsey and Ashley walking slowly into the room, holding on to each other. "You two look absolutely fabulous!" Lloyd's mouth gaped, as he looked at his two daughters.

"I'm the luckiest man in the entire world! Two fabulous young daughters. Wow!" He gave each a loving hug. Lindsey beamed. She felt electric; her father's word hung in her mind, fabulous. She did indeed feel fabulous.

Fred simply cried and went to hug Pam. "You are stunning, Pam. You are so radiant, so gorgeous in that gown! I can't keep from crying." She hugged him.

Henry, who had just returned from his long day at the hospital, looked at his eldest daughter, rushed to her, and hugged her tightly, whispering in her ear, "Monique, you look stunning! I'm so proud of you!"

R. B. looked at Amanda and gave her a hug. "You have blossomed into the prettiest flower in the whole wide world! You are my greatest treasure." He gave her a long, loving hug as well.

The dresses lay bare across their top, only the frilly, lace touched their shoulders, forming a short sleeve about two lacy inches down their shoulders. Nearly strapless, much of their chests were bare. Wilma suggested that they needed to wear some jewelry, perhaps a dangling necklace or pendant. Earrings were going to be needed as well. However, the biggest consideration was the heels and the billowing dresses, which hid their feet. Each dress flared outward nearly three feet all around them. The material was satin with a good deal of lace trimming. All five felt moving about was awkward. "We are really going to need to practice walking in these heels!" Ashley declared.

"We ought to wear these dresses for a time every day to get used to them, perhaps wear the heels lots more around the house. They need to be broken in as well as us getting used to walking in them," Pam declared. Polly, Wilma, and Monane also agreed. They went to get their identical heels and when they returned, they more than seconded Pam's suggestion.

"What we women do for fashion," Polly declared.

"But I feel like a million!" Ashley replied. "I've never felt quite like this before." Lindsey smiled; neither did she. "How are we supposed to dance in these heels?"

"I think that we ought to practice that too," declared Pam flatly. "We have only six days left, so we'd best spend time every day on it."

Later that night as the girls were undressing, Ashley commented, "Wearing this gown and getup, I feel incredibly sexy. Am I supposed to feel like this?"

"Absolutely, Ashley," Monique replied. "We look like a million. Our opinions of ourselves are what matters. You should feel fantastic about yourself and your appearance. I mean, how often in our lives do you suppose that we will get to dress up in such fancy gowns and go to the most formal ball in our country? Wearing this outfit, I feel so sexy I can hardly stand it!"

Polly stuck her head in, "Girls, we've been discussing everything, and we will need to get our hair and nails done professionally. Also, you should consider using some makeup as well, at least a little lipstick and blush."

"I think that they ought to have their eyes done as well: mascara, liner, shadow," Monique added.

Inspired and feeling incredibly good about herself, Lindsey said, "Okay. Tomorrow, let's see about getting our hair and nails done. Then, let's have Monique help us get what she thinks we need, and then I will splurge and buy us all a matching emerald pendant and earrings. That way we will look alike. How's that?"

She got a huge round of thank you's. Polly replied, "Okay girls. I will check into the hair and nails. We probably ought to look like the others who will be there. I doubt that cherry red lipstick is in order, nor cherry red nails. Sorry Monique."

Monique grinned. "For once, you're right. I think cherry red is out for this formal ball. I ought to take another look at the video of the previous ball and go from there." Lindsey breathed a sigh of relief, because she had been worried that Monique would want her to wear a gaudy shade of red.

Later that night, Monique reviewed the video with Amanda looking over her shoulder. Her folks and Ellie had already gone to bed. She had made her makeup list, all light shades. Now she was zooming in on the women's nails. "Gosh, do they all have such long nails?" Amanda asked.

"Sure looks like it. Let's try some others." Indeed, nine out of the ten women they examined up close had long nails. "Surely those are acrylics. They all can't have such long nails normally," Monique stated. They decided to see what Polly would suggest in the morning.

At nine the next morning, the women and teens walked into Lois's Beauty Parlor in Denver. Polly had brought them to a very exclusive shop, one that used magic to create the styles. She explained that normal women went to beauty parlors and spent a good deal of time getting their hair done. However, even sleeping would begin to take its toll on the hairdo. Using a magic styling shop, once they had the style they liked, they would be given a magical command, which would automatically redo their hair in the chosen manner. The spell effect would work daily for at least a week, often for two weeks, before needing to be redone.

Lindsey and Amanda chose to retain their long hair, but allowed it to be fluffed up so that it appeared they had much fuller hair. Ashley's, which had been growing longer, was done up with a lot of body, making her look even more like a fashion model. Pam's mostly unruly hair was worked over until she too had a regal look.

After much discussion, the stylist convinced them that nearly all the women attending the ball would be wearing at least two-inch nails. They opted to get their nails magically lengthened instead of gluing on nail extensions. Their nails looked real and were real this way. An hour later, all sported long, gorgeous talons painted in subdued colors that wouldn't clash with their dresses. Pam's comment was apt, "Now we have another thing to get used to living with." They all chuckled.

An hour later, Monique had picked up all the cosmetics on her list. Now they headed to a jewelry store that Polly recommended. After some discussion and after Monique showed a picture of themselves in their gowns that she had taken last night with her cell phone, they found the perfect pieces. Each teen had a large emerald pendant necklace, adjusted so that the jewel lay just above the edge of their cleavage and dress top. However, their matching earrings, which came with the set, hung down all the way to their bare shoulders, a look that the jeweler highly recommended. Lindsey bought the five matching sets.

Once home again and lunch handled, which required a good deal of getting used to their long nails, they set about practicing walking in their heels. After supper, they again got into their gowns. While they slowly became more skilled in putting on their outfits, they found they needed to continue to get used to their nail's new lengths. They then spent the evening practicing their dancing in their gowns and heels. All eight women knew that they really did need the practice. Ashley's comment was appropriate, "Gosh, we are all a bunch of klutzes! We need more practice!"

The next night, Alister brought Deiter with him, and they, along with Fred, wore their tuxedos and practiced their dancing and escorting of the women. Deiter just could not believe how utterly beautiful all five of the girls looked. Lindsey thought that he looked handsome in his new fancy tuxedo as well. Yes, the men needed the practice as well, especially learning how to walk slowly enough with the women, who had to take unusually small strides in their heels. Alister was leaving nothing to chance, knowing that this formal appearance would have both far reaching and long reaching consequences, though he did not know the specific details yet.

The next day, Pam's new surveillance equipment arrived by Mag Post. The camera itself was incredibly tiny, which she inserted in her hair. This way the camera would pick up whatever she was facing. Further, by looking slightly downward, which she would be doing anyway in this gown just to see where she was going, the camera would point to people's hands. The tiny unit could only transmit its signal a short distance. Hence, she had acquired a long distance transmitter. This they would have to place close to the ballroom. After reviewing the video of the last ball, she decided to have it placed on the flat porch roof over the stone columned entrance.

The transmitter would then send its signal back to a receiving unit. From there, the video would be uploaded onto her secure server that her father had secretly setup for her at the High Plains Department of Magical Misuse in Sterling. However, someone would need to monitor the feed, someone who was part of the Rodent Pack. She elected Lloyd to handle this. She got her laptop setup for him and drilled him for over an hour, making sure he knew what to do. "If things go wrong, just Message me, and I'll find a way to get back to you," Pam insisted. She wished that she were here to make sure it recorded perfectly. Four hours of live video feed would take up a lot of disk space and over such a time span, she was sure something would go wrong.

New Year's Eve, Lena decided they ought to hold a dress rehearsal for the ball and celebrate the coming of the New Year. The girls spent an hour after the early supper getting dolled up, including their makeup. Pam got her video camera working and set up the transmitter for Lloyd. At their rehearsal, both she and Lloyd would get some practice at the real thing.

While the other girls helped the five dress, Audrey kept giggling, and Lindsey just could not get a straight answer out of her about what was so funny. Audrey kept saying, "You will see." Lindsey didn't like being kept in the dark.

Promptly at six, Alister and Deiter arrived, dressed in their tuxedos. At last, the five teens and the three older women, along with Fred joined everyone in the large living room. The other teens had been busy moving the furniture out of the way and decorating for the party. Audrey spied Deiter and giggled again.

Deiter walked up to Lindsey and bowed. "I have a little something for one of the prettiest girls I've ever known." He handed her a small box. Lindsey opened it and saw a beautiful golden ring with her birthstone in it.

"It's fabulous, Deiter! Thank you!" She gave him a kiss and he blushed. One by one, Deiter went to the other four and gave a similar speech, handing them each an identical small box. He had gotten all five a very nice birth stone ring. Finally, he admitted, "Audrey's doing. I didn't know your birthdays, so I had her tell me. She's been in on it." Audrey giggled once more. Now, she thought, the five looked perfect. Yet, did they trust this Black Hall boy? That thought drifted in all five minds.

When the old year finally ended and the new one arrived, the party broke up to get some needed sleep. All were extremely excited about the ball coming up this evening. However, Pam had checked on the video feed with Lloyd ten times during the evening. Yet everything had worked perfectly. She put fresh batteries into both devices before finally going to bed.

The problem the girls faced was the same one that Deiter faced as he lay in his bed that night. He was too excited to fall asleep easily. Visions of the five fantastic looking girls filled his mind along with the upcoming ball. He was nervous, more so than he had ever been before. After all, only a few hundred people out of all the millions in the country ever went to the Presidential Inaugural Ball!

Chapter 19—The Inaugural Ball

"Emotion: Calm!" Lindsey cast the spell on herself for the twentieth time so far. Now that the big day had come, everyone in both households was nervous, excited, worried, stressed, and elated—a bad mix of emotions that left no one wholly unaffected.

Lena was exasperated with the continuous, "Now how do I look?" coming from one of the eight women or teens. She pretended to be distracted by Jonathon needing a diaper change or a feeding. As the afternoon ended, Lena was grateful to head to the kitchen, where Audrey and Ellie had also taken refuge, to fix supper for the big bunch,. She put them to work helping her make dinner.

"I'm sure glad I'm not going," Audrey said, as she peeled the potatoes. "They are so nervous it's not funny. Even Polly is bouncing off the walls."

"But Monique looks just fabulous, don't you think? She's like a beauty queen or something. I think so anyway, but then they all do," Ellie commented, very much impressed with her older sister and the other girls' new appearance. "Moni says that I can try on her heels tomorrow. You don't suppose anything bad will happen do you?"

"Nah, or I would have sensed something, maybe anyway," Audrey replied. "Hi Fern, how's Amanda doing?" Fern just arrived carrying a large pan. Luci had prepared the roast beef for the dinner. Both families would spend the last hours together, before they left for the ball.

"I've never seen her so nervous! Honestly, I had to cast Calm on her twice because she was so befuddled she couldn't do it herself. Really," Fern had a dismayed tone in her voice, but with more than a little hint of jealousy.

Alister and Deiter arrived for supper, and the huge group dined together. Once that was finished, Alister took Lindsey and Pam aside. "We will not be allowed to enter the ball with the video camera on us. We will need your unique services, Lindsey. As we approach the entrance, I will hand you the transmitter. Without using your wand, place it on the roof, where Pam has showed you. Then, I will Vanish the camera as we enter. Once inside and past the heavy security area, I will Reappear the camera and affix it to Pam. Are we all set?"

"Honestly, Alister, we are all very nervous," Lindsey admitted.

"That is only natural. So am I," he gave her his reassuring wink, and Lindsey relaxed. Somehow, when he gave that certain wink of his, she felt calm, that she was now safe. Right now, she needed that bit of reassurance.

Alister got everyone together. "Here's how it will go. For security reasons, no one is allowed to apparate directly upon the grounds. Hence, I have arranged for a limo to meet us and drive us the short distance to the Ballroom. Are we all ready? Got everything? Girls, your purses? Wands?"

Two minutes later, Alister, Deiter, Fred, Polly, Wilma, Monane, Ashley, Pam, Monique, Amanda, and Lindsey stood on an apparation platform about a half mile from their destination. A large limo pulled up, and the gentlemen helped each of the ladies get inside. All the while, Lindsey watched other couples dressed much as they appear on the platform, then head off to their waiting limos. It was dark, so they could not see much of the capital's sights; besides, they were not interested in its landmark buildings just now.

The limo pulled up at the entrance to the Ballroom, where a dozen security men were inspecting those who had arrived ahead of them. Additionally, Lindsey spied several Secret Security men and women observing the proceedings from the background. Each wore a head communications device. It was all very unnerving, so much security. As they got out, Lindsey silently cast her Move Object and placed the transmitter on the roof, right where Pam had requested it be placed.

Deiter then moved to put his right arm around her waist, while putting his left arm around Ashley, just as he had practiced. His job was to steady the two as they walked. Fred did the same with his wife and Pam. Wilma and Monique held on to each other, while Alister steadied Monane and Amanda.

Alister led the way. After passing through the security lines, an usher took Fred and Alister's invitation cards and led them to their waiting room.

He explained, "You are to wait here until the doorman comes. He will announce your party, and then you may make your grand entrance. Of course, the President will enter last. Please enjoy your ball, compliments of President Missy Snow." He bowed and left. Everyone sat down, and Alister took this interlude to position the camera properly on Pam. Pam had Lindsey Message Lloyd to see if it was all working properly. Shortly a Message floated before her eyes, and Lindsey reported that all was just fine. While they were waiting, the ladies continuously fiddled with their dresses and appearance.

Deiter whispered to Lindsey, "You look gorgeous." She flashed him a smile. He added, "I'm really nervous. Are you?"

"Really, really nervous! I hope I don't trip in these heels or fall down or whatever," she admitted.

"I'll be holding on to you as much as I can," he tried to alleviate her fears.

Finally, another man dressed even finer than Alister and the men entered; he was the doorman. He took the invitations from Alister and Fred. After looking over the names, he checked the pronunciations and then said, "Mr. Betts and his party will be introduced first; he out-ranks you, Governor Broadwell. I'll give these invitations back to you once I have read your names. I must say your women look extremely attractive. Please enjoy your ball. Are you ready?"

Lindsey desperately wanted to call out, "No!" She bit her lip in silence. "Please don't let me fall in these heels," she thought to herself and clung onto Deiter.

The doorman threw open the doors, revealing a huge, elegant ballroom. The floor was polished marble; great draperies hung from various columns surrounding the massive dance floor. A small band was seated in one corner. Opposite them, refreshments lined many tables. On the other two sides, small tables and chairs were arranged. Already something like fifty men and women had entered, and they looked at the newcomers, as the doorman spoke loudly but clearly.

"Colorado High Plains Department of Magical Misuse,

Mr. Fred Betts, his wife Polly, and daughter Pam. His sister, Wilma Weltsi. Mrs. Monane Tumble and her niece Miss Amanda Whitewater. Misses Monique Blackburn, Ashley Stokes-Compton, Lindsey Barron. Governor Alister Broadwell of Bradbury's School of Magic and Mr. Deiter Cross." He handed the invitations to the two men. A brief fanfare accompanied them as they slowly walked out onto the marble floor, the women's heels clicking on the stone surface. Many of those watching gave a round of light, polite clapping. However, the women noticed that everyone was indeed looking at them.

As Deiter led Lindsey and Ashley into the room, Lindsey's attention went to how the other women were dressed. She saw that nearly all had formal dresses similar to theirs. In this she took immense comfort, because she did not look at all out of place; she just felt out of place—big difference in the mind of a young teen.

Fred whispered to the group, "Minor officials. Looks like all the bigwigs will be introduced after we lesser ones arrive. Say, let me introduce you to my boss. I know some of these people." Fred led the group over to where two elegantly dressed couples stood chatting among each other.

"Gang, this is Mrs. Kathy Jakes, head of the Colorado Department of Law, and this is my boss, Casper Williams, Head of the Colorado Department of Magical Misuse. I'm afraid I don't know your spouse's names." He proceeded to introduce his group. Pam made sure that she got a good view of their hands and those of their spouses.

After the usual polite chatting about how great everyone looked and the frequent interruptions of new arrivals being introduced, Kathy said, "I have wanted to meet you students for some time. Miss Betts, I do hope you consider a position in the Department of Law when you graduate. That presentation you did on the now ex-Governor General was most impressive. And Miss Barron, I hear that you are following in your father's footsteps, a Dispeller, incredible. I'm sure a job awaits you when you graduate. Miss Stokes-Compton, I've heard how you are developing as a Diviner. Please keep up your studies. We need competent Diviners of your caliber, though I suspect that you would much prefer a modeling career. Oh, excuse me, I must greet Phillip." She and her husband dashed off to meet another arriving couple.

"Oh don't pay her any mind," the lovable, older Casper Williams spoke up, observing the effect of Kathy's blunt exit had on the girls. "A lot of that will go on tonight. Brown nosing with the uppity ups is the name of the game for political advancement. Guess that's why I am still where I am at, head of the Colorado Department of Magical Misuse. I'm your father's boss, Pam. Oh say, here comes the rest of our department. Felix Jones, head of the Denver Department of Magical Misuse, and Rachel Smith, Mountain Region. I oversee these three, you see. I'd like you to meet. . ." With the help of Fred, the group was introduced to the two peers of Fred.

"Oh I see you've brought along half of Bradbury's with you," Rachel teased Fred, as she began shaking hands with the girls. Lindsey thought this middle aged woman was friendly enough.

Felix commented sarcastically, "You know as well as I that he was ordered to bring the girls. Dominus requested their presence here." Lindsey didn't like the antagonistic tone of his voice. A moment later, she spotted the telltale bulge on his ring finger! He was under the control of Dominus! As far as she could tell, neither Casper nor Rachel was.

"We should make it educational, Felix," Rachel interrupted him. "Everyone here so far are us junior members of both the magical side of the government and the newly appointed norm side. Take our department for example, Magical Misuse. Each ball, a fifth of the States send their Department heads here. This year is Colorado's year, which is why we are all here. All the fifty heads of the statewide Department of Magical Misuse report to the US Head of the Department, which would be Karl Jones. Kathy, who just ran off, she heads the Colorado State Department of Law now, and she, along with forty-nine others report to the US Department of Law, run by Geneva Holmes."

"The head of the US Department of Defense—Magical Branch is run by Misty Wells. Agatha Brighton is head of the US Department of Healing, while Sam "DNA" Spade is head of the US Department of Records. Those five are the bigwigs and report to the US Regent, Thomas White. He is on the worldwide Board of Regents. Also, the US Governor General, who oversees all the magic schools, reports to Thomas as well, that would be Lacy Broom, who replaced Henry Albright, who is in prison, thanks to Pam Betts."

"These bigwigs will be announced near the end, just before the new Secretaries of Missy Snow's new administration. Missy will be the last one to arrive."

"You forgot Dominus," Felix glared at her. "Dominus will be announced just before Missy Snow, if I have it correct." Rachel glared back at him.

She said, "Say, let's move over this way, and I'll introduce you all to the head of Colorado's Department of Healing." Slowly, the group moved a hundred feet, and Rachel introduced them to Merke Lemkey.

When Monique was introduced, he commented, "Say aren't you Doctor Henry Blackburn's eldest daughter? I hear that you are planning to go to Denver Magical Healing College this fall." The two chatted for a bit, though Monique wondered who all knew that she had made this career choice!

While they were chatting, a hearty voice called out, "Hey Fred, got your whole group with you I see. You've got to introduce me to all these charming young ladies." Ace was barely twenty-one, a handsome young man, in charge of the Colorado Department of Defense—Magic Branch. He had only recently been appointed to the position, replacing the retiring head.

Ace was duly introduced to the group. He was not married and had not brought any one to the ball. However, he was instantly smitten with Monique. "Fred, you have too many beautiful women and way too few escorts for them. Miss Blackburn, if you will allow me, I would be most honored to be your escort this fine evening." He put his arm around her. He whispered into her ear, "I've heard those heels can be treacherous. Just hold onto me this evening." Monique noticed that he did not have a Dominus ring underneath his skin on his fingers and so agreed. He was very charming, she thought.

Many others came up to introduce themselves as the

minutes counted down to the major arrivals. A middle age couple, dragging a young teen came up, "Hello, I am Britt Ryker, head of Arizona Department of Law, my wife, Elaine, and our son, Tom." Fred did the introductions for his group. They all began chatting about the unusual and unexpected pardon of Dominus Malefic.

Meanwhile, Tom, who was a fourth year at the Phoenix School of Magic, came up to Pam. He'd heard the introductions. "Excuse me, but are you *the* Pam who got Governor General Albright arrested?"

Pam flushed, "Yes, he committed very serious crimes." She went on the defensive. After all, she had only met this boy. He seemed a bit shy, and he certainly was not handsome like Ace, or as gallant. In fact, she sensed that he was downright nervous.

"Wow. Way cool. We heard about it at school. I thought that was an incredibly brilliant piece of detective work! You were able to match fingerprints? Or was it the DNA that gave it away?"

He seemed genuinely interested, so Pam answered, "Fingerprints led me to the underlings that Albright hired to do his dirty work, but it was his emails to and from his underlings that hung him as the mastermind behind the bombings. Three of our staff was killed and nine horribly burned, you know."

"Incredible! Email. I would never have guessed that. Can you tell me about it? I mean if you don't mind. I'm new here. I don't really know what I am supposed to do. Are you nervous? I sure am. You look very pretty and elegant, Pam." She blushed. The two began chatting, but as their group moved a little, Pam reached out for him to help steady her walk. He responded by putting his arm around her to steady her. They chatted away, interrupted by other introductions.

He said, "I don't have anyone to dance with. I sure don't want to be *seen* dancing with my mother! Would you mind if I danced with you, Pam?" Tom asked. Pam agreed, though she didn't know why. She had planned to dance with Monique, but she saw that Monique was being monopolized by Ace. Hence, she agreed.

A short while later, a fanfare interrupted everyone. One by one, the US heads of the five magical departments and their groups were announced. Misty Wells, Department of Defense—Magical Branch, Geneva Holmes, Department of Law, Karl Jones, Magical Misuse, Agatha Brighton, Healing, and Sam "DNA" Spade, Records. Half of the crowd chuckled over the "DNA" nickname, but he was the one in charge of the entire country's DNA samples. Finally, Lacy Broom was introduced, the new US Governor General who oversaw all the magical schools. She had only been elected less than a year ago, replacing the imprisoned Albright.

Next, all the newly appointed Secretaries of President Missy Snow were introduced. Pam tried to get as close as possible so she could video their hands. Many of the names she didn't catch. A few posts had not yet been filled. However, she did get a good view of the Secretary of Justice, the Attorney General, Amos Fudge. Her video clearly showed that he wore a Dominus ring. She also got a clear shot of the Secretary of Defense, Miles Standford. He too was under the control of Dominus.

An even louder fanfare called everyone to attention. The doorman announced, "Dominus Malefic and his wife Nadia." A hush fell over the entire ballroom, as all eyes stare at the two as they slowly walked into the room. Many were intensely curious to see this man in person. Others saw the man that they had been trying to apprehend for the last few years. Others saw their silent, unspoken leader.

Dominus wore a very expensive, handmade silk tuxedo, sky blue in color, in contrast to those worn by most other men here. Lindsey gazed at his face. He seemed calmer and more relaxed than the other times she had been with him. He seemed totally in control, according to her observations.

Yet, all eyes soon focused on his new wife, Nadia. Lindsey could see why! Unlike the gowns that the others wore, Nadia wore a handmade, strapless satin gown that was truly form fitting. She had a form to fit! Her arms, or what was left of them, were barely two inches long. Her huge bust was similar to the five women that Lindsey had rescued, enormous, outlined superbly by the top of the sky blue satin dress. Her waist was incredibly tiny, accented even more by her huge bust line. The tight dress hugged her legs all the way down to near her ankles. She too wore oxford pumps, but hers were well over an inch taller than everyone else's and matched her dress. So tight was the dress and so tall were her heels that she could barely walk, taking very tiny steps, rolling her hips with each step. She certainly needed the arm of Dominus around her waist to help her keep her balance. She wore a diamond-studded tiara in her hair and a large diamond necklace that spread out over the front of her chest. Her makeup was very well done, and she looked stunning, both captivating and demanding the attention of everyone.

"Now that *is* a fetish outfit!" Monique whispered to her new friend, Ace. Dominus and Nadia walked only a little ways into the room before stopping and turning to face another door. Now the musician began playing "Hail to the Chief." Lindsey knew that President Missy Snow was about to make her appearance.

"I give you the new President of the United States of America, Missy Snow, and her vice-president and husband, Herman Snow," the doorman called out. Her arm around her husband, Missy walked grandly into the room and to the microphone. Lindsey saw that she too wore a dress very similar to those that she and her friends were wearing. Now Lindsey felt even more comfortable; she fitted in with everyone else.

"Good evening ladies and gentlemen. Thank you all for coming to my Inaugural Ball. We have fought a long, hard battle to win the Presidency. Tonight, we celebrate our victory. However, before the dance begins, I would like to express my thanks to Dominus Malefic and his charming, fetish wife Nadia for gracing us with their presence. It is time that we let go of the past and move forward in peace and harmony. It is time that we all work together, shoulder to shoulder to improve our glorious country. I know that some of you have not agreed with my decision to pardon Dominus. I respect your opinion, your point of view, *as* I would expect you would mine. I ask you to put your hatred behind you and work toward peace and harmony. Let us all work together and make this country of ours great once more. I will try to visit with all of you this evening. Now I've talked enough. Band, let's get this dance started!"

Deiter and Lindsey began to dance. She commented, "How on earth can she dance in those heels? I can barely in mine, Deiter."

Ace swept Monique onto the dance floor. Tom began dancing with Pam. Fred, seeing that Pam was dancing, took Polly in his arms. Alister took Ashley as his partner. Amanda, Wilma, and Monane were suddenly asked to dance by three others whom Lindsey had not yet met. Since the three seemed to be enjoying themselves, Lindsey stopped worrying.

A short while later, Dominus and Nadia came close to Lindsey and Deiter. They stopped to chat, and at once Ashley, Alister, Pam, and Tom moved to get closer, just in case. Alister was very worried about how Lindsey would handle coming face to face with the man who had kidnaped her twice now, cutting off her hands and then arms, to say nothing of the rest.

"Good evening, Miss Barron. I must say you look positively stunning. That dress suits you very well. I hope there are no hard feelings between us. I certainly hold none against you." His voice dripped with polite covert hostility. Lindsey knew the opposite must really be the case. However, she found that in spite of what all this man had done to her, she did not hate him. She did not get angry or even hostile towards him. Deiter fought hard to keep himself under control, however.

Lindsey replied, "Thank you. I'm not angry with you, if that is what you mean. I do hope that you will help people from now on instead of hurting them."

"I've turned over a new leaf. Look, I have even gotten married to this incredible beauty. Have you met my wife, Nadia? Isn't she the most spectacular woman at the ball?"

"Hi Nadia, congratulations. You certainly are attracting everyone's attention. That is an incredible dress. I do like the color. Everyone else is wearing faint pastels, so you look like the flower in this crowd." Lindsey felt she ought to be honest with Nadia and point out what she could that was positive."

"Thanks, Lindsey. I'm glad you see it as I do. All these faint hints of color I find disgusting. We should celebrate with colors of life. We, Dominus and I, are reflecting the sky above."

As Ashley moved closer, hanging on to the arm of Alister, Dominus greeted her. "Miss Stokes, I see that you have chosen to re-gain arms. Pity. I swear that you were an incredibly sexy without them. Still, you are one of the prettiest young women at the ball. You look absolutely radiant, my dear."

Ashley didn't know how to respond, but spoke from her heart, honestly. "Arms have made my life better in many ways, but not so good in others. I still can't shoot pool worth a darn with my arms, yet I can clear the table with my feet."

"See Nadia, it is as I have always said; women really do not need arms. Miss Stokes is living proof of that. She made it all the way through third year magic school without needing arms. If Miss Stokes can do it, so can any witch worth her salt. I must compliment you, Miss Stokes; tonight you look like the young flower of the ball! Please enjoy this evening as one to remember always. I know I will with Nadia on my arm."

Just then, Attorney General Amos Fudge came up to the group. "Excuse me, Dominus, but President Missy Snow would like a private word with you now."

"Will you excuse me? Our President is calling. Say, Miss Barron, would you be so kind as to dance with Nadia for me? Hopefully, I will only be a minute. Thank you." Amos led him off.

Lindsey moved over to face Nadia. Embarrassed, Lindsey whispered, "Should I put my arms around you?"

Nadia grinned, "Please or I will embarrass everyone by falling down! I need someone to help me keep on my feet—these heels you see. They are incredibly sexy, but not made for much walking." Lindsey put her arms around Nadia's waist and held her against her body.

"Want me to lead," Nadia whispered. Lindsey flushed, that was just what Lindsey was wondering next. "Very small steps." Nadia pressed her body against Lindsey's, and the two began to waltz to the slow tempo music.

Indeed, Lindsey felt Nadia leading her by putting slight pressures on her body with hers. Nadia then said, "Lindsey, I really, really want to talk with you and soon. I will be forthright and honest with you. I have never committed any murder or crime. You can check the records if you don't trust me. You are following me very well, by the way. You are a good dancer. You like to dance a lot, don't you? I can tell. We women do love to dress up like this and dance. Say, do you find that time just vanishes when you dance?"

"Yes, how did you know that? It's like I get started, and then it's ten p.m. all at once!"

Nadia smiled, "Yes, it's the same with me too. I can tell by the way you move; you follow me really well, far better than Dominus. Can I ask you something personal? If you don't want to answer me, that's okay. I understand, so many think such evil of Dominus and me."

Lindsey had no idea what Nadia wanted to know, but she was polite. "Sure go ahead, ask."

"I have heard that you can cast many of the Grade spells non-verbally and without a wand. Is this true? I know when I was a sixth year student—at Amsterdam School of Magic—I'm Dutch you know—I worked hard to do this, but was unable to even cast a Clean spell without my wand."

"Yes, I can cast many spells that way, though I'm still learning," Lindsey replied, trying to answer the question without giving away too much detail.

"I thought as much. Lindsey, I have so few girlfriends. I would dearly love to spend some time with you, getting to know you better. You are surprisingly different. You're not like most all the women gathered here tonight. You are very special, and I would love to make friends with you. I know that you and Dominus have had bad times together, so I would suggest that we meet, if you are at all interested, at times when he is away on business trips and when you are not in school. Believe me; I know just how much homework gets dumped on you. It only gets heavier the last two years."

She continued, "We have bought our first home in a suburb of Denver. It is difficult for me to come to visit you, though I wouldn't ever expect you to invite me into your home just now. Perhaps if we can become good friends, that day may come. I hope so, anyway. You see, I'm really still learning to adjust my life as I am now, like this." She shrugged her shoulders and wiggled her arms a little bit. Lindsey got the idea loud and clear.

"As I said, I have a hard time getting around on my own. It will get easier the more practice I get, that I'm sure of. Would you consider coming to visit me one day when I can guarantee Dominus will be gone, and it'll be just the two of us, plus my handmaiden, who helps me with things I can't do yet? If you will come, I'll make it worth your while, even if you find you don't like me and don't want to pursue a friendship with me. You see, I have had to get a completely new wardrobe, since I got married. With this bosom and tiny waist, none of my old clothes remotely fit any longer. I hate to throw them all away. You are just the size I used to be, so I know that most of them will fit you nicely. Please, Lindsey, will you come and visit me, chat with me, see if you can possibly find it in your heart to like me, even a little bit? I'm not like Dominus. You'll see."

Lindsey had to make a decision on the spot. Here was her enemy's wife asking her to come and visit in the lion's den, so to speak, though the lion would be out or so she claimed. Yet, something in the way this woman spoke to her suggested to Lindsey that Nadia was sincere in her desire. She could detect no hostility towards her, either overtly or covertly. Indeed, she shared a love of dancing, and she really did understand how time flew when she danced. If this was a trap, Lindsey thought Ashley might be able to detect it ahead of time, and she could decline at the last minute. Further, if she could master the Teleport spell as a non-verbal, non-wand spell, then she could instantly extricate herself should she find herself in a trap of some kind. Yet, would Dominus even be trying to harm her now? If he was pardoned, what did he fear from her now?

"Okay, Nadia, I'll come to visit one day," Lindsey answered her.

Nadia's face lit up; she became more radiant than normal. "Thank you so much! Please, do not say anything about this to Dominus. He'll be gone on a trip the entire second week of January. He is starting a new business, a fishing business, and will be off buying boats and stuff in

Florida all that week. I'll be on my own then." She gave Lindsey her email address, and Lindsey told Nadia hers, Nadia repeated it several times, memorizing it, though it was plainly obvious, LindseyBarron@Bradbury.edu.

"Ah, there you are, my queen," the voice of Dominus broke in on the two. "I see that you are enjoying the company of my wife too. Isn't she just the fetish queen? Darling, may I cut in on Miss Barron?" he grinned at his wife; she grinned back. Lindsey could tell that Nadia did have a strong bond with him, though she could not see why. "Miss Barron, thank you again for looking after Nadia for me. I appreciate it." Lindsey nodded and backed away.

Shortly, Deiter's arm went around her waist, steadying her. "Thanks, it's daunting to be standing all by myself," she whispered to him. Deiter grinned.

"I know. What was that all about?" he asked as the two resumed their waltz. Lindsey explained what Nadia had told her. "Do you trust her? I mean, she's the wife of Dominus. How can she not be a criminal?"

"Don't know, Deiter. It's just that I didn't detect anything amiss. I'll talk to Alister about it, first."

"Excuse me, Master and Madam, the President wishes a word with you at this time. If you will follow me, please," the aide interrupted them. Lindsey saw that their whole group was being escorted over to the President's table.

"President Snow, allow me to introduce our party," Fred Betts took the initiative and introduced each person. As they were introduced, President Missy Snow shook their hands, giving each a warm greeting.

"Thank you for coming to my Inaugural Ball. It is always such a nice thing to see our young people taking an active interest in our government," she said in a slightly condescending manner, at least Lindsey thought it was. "I trust that you will always study hard to become the best wizard and witches this country has, and then when you graduate, remember to do your very best to help make our country strong and peaceful. I understand that Miss Barron has had some run ins with Mr. Malefic before. I do hope that you can see the great benefits to our country of my giving him a full pardon and that you will not harbor ill will towards him or his men."

"How would you feel if he stunned you making you completely helpless and then cut off your hands and arms and sewed your mouth shut? Warm and friendly towards him? Bosom buddies now?" Pam burst out towards her. If no one else was going to say anything, she sure would. "Dominus is an evil sadist and murderer. That's the man you've pardoned," she added.

"Surely he had his reasons, but we must try to put that into the past and look forward to the future. Dominus is a powerful wizard, who, if given the *proper* direction, can do *great* things for our country," President Snow countered. "Besides, look at all the time and money the government has spent over the last nearly four years trying to track him down and apprehend him! Four years with nothing at all to show for it. Yet, within days of his pardon, here he is being an active, contributing member of our society once more. You must put your bias and prejudice behind you and embrace the future. Mr. Malefic will do great things for our country. He is a reformed man now and will be of immense value to our land."

She looked at Mr. Betts, "You have gotten the Attorney General's orders to cease all investigations of Mr. Malefic, have you not, Mr. Betts?" She gave him a cold stare, as though he was openly violating their orders, putting him on the spot. Pam saw that her outburst had only gotten her father into hot water and wished that she'd kept her mouth shut.

"Of course, Madam President. All records have been purged; personnel reassigned to other investigations," Fred stated factually.

"Good, we must look to the future and forget the past, Mr. Betts. We need all the assistance we can muster to get this country back on the road to health and prosperity," she continued.

Deiter saw that Fred was being pressured and decided to take a different tact. "President Snow, I see that you have given the word Justice a new meaning. Might I suggest that you have the families and relatives of those whom Dominus has murdered in the last four years and those women who he had kidnaped, cut off their arms, blinded, and repeatedly raped kept under close scrutiny? I believe you'll find they will have a very difficult time accepting your Justice. You need to keep an eye on them; they might not be looking forward to the bright, peaceful, and hopeful future that you and Mr. Malefic are planning. It would look bad for you, if one of these women tried to take revenge into their own hands." Deiter said all this very covertly.

"Oh, such wisdom from one so young! Governor Alister, Mr. Cross is a great credit to your school. We will certainly keep, as you suggest, our eye on them. Well, if you will excuse me, I still have hundreds more to meet. It has been a pleasure speaking with you all. Remember to work towards peace and cooperation. We must all don the mantle and do our fair share to help our America grow strong and prosperous."

This was a dismissal, and the aide gestured for them to move back onto the dance floor. Another group was nearby, making their way to chat briefly with the President. When they were out of earshot, Pam declared, "Deiter, I can't believe that she totally bought your sarcasm! She must be a complete dope to have believed that you were sincere!"

"Thanks for sticking up for me, you two," Lindsey added.

"I'm sorry, dad. I didn't mean to get you into trouble. Do you think you will have more repercussions because of what I said to her?" Pam asked, her face crinkled with worry lines.

"Probably not. I suspect that she is hearing quite a lot of that kind of thing tonight. After all, she's managed to upset three quarters of all the people in the law enforcement departments of the entire country! I'm sure she's heard vastly more severe criticism before now. I think it was good of you to stick up for Lindsey. You too, Deiter," Fred replied.

"Well, I made quadruply sure that I got good shots of her hands. She's wearing quite a few rings," Pam declared.

"Three were magical rings," Lindsey spoke up. Alister looked down at her, and she smiled. "Well, I just took the opportunity to practice my Identify spell lessons," she cleverly added. Everyone chuckled. "One is shielding her from up to

Grade 3 spells. Another prevents anyone from reading her mind, and the third is keeping anyone from scrying on her thoughts. One was just a wedding ring, expensive though, I think."

"Well done. I will relay to Mary Ann that you have practiced her spell well tonight," Alister chuckled once again. They resumed their dancing once more.

A bit later, Lindsey tripped. Deiter elegantly held on to her, moving her body along the same path as she was falling, as if they were doing a dip. Then, he got her back on her feet. Lindsey looked pale. "What happened?" Deiter asked.

"Someone deliberately cast a Trip spell on me. I think someone wanted me to take a fall and become totally embarrassed!"

Deiter covertly glanced around the room, his eyes landing on Dominus, as his first thought. However, Dominus had his back to them, chatting with another group and had not even seen Lindsey take a dip. "Wasn't Dominus," he whispered. "He's got his back to us. Who else would want to have you make a fool of yourself?"

"Dunno. Just keep a tight hold on me in case they do it again," Lindsey replied, nearly petrified that she had nearly disgraced everyone by falling down on the dance floor.

A bit later, Tom Ryker managed to catch Pam, who also suddenly tripped. He cleverly turned it into a dipping back swoop, then gently raising her back up. Pam looked ashen and shocked. "Someone tried to Trip me!" she whispered.

"I know. I saw that man over there doing something subtle with his wand. The second you started to fall, I acted. I think everyone just thinks we did a cool back swoop, Pam," Tom said. "You are too good a dancer to trip."

"Thanks, Tom, you saved me! I would have embarrassed everyone if I'd tumbled onto the floor. Let's dance a little closer to that man so I can get a good look at him." A minute later, Pam turned in a circle move and got a very good look at his face, though he was no longer paying them any attention. Then, Tom moved them away from him.

"Well, he is not a known Death Stalker; at least I don't recognize his face from the files. I think he is probably one of

Madam Idiot's Secret Service men. That would make sense, if she wanted to get back at me for speaking out like I did."

"What did you say to her anyway?" Tom asked, very curious about it. Pam blushed and repeated their conversation highlights. Tom chuckled, "Way to go Pam. I like that about you. You have more guts than any girl at Phoenix!" He gave her a little bit of a hug. She blushed.

Not long after that, Alister announced, "It's time for us to go."

"What? How did it get to be ten o'clock already?" asked Lindsey, who would have sworn it was no later than nine.

"Yes, it can't be that late already," Pam added, still holding onto Tom.

Tom giggled, "It's midnight, Pam. I have really, really enjoyed your company tonight. You are the greatest!" He gave her a loving hug and left to find his parents. He didn't see Pam's face turn a deep pink. Pam suddenly felt very hot.

From the corner of her eye, she saw Ace giving a passionate good night kiss to Monique. Her eyes fixed on them, as she began moving with the group. It was the first time that she had seen a boy kissing Monique, and Monique seemed to be enjoying it. Strange emotions filtered through her body. Then a bubbling Monique caught up to her and took her hand.

"Wow, that Ace Brill is really a nice fellow. How was Tom? He seemed to monopolize you all night, Pam."

"He is really nice too. He saved me from falling. A Secret Service man attempted to Trip me and embarrass me."

"What? You too?" Deiter interrupted her. "Someone tried to Trip Lindsey. I kept her from falling and made it look like it was a dance move." They chatted about the significance of this as they left the ballroom. Outside, Lindsey Moved the transmitter from the roof, shrunk it into a very tiny object, and placed it cleverly into Governor Alister's hand. He gave a fleeting grin as he felt it appear there. A minute later, Lindsey was standing before her porch, home at last.

Just as soon as they entered the house, Wilma exclaimed, "Off with these heels! Oh do my feet hurt. I can tell I'm not used to wearing them." However, the girls also began changing. Lindsey didn't want to risk snagging a run in her nylons. Neither did the others for that matter, not at twenty-five dollars a pair. Considering the hours spent dressing, they all wound up in the kitchen in less than ten minutes. All were famished and Lena and Lottie had a midnight supper waiting for them, expecting just this.

The conversation was light, except for Pam's query about how the video recording went. Only after Lloyd assured her that it went like clockwork did she relaxed. Considering the late hour, Lena insisted that Alister and Deiter stay the night. She had already contacted the Cross's and gotten their permission. Lena had also arranged for Ashley's grandparents to be here and spend the night. Ashley, delighted, spent most of her time chatting with her grandparents, who could not have looked any prouder of their granddaughter. In fact, none of the parents could have. It was an event to tell their grandchildren about, Lena kept saying, much to the embarrassment of Lindsey, who had no such thoughts.

Around one in the morning, they finally went to bed. As Pam closed her eyes, she reflected upon the entire evening. No, she didn't think about the spying and the video recording conspiracy. Rather, it was her emotions. This evening she'd felt things that she had never felt before. Still too keyed up to sleep, she began to use her normal analytical skills on her emotions, as she always had. Unfortunately, her feelings did not yield to analytical thought.

She had felt beautiful this evening, really beautiful, not the homely girl she had always seen in the mirror. Analytically, this made no sense, since she was still Pam. Yet, she had felt this way all evening long, and she *loved* that feeling! Then, her mind saw Ace kissing Monique. It was a passionate kiss, just the way she and Monique always kissed in private! Pam suddenly realized that she was jealous of Ace!

After a while, images of Tom appeared. He had definitely gotten her attention. He was not anywhere near as handsome as Ace, but something about him had kept her attention on him all night long. She just could not figure out what this feeling in her stomach was or meant, only that she had felt it all evening. Then the morning came unexpectedly.

Monique also had wild, raw emotions all evening. Ace was handsome and understanding and kind, and, well, she had so many 'and's' that the list seemed endless. "Oh, I've a crush on Ace!" she realized, but then thought at once of Pam. She fell asleep dreaming of how she could have both Ace and Pam at the same time. Both teens were profoundly changed from the ball and in ways that they could never have imagined beforehand.

Chapter 20—Aftermath

Everyone rose late the next morning. Lloyd was up first, going to answer the door. Via Mag Mail, Deiter's parents sent him everyday clothes, which pleased Deiter, who was worried that he would have to wear the tuxedo when everyone else was wearing jeans.

As everyone wiped sleep from their eyes and devoured the stacks of pancakes, bacon, and eggs, Lloyd again had to answer the door, another Mag Mail delivery. "Whoa, this one is for Miss Ashley Stokes-Compton," Lloyd teased her, handing her the package.

"Hurry up open it. Who's it from?" asked Lindsey, rather excited. Ashley almost never got Mag Mail.

Ashley flushed and replied, "Teen Fashion Magazine. What could they want?" She opened the package and read the cover letter. The latest magazine was enclosed along with a legal contract. Ashley read it, but was too embarrassed to read it to the others. Instead, she handed it to Lindsey who read it aloud to everyone.

Dear Miss Ashley Stokes-Compton,

Teen Fashion Magazine is proud to offer you a photo shoot modeling session for our main feature article and cover for our May issue. The theme this year is Swing into Spring. The interview and shoot will take the better part of one day. We know that you will be heading back to school shortly and we would like to do the shoot before then. Your remuneration will be our standard cover model payment of $10,000.00!

Lindsey shrieked when she read the amount! "Blah, blah, oh, it says you are to reply today if you are interested, either by Mag Mail, fax, or email. Blah, blah, oh, it says you must bring along one parent or guardian but you can bring along other friends if you like."

"How do they know Ashley lives here? How do they even know about Ashley, let alone that she is pretty enough to be their cover model?" declared Pam, seeing a mystery brewing.

"Blah, blah, blah," Lindsey said as her eyes skimmed over the letter. Oh, it says that a Miss Kathy Townsend sent us your name, photo, and pertinent data. Kathy, way to go!" Pam's great mystery evaporated.

Ashley couldn't believe it. "Ten thousand dollars for one day's work? That'll double my savings! Do they really want to take my picture? Me?"

"Ja, sure, you should do it," Katja encouraged her.

"Ja, you should, you are more than pretty enough," Jeannette added.

"Mom?" Ashley looked to Lena for help and reassurance.

Lena deferred to Lloyd. "I've never seen the magazine. Do you suppose she ought to do this?"

Everyone decided to look over the March issue. It was tasteful and anything but sleazy. Both Lloyd and Lena said it would be fine, but only if she wanted to do it. Ashley decided that she couldn't turn down the money. Lloyd and Fred went over the contract and found nothing amiss or harmful. A half hour later, Lloyd sent off the Mag Mail for her. Later that day, by return Mag Mail, they learned the shoot would be on Friday in Denver. Because of the baby, Lena couldn't go with her. Hence, Lloyd would go, along with Wilma and Monane, giving her needed protection, in case something went wrong. Lena also decided to send Katja and Jeannette along with her. This would certainly be something the Dutch students could share with their families and friends when they returned. Both girls were ecstatic over going with Ashley to see a real photo shoot!

When the excitement died down, Lindsey had a long talk with Alister about Nadia's desire to make friends with her and to have her come and visit her at her new home in the Denver suburbs. "Honestly, I think she was being sincere about it, Alister. Besides, I can perhaps learn more about our adversaries this way." Alister insisted on Ashley's opinion. Try as she might, Ashley could not sense anything bad happening as a result of her doing this. Satisfied, Alister gave his okay on two conditions.

"One, you must be able to cast Teleport sans wand and

non-verbally. If things go wrong, I want you to be able to get out of there fast no matter what happens. Two, you can't go alone. I and some others will go with you and stay invisible just outside the home. If they try any trickery, we will be at hand to put an end to it. Is this agreeable?"

"Oh sure. However, these Grade 5 spells are so tough that I haven't had time to work on casting them my special way. I guess I have been too lazy this vacation. I better get to work."

"Considering the importance of this, Lindsey, I will stay today and work with you myself. She did indicate that the visit ought to be this week. We must have you able to Teleport if it becomes a trap." Lindsey grinned; this would be fun! The two then bundled up and went outside to begin working on the spell.

Deiter took this opportunity to have a private chat with Pam. "Anything on our mysterious Mr. Greeley Longsteen?" He was referring to the strange wizard who had published a paper thirty-five years ago on how the Teleport spell worked, and that when one teleported, he or she moved out of this universe, passing through a bit of space of another universe, which has been called the Beyond, and then re-appearing back in our universe. He had claimed that this Beyond had inhabitants called goggles, whose description sounded much like ghastly looking dogs. Their problem was how to contact the man. He had no phone number, no email address, no nothing, except a house in Leadville. He was born in Yorkshire, England, went to Oxford School of Magic, attended Oxford University, and graduated with a degree in physics, before moving to New York, where he published his paper. He then moved to Chicago, and then to Leadville.

"I wrote him, but got no answer," he said.

"Deiter, I have now written him ten letters! He has not replied to one of them. They did not come back so I know he must have gotten them. I just don't know what more we can do, except go knocking on his door or something."

"Wow. Ten! Pam, thank you!" Deiter exclaimed, excited that she had taken him seriously and made such an effort on his behalf. "Wonder why he won't reply?"

"Dunno, maybe thinks we are more crackpots or journalist out for a twisted story on him or something equally dreadful."

"Perhaps we should pay him a visit. After all, we still have some days before we have to go back to school. I'm sure we can get someone to go with us," Deiter replied confident that they could do just that.

"Well, I suppose so," Pam slowly admitted. She didn't want to sound very excited about Deiter's special research project, although she was. "But we should probably first chat with him and tell him that we're coming. It's not polite just to show up on someone's door. Besides, he might be out at the grocery store or something when we arrive."

"Yes, but how do we chat with him?" Deiter asked, both confused and excited.

"We Message him, of course," Pam said flatly, as if she were addressing a first year.

"Cool! Ah, you better do it, since you've been writing the most letters," Deiter suggested, more than a little nervous about doing this. He suddenly realized that Pam was braver than he was! He was startled by this revelation, which shouldn't be. After all, he was Black Hall and she, Yellow Hall.

"Okay, let's sit down and do this. I'll send him a message similar to the letters and then add that we are coming for a visit. Then, I'll ask him what day. That way, he'll realize that we mean business." The two sat down in Pam's bedroom, and she waved her wand, composed the message, and sent it to Mr. Greeley Longsteen.

"Well?" Deiter asked a moment later.

"The spell worked. My Message was sent and was received—that much my spell can tell, nothing more, of course. I guess we wait for his reply." Both sat there waiting expectantly for a magical paper to appear before Pam's eyes.

Never in a million years would either of them have predicted what happened next. No, a Message paper did not appear before Pam's eyes. Instead, the head of an old man, with a long beard streaked with grey, wearing very thick glasses, materialized above their heads. Only his upside down head appeared. It was as if the rest of his body from the neck on down was somewhere up on their roof. Both teens craned their necks upwards, staring at the weird sight!

Pam found her voice first, after clearing it twice. She did not want to sound totally freaked out or startled by his upside down head hanging from her bedroom ceiling. "Mr. Greeley Longsteen, I presume?"

"He he, yes, yes, I do believe that is the name I had. You are the two who keep sending my house the letters?"

"Well, yes. We wish to discuss with you the Beyond and what lies there. Deiter has already seen the goggles, well once, when he was being teleported while he had his magical eye extended."

The thick glasses stared at Deiter for a moment. "And you didn't get the heebie jeebies?"

"Well, yes, my body got sick, sort of freaked out, but I've recovered, and I know that they are real and are there. Apparently, no one else but you knows about the Beyond and the goggles. Please, Dr. Longsteen, we would really like to come and visit with you about all this. We really do. I know that others have called you a crackpot and worse, but we know better."

"Blimey, you are sure that you want to do this?" he asked. His voice was fairly high pitched, and he had a distinct English accent.

"Of course, we are and do. Why else would I have written you ten letters?" Pam answered flatly and didactically, again as if he were a first year.

"Well, then do a Half-teleport."

"A what?" asked Deiter, quite confused, wondering what is a Half-teleport spell.

"Oh bother," the bespectacled man said. He lowered an arm to the two. They saw his arm suddenly protruding down from the ceiling, not otherwise connected to anything. Fully extended, his reach was just beyond theirs. Hastily, Deiter stood on his chair. Pam followed suit. They both held on to his hand. The next instant they arrived in the Beyond.

"Welcome to the Beyond and my home," Greeley said, only now they saw that he indeed had a complete body. His clothing was definitely of English origin. Pam looked around and saw nothing but blackness in all directions including up and down. However, there stood Deiter and Greeley. Deiter was just as disoriented as she was, which she found comforting. She was not imagining this.

"My home is this way," he said. Pam noticed that he did not open his mouth to speak. "There is nothing here. It is the Beyond. Thoughts rule here. Think and we will hear. Think that you are moving, and you will move. Oh here, take my hands," he extended one to each of them, a little exasperated by the two gaping youngsters.

"Way far out cool!" Pam thought.

"You can say that again, incredible! It's just like I saw it, Pam," Deiter added.

"Here's my house," Greeley said to the two. Lindsey saw a quaint English cottage floating in the middle of this void. He led them inside. Just as they entered, two large goggles appeared and began barking. Unnerved, Pam jumped back, suddenly quite frightened. They looked ghastly or ghostly might be a better way of putting it. Nearly transparent, the goggles looked like a dog, in that they seemed to walk on all fours and did not have hands as a human would. Their long yellow fur was reminiscent of a lion, as were their overly large canines and loud growls.

"Oh look, Elmoid; we have scared the creature!" one of the goggles said.

"Mellor, that's what we are supposed to do. Haven't you been paying Greeley any mind at all? Growl. Growl," the other added.

Greeley laughed, "Good show, Elmoid, Mellor. Perfect job." Deiter just stood his ground, staring at the creatures like those that he had seen that fateful day when he was teleported. Seeing them again did not cause him to froth at the mouth or convulse. In fact, he wondered why he had done that in the first place.

Deiter said, or rather thought, "Hey, you can talk! Cool."

"Duh, the small one talks," Elmoid commented.

"What's he think we are anyway," Mellor added, "a couple of doggies from his world?"

"Probably," Greeley explained. "I say, we have company. This is one called Deiter Something and Pam Something. These are my dear friends, Elmoid and Mellor. They are staying with me at the moment."

"Now we thought Greeley was an awfully strange thing to be called, but Something? That is even stranger," Mellor replied. "Still, we are pleased to meet Deiter and Pam Something."

"Cross, Deiter Cross, that's my name. Greeley meant that he didn't know our full names. Pam Betts," Deiter took charge. Pam was still recovering her senses.

"Ah, even stranger, don't you think, Mellor?"

"Yes, I think I preferred Something to Cross and Betts. Ah well, so much for names."

"Oh yes, we have guests! Now let's see what am I supposed to do?" Greeley muttered to himself, as if trying to remember some fact lost somewhere in the vast, distant past. "Ah, tea! That's what it was called." Turning to the two, he said, "Would you care to take tea with us?"

"Sure," Pam replied mechanically, out of habit.

"Ah, now let's see, tea. It was hot, if I remember right. Oh and it tasted good. Sugar, yes, I'm supposed to ask if they want sugar when I serve it. Let there be tea and sugar. Oops, well not that much sugar!" A teapot with five cups appeared, steam tendrils rising into the room. A twenty-pound sack of sugar also appeared momentarily until it was replaced by a sugar bowl and a spoon.

He poured everyone a cup, though Pam swore that his hands did not actually touch the teapot itself. He noticed her noticing him, "Just think it, and it is here in the Beyond. Much more convenient, I find. Besides, the pot is hot. I wonder if I could actually get burned or would it be me just thinking that I was burned? Is that another conundrum I wonder? Well, here's to your health." He raised his cup and took a sip.

Hesitatingly, Pam raised her cup and investigated. She certainly didn't want to drink anything unhealthy. It smelled like a strong black tea, however. So she ventured a sip. Tasted like a strong tea, she decided. Deiter, however, added several teaspoons of sugar to his.

"I say, perhaps you two could help me with a little problem that these friends of mine saddled me with. Imagine a pole twelve feet tall. Imagine a worm who wants to climb to the top of the pole." As he said the words, indeed a pole and a worm materialized in the middle of his room. "Now the worm is industrious and patient, or so Mellor claims. During the day, it climbs up three feet. However, at night, it falls asleep and slides back down two feet. The challenge is to tell Mellor and Elmoid here how long it takes the worm to get to the top. I've been insisting that the worm takes twelve days. Mellor insists that it does not. Can you explain?"

"Oh that is an old children's teaser. It takes ten days, because on the tenth day it reaches the top. The top of a pole is flat, so it can't slide back at night," Pam explained.

"She's a sharp one, Mellor," Elmoid replied. "Yes, that is what we keep telling Greeley here. He says the pole is round and so it slides off at night. It boils down to the shape of the pole. What shape is a pole?"

"Hey, a pole can have any kind of shape on its end," Deiter answered. "I've seen pointed ones, rounded ones, and flat ended ones, so I guess you both are right."

"Wise, this Deiter is," Mellor replied.

"Ask another, Mellor," Elmoid said.

"Okay, if you have a three-dimensional coordinate system and x goes this way and y goes that way, which way goes z?" Mellor asked.

"It all depends on whether you are using the right hand rule or the left hand rule, you just have to remember to be consistent in its application," Pam declared.

"No dummy, this Pam is," Elmoid replied. Deiter remained silent. He had no idea what they had asked or what Pam had answered, save it was correct.

"I've got one. Pam Something, we want to know if a number is a prime number. Do we need to try dividing it by all the numbers from two on up to that number to see if it is evenly divisible?"

"Of course not; that's a waste of time. Just check up to the square root of the number. Saves you half of the work," Pam answered.

"Oh this *is* fun! We have another Greeley with us!" Mellor exclaimed very excitedly.

"Whatever do you mean?" Pam asked, slightly baffled by all these questions.

"It is her first time in the Beyond, Mellor, I so believe," Greeley explained. "Up here in the Beyond, everything you do is controlled by your thoughts. Only the very intelligent of beings can manage to travel to here, wherever here might be, since it is nowhere. Obviously, you two are here, so you must be very bright students. The goggles are just having a little fun with you, that's all. We so rarely have a visitor up here, you see."

"None but Greeley, from your world," Elmoid pointed out.

"Er, well, now you've seen two more, so that makes it a two hundred percent increase from my world," he teased the two.

He took another sip and added, "Anyway, if you cannot handle your thoughts properly, if your intelligence is not up to par, you would have not been able to come with me when I Half-teleported you here. I suspected you wouldn't actually make it, and so I was more than a little surprised when you materialized at my side out there. I spend most all of my time here in the Beyond. It is so much more enlightening to spend time with fellow intelligent beings than the dopes back down there, wherever there is."

"Tell them about the light show, Greeley," Mellor suggested.

"I suppose I ought to present our current theories first. After all, this is their first visit. You see, when we use our Teleport spell at point A in our world, we step momentarily out of it and, by the power of the thought of your spell, appear here, where that power places you at point B, the destination you intended. As far as you can tell, it is nearly instantaneous, but up here in the Beyond, you can see them, as they suddenly appear here in the Beyond and then zip across the nothingness, and then disappear back into their world. The streaks are our light show. To find you a bit ago, I merely followed the streak of energy down to your world and poked my head in. Once you get the hang of it, you can just poke your head in nearly anywhere, as long as you know where it is that you want to poke it. That's the hard part. Sometimes, when we get bored, we begin to randomly poke our heads through, just to see where it's at. I once stuck my head into a sun. That had to hurt, but since thought rules here, Mellor just had me change my mind about it, and I was fine."

"Come on; let's watch," Greeley suggested. They went outside and sat down; at least Pam thought that she sat down. Her body did appear to be sitting, but on what, she had no idea. In a sphere around her, all was a black void.

Suddenly, she saw a streak of white light. "Ah, there goes someone now," Greeley pointed out.

"So that is what we look like when we are teleporting?" asked Pam.

"Bloody well yes," Greeley replied enthusiastically. "Whee, there goes another one. I've told my friends here that the most frequent light shows occur in the morning and evenings, as people of our world got to and from work. It lights up like Trafalgar Square at night. Bloody cool."

"I notice that the light trails take a bit to dampen out. Why is that? Anyway to identify who the person or being was that just teleported?" asked Deiter. "And how is it that we could get here to visit you by ourselves? That new spell you called a Half-teleport?"

"Lots of questions, has he, eh, Mellor?" Elmoid chuckled.

"He's on to our project, that he is, Elmoid," Mellor replied. "That's why we are here, Greeley too, we think. Why do the light trails take time to dampen out? That is our research project. Unfortunately, we have not gotten very far with it yet. Big problem face we: what is time if there is nothing by which to measure it, except by our own thoughts about it, eh? Conundrum indeed."

"Oh, you could just go to the endpoint of the streak and pop your head in, like I did and see who it was," Greeley answered the second question. "You get here by your own thought, as I said; thought is all that is here. Half-teleport is my word for it. You start your Teleport spell and have your mind go blank just after your wand fires. Poof, you get here, kind of like waiting for the destination thought to arrive. If it doesn't, why, you are here."

"How do we get back? I mean to my bedroom, when we want to get back?" Pam asked, becoming very curious about this whole Beyond thing and how it operated.

"Think upon your destination, decide to be there, and you will be there. Bloody simple, a child could do it," Greeley replied.

"Another question, if I may," Pam asked. Hearing no objections, she continued, "Since out there is, well anywhere, how could I sort of move to some spot I know in my world and stick my head in there? I mean, suppose I wanted to peek at my house in Sterling, Colorado. Where out there would I think myself to, and how do I pop my head in to take a peek?"

"Since here is there and there is here and all is but where you think it to be, you can say you are there and there you are, if you so think that you are. Me, I think I am bending down and pulling my head into the world, like I used to do when I peeked under the covers at me mom and dad when they were sleeping," Greeley answered her.

"So you're saying that if I say right here," Pam moved a bit to her left, "this is my home in Sterling, if I bend down and pretend that I'm peering under my bed, I can see. . ." She didn't finish her sentence. Deiter saw her head totally disappear! At first, he panicked, believing that Pam had just somehow decapitated herself! However, he didn't see any blood and calmed down.

Pam's head appeared high in the sky over her family home in Sterling, just her head peering into the world from on high. She suddenly realized a small child playing in the snow near her house was looking up and pointing to her head in the sky. Quickly, she thought herself back with Deiter, and so was.

"Way unbelievably cool! Deiter, my head was over my house, in Sterling. Some girl looked up at me. I think I spooked her, though."

"Suppose we should be a bit careful," Greeley suggested, "though they won't believe it anyway. Sometimes I wonder why it is I ought to worry."

"Don't you have to eat up here?" asked Deiter, who was getting hungry.

"It is mere consideration. Think yourself full of lamb chops and so you are," Greeley replied.

Deiter never had lamb and decided to have a large roast beef sandwich. He tasted it in his mouth, and his stomach felt full. "Amazing."

"Don't you ever go home to your house in Leadville?" Pam wanted to know.

"Why? Is there something there I should know about? Well, I do check on it now and then. Get all these letters from you two," he chuckled. "Seriously, there is nothing down there of interest to me really. My pals here, Elmoid and Mellor, are actually geniuses. We have the best conversations and adventures. Honestly, Pam, up here in the Beyond, you only meet the most intelligent beings in the universe, though we're not sure that is quite the right word for it. Mellor suggests that there are many such universes, but we wax philosophical on you now."

"Say, how do you judge time up here? I mean we left without telling anyone, and we could be giving everyone a terrible scare if we're missing for a long time," Pam suddenly remembered what they had done. Even Deiter suddenly got worried about it as well.

"Oh no problem, for what is time in the Beyond. Merely state your arrival time as you return. I suppose you ought to be returning now. Please feel free to come and visit with us again. I have in fact rather enjoyed chatting with you two. I didn't think that I would, which is why I ignored your letters, Pam Something. However, it has been fun, especially remembering the teatime. Just decide it is a minute after I came and reappear there."

Pam offered Greeley her hand, as did Deiter. "Bloody well forgot about handshakes!" Greeley replied shaking her hand.

"Hey, how about us?" Mellor asked, a human hand suddenly appearing out of his middle. Pam giggled and shook it too. Mellor seemed to get a kick out of it. Elmoid followed suit. "Do come back for a visit."

Deiter and Pam concentrated on it being a minute after they had gone, decided they were back standing on their chairs, and so they were.

"Wow! Pam! Was that ever cool! It was real, wasn't it?" Deiter asked.

Pam sat down on her chair. "That, Deiter Cross, was the single most important thing that I have ever learned! I think for now, until we know more about the Beyond, we should keep it to ourselves. After all, remember what happened to Greeley, when he went public with it thirty-five years ago."

"Yeh, I see your point. They might try to throw us into the looney bin. Okay, mum's the word. I don't know how I'm ever going to repay you for helping me with this! You ever need something, I'm your man!" Deiter gave Pam a big hug. He then left to see how Lindsey was doing; he rather missed her.

Pam sat there in thought for some time. This was an incredibly important discovery, monumental in her opinion, but not believable by the average person.

Deiter found Alister and Lindsey outside; she was practicing her spell. "Hey, how's it going?"

"Hi Deiter. Alister really knows how to help me. Watch this. Teleport: Barnyard." Of course, he didn't hear the destination, but saw her waving from the vicinity of the barn. A moment later, she reappeared beside them.

"Way cool, Lindsey! No wand. Fantastic. I wish I could do this one spell that way too."

Alister explained kindly, "In sixth year, Deiter, we will work on it. Cover the theory first. Only a very few ever do manage to do one or more spells non-verbally, no wand. A little patience and you may get your wish, but then you may not."

"Great. Well, I best get going; my folks want me back. Goodbye for a while, Lindsey; thank you for a wonderful ball." He gave her a hug, and she returned it. She and Alister watched him teleport safely home, before resuming her training. By suppertime, Lindsey had the Teleport spell down perfect, even when Alister was purposely harassing her, as if he were trying to prevent her from escaping him. When the two came inside for dinner, Lindsey was very pleased with her success, though she now realized that these more difficult spells would be harder for her to get down her special way, unless she practiced them a whole lot. This she vowed to find time to do when they got back to school.

During supper, the conversation was on Ashley's photo shoot, scheduled for Friday, now three days away. Just after supper, the monotone voice announced, "Miss Kathy Townsend is arriving." Ashley rushed to the door to let her in.

"You did it, Ashley. I knew you could. I'm so glad I sent it in. I hope you aren't angry that I did that," Kathy said, entering and giving Ashley a hug.

"Well at first, I wanted to kick your butt," Ashley giggled, "but then I changed my mind. I get ten thousand dollars for letting them take pictures of me for one day. Can you believe that?"

"Sure can. They make millions of dollars from their magazine. Lots of us use it to know what to buy," Kathy answered. "Now tell me all about the Inaugural Ball! I have to see your dresses! Honestly, did they cost four thousand dollars each?" Kathy asked awed. The girls all disappeared for hours in their rooms.

Just after Kathy came, Lindsey had an email reply from Nadia. She showed it to Alister. "Darn, she wants us to get together on Friday just after lunch. That's when Ashley is doing her photo shoot. Should I cancel?"

"No, I'm available, and I know several others who will lend a hand. Go ahead and set it up. Make sure you have very good directions. I don't want you teleporting yourself into the ground or half into a tree," he teased. "I'll come to pick you up at say 11:30 on Friday and make sure you get there safely. Just be sure to send me the directions as soon as you get them from her. I wish to verify them beforehand, just in case. Remember, we are dealing with Dominus, who will stop at nothing to achieve his goals." She agreed, and Alister said his farewells and left. Lindsey joined the others, showing Kathy their dresses.

Chapter 21—Friday Events

"Honestly, Lindsey, I don't sense anything bad is going to happen to you today," Ashley told Lindsey. It was early Friday morning. Ashley was just about set to go to her Teen Fashion Magazine photo shoot. Polly, Monane, Wilma, Lloyd, Kathy, Katja, and Jeannette were accompanying her. Since Kathy had sent in her name and photos, which resulted in her getting this job, Ashley had asked Kathy to come too, something that utterly thrilled the young teen.

The group vanished from their front porch a few minutes before eight, arriving at the designated studio in Denver. At once, they rushed Ashley into the makeup and hair styling department. A reporter with a recorder followed her throughout the day, asking her many questions, preparing the interview with would accompany the spread.

During the day, Ashley wore four completely new outfits, designed for the summer season, even though this was the dead of winter. The studio was well heated and the fake backdrops looked real enough, though Ashley realized that no one would be looking at the backdrop. She was very surprised at the end of the day when her host gave her a bag containing all the clothes and shoes that she had worn. This was a fringe benefit, she discovered.

All had gone well. The teens were thrilled to have seen it all and spent the evening telling everyone about it. Kathy had even snuck some pictures with her cell phone to show everyone. Ashley proudly showed everyone her check for ten thousand dollars! "Now you are a teen fashion model, Ashley!" Kathy declared proudly. She had been saying all along that Ashley had the looks for it; her conviction had been accurate indeed.

Shortly before noon, Alister arrived. "We are all in position, Lindsey. Professors Cho Lin, Huan Su, and Delius are watching the place as we speak, Invisible, of course. Her directions are very well done. Dominus is not there and has not been there for a few days. As near as we can tell, he is not due back until at least Monday, though we shall see about that. Their place is an expensive new home in one of the wealthier suburbs. By all appearances, everything looks as it should. Delius detects no traps yet. I will say this: Delius was quite upset that I was allowing you to make this visit into the lion's den, as he put it. However, when I explained that you could now Teleport sans wand, sans words, and while being distracted, he changed his opinion. Actually, he was rather surprised that you could do this."

He went on very seriously, "He still thinks that you could be drugged or poisoned or worse, so do be careful. Alert us at the tiniest sign of anything amiss, please. Your safety is our prime concern."

"I will. I think that this may be a golden opportunity to find out useful information, especially now that he has been pardoned and is free to do whatever he wants," Lindsey replied. Alister cast Invisible on himself and teleported the two to the large, green mansion. Lindsey took a deep breath and walked up to the front door. The home was very large, very expensive, and very modern looking from the outside. A light blanket of snow covered the lawn, which she suspected was green in the summer, probably well watered.

"She's here," an excited Nadia called out to her constant companion and fellow Dutch woman, Jolina Wessel. "I'm coming," she added, hoping that Lindsey could hear her. She was wearing her latest fetish outfit, a pale green satin hobble dress that fit her every curve on down to her ankles, where she had barely enough room to put one foot in front of the other. That didn't matter, because she wore matching spiked metal heels that allowed her to only take such small steps anyway. The bottom of the dress at her ankles suddenly flared outward about five inches, like a starched ruffle. She wore a matching striped pale green and white corset on top of the dress, setting off her remarkable body shape. Her heels clicked on the polished marble of the entrance hallway, as she moved to her front door. "Coming," she called out once more, again hoping Lindsey would be patient with her.

The chain deadbolt she was able to undo using her tiny

two-inch right arm, but getting the doorknob turned proved more of a challenge. Unable to bend, she squatted down and after some struggling, managed to get the knob turned. Lindsey saw her slowly rising as the door opened, and realized Nadia had actually opened the door herself, rather surprising Lindsey, who had expected her maid companion to be welcoming her.

"Hi, come on in, Lindsey! So glad you could come. Hurry up; it's chilly outside today. I don't like the snow and cold very well myself." Nadia's face looked radiant, though perfectly made up with her eye shadow done in the same shade of green as her dress and with a bright shade of red on her lips. "I'm a little out of breath from hurrying to the door. Tight corsets. What do you think of my latest fetish outfit? Do I look good in this pale green?"

"Stunning, I'd say, but isn't it awfully constricting, tight, and awkward for you? I mean with your lack of arms, it has to be terribly difficult for you," Lindsey asked, looking her over and being surprised with the way she appeared.

"Yes, but that's the point of it. Come on in. You can put your coat in the hall closet here. I'm being a bad hostess. I can't take your coat for you and hang it up. Sorry, I haven't figured out any way to do that yet, but I'm still learning." Nadia stopped panting with shallow breaths, evidently catching her breath at last. Lindsey took off her down parka and hung it up. She was wearing her super warm fleece lined pull on leather boots, a stark contrast to Nadia.

"I didn't realize that I was supposed to dress up, Nadia. Sorry about just wearing my jeans," Lindsey said. Obviously, Nadia was dressed very formally.

"Oh no, Lindsey. Please don't take offense! I dress this way every day for lounging around the house. These are my everyday clothes, kind of like your jeans."

"Your everyday clothes?" Lindsey asked surprised. This, she had never even considered to be the case. "Well, you look absolutely great, that's for sure, but I don't think I could ever possibly manage to wear something like your outfit. I bet it cost a lot. It sure fits tightly all the way down, doesn't it?"

"Yes, it did and does; that's the whole point of this

dress, to follow my curves, though I'm sure you could manage it, but it does take a good deal of practice and patience to wear it. Come on, Lindsey. I'm dying to show you my new house!"

"Hi Nadia. All going okay?" Jolina Wessel appeared at the other end of the marble hallway that led into the front room. Jolina appeared to be the perfect fetish maid. Lindsey stared at her outfit. The little black and white maid's outfit barely covered her. She wore black nylons and a black and white corset over the top, similar to Nadia's. She too wore very tall metal spiked heels. She had done her makeup similar in style to Nadia's, in that her eye shadow matched her dress. Both wore the same shade of bright red lipstick, leaving Lindsey wondering if they had been Red Hall students when they were in magic school. Both women had similar long blonde hair and blue eyes. Nadia had let her hair grow very long down her back, similar to the way Lindsey wore hers. Jolina had pretty bangs over her forehead, while the rest fell gently below her shoulders. In many ways, both women, Lindsey guessed could have been models. In her eyes, they were every bit as pretty as Ashley, though of course more mature.

"Lindsey, I'd like you to meet my very dearest friend and maid, Miss Jolina Wessel. She and I both came over to your country three years ago, when we were twenty-one. We grew up in Amsterdam and went to the Amsterdam School of Magic, Red Hall." Lindsey smiled. She was right about Red Hall, and she now knew that the two were probably twenty-four years old. Yet Dominus, her husband, was in his early forties, though he looked to be at least fifty at the Ball. She guessed that magical aging was taking a toll on Dominus because he had used the Restricted Wish spell so many times, prematurely aging him.

"Hi Jolina. You must be really a good friend of Nadia's to take care of her needs, Jolina. We all need really good friends."

"Ja, ve do at that, though I didn't expect it to be quite like dis. Fetish yes, but like dis?" she grinned. Lindsey figured she meant the fact that Nadia had lost her arms and now needed Jolina more than ever before. "Sorry, my English is not as good as Nadia's."

"Het is fijn. Ik spreek een weinig Nederlands," Lindsey replied using the basic Dutch she had been learning. Both women cracked a very big grin, pleased with this little treat.

"Nadia wants to show off our new house. I'll make us some tea," Jolina replied. "Holler if you need me." She headed off to the kitchen.

"Come, you must see this fabulous house, Lindsey. This is our front room and entertainment center." It was spacious and luxurious, but nowhere near the size of Lindsey's front room. "Ve like the marble floor; it is so easy to keep clean, unlike rugs, though it is a bit noisy. I've put up those heavy draperies hoping to dampen some of the sounds. Do you think that they look good in this room?"

"Sure, the colors match. I think it was a good idea, cuts down on the echo in here. You have good taste, Nadia." The woman seemed very pleased with Lindsey's sincere compliment. If nothing else, Nadia did have a sense of style.

Nadia walked along the hallway, ever so slowly as far as Lindsey was concerned, each measured step barely eight inches long, if that. Nadia seemed to be really enjoying showing Lindsey her home, so Lindsey followed along, trying not to look like she was hurrying. Their master bedroom was red velvet. Lindsey was not surprised by this, since Dominus seemed to have a passion for red velvet at the house in Telluride where she'd rescued his kidnaped women. She had no idea why they would want mirrors on the ceiling over their bed, but thought better of asking.

"Our wash closet, oops, bathrooms, I keep forgetting your word for it," Nadia pointed her short arm into the elegant bathroom. Gold fixtures predominated. A shower and a giant bathtub dominated this large room.

"Now on down the hall here is our very special dining room. You will see why. When I saw this room, I fell in love with this house. The room had an amber theme, from the tiles to the panels. The entire western side was large, glass windows, which framed perfectly the dark, tall Rocky Mountains, like jagged teeth biting into the sky. "You should see it in the early morning, when the sun shines off the snow

344

covered peaks! Beautiful indeed." Nadia definitely had picked a house with a view, Lindsey thought.

"What a view, Nadia! I can see why you would really enjoy dining in this room. I live on the High Plains, not much of a view, just flat lands. Did you pick out the drapes in here too?"

Nadia flashed her a big smile, pleased that she noticed, "Yes. Fits well, don't you think?"

"Tea ladies?" Jolina interrupted them, carefully carrying a tray into the dining room. "Looks like I timed it perfectly."

"Thanks, dear. Join us?" Nadia asked. Lindsey guessed that it was her polite way of asking for some help handling her tea, what with no arms. She was pleasantly surprised to see this was not the case. After pouring the cups, Jolina put a straw in the one for Nadia and set it before her. Nadia was being independent, at least in sipping tea.

"Have you shown her our car yet, Nadia?" Jolina asked with a twinkle in her eye. Lindsey guessed that Jolina must be impressed with their car. Lindsey had mostly been ignoring cars. After all, she could teleport, why use a car?

"Not yet. I figured I'd show our pride and joy to her after tea. Lindsey, you are what, about sixteen now?" Lindsey nodded, while sipping. "Thought so. We're twenty-four. In Amsterdam, we tried out the gothic style, but soon gave that up. Pointless. Then, we bounced around the club scene in Amsterdam, but it just wasn't for us. As soon as we turned twenty-one, we came over to the States."

"Miami, to be exact," Jolina added.

"You see, we both are into wearing fetish clothing, and it just didn't fly well in Amsterdam. At a club there in south Florida, we ran into Dominus, who seemed like a nice man. Well, he was nice to us, at least. We hit it off, and he began taking us on his yacht," Nadia felt like explaining her situation.

"He promised us many things, not the least to wear the clothes we desired," Jolina continued. "But we kept sensing that there was more to him than he told us."

"Yes, when we found out about what he did to the women at his play house in Telluride, we insisted on visiting there with him. Well, they were fetish dressed, but we were appalled that he was holding them captive," Nadia went on with the story. "Well, he said that his sexual drive got all bent out of shape by being imprisoned fourteen years. We rather bought his explanation." Her voice trailed away, as if she was ashamed of what she had seen or done or not done. Lindsey couldn't tell which.

"Yes, but Nadia right away got Jack to take over watching them and cooking for them. He's a really good chief and was not interested in, well you know, taking advantage of them," Jolina added, hesitant to say more because of Lindsey's youth.

"We just want to be fetish. Well, okay, I wanted to be the Queen of Fetish," Nadia admitted shyly.

"Well, we are now, Nadia!" Jolina added with a wry smile.

"Yes, we sure are. It's really great, Lindsey. Just so you know, as far as we know, all the money Dominus has spent on us he earned from his businesses. Several times, we have put our feet down on him when he tried to spend stolen money on us. Right now, he is starting a new fishing business in south Florida."

Jolina added, "As far as I can tell, he has made some business deals with the really large corporation called Mac Fluide Enterprises. We believe that they are fronting him the money to get the fishing business started."

Lindsey found this interesting data. However, she could not see how these two girls could ignore all the murders and crimes that Dominus had done. "But what about all the murders he's committed?"

"We have no proof that he did any of those things that people say he has done," Nadia defended her husband. "We've never seen him do anything, except protect himself. Like once, we were on his yacht off Cyprus last year, and someone was shooting lightning bolts at the ship. I fired back. I think people are gunning for him or something. Do you think that he is in danger from some people who want to take revenge on him for something? We are beginning to think so. We've received veiled threats in the mail." Lindsey was a bit surprised. The yacht attack was herself and the others trying to rescue Governor Alister, who Dominus had kidnaped and was attempting to drown in the sea as the tide came in.

Lindsey answered the question though, "Dunno on the threats, Nadia, but there is overwhelming proof that Dominus has murdered many people, to say nothing of other crimes. I would be very careful around him. He is an evil sadist, in my opinion. After all, he did cut off my hands once and my arms like yours once."

"Really? Then those rumors are actually true?" Nadia asked. Lindsey wondered if Nadia was playing games with her or if she really had no idea of events. Lindsey told the two women about the two times she had been victimized by Dominus.

"You mean he was causing that awful hurricane?" Nadia asked, finding it almost impossible to believe what Lindsey was saying about her loving Domi.

"We should try to check on that, Nadia," Jolina suggested rather seriously. Lindsey just could not believe these two were so ignorant of current events, but then they were from Amsterdam and not too familiar with things Stateside. Lindsey suggested that they surf the Bradbury website and read the several school newspapers that Ashley had done.

"Well, you just have to see our dream car," Nadia changed the subject. "Jolina and I have been drooling over this car since we were eighteen. Now we have one of our own. It's in the garage below us. Come on; you have to see it. We've been saving for years to get it. We may be broke now, but we've the car of our dreams!"

Again, Lindsey purposely had to walk very slowly. Nadia could only manage small steps, between her heels and the tightfitting dress. When they got to the stairs, Nadia sighed and looked at Lindsey, "I'm afraid I need some assistance getting safely down the steps. I can't see my feet over my bosom, and this dress is so confining that I can just barely take one step down. If you will support me, I'd be grateful. If you'd rather not, I'll get Jolina."

Lindsey had no problem putting her arm around Nadia, giving her the needed balance to go down the steps, but it was very slow going. Nadia's fetish dress just barely allowed her to take one step down at a time. In the two-car garage, there was no mistaking Nadia's bright red Ferrari, fully equipped with every luxury imaginable, including GEOSAT driving controls, similar to the Bradbury school bus. Nadia pointed out that all she had to do was enter the destination, and the car would automatically drive them there safely, but in a grand style and at great speed. Looking inside, Lindsey got a goof whiff of that brand new car smell.

After Nadia showed off the many features of the car, the two headed back upstairs. Nadia had to stop to catch her breath several times on the way up. Jolina met them at the top of the stairs.

"Cool car, eh? Hot car for hot babes!" Jolina exclaimed.

"I've never seen anything like it," Lindsey admitted, which was true. She'd only seen the car that Aunt Wilma sometimes drove to the Whitewater ranch, a deluxe Cadillac.

"Sometime, you'll have to go for a spin in it. Nadia can still drive it. Actually, it's part mine too; we bought it together. Our big play toy," Jolina added. She too was very proud of their car.

"Have you got all the clothes ready for her?" Nadia asked.

"Ja, all ready."

"Lindsey, as I said before, when I got my body altered like this, all my old clothes no longer fit, not even remotely. Jolina took a few that fit her, but most don't. I saw that you and I were about the same size, before I got enhanced, that is," she giggled. "So I thought why not give them to you? Honestly, Lindsey, I spent about twenty thousand dollars on them over the years. If it is true what Dominus did to you, then I really would like to give them to you, if only as a small, tiny bit of compensation for what you endured. Jolina and I realize that you are still growing and at school, so you will probably not have any real need for a lot of them right now, but later on, you may."

She went on with her explanation, "I even spent the last of my savings on the wardrobe box. It's magically enchanted, you see. It opens up to form a complete walk-in closet of clothes, but then folds up into a small hand briefcase. This way you can carry your entire wardrobe with you when you travel. Here we are. This whole wall closet is the magical wardrobe. All the clothes and shoes you see in here are for you, if you will accept them. Some you can give to your friends if you like. I just hated throwing them away. Please, look them over and take these as a small gift from me. No strings attached, really. If you find you enjoy wearing even one outfit, then it makes me feel really happy."

"We know you are still very young," Jolina added, "but you will be of age before you know it. We'll let you in on a little secret. When we wear these, we feel incredibly sexy. Guys really notice us, which is both good and bad, of course. It can get annoying."

"Didn't you feel super special at the ball the other night?" Nadia tried to make this real to Lindsey. "You wore a fabulous gown. Didn't you feel just super, elegant, refined, sexy? Just a little?"

Lindsey giggled, "I felt very special that's for sure. I don't quite know what this sexy thing is all about though." Nadia smiled, relieved.

"I've had all these cleaned, so you won't have to even think about anything being dirty or anything like that. If you want to try on some of these, Jolina can help you get into them. What do you think?"

"Way cool, Nadia. I've never had so many clothes in my life. I'm not sure when I would wear half of them, though." Both women giggled.

Jolina explained, "When you want to excite your boyfriend, wear anyone of these. Later on, if you get married, you can drive your husband wild by wearing many of these. Honestly, quite a few of these are really home-bedroom wear, you know, just for your husband. I don't reveal myself for anyone except the one I am in love with." Lindsey noted that Jolina didn't say who that might be, and she wondered where he might be and if he too was associated with Dominus.

Nadia added, "Also, I got you a dozen new pairs of really stylish nylons to wear with these. I figured that you might not have many, and I so hoped that you would accept my little gift."

"Sure, I'm really honored that you would want to give them to me, thanks a bunch. They are really something." Lindsey didn't quite know what to say, except that she certainly could not say no. That would definitely hurt Nadia's feelings. She added, "Nadia, if I accept all these clothes of yours, is there anything I can do in return for you to help you?" There, she played the card that she had calculated from the moment that Nadia had suggested this private meeting: that Nadia desperately wanted something from Lindsey.

"The croissants are ready, Nadia. Should I serve them in the dining room?" Jolina cleverly interrupted.

"Perfect! Lindsey, Jolina bakes the most fabulous pastries. Come on. Let's sample them, and we can talk." Lindsey followed the two women who walked very slowly together back into the kitchen. Indeed, the pastries were fantastic, melting in their mouths. Lindsey complimented Jolina heartily, which pleased her immensely.

"Lindsey, before I answer your question, I need to ask you something personal. If you don't want to answer it truthfully, I can understand. Just tell me it's none of my business. Okay?" Lindsey nodded, wondering what this was all about.

"I've heard rumors that you can cast a very large number of spells sans wand, sans words. Is this correct? I need to know this if I am to answer your question honestly."

"Yes, I can do a bunch this way. Why is this so important?"

"Then, perhaps there is one thing you could do for me, something I would value most highly now. However, I know you might not be able to help me with it, but I have to ask. You see, I love my new look, like this," she shrugged her shoulders, "very, very fetish. I've gotten my wish to be the Queen of Fetish, but. . ." her voice trailed off.

"Without arms and hands, life is really tough?" Lindsey said what she though Nadia was ashamed to admit.

"Well, sometimes it is. I didn't think so when I got transformed, but sometimes it would be really helpful if I could cast my Morph spell without my wand. I've no way to use my wand like this. Sometimes, I feel that I have given up too much of myself to be fetish. I don't want or need to cast anything more than the Morph spell. If I can somehow manage that one, I can change into someone with arms and carry on from there, you see. Jolina and I have given this a great deal of thought these last many weeks. If I could somehow do this on my own, without depending on Jolina, that would be just perfect. I hate like heck waking up Jolina to help me go to the bathroom. If I could just do this one thing for myself, all would be perfect. Is there any possible way that you could help me to learn how to do this one spell sans wand?"

Jolina quickly added, "I've been working with her on it nearly every day now, but there is something that is not quite right. Please, can you help us?"

Lindsey didn't see any harm in this, besides being able to Morph into someone with arms would really help this woman out a lot. "Okay, I'll give it a try. I can't guarantee anything, though."

They returned to the front room, where her wand was located over the mantle. Lindsey had the two women go through their attempts to have Nadia cast the spell. Indeed, something was slightly off. Lindsey cast her Slow Motion spell and had Nadia do it again a couple more times.

"Ah ha. I see what is going wrong, Nadia." She gave the woman some specific instructions to follow. Nadia worked hard and concentrated fully on what Lindsey was telling her. "Now try it again. That's much better. Once more, keep your mind fully focused on the end form you desire to take. Give it another try."

Nadia concentrated and magical energies flashed. Lindsey blinked; two Jolina's stood before her. "Way to go, Nadia you did it!" Jolina-Nadia jumped for joy, nearly falling over, having forgot that she was wearing the stilettos.

"I did it! I did it!" Nadia exclaimed.

"Yahoo!" Jolina added, "Finally! After all these days of trying!"

Lindsey had her practice the spell another ten times until she felt certain that Nadia had it down pat. "How can I ever thank you, Lindsey? You've given me back my witch's life without my having to depend on someone else to do it for me. I'm so happy I could hug you!" She pushed her body into Lindsey's and pressed her tiny arms against Lindsey's shoulders. Lindsey gave her a big hug as well.

"We like to dance. How about you, Lindsey?" Nadia asked after she calmed down.

"That's a magic word," Lindsey laughed. "I love it—just cannot get enough of it."

"We've been acquiring a whole lot of antique rock and roll disks. Jolina, put on some, and let's have a dance party, unless you'd like to change into one of your new outfits first."

Jolina laughed, "Party time! Well, Nadia, you ought to change too, if you want to really dance. That dress is too tight and confining for good rock and roll."

"You're right. Okay, I'll wear my maid's outfit like yours. Lindsey, since I am going to have to change, how about you? Care to try on the new maid's outfit? It's just like ours. Wear those black pumps, if you do."

"Well, okay, I'm game," Lindsey agreed. What teen could resist trying on clothes, especially expensive ones? Nearby, Jolina undressed Nadia. "Say, can I ask a stupid question?" Lindsey asked. "We were never quite sure, but do the panties go on first or the garter belt?"

Jolina giggled, "It all depends on whether you want to quickly take your panties off for your boyfriend or not. Probably best put them on first," she giggled. Lindsey flushed, but now got the significance.

"How do I look?" she asked after she had gotten the maid's outfit on properly.

"Perfect, I said they would fit you well, but you need the pumps. Don't forget to put that blue gel pad in your shoes first; it really helps cushion your feet when you wear heels this tall," Jolina advised.

"Whoa, these are really tall!" Lindsey exclaimed. The three headed slowly to the living room, and Jolina turned on their Antique Rock disks. Soon all three were gyrating to the heavy, solid beat of the music. Lindsey soon discovered that these two women were superb dancers and loved to dance every chance they could make.

Finally, Lindsey realized that she had to head for home soon. Jolina helped her change back into her jeans. Once that was done, Jolina showed her the command words to activate the magical wardrobe. Lindsey spoke the command words. She stood there completely amazed, as the closet began closing, folding upon itself repeatedly until only a small briefcase sat on the floor beside her.

"Super way cool!" Lindsey exclaimed.

"Ja, it is," Jolina gave her the key, and she locked it. "There, no one can open it, without the key."

Lindsey again thanked Nadia for the gift, and Nadia thanked her profusely for what she had done for her. "Please, come back for a visit whenever you have the chance. Just email me, and I can tell you when Dominus will be out. I don't think you want to be here when he is, right?"

"Right." Lindsey gave both women a farewell hug and left. As she began walking down their front sidewalk, she felt the gentle touch of Alister on her shoulder. At the street, they teleported and stood before her porch. She opened the door and the two went inside. Ashley was not back yet, so she told Alister and the others about her unusual visit with Nadia.

Alister checked over the wardrobe, pronouncing that it was merely what it was supposed to be, a magical wardrobe. "One of these probably costs at least five thousand dollars. Some gift she bestowed on you, Lindsey. I will not embarrass you by checking all the contents. Please cast your Identify spell and go over everything inside the wardrobe. If you find anything magical or suspicious, let me know immediately and do not touch it! It could be very dangerous to you. I believe that we can trust Nadia to be what she claims."

"Thanks for waiting outside for me today and looking out for me. Please tell the others thanks for me." He grinned and left.

Lindsey then went into her room and did as he asked, quickly checking for additional magical items within the wardrobe, among the clothes and shoes. She found nothing at all; everything appeared to be what it was supposed to be. Lindsey relaxed and closed the wardrobe. She heard Ashley arriving and raced out to greet her model sister.

On Saturday, Lindsey showed her friends the wardrobe from Nadia. The girls giggled for hours over the fancy, expensive, but very definitely fetish outfits. A few Lindsey figured she might be able to wear to their dances, so she decided to bring it back to school with her. Everyone teased her, saying that now they knew who to go to in order to borrow something sexy.

Saturday, Pam added the latest bit of news to her many sleuthing projects: that Dominus was getting funds from the Mac Fluide Enterprises and that he was starting a fishing business. Pam punned, "Sounds fishy to me." An hour later, she found the legal documents that did indeed show that Mac Fluide Enterprises had set Dominus up with a million dollar loan to open Ace Fresh Fish Supply, based in Miami. That part checked out. She went back to work studying the four hours of video taken at the ball.

Monique came over Saturday night with some news for Pam. For some reason, Pam was a bit chilly to her; and she, to Pam. "I have proof positive on President Missy Snow. Here, look at these two enhanced video excerpts from press shots. This first one shows her being admitted to the hospital. You can see clearly that she has no ring on that finger. Now this next one, I finally found posted in MySpace2100. Look closely; she's leaving the hospital, and there." She froze the video and toggled her enhancement software, zooming in on the same finger. The tell-tale sub-dermal ring bulge was clearly present."

"Excellent work, Monique. Clearly, someone got to her in the hospital and put the ring on her, probably when she was sleeping," Pam reached a logical conclusion.

"That's not all. I took those names you gave me, the top officials, and did more checking. The Attorney General Amos Fudge was quietly supporting Dominus for President. Her Secretary of Defense Miles Standford was likewise a silent supporter. Both probably got one of the diamond ring variety," Monique theorized.

"What makes matters really bad is that the US Regent, Thomas White, who is over all the magical departments, is an open Dominus supporter and has a ring. Worse for us, right here in Denver, the head of Denver's Department of Magical Misuse, Felix Jones, is also a Dominus supporter with a confirmed ring. His superior, Karl Jous, the head of the US Department of Magical Misuse has a ring, a quiet supporter I believe as well. Your dad is in tight waters, Pam. They also got to Geneva Holmes, the head of the US Department of Law too, though I cannot find any evidence that she was supporting Dominus in any way. Perhaps they snuck it onto her finger as they did Missy Snow."

"So Dominus has the top Regent and the two key US department heads of Law and Misuse under his control. He certainly went for the jugular vein," Pam stated flatly.

"Yes, he probably cares nothing for the Department of Defense. They only provide security, which he seems able enough to circumvent," Monique replied. "The only bright spot is Lacy Broom. She is over all the magical schools and is on our side."

"He probably doesn't consider kids to be a threat," Lindsey finally found something to add to their conversation.

"True. I'm going to suggest to Alister that we find some way of finding out which state department heads in Law and Misuse are not under the control of Dominus," Pam concluded. "I guess we have done all that we can from the video." All agreed with her.

"What I don't understand, Pam, is what is Dominus really, actually trying to do? I mean this whole bid for the Presidency was a sham. What's he trying to accomplish? Getting himself pardoned?" Monique asked.

"Hardly likely," Lindsey said thoughtfully. "Look, he's killed, stolen, and raped too many times to suddenly turn over a new leaf and be a normal person. Look what he did to Nadia just so he could marry her. No, there must be something we're not yet seeing."

"Hum, now that is an interesting thought, Lindsey," Pam commented, still thinking about what she just said. "Alister says he is methodical to a fault. That must mean that this whole election thing was very carefully orchestrated by him for a key purpose. Perhaps to get the rings into circulation. Yet why the pardon? Obviously, he's never been seriously worried about being captured, so that can't be the reason. I think Lindsey might be on to something. Being a normal, accepted citizen, not a wanted criminal—this must be or play a key role in his overall plan. Otherwise, he would not have wasted time in obtaining a pardon. What can he do as a normal, respected citizen that he can't do as a wanted criminal? That is the key question to ask, I believe."

"Well, he got married too. He looks like a respectable business man now," Lindsey replied.

"Yes, being married just now must play a role in his plans. Dominus isn't the kind of man to marry and settle down. Besides, Nadia is nearly half his age. No, if I were Nadia, I would be very, very worried. Dominus must have some use for her in mind or he would not have married her," Pam concluded. "I wonder if we will ever know?"

"I sure hope Nadia and Jolina come out of this all right," Lindsey added. "They seem like innocent, but foolish young women."

Chapter 22—Back to School

Mid-January arrived, and everyone headed back to Bradbury's for the spring term. Upon arrival, Lindsey had a MagMail post waiting for her. When she retrieved it from the Bookstore, the package contained a dozen red roses and a card from Nadia, expressing her undying gratitude for her assistance. She smiled and brought the roses into her room. Of course, everyone wanted to know who had sent them, and they giggled when Lindsey told them it was Nadia.

Their Dutch friends spent their free time with each other, telling each other about their different vacations. Pam spent hers researching the Mac Fluide Enterprises and how this huge corporation could be working with Dominus. Lindsey asked Amanda and Ashley to help her work on getting some more of their new spells learned in her special way.

The Sunday announcement ended Ashley's aid, though. Governor Alister made a school-wide speech. "It is with great pleasure that I'm able to announce that Bradbury's School of Magic now has both a school swimming team and a diving team. Mr. Deiter Cross is the captain of the men's swimming team, while Miss Peaches Colt is the captain of the girl's diving team. Let's give them a bit round of applause for establishing these two teams." Around the dining hall, clapping and hooting pleased both Black Hall students.

"In conjunction with the formation of our teams and in celebration of International Relations month, I am extremely pleased to announce that in April, Bradbury's will be hosting the swimming teams from the Singapore School of Magic. Indeed, Governor General Pina Pong of the entire Southeast Asia area will be accompanying them here. We will hold a swimming and diving tournament, showcasing these fine athletes."

Katja, Jeannette, and Ashley were on Peaches diving team. "We've got to spend all available time practicing," Ashley explained to her friends. "We certainly don't want to get routed by the Singapore team!"

By Monday, Lindsey was ready to get back to the business of learning new things, just not for the homework loads the professors gave out. Physics was interesting now; magnetism was the topic along with electrical effects. Electricity through a wire could produce heat. For Tuesday, they had to calculate the amount of heat energy that running various devices for one minute produced. Since the time was being held constant, as was the voltage at 110-volts, she discovered she only needed to find out how many amps the device drew. The heating calories would then be .24 x 60 x 110 x amps. Off she went, eagerly in search of the data.

On the other hand, Spell casting class with Professor Delius became a nightmare for the girls. For two weeks, they pretended to be learning Create Skeleton and Create Zombie from various skeletal bones and dead corpses. Lindsey found this to be utterly revolting. Besides, she had seen Professor Delius do just that, raising dead creatures to help defend their position last year, when the band of Death Stalkers attacked them while they were rescuing Governor Alister. These undead creatures had not stopped the onrush of their attackers much at all. Additionally, she thought, it was not right to do this to the remains of a person whose body died. She wondered if he'd become a grave robber or something.

Pam did research where these body parts came from, only to discover that he was using bodies, which had been donated to science when the person had died. Still, Pam wanted nothing to do with this spell. Deiter and Peaches were elated with their creations. Their animated skeletons and zombies began wandering about the large classroom. "It cannot get any worse," Lindsey suggested to her friends.

It did. The next week Professor Janice began to teach them their new enchantment based spells. The very first spell was the one Dominus had used on Pam, Idiot Mind. When it was cast, the person wound up with the intelligence of a very little child at best. Worse still, the spell's effect was permanent. Hence, Doctor Carterwall was present at each class. Once the spell was successfully cast, the person on whom it was cast became an idiot, permanently until he or she was fully healed. The good doctor hated this spell, primarily because he constantly had to perform his cures on the students each year, usually several times.

Because of the serious nature of the results of this spell, Professor Janice, for the first time, spent an awful lot of time going over details on how best to defend against this spell. It was most effective against an unsuspecting victim, she explained. Professor Janice then worked with them so they would be able to detect the symptoms of that spell being cast upon themselves, perhaps while they were looking another way. The only thing that kept this from causing major problems with the students was the fact that, if the doctor administered his potions the very instant someone became an idiot, the healing time was reduced to around a day. Still, many students had to assist their temporarily idiot classmates get through the evening meal and to bed. There was no chance to do any homework that night for those afflicted.

"Have you noticed that this is the only time that Professor Janice has not been laughing at us and teasing us about the spell's effects on us?" Amanda noted to her friends at supper.

"Who's Professor Janice? What is a tease anyway?" asked Lindsey, who was recovering from Amanda's spell an hour before. Everyone ignored her.

"Must be because of the really seriousness of the spell," Pam concluded.

"No, it is because she will be in really big trouble with all the other faculty if one of you loses more than one evening of study," Jim broke in on their conversation. He'd come to chat with Ashley, who still had a headache from the day before when she had become an idiot.

He continued, "Just hang in there. By the end of the week, you all will be very likely to be able to throw off this spell's impact on you or just dodge it."

"What's a Dodge? Is that a car?" Lindsey asked innocently.

However, the following week, Professor Janice was back to her normal, covert self, making fun of those who fell victim to the spells they were now learning. "This week, we are going to learn how to Force Your Will onto Another. When successfully cast, you form a bond with the other person's mind and can then make them do what you desire. Mind you, if you attempt to force them to do something that is really against their basic nature, you run a real risk of them breaking the spell."

By Tuesday, many were finally able to dominate others with this spell. Deiter was the first to dominate another successfully. He had Peaches give a passionate kiss to Pam, who tried to fight off the advances of Peaches. Soon, the others in the class attempted to force their victims into doing similar things. Peaches got even with Deiter, when she finally Forced Her Will onto him. She had him trying to kiss Lyle passionately. The class roared with laughter, none more so than Professor Janice.

Pam found this spell particularity interesting. She wondered if there could be a connection between this spell and the effects caused by the rings given away by Dominus Malefic. She chatted to Governor Alister about this possibility. "Yes, that is part of the ring's effect, Miss Betts." She felt better; at least, she now had something more tangible on which to base the effect of these rings.

The next week, they learned an even more powerful way to create massive confusion among a group, the Total Chaos spell. By the end of the week, many in the class had bruises and bloody noses and such. When the spell detonated, some would stand totally still doing nothing, completely confused. Others would wander off, keeping Professor Janice on her toes, ushering them back into the classroom. However, more than likely, those affected would begin fighting with anyone around them, hence the battered bodies come Friday.

The following week, Professor Janice brought back her caged wolves, four this time. Now the students had to learn how physically to hold them still. Before, they learned to Charm Animal; now they had to go further and physically restrain them. Pam liked this spell. To be able to freeze an attacking rabid animal appealed to her and to many others as well. Kathy thought this was a particularly useful spell.

Potion making finally got to Lindsey. The ingredients became more and more gruesome, and the smell while it was brewing made her vomit more than once. Indeed, Deiter very nearly gave up the course entirely, after he got terribly ill from the fumes. Only when Professor Delius explained to him that he had completely messed up the potion that he was making did Deiter calm down. "Oh, well then that explains it," he muttered. His mistake had turned his potion into a noxious poison.

Finally, Kathy gave them her successful tip. "Here, put this clothespin over your nose. If you cannot breathe through your nose, you cannot smell it." The remainder of the week nearly everyone in the class walked around with a clothespin on their nose!

Early February, Professor Blake taught spell casting and conjuring was the game. First, they learned to conjure a Secret Chest in which to store valuable things. When the spell was successfully cast, a three foot by three foot by two foot chest appeared. After one stored their valuables inside, the two command words were: Store and Retrieve. When the Lindsey succeeded with her spell, she gave the chest the command to Store. The large chest vanished, leaving a very tiny chest replica in her hand, much as might be found on a charm bracelet.

Pam insisted on knowing just where the chest disappeared to, "Professor, this is all well and good, to conjure a fine chest, but just where does it go when you say Store? I mean, isn't it likely that someone could find it and rob you? It has to go somewhere. I would think that mischievous wizards like Dominus would research this spell to find out where the chest goes and then go rob them."

"There are a number of theories about where the chests go, Miss Betts. No one has proved conclusively their destination. The most likely is that they go into the uninhabited Beyond. Thefts are very rare, but have been known to occur. Let me see. I have that number here somewhere." He fumbled through his notes. "Ah, yes, one theft per ten thousand chests. Not very likely at all."

Pam looked at Deiter, who looked at her. Both knew that the Beyond was not uninhabited. If these chests appeared in the Beyond, they were quite vulnerable, if they were found. Pam wondered if perhaps the goggles sometimes came across these chests and rifled them. She resolved to ask them the next time she visited the Beyond.

Conjure Hound was the final spell from Professor Blake. Essentially, one could conjure a dog to serve you for a period, normally about twelve hours. As one cast the spell, one had to specify what skills this dog would have. Amanda chose Tracking, while Pam chose Protection. Lindsey experimented with Guarding, while Deiter chose Hunting. In the end, nearly everyone found good uses for this helpful spell.

By the time that March came, Professor Cho Lin became their teacher for her illusion-based spells. When she finished with them, they could now create very realistic illusions, complete with sounds, sights, smells, and tastes. These illusions were very hard to detect as not being real, which was the whole point of the Real Illusion spell. Next, they could cause another to have nightmare dreams or any kind of dream that they desired. Lindsey didn't particularly like this Fabricate Dream spell, however. "My dreams are my dreams," she insisted.

"The rest of your spell casting time this term will be spent on a very critically important spell. A very few of you may learn enough actually to be able to create and sell magical items, such as rings and staves. Frequently, part of the construction phase requires the Creation of Object spell. With this spell, you can actually create any material. For example, who would not like to create a gold coin, eh?" Of course, this got everyone's attention.

"Don't get too excited about this just yet. The things that you create will have a short lifetime. If you create say a wicker basket, it will remain for several hours before vanishing. However, the more valuable the object is, the shorter it stays in existence. If you create a gold coin, don't expect it to stay around for more than twenty minutes at most. Valuable gemstones stay around even less. Naturally, this spell would then be followed immediately with additional higher Grade spells, to make the object remain permanently. This week, we begin by creating a bit of hemp rope. Once you have this mastered, we will create a bit of steel, before moving on to precious metals. Your passing standard is to create a valuable gemstone for me."

Lindsey had never seen her classmates throw themselves into the learning of a spell as they did on this one. Perhaps it was the lure of being able to create gold or gems that inspired them, she didn't know. For her, it was all about being able to know how to create magical items. Amanda thought along similar lines. After all, R. B. was an inventor of magically enchanted items.

During January, Peaches and Jeannette worked with the diving team, holding a practice session every evening for an hour. These two were the best divers. Katja was just not as skilled or as inventive as these two. However, Ashley found that she was a natural born diver, fearless now that she had conquered her terror of diving head first into the waters. Additionally, the fifth member of their team was a Blue Hall student from Denver, a fifth year named Sally Long, a shorthaired brunette who had spent many years as a lifeguard at the largest public pool in Denver.

Similarly, Deiter held swimming sessions three times each week. Theirs would be a speed contest, using various strokes. Hans and Klaas were excellent swimmers, far better than Deiter, who constantly picked up pointers from them. Joining them were Marshall Boggs and Fred Smith, both sixth year students from Blue Hall. Marshall grew up in Florida and Fred, in Alabama. Both had been strong swimmers all their lives. Now they relished a chance to swim in an official competition. Neither minded having a fourth year be their captain, even though they both knew far more about swimming competitions than Deiter. They were just grateful that Deiter had managed to put together a swim team.

Finally, Valentine's Day came at last. All the fourth years were looking forward to this day, not so much for romance as for the chance to get away to Telluride for the day. This was their much needed time-out from their intense studies. Once more, Governor Alister issued his orders that everyone had to travel about in larger groups, nothing smaller than a half dozen. The day was cold, and they all knew that skiing was on the agenda, particularly because of the Dutch students' love for skiing.

Lindsey and her large group wandered out onto the snow-covered sidewalk of Telluride, just as the clouds broke. "Hey, it's going to be sunny anyway," Jim commented, eager to have some fun.

Just then, a Message flashed in front of Lindsey's eyes. "Over here!" a familiar voice called out. Everyone looked, there was Nadia and Jolina, the latter waving her arms to get Lindsey's attention. The message had been from Jolina, naturally, on Nadia's behalf. Both were standing beside their super fancy red Ferrari. Lindsey and her group made their way to the two women.

Nadia and Jolina wore matching expensive parkas, with long, soft fur around their hoods. They wore jeans but she could tell that their boots had heels. "Everyone, this is Nadia and Jolina." She then began the lengthy introduction of all her friends. Naturally, Jeannette, Hans, and Katja chatted with them in Dutch, while Lindsey struggled to follow them. They talked much too fast for her basic Dutch, she concluded. Finally, Lindsey asked, "So what brings you to Telluride today?"

Nadia grinned, "I promised you a ride in our super Ferrari. Would you like to go for a ride? We figured you will have to ask permission or something."

Lindsey did just that, Messaging Alister. Promptly she received a reply and whispered something to Ashley, who just giggled and said, "No."

"Okay, I have permission as long as someone comes with me," Lindsey said, a bit excited by the prospect of going for a ride in such a hot car.

"You are not leaving my sight," Deiter spoke up before anyone else. "I'm going with you, Lindsey. Besides, do you know what kind of car this is? A Ferrari 2000! Only the fastest thing on four wheels! I can't believe you have one of these!"

"Ja, sure ding, Deiter. Ve saved for years to get dis Ferrari. Got ever extra they have. Ve now broke," Jolina grinned, "Come on; let's get inside and drive. Ve'll only be a couple minutes. Does anyone else want a ride too?" Of course, everyone wanted to get inside this car! It retailed for over five hundred fifty thousand dollars!

"Way cool, a Ferrari is just about the hottest car in the world!" Deiter exclaimed as he climbed into the leather covered rear seat alongside Jolina. He noticed that her boots had three-inch heels.

She saw him staring at her boots. Jolina explained, "I know, low heels, but we can't walk in de snow wid our usual heels, you see. Ferrari 2000 is de hottest car in de world. Dat's why ve got dis one. Hot car for de hot girls." He flushed. That he was sitting beside a very beautiful woman was on his mind almost as much as the incredible car.

"Fasten your seatbelts," Nadia called out. "Will you fasten mine please, Lindsey?" She did, noticing that she too wore much lower heels and sensible jeans. However, she wondered how Nadia could possibly drive the car. She watched as Nadia pushed a button with her stub and then spoke clearly. Properly programmed, the car moved off onto the road that led out of Telluride. "See, I can steer with my arms, if I have to, but the computer usually does it for me."

They drove around onto the main north-south highway for a bit. Then, on a long open stretch, Nadia opened it up full throttle. "Whoo hooo!" exclaimed Deiter, very much impressed with the acceleration that flattened him back against his back seat. Ten minutes later, they were back at their starting point.

Deiter asked, "How could you possibly afford this hot car?"

Jolina answered, "It was not easy. We saved every penny for years to buy it, except for what we spent on clothes."

Nadia chuckled. "Ja, we could have gotten it sooner but we spent too much on clothes."

For the next hour, Nadia and Jolina proudly gave the others a quick spin in their super car. Since it was almost lunchtime, Lindsey asked, "Say, Nadia, want to hang out with us today? We are heading to Domino's for lunch. After that, we are all going skiing. You are welcome to come with us, if you want to and have the time."

Nadia's eyes lit up; Jolina's too, although only Deiter saw hers. "Ja, super, sure, ve love to!" She spoke so fast that her English suffered slightly. Leaving the car parked in a parking lot, the two older women joined Lindsey's large group. Jolina carefully put her arm around Nadia to steady her as they walked carefully along the snow-covered sidewalk. Deiter gallantly put his arm around Jolina to stead her, and Lindsey, seeing this, put hers around Nadia as well.

Nadia and Jolina, though eight years older than most of the teens, fit right in with them. They still had their youthful outlook. As they walked along, Nadia asked Katja about current events back in their home country. She had been very out of touch for several years now.

Inside the packed pizza parlor, Jolina began to feed their pizza to Nadia, who looked a bit embarrassed by having to be fed so openly in such a public spot. However, Peaches insisted Deiter do the same for her, claiming it to be so romantic. Ashley explained that she had started this last year, and Jim began feeding her as he had done all last year. This brought a hearty laugh to everyone, especially Nadia, who began to feel far more comfortable around all these new people.

After spending an hour at Dominos, the bunch divided. Lindsey and her half, along with Nadia and Jolina, headed back up to the ski resort. "Don't worry, Nadia, you can manage to ski too," Ashley explained as they walked along. "Jim took me on the beginner's slope when I had no arms at all. If I can manage with no arms, you should be all right because you still have some."

"You vent skiing wid no arms?" asked Nadia, very excited and impressed.

"Yes, I did everything I could possibly do. I don't take no for an answer. I just found other ways to accomplish things. Sometimes it took forever, though. Still, I'm a terrible pool player with my arms, right Jim?" Jim nodded, as well as Deiter.

"Yes, she ran the table on me, when she didn't have arms," Deiter added. "Shocked the heck out of me, she did. I expected that she might be able to maybe somehow sink one ball, but clever Ashley sank them all, and I didn't get one shot!"

Katja, Jeannette, Hans, and Klaas wanted to go cross-country skiing. Bale Volker also wanted to join his fellow Dutch friends, so Peaches tagged along to make it six. The rest opted for the beginner's slope once more. Lindsey was not ready to try anything harder. They rented their equipment and lockers. Lindsey kept an eye on Nadia to see if she needed any assistance, but Jolina was right there and helped her put on the ski boots. Since neither woman had ever been skiing, Jim began instructing them just as he had done for Ashley and Lindsey.

Two hours later, covered with snow from their many falls, but elated at the sheer fun of it all, they returned to their lockers and changed. Jim returned all their equipment.

Deiter complimented the two women, "I say you did really well for your first time on skis, especially Nadia. That has to be hard for you, I mean trying to ski with no arms. I bet you really miss having them. How about I buy us all a round of hot cocoa here at the inn?"

"You're on!" Lindsey exclaimed, "My feet are freezing. I'm not so sure I really like this cold weather skiing." Nadia grinned, pleased with his compliment, but didn't reply about missing them just then.

Inside the warm ski lodge, with warm cups before them, Nadia finally said to Deiter, "Ja, times like this I miss them, but usually I don't. Jolina and I are into the fetish scene really. This way, I am unusual. We find fetish to be really sexy."

Deiter blushed. "Er, sorry, I really don't know about it. I mean, well, I'm only sixteen."

Nadia laughed, "Ja sure, sure, but don't you think that Lindsey looked really hot when she wore that gown at the ball a few weeks ago? We find wearing exciting clothes is a big turn on for us. We really enjoy dressing up. One day when you get older, you may see what we mean. I have always wanted to be the fetish queen, and now I actually am one. I am very happy with the way I am."

"Yes, but I don't understand how losing your arms makes you a fetish queen," Deiter persisted. He just could not fathom why anyone would want to lose their arms for any reason.

Nadia, for the first time, flushed, and looked slightly embarrassed. Jolina wiggled involuntarily. In a soft voice, Nadia admitted the truth, "Dominus promised me that I would be a fetish queen if I did this for him. He didn't lie. Now I am one. I've gotten my dreams. The price has not been too great. We never could have succeeded unless I did this."

Deiter saw that Nadia had revealed something very personal and was kind. "Thanks for telling me." After a pause, he asked, "Nadia, maybe it's because I don't know much. But does becoming a fetish queen mean that you have to lose your arms to become one? I don't quite understand this thing."

"Oh no! Fetish queen has nothing to do with my giving up my arms. That was the price I had to pay for him setting us up with all our fancy fetish clothing, close to thirty thousand dollars' worth. We were totally broke, having just bought our Ferrari. We didn't have any jobs, and we figured by the time that we could possibly have earned that much money, we would be old and grey. Then too, I thought I was in love with him, so I wanted to please him. Lots of reasons why."

Deiter scratched his head, "You mean that you gave up your arms so that you could get a whole lot of expensive clothes to wear? Women, I just do not understand you at all." He said it jokingly, and everyone one roared with laughter, but Jim and Andy felt pretty much as he did, though.

Pam butted in, "That's because you *men* don't have to look pretty and attract the attention of others and all that. In our society, women are *supposed* to look pretty in whatever way appeals to them. When you look as *homely* as I do, then you would see what I mean. Deiter, how many times have you seen an ugly girl and felt yourself attracted to her, huh? Zero! I saw the way you have been looking at Jolina all day." Deiter's face felt very hot.

"You've never looked at me *that* way." His face grew even more scarlet. "See what I mean? I don't give a rat's bottom about how I look. I've given up all desires of ever looking anywhere near as good as either Nadia or Jolina or Ashley or Lindsey or Amanda or Kathy or Monique or Katja or

Jeannette. So while I certainly would not give up my arms to look great, I can totally understand why Nadia did it for herself and Jolina. Just try to buy a designer outfit on a waitress's salary sometime, Deiter."

"Ja, the world is male dominated, that's for sure," Nadia admitted, easing the situation a little. "Missy Snow is only your third woman President ever. It is so even in the world's magical departments, far more men in power than women."

Pam added, "There are more women in positions of power in the world's magical departments, primarily because the ability to cast spells plays such a vital role. Otherwise, there would be far fewer women in the departments. According to the latest Mag Job Survey, normal women are still earning less than fifty percent of men, while it is thirty-three percent in the magical community."

"I didn't know," Deiter admitted. "I'm sorry if I offended any of you."

"You've not offended us," Nadia replied kindly. "Rare indeed is a man who truly understands a woman. I think it is easier for us to understand you guys than it is for you to understand us." The teens giggled.

Lindsey felt for Deiter and added, "We appreciate the kind, little things you do, like sending us roses. It shows us that you care for us, that you are thinking about us." Deiter smiled recalling that this was just what his mother had told him last year. He felt he was finally on solid ground, but he dare not tell Lindsey this.

"Well, we had better get going," Nadia suggested. "We've a good distance to travel to get back to Denver. I honestly have to admit I've had a grand time with you all today. Thank you so very much for sharing your day with us."

"Yes, me too. It was fun. Thank you very much," Jolina added. They left in their Ferrari, while the others, now joined by the cross-country skiers, headed back to the campus.

"Nadia is all right," Jim began, "Jolina too. Shame that she got herself married to about the worst man in the world."

Pam suggested, "I think that she took advantage of him, Jim, to get what she and Jolina wanted. Still, it's a shame. I think that those two are selling themselves short. There are other ways to get what you want, clothing-wise, than to get your arms hacked off."

When they got back, the girls had to rush to shower and change into their gowns for the Valentine's Day dance after supper. Because of the many requests, they donned their very expensive gowns they had worn for the Inaugural Ball. Lindsey had been pestered by many to wear it so they could get a close up view of the dress.

"You look incredible," Andy exclaimed as he took Lindsey's arm when she made her grand entrance, along with the others. Jim proudly escorted Ashley onto the dance floor, whispering to her that she was the prettiest girl in the room. All that evening, Lindsey saw that Andy kept casting glances at Peaches; Deiter kept glancing at her; and more than once Peaches stared at Andy, when she thought no one was looking. Lindsey didn't know what to make of this, however.

Around nine, she decided to try something. "Say, Andy, would you mind dancing with Peaches for a while? I would like to have one dance with Deiter." Andy's sudden grin told her lots. Deiter was very surprised that she asked to dance with him. Peaches didn't conceal her pleasure when Andy cut in on Deiter.

"What's this all about?" Deiter whispered to Lindsey, as he put his arm around her waist and began dancing.

"I think Andy really likes Peaches," she whispered back.

"Sure does. I caught her looking over here at Andy several times, when she didn't think I was looking. I know everyone thinks that Peaches and I are a couple, but really we aren't. We've just been friends since we were kids. I suppose I ought to tell Andy that, what do you think?"

"I agree; you ought to. I think Andy is too shy to say anything," Lindsey replied.

"Cool. Say, you don't mind dancing with me, do you? I mean Andy's with Peaches now." Deiter fumbled trying to be polite, but more or less messed it up.

"No, you are a good dancer, Deiter." He smiled, and they continued to dance until ten p.m. came. Once more, it came way too early for Lindsey.

As the music ended, Deiter whispered in her ear,

"Lindsey, you are the greatest girl in the world!" She flushed and smiled. She watched him as he walked to the stairs leading to the boy's side of the dorm. Lindsey didn't know why she watched him, only that she felt compelled to do so.

During January and February, the forth years had two more mock battles under the guidance of Professor Delius. For Lindsey, these practice sessions were valuable, and she continually worked on anticipating who would cast what spells. Indeed, in her Dispeller Theory class, Lindsey was being trained to anticipate spells based upon the caster. However, she also noticed a big change in Deiter's attacking mode. He pushed himself to become blazingly fast, firing off spells very rapidly, though good ones. She began to have the feeling that this was in reaction to having become part of the Rodent Pack, that one day soon, he would be called upon to attack to save the day, and he wanted to be prepared.

At the end of February, Pam met with Governor Alister and Professor Cho Lin. She wanted to discuss with them the results of her latest Sleuthing Theory II class assignment. Admittedly, she had given herself this assignment. "Okay, thank you for agreeing to meet with me. First, may I ask if there are any further findings on Dominus rings? I mean, I thought that perhaps he had enchanted them with a Force Your Will on Another spell."

"Still working on it Pam. Yes, that spell would seem to fit. However, R. B. and I believe that he has in some way altered that spell slightly. We are not sure just how. For now, we believe that the results of the ring upon its wearer are roughly the same as you would get from that spell."

"Okay. Thanks. Now as my research project for Professor Cho Lin, I chose to track down just how Dominus has been able to interrupt the major television stations with his pirate telecasts during the Presidential election."

Alister chuckled. "Pam, the electronic wizards have been all over this one already."

"Yes, but they didn't solve it, did they?" Pam grinned, and Alister chuckled, prepared to be surprised once again by this incredibly bright young woman.

"I began by reviewing all that the previous investigators had done and the data that they had gathered. They are essentially correct. The feed did come via satellite. I went farther. I decided to find out just what equipment and actions would be needed to hijack the satellite, along with what equipment would be needed to produce the high quality video signals."

"On the screen is a listing of what I believe Dominus would have needed to create and produce the actual TV presentations that he made. Notice the cost column and the bottom line. Next, the space requirements is shown here. Notice that we are talking an actual recording studio setup. His was not some flyby night production. On the contrary, it was made with state of the art digital equipment, which as you have seen is very expensive."

"Next, I made the assumption that Dominus had with him the needed know how and personnel to acquire, use, and produce his TV shows. That being said, I then looked into all major purchases of the above listed equipment, going back a full year before he made his first broadcast, knowing that he is methodical and would have been planning this for some time. As you will note on this screen, during this entire time span, while some of the equipment has been bought, not all of it has been. Assuming that no other organization in the country ordered any of this equipment during this time span, you will note that it is still not enough to equip his studio, not nearly enough."

"Conclusion: Dominus used some existing facilities somewhere in our country or perhaps overseas. Before we continue following this line of inquiry, we need to examine the technology, equipment, and facilities needed to hijack a television satellite. This is a listing of the equipment and suppliers. The actual method I will not disclose, unless someone insists on it. That is currently classified information. The equipment is not classified. Now this next is a listing over the same time span of companies and individuals who purchased such equipment, at least the ones that we know about, I decided not to break the law and hack into the manufacturer's databases."

"You will notice that all the major broadcasters have been replacing equipment; this is routine. Please notice this one company: Mac Fluide Enterprises. They purchased every item that I deem required for satellite hijacking, though they may well have valid other uses for said equipment. Now, let us return to the probable use of existing facilities in which to record and produce his shows."

"This listing shows highlighted in yellow one of the subsidiary companies that Mac Fluide Enterprises owns outright: the Miami Commercials Production Studio. This is a fully equipped facility, which has produced high quality television commercials, high digital quality, not necessarily good advertising. Now for their tax returns. This listing shows the last five years. They average three commercials per year. The next listing shows who has contracted for these. Via these, I managed to view several of the final products, just to verify that the digital quality was there—awful commercials, as far as content is concerned, which is probably why they sell so few."

"Anyway, the average is three. Now look at their reported utility expenses for the past five years on this listing. To the right, is the average for the first four years, and that is written next to what they claimed for this past election year. Same number of commercials, three. Utility expenses are up by a factor of eight over the same time period."

"Conclusion: the studio was in full production use way beyond what they claimed in income. Based on this, one can estimate that they produced nearly two dozen television commercials during last year that they did not report. I tracked down the number of Dominus for President spots. They number over two dozen. Interesting correlation."

"Final conclusion: either they had an incredibly bad string of luck producing those three commercials, having to redo each one completely from start to finish nine times, or this is the studio where Dominus made and produced his videos and from where they have the equipment to hijack the television satellite." Pam sat down, satisfied with her presentation.

"Wonderful piece of Sleuthing, Miss Betts. I believe you

are on to something here. If you don't mind, I would like a copy of this report. I will see that it surreptitiously lands with the IRS. Let them see the apparent anomalous tax report, and let them look into charges of tax evasion. This will gain us more information, while none of it will look like it is coming from the departments who have been ordered to lay off of their Dominus investigations," Governor Alister explained.

Pam thought his idea was cleverly devious and diabolical, thoroughly approving it. Professor Cho Lin merely gave Pam an A for the term, telling her she had fully passed all the course requirements, giving her more free time for her other studies. Pam thanked her, but had other ideas.

What was this connection between the Mac Fluide Enterprises and Dominus Malefic? This question continued to burn in the back of her mind, especially since Nadia told her that Dominus and his new fishing company were being financed by this corporation.

Chapter 23—Singapore Comes to Bradbury's

On April 1, Kathy came running into their dorm room, waving a magazine she had just received. "It's here! Ashley, it's here! You are on the cover!" Everyone dropped everything and crowded around Kathy, who laid the May issue of Teen Fashion on Ashley's desk. The glamorous model wearing an evening gown stared up at them.

"Wow! That's me? I don't believe it, Kathy," Ashley exclaimed. What she saw was a very beautiful young woman, not at all what she thought she saw when she looked into the mirror.

Rapidly, everyone thumbed through the pages, emitting various squeals, and oh's and ah's at each of the various outfits worn by Ashley, who was shown in many different poses. "Sis, you are a knockout!" Lindsey exclaimed, "Wow!"

"Yes, and there is a four page interview with Ashley on page 8, but it gets continued back on page 24," Kathy added. "But look at this picture!" They stared at the caption: Ashley— as she is without her arms spell.

"I didn't want to reveal what Lindsey did, so I called it a spell that they were seeing, my arms, I mean. After all, it is a spell that got them back." Ashley defended herself.

Pam said quietly, "Ashley, if I looked that good, I wouldn't mind not having arms. You look fabulous no matter what. You realize that you will likely become something of a celebrity on campus, once this gets around?"

"Oh, no. I hadn't thought of that," Ashley replied.

By Monday, over half of the girls on campus had a copy. Everywhere Ashley walked, someone came up to her with their copy asking for her autograph and asking about her arms. Were they a really good illusion? How often did she need to recast the spell? Similar questions. Ashley figured it would die down in a couple of days, once she signed a bunch of autographs.

It didn't. Other girls who didn't routinely get that magazine ordered themselves a copy and then came after her signature. Worse, nearly every fourth year boy on up called out a greeting to her everywhere she went. "Hi Ashley!" was the most commonly heard phrase around campus all during April. Unused to attention of this magnitude, Ashley wanted to find a hole to hide in, even considering magically donning a disguise. Pam pointed out that if she did that, they would soon be on to the deception, causing more embarrassment than it was worth.

Lena sent her a wonderful letter, praising her good taste and telling her how proud she was of her daughter. This meant everything to Ashley. She saved the letter for all time.

Two days after the magazine came out, the bus bringing the swimming team from Singapore School of Magic arrived in their parking lot. "They are here!" Ashley called out. Everyone headed down to the dining room where the visitors would be introduced. Outside, a foot of snow still covered the grounds. Blue Hall monitors were assigned to greet the arrivals in the parking lot, move their bags to their rooms in Blue Hall, and lead them through the tunnels to the dining room.

When Lindsey, Ashley, and their gang arrived, they found their dining hall decorated in an Asian flavor. "Cool!" Lindsey exclaimed, looking over the unusual tapestries that hung on the walls. Governor Alister soon came walking in leading the procession of visitors and Blue Hall monitors, who were chatting with their guests. Lindsey guessed that many of the visiting swim team members were Blue Hall, a fact not hard to guess from the blue arm bands more than half wore.

Ashley had expected to see them all wearing strange clothing, strange at least to her, but all were wearing jeans and tee-shirt tops that advertised Disneyland. She smiled; evidently, their visitors had made a fun stop along the way. Pam whispered, "Isn't that Pina Pong, the South Asia Governor General and Lacy Broom, our new US Governor General?"

"You are right! I recognize Pina from our research two years ago. She was at the Board of Regents meeting here where you made your presentation that got ex-Governor General

Albright arrested!" Lindsey replied. "What's she doing here?"

"Maybe representing her area?" Pam suggested. "I think it is a bit unusual, though, especially since Lacy is also here. I mean if this is just a swim meet between two schools, I'd expect to see only the school Governor present. After all, only Governor Alister was at all the National Track Meets in Des Moines."

"Gotta go get in line," Ashley called out, and she went to join Peaches. The Bradbury swimming teams lined up beside their coaches on the Yellow Hall side of the room. The Singapore teams lined up on the opposite side, over by Black Hall. Betsy and Hank, the PE teachers, joined the Bradbury group, while two other adults stood beside the Singapore team, evidently their coaches. Lacy Broom, Pina Pong, and another man followed Alister to the front professor's table, pivoted, and faced the large gathering.

Governor Alister spoke first, "It is my great honor and pleasure to welcome our esteemed colleagues from the Singapore School of Magic to Arthur Bradbury's School of Magic to engage in our first ever swimming and diving competition. Here in the landlocked Rocky Mountains you would not expect to find excellent and accomplished divers and swimmers. Skiers would be more like it. That's a joke, by the way." Scattered chuckles echoed around the room.

"Yet, it is with extreme pleasure that this year Bradbury's is able to field both a diving and swimming team, our first ever. To celebrate our achievement and in recognition of World Culture Month, the superb, excellent swimming and diving teams from Singapore School of Magic have graciously accepted my invitation to spend two weeks here with us and vie for the First International Swimming and Diving Cup."

"At this time, I would like to introduce the Southeast Asian Governor General Pina Pong and her Governor Lin Yan of the Singapore School of Magic." A loud round of applause greeted the two, who smiled and graciously accepted the warm welcome. Pina was thirty-seven. She wore her thick, black hair long down her back, with bangs across her forehead. Her makeup was light. In her grey tweed business suit, Pina looked quite the professional. Lin Yan looked to be around fifty, with piercing black eyes and a hint of a moustache. He too wore a grey tweed suit.

"Accompanying them is our very own Governor General Lacy Broom." Again, a round of applause greeted her. Lacy was thirty-five, with short brown but curly hair, nicely done. She wore a light brown skirt, white silk blouse, with a matching light brown jacket. She had blue eyes that seemed to take in the entire group sitting before her. Lindsey suspected that this woman was a keen observer.

Lacy spoke first, "I would also like to extend my hand in international goodwill and cooperation between schools of magic. As Governor General, I feel it is my duty to do everything in my power to foster exchanges between our schools. During these next two weeks, I invite you to open your minds, to make new friends, and to share your experiences and culture with each other. In trying times like these, we must do all that we can to foster strong bonds between all young wizards and witches of our world. Thank you." Lindsey thought that she sounded like she was giving a political speech, not addressing them.

Pina stepped forward, "Greetings Bradbury students, one and all. I am Governor General Pina Pong. I too feel as Lacy, that in these dark times, we must do all that we can to foster goodwill and understanding among you, our new generation of wizards and witches. It is with great pleasure that Governor Lacy and I have been able to arrange this swimming meet. I would like to extend my compliments to all the young athletes who are going to compete, especially to the Bradbury students, who have formed your school's first swimming and diving teams. During our stay, I hope to get the opportunity to meet with some of you personally. Now I would like to present Governor Lin Yan of the Singapore School of Magic. Lin?" She gestured to him and stepped back.

"Greeting to all of you fine young wizards and witches. When I received the request to schedule a diving and swimming meet with your school, frankly I was most surprised. Bradbury's is known the world over for the high quality of its graduates. Yet, as Governor Broadwell says, you are in the Rocky Mountains, which I must add we have just toured, very impressive; we have nothing like this at home. It was with surprise that I learned you have such excellent divers and swimmers. In Singapore, everyone learns to swim at an early age, so we have always had such teams. Indeed, we have Hall Competitions each year, much as I understand you have Hall track meets."

He grinned good naturedly, "I hope you will not be too disappointed if we, as you say over here, skunk your butts. But it is all in good fun. We have toured your Disneyland, can you tell?" Many laughed over this jest; one would have to have been blind not to notice his team's tee shirts.

"Now I would like to introduce the members of our diving and swimming teams. They are all sixth year students and several hope to go to the next Olympics representing Singapore there." One by one, he introduced the team members. As with Bradbury's teams, girls formed their diving team, while the boys, their swimming team.

After Governor Alister introduced his team members, he announced that lunch was served. The guests had tables of their own near the Yellow Hall side, between the professor's tables and those of Yellow Hall. However, today, both teams sat at these same tables, chatting among themselves. One girl asked Ashley, "Say, you look an awful lot like the fashion model featured on the cover of May's Teen Fashion magazine. Have you seen it yet? I got a copy at Disneyland."

Ashley flushed, "Yes, that's me. It's my first modeling session."

"Way coolest!" she replied, hastily telling all the other girls, at which point all six began chatting with Ashley. What it was like, was it hard work, did she get to pick out the dresses and so on? Peaches giggled, thankful she did not have to face all these questions from strangers.

Lunch finished, visiting students and coaches took off on a guided tour of the campus. Meanwhile, Alister, Pina, Lin, and Lacy met in private in Governor Alister's office. As the four entered, he checked on his security. Satisfied they were still in place, he said, "We can speak openly in here. No one can eavesdrop."

"Good, Alister, what the devil is going on over here?"

Pina burst out. This question had been burning within her, desperate to get out at the first opportunity. She didn't wait for any other pleasantries.

"Dominus Malefic has been active, Pina, far, far more than anyone could have possibly guessed. You remember Miss Pam Betts and Miss Lindsey Barron?" Pina nodded. Lacy looked at him quizzically, as if to say what have these two students have to do with this. "As part of their special educational courses, they have been gathering valuable data for us. This whole presidential run by Dominus was a smokescreen for his real purpose. Pam discovered the connection. You recall his theft of gold bars from Fort Knox?"

"Well, yes, but he's stolen three times that from vaults in Southeast Asia," Pina added.

"Interesting, fits. Also, some fifteen or so years ago, Dominus robbed two Amsterdam gem cutters, the grandparents of three of our foreign exchange students from the Netherlands. Dominus turned the gold and diamonds into rings, which have been magically enchanted with a spell or spells unknown to us, though Miss Betts has identified the base for the spell, Enforce Your Will over Another. There is more to it than that simple spell however. Using the campaign as a cover, Dominus has given out a very large number of these rings to his supporters and others. Here is one that we have recovered from one of our students. Do not put it on!"

While they looked at the ring, he continued, "Immediately after the election was over, Dominus performed some kind of mass activation of these rings. Yes, we did a good study of a few of these rings beforehand and found only the tiniest trace of potential enchantment, not enough to pin anything down. However, the activation process was something quite unexpected. It seems that the rings somehow blend into the person's body, sub-dermal; skin now covers completely the rings. The rings fuse onto the bone of the finger. Only a telltale raised area is visible where the ring is beneath the skin."

"Now they radiate strong magic. Via these rings, Dominus is able to control the person, making them do what he desires. Pam has discovered that President Missy Snow entered the hospital after the terrorist attack on her with no such ring, an accident that was probably Dominus-caused. However, she has found video of Missy leaving the hospital wearing one of these rings. Someone probably put it on her while she was unconscious, and she was helpless to prevent it from happening."

"Pam secretly recorded everyone at the Inaugural Ball, focusing on ring fingers. From the hours of video, we have established the identity of many who are now under the control of Dominus. These include the President, the Attorney General Amos Fudge, the Secretary of Defense Miles Standford, the US Board of Regents Thomas White, and the US head of the Departments of Law and Magical Misuse Geneva Holmes and Karl Jones. Fortunately, the Colorado heads of these two departments, Kathy Jacks and Casper Williams, do not have rings, as do the High Plains and Mountain Departments of Magical Misuse, Fred Betts and Rachel Smith, though Denver's head is wearing a ring. We are slowly compiling a secret list of what officials are under the control of Dominus."

"As you know, both departments have been ordered to cease and desist all further investigations of Dominus Malefic and his Death Stalkers. We believe that Dominus forced President Missy Snow to pardon him and his men. I know that it is hindsight, but Pam Betts has worked out the likely location from which Dominus produced his campaign videos and hijacked the television stations."

"Further, Miss Barron has struck up a friendship with the new wife of Dominus, Nadia van Nye Malefic. From all indications, this woman and her companion are innocent victims as well, and they do not sport any rings. Via Lindsey, we know for certain that Dominus is starting a fishing business and is pretending to be a 'normal citizen.'"

"Incredible, Alister, just incredible!" Pina commented at last.

"Darn it. Why didn't I know about all this, Alister?" Lacy demanded to know.

"Lacy, you understand the gravity of the situation. All the top law enforcement officials, including the President, are under the control of Dominus. Everyone in these departments is under dire jeopardy if they even *seem* to be violating the top orders. We must be very secretive about this and cautious. Some of this information, Lacy, has only recently become known. Further, we have no secure means to relay data without fear that it could be intercepted. I wouldn't give a rat's hair for the life of anyone in these departments who is discovered working against Dominus."

"Lacy, you are now being told. I trust you will keep this between us. Some of us have formed a counter task force, the Rodent Pack. I'm entrusted to invite all three of you into our conspiracy, if you so desire. If you feel this is too risky for you, there's the door. No one will ever again approach you about this." No one left.

"Good. Pam Betts is our official record keeper. She is compiling the definitive database of all the criminal activities of all parties in anyway associated with Dominus. Trust me. It is secure and will one day be used to bring all of those who are guilty to justice." He went on to identify the others in the pack.

"Currently, R. B. is working on the rings and their enchantment. Top priority is finding an easy way to identify who may be wearing one. Estimates suggest that number may be in the millions! We've positively identified only close to twenty-five thousand of those. His next priority is to find a way to nullify the ring's effect. Removal is only accomplished right now by cutting off the wearer's finger. He will work on bettering that as his third priority."

Pina toyed with her long hair, "It seems that Dominus has really gained solid control over the US at this time. However, overseas, such is not the case. He and his men are still committing robberies and murders in Southeast Asia. Our authorities are not yet under his control. Perhaps an international tribunal can arrest him."

"We thought of that, however, you must obtain US permission to enter and arrest him. You will not get such permission I'm sure. However, perhaps later this method can be used to bring him down, Pina."

Lacy ran her hands through her short hair, puffing it up a bit. "What I don't see is what is he attempting to do? Surely, it must just be an elaborate scheme to obtain a pardon for his past crimes."

"As I have said many times, Lacy, Dominus is methodical to a fault. A pardon is only a tiny stepping-stone for his ultimate goals, Lacy. I believe his Manifesto may give us a clue, world domination. Admittedly, none of us can see what his next move may be; we certainly didn't anticipate these rings. Yet, these rings must play a critical role in his overall plan, whatever that may be."

Alister sighed and continued, "Right now, the best thing we can do is organize secure resistance pockets. When we can finally figure out his next move, we will be in a better position to counter him."

"Makes sense; you can count on us. I suspected something was brewing," Pina commented. "That's the main reason I suggested we make this visit, a perfect cover for this meeting."

"Indeed, now I would like to show you some video taken at the ball by Miss Betts. Play close attention to the ring fingers, so that you can easily identify who may be wearing one." He played ten minutes, showing many closeup views where the bulge was clearly visible beneath the skin's surface.

"Unbelievable! The rings have melted into their skin!" Lacy commented very surprised. "How is this possible?"

"We don't yet know that answer," Alister replied. "I am researching that one. Once I know the how, I can probably work out a way to undo it."

"How do we communicate securely with you when we have something to report?" asked Lacy.

"Encrypt your files with the phrase 'Alice in Wonderland' and send it to this secret site." Alister wrote out Pam's secret server's entrance portal. "Memorize it. Do not write it down."

"Could we meet with Miss Betts and Miss Barron, Alister? I would like to thank them personally," Lacy asked. He smiled and Messaged the two.

"What's Alister want with us?" Pam asked as the two left their dorm room. Lindsey cast a Magical Door, and they stepped through it, arriving before his office door.

"Dunno, I don't think we've goofed up anything," Lindsey replied.

"Come on in, Miss Betts, Miss Barron," the kindly voice of Alister welcomed them. From his tone, both girls knew they were not in trouble. Both were surprised to see the three other adults present, though.

"I would like you two to meet the three newest members of the Rodent Pack," Alister said. He then did the introductions.

"I wanted to thank you both for all that you have done. It is amazing, thank you," Governor General Lacy said shaking their hands.

"We meet again, Miss Betts, Miss Barron. Last time you made an indelible impression on me with your evidentiary presentation leading to the arrest of ex-Governor General Albright," Pina said. "Now you have outdone even that. It is my pleasure to meet you again. How did you ever work out these things?" Pam launched into a lengthy discussion of how she'd made her discoveries and the logical conclusions derived from them. She was pleased to have such an attentive audience, especially these in positions of high power over the schools of magic.

"The more people that can understand just how I worked these things out, the better," Pam finished up.

"Miss Barron, please be extra careful with this Nadia. She is the wife of the world's most evil wizard. You are playing with real fire there," Lacy warned Lindsey, a serious tone in her voice.

"Honestly, I think Nadia and Jolina are just duped, innocent victims who are being used by Dominus. He is quite sadistic. After we saw what he did to those six women that he kidnaped and kept as his sexual play toys, I wasn't surprised in the slightest to see what he wanted his wife to look like. It's just plain twisted. Actually, I think that it is Nadia who is in the worst danger. I've been asking myself why would he want to keep five play toys?" She was trying to express her idea without becoming too graphical, because she found it too embarrassing to discuss more explicitly.

"My guess is that his sadistic drives cannot be satisfied

by one woman. That's why I think that Nadia is in danger. I mean he is now a married man, but she's only one woman. Sooner or later, I predict that he will tire of that, and then she is in big trouble," Lindsey confided what she had been constantly worrying about ever since spending the afternoon in her house back in January.

"I see your point, though it is hard for me to think the way that he must be thinking. Such perversion, such sadism, is beyond my imagination," Lacy answered.

"When you see those poor women and have to help them, you get a real indoctrination really fast," Pam added.

"Well, let's get our immediate priorities ironed out," Alister took back control of the meeting. "What we most critically need to know are two things: one, what other high level personnel are under his control via the rings, and two, what is his next step, his next move? Pina, Lin, please see what you can discover about those in power in Southeast Asia. Lacy, can you find out how many of the other magic school governors are under the control of Dominus and any other officials that you may come in contact with, please? As far as his next move goes, I must admit I am baffled on any method to proceed."

They chatted a bit longer, and the meeting broke up. As the two girls walked back through the tunnels, Pam said, "I wonder how we might be able to figure out his next move, Lindsey? This is a real sleuthing challenge, perhaps the greatest I've ever attempted. Yes, I am somehow going to work out logically what his plan is at this point!" Lindsey never saw her more determined to solve a mystery.

Because so many students wanted to watch the swimming meet, Alister and his staff magically enlarged their indoor pool's seating area. Six hundred students swarmed onto the bleachers to cheer on their team.

Governor Lin officiated the meet, "Let me begin with the diving contest rules. Two contests will be held: perfunctory dives and free-style-magic dives. Each is scored differently. In the perfunctory dives, each diver will perform six dives. The categories that they must choose from consist of a front dive, a back dive, a reverse dive, an inward dive, a twisting dive and an arm-stand dive. Each contestant will perform one from each category. Within a category, there are many to choose from, but some are vastly more difficult than others are. The difficulty is taken into account in the scoring. The judges will be assigning points on each dive based on how well the somersaults are executed, the diver's flight position, the quality of their twists, their angle of approach, and finally how they enter the water."

"Once each judge has marked their score, the total points are added and then multiplied by the degree of difficulty. The team with the highest score wins the meet, but the team member with the highest score wins the personal achievement trophy."

"In the free-style dives, each participant is allowed five dives. Again, they are scored similarly. However, points are also awarded for creativity and expressivity of the dive. The team with the highest score wins the meet, but the person with the highest score wins the personal achievement trophy."

"The men's swimming competition is far simpler. It is essentially a race, and the team with the fastest total times wins the meet. Three races are done. In each, only one type of stroke is used: the front crawl, the breaststroke, and the butterfly stroke. Each race will be ten laps of the pool. Additionally, the person who has the fastest ten laps in any of the three races wins the personal achievement trophy."

"Because the men's races are fatiguing, they need some recovery time. Hence, the competition begins with the front crawl race. Then, we will conduct the women's perfunctory diving contest. Next comes the men's breaststroke race, followed by the women's free-style diving competition. The butterfly race will mark the end of our meet."

"To judge the meet, we have brought in five judges from Florida, who frequently judge the US Nationals. You have fair and unbiased judges. Now, let the meet begin!"

The Singapore men won the first race, though Hans and Klaas were close. A dejected Deiter joined them in the stands to watch the diving contest. He'd come in last out of the eleven racers.

"Look, you are racing against six boys that are two years

older than you. Plus, they are larger and stronger than you, Deiter. I thought you did well. How many other boys at Bradbury's were racing, eh?" Pam flatly replied to his melancholy.

He brightened up, realizing she spoke the truth. They were way bigger and stronger than he was. "Two more years," he told himself.

The perfunctory diving contest was also not very close. Peaches came in second and Katja, fourth. Jeannette came in seventh, but this was not her specialty. As Peaches dried off and came to join the group, Lindsey and all those around her complimented the Black Hall girl. "You are an incredible diver, Peaches," Lindsey said. "None of us knew you were this good."

She smiled, "These Singapore girls are really excellent, technically spot on. Now I can see where I need improving. Before today, I had nothing to really compare myself against, except what I could occasionally see on TV."

The breaststroke race was once more won by the Singapore men; only this time, Hans came in second with Klaas, third. Deiter finished last again, but he was in better spirits when he rejoined the others. "Hey, someone will be last. I'm the weakest swimmer of the lot. Good going Hans, you nearly caught him. You too, Klaas." As captain, he continued to encourage his team. Lindsey took note of his attitude change.

The free-style diving competition was won by Bradbury, no contest. True, Peaches came in last overall, but the top three spots went to Jeannette, Ashley, and then Katja. The grace, style, and inventiveness, to say nothing of Jeannette's clever use of magic, which she had developed while diving with no arms, landed her in the top spot, several points ahead of the more inexperienced Ashley. Katja was nearly tied with Ashley, however. Bradbury's crowd exploded when the three winners were announced.

Finally, the butterfly power stroke race finished off the meet. The two Blue Hall students came in third and fourth, amazingly enough. Shortly after that, the trophies were presented. Each participant received a participation medallion. The Singapore teams won the perfunctory diving trophy and the swimming trophy. The Bradbury girls' team won the free-style diving trophy. The first place individual trophies went to two of the Singapore athletes, while Jeannette picked up one for Bradbury's. Ashley was very pleased that Jeannette had won the trophy; she would have something to take back home with her to show her parents and her school.

On Monday, after their guests had left, Spell casting class with Professor Cho Lin took an entirely unexpected turn. "Today and for the next six weeks, you will be learning how to drive a car. At the end, I expect that each one of you will pass the written and practical tests, and get your official Colorado driver's license. I would like to introduce your instructor, this is Max Belt." Professor Cho Lin turned her class over to this little man from the Colorado Driver's License office.

"I didn't know we had to learn to drive a car," whispered Lindsey to Pam.

"I didn't either."

"Sorry, I forgot to tell you," Ashley whispered, "Jim told me about it, but I was so busy with the diving that I forgot."

After easily passing their rules of the road test, next they received their behind the wheel instructions, four students per car. Lindsey learned that some cars were still manual, in that the person actually had to steer it, shift gears, and handle the gas pedal and brakes. This took the students the longest time to master, though most of the boys had it down far sooner than the girls.

The last week was spent on learning how to operate all the automatic controls that most new cars were now equipped. "Compared to spell casting, this is a piece of cake," Lindsey commented to Pam, who agreed, seeing no challenge in it at all. Indeed, Pam wondered why they even had a course in it. By mid-May, they all stood in line to get their photo-id driver's licenses from the official mini-portable station, operated by Max.

Chapter 24—End of Term Again

May Day came, and Lindsey prepared for her last trip into Telluride for this school year. The weather was warm, though not hot, light jacket weather. The day was sunny, perfect for an outing. Deiter had taken the initiative, asking her for a date. Andy, greatly relieved that he had done so, quickly asked Peaches for a date.

"Nadia and Jolina will likely be meeting us today. I hope that's okay with you, Deiter," Lindsey explained, as they began their long walk down the underground tunnel towards Telluride.

"Oh, I am mortally wounded. I had so hope to have a romantic outing with my fairest flower. I am so crushed," Deiter playfully teased her. Lindsey giggled. This was a side of Deiter she had not seen, but she liked it. He became serious, "Gosh, I hope everything is okay with them, you know, that Dominus hasn't hurt them any."

"Me too, me too." They joined the throng heading into the mountain town, reminded once more to stay in large groups. Ashley, with Jim on her arm, joined them.

Ashley whispered, "Let's try to get Nadia and Jolina kind of apart from everyone else so they can freely talk, Lindsey. I've had a premonition that Nadia has had some trouble, probably with Dominus." That put a somber edge on the sunny day.

Pam and Monique caught up with them. The Red Hall girl said, "Gang, this is my last trip into Telluride. I want to make it very special for all of you. I count you as my very best friends ever. I have to take you to one particular store sometime today, whenever we can work it into our schedule. I'm off to the Magical Medical Healing school in Denver. I can't believe that they want me to start June 6! I get five days to get home and get there."

Jim added, "Me too. I have arranged a very special lunch for us all. If we are separated because Ashley and I want to shoot a final game of pool, you are all to come to the ski lodge for lunch. I have reserved the whole place for us. Noon, don't forget or you will wish you hadn't!"

"Hey look, it's Nadia and Jolina again. Invite them too," Jim added, waving to the two young women, as they stepped out onto the main street.

"Hi ya. Miss us?" Nadia said with more enthusiasm that Lindsey would have expected. Both women looked very well dressed, fetish-wise, that is. They wore matching outfits: pale blue satin tight, form-fitting dresses with only a tiny walking slit, matching corset in pale blue and off-white strips worn on top of the dress, and tall matching pumps. A tiny matching jacket was thrown over their shoulders, which hid Nadia's tiny arms from view. Their hot Ferrari was parked nearby.

"We wore lower heels so we don't hold you up so," Nadia teased. Lindsey thought that these were not significantly lower, however.

Slowly the large group of students, many of whom stared at the sight of the two women, fanned out through the town. "Hi Nadia, Jolina. You two look like you are dressed for a party," Lindsey said.

They both smiled. "You don't mind having a pair of fetish queens with you today, do you? I mean we just showed up, uninvited and all that," Nadia asked, her voice becoming rather serious.

"Heck no, we're out for a fun day. It's Monique and Jim's last time here. They graduate at the end of the month," Lindsey answered. "So where to first?"

"Pool hall for us," Ashley answered.

"Say, Ashley, that was a fabulous shoot in the Teen Fashion magazine. We got a copy and read your article," Jolina interrupted. "Did you really shoot pool with your feet?"

Ashley giggled, and Jim replied, "You bet. Shooting with her feet, she has skunked everyone she plays. Now we make her shoot with her arms so that we have a chance."

Deiter just couldn't resist adding, "He's right. I'm a pretty good pool player, and she ran the table on me when we first shot pool!"

"Thanks, I did have fun doing the modeling. I got to keep all those neat outfits," Ashley acknowledged Jolina.

They decided to visit the pool hall first. As before, Lindsey put her arm around one side of Nadia, Jolina the other, and Deiter put his around Jolina's waist. This way, the two were steadied as they took their very small steps in their sky blue heels. Three others were in the pool hall, all locals. They greeted Ashley, Jim, and Deiter, having played a number of games with them. When the two other women came in, they whistled at them, as well as stared at them, making no secret that they were attracted.

Jim and Ashley racked up the balls on one table. Deiter asked if anyone wanted to play him. Surprisingly, Jolina volunteered. "I've played a little, though I'm not so good."

"Cool, I'll rack them up," Deiter could not believe his good luck. He was playing a game with such a knockout woman. He could see the three locals watching their every move.

Nadia walked to Ashley and Jim, "Ashley, could you show me how you shoot pool with your feet? Jolina and I just cannot believe it. If it is too embarrassing, we understand."

Ashley agreed, "One game, then I'll show you how bad I am with my hands; that way Jim can win at least one game," she teased. Jim gave a fake moan, while she grabbed a tall stool and took off her warm boots and socks.

"You break, Jim." He moaned again. Nadia looked confused, so Ashley explained, "With my feet, I can't get any real power behind the shots, so I can't break well at all, terribly, actually."

An hour later, Jolina and Nadia were dutifully impressed, fascinated, and educated. Ashley had indeed run the table on Jim, after he initially sunk two solids. When she used her hands the next game, Jim took her, but only just barely

Meanwhile, Deiter won both games from Jolina, but she was a descent shooter, nearly at the same skill level as he was. Pam and Monique had stayed to watch, primarily because they had never seen them shoot pool, plus they were a bit worried about Nadia and wanted to keep an eye on their friends. Safety in larger groups, Pam kept repeating.

Now the group headed to the jewelry shop, where

Monique had arranged her farewell gifts. "I wanted to give you all something to remember me and our times together after I take off to med school. I've had these bracelets specially made for us—all identical, kind of like a sisterhood of witches."

Neither Ashley nor Lindsey had any bracelets, so these added to their small jewelry collection. Made from 14-caret gold and set with small diamonds, each had seven small charms on them, representing the seven girls: Ashley, Lindsey, Pam, Audrey, Kathy, Amanda, and Monique.

Next, they headed for the ski lodge at the other end of town. Because it was a fair walk for the women in heels, they headed there sooner than they might normally have. "You are sure that you want us to join you for your farewell party, Jim?" Nadia asked.

"Sure, why not?"

At the lodge, Jim had indeed arranged for their private lunch. A huge round table in the center of the A-frame had a romantic view of the tall mountains and the fields of blossoming wild flowers. The waiters served a roast duck dinner, compliments of Jim, who wanted this to be a special memory for Ashley.

Pam, Monique, Ashley, Lindsey, Deiter, Amanda, her boyfriend Henry, Kathy, Emilio, Audrey, and Fern were there, along with Nadia and Jolina. The fancy lunch was even more memorable. Jim hired a traveling Mexican mariachi band to play for them while they ate.

As they ate, Henry, Amanda's boyfriend, explained sadly, "This is my last time here too. My dad has taken an accounting job in Chicago. He gets a big pay increase, and we are moving in June. I tried to get him to let me come here for my last two years, but," he sighed, "I couldn't. I'll write to you, Amanda, every week, though. I'm going to miss all of you, especially the dances."

Jim and Fern knew how badly Amanda was going to miss Henry. After all, they had been dance partners at every dance for the last four years. Amanda didn't quite know what to say. Henry had just dropped the news on her.

"So what are you plans when you graduate?" Monique asked Jim, breaking the awkward silence.

"I'm not like Tom. I don't want to go to college. I'm a lot like Ashley, a free spirit. If I could get away with just playing around, goofing off, I would. However, I can't. Dad's orders," he teased his two sisters.

"Seriously, what with all the trouble from Dominus and the Death Stalkers, er sorry no offense to you Nadia, I've taken a job with the Colorado Department of Security. They like my rogue ways and think I will do well protecting others from harm. The main thing I will be doing is waiting on my Princess here to graduate, and then maybe we can get married." Ashley blushed; Jim had already suggested this to her, and she had agreed, though she insisted he formally propose only after she graduated. After all, a lot could happen to each of them in two long years.

Pam thought this was very sensible of him. "Honestly, the Department of Security is spread so thin since Dominus and his vile men escaped from prison that it's not funny. We need lots more security forces, Jim. I'm sure you will do well at it." Pam wanted to ask Nadia what her husband was up to now, but thought better of it.

A bit later, many left to do other things, leaving Jim, Ashley, Deiter, and Lindsey with Nadia and Jolina. "So how has everything been with you ladies?" Lindsey asked, deciding now was as good as any to probe a bit, following up Ashley's premonition. She saw Nadia flinch and knew she hit a sore spot.

Since they were in a very private location, Nadia admitted, "Not so good. You may be right about my husband. He is changing on me."

"Go ahead and tell them, Nadia," Jolina encouraged her friend, adding, "or I will."

"When we married, I thought my taking this form would be all that he would desire. And it was for a number of months. Now he has been getting rougher with me. I have bruises on my shoulders and back. He's been making me wear impossibly high heels, blinding me, and then making me try to find him. If I complain too much, he puts this gag with a ball on it in my mouth to silence me. Jolina has tried to intervene, but he nearly knocked her out. Yet, each morning, he does apologize to me and cancels the Blindness spell, so perhaps it is not so bad after all."

"I think you should get out of there, get away from him before something really bad happens to you," Lindsey stated emphatically.

"We've been thinking about that. Jolina thinks I can easily get a divorce on cruelty grounds. We'll see. Maybe he will calm down; perhaps his fishing business is not going so well," Nadia tried to make a reasonable explanation for her husband's conduct. "At least we don't argue. I know many married couples argue, but we certainly don't do that. He is a good provider, and we do not lack for good housing. We always have plenty of good food, spending money, and of course, lots of fancy clothing. He takes us to many nightclubs, formal dances, and affairs. So it is perhaps not as bad as you think."

Lindsey wrote down her address on a napkin. She handed it to Jolina. "Punch this into your Ferrari's computer when you get back to your car. If you ever need to find me during the summer, try here. Once you enter it, burn this napkin." Jolina agreed to do it and looked relieved.

"I want to take my Princess here on a stroll in that flowered meadow out there, where we went skiing in the winter. You are welcome to come too," Jim suggested. The six headed outside. Lindsey and Deiter purposely hung back with the slower moving women, giving Ashley and Jim some private, personal time together.

"They are like two feisty peas in a pod, aren't they," Jolina commented. Lindsey grinned. She was right. Neither of those two took anything from anybody; both had a bit of rebel in them.

Later, Lindsey and Deiter walked the two women back to their car. As promised, Jolina entered the address, labeling it Fire Department, in case anyone got curious. Deiter cast a quick Flaming Fingers spell and destroyed the napkin.

"Thank you again for a really wonderful May Day. We've really, really enjoyed it. Have a good summer you two. Jim, thank you very much for allowing us to attend your farewell lunch. It was excellent. Bye, bye for now," Nadia said.

This time, Jolina got to drive them home to Denver.

"I think she is being naive," Pam said, as they walked back down the long tunnel to the campus. Lindsey had told her what Nadia had said about Dominus and his treatment of her. "Mark my words, one day we will read her obituary in the news." Pam was more than a little glum as they walked back. Lindsey suspected this was because Monique was leaving her for med school, but that was not what was bothering Pam. She was too confused to put the real source of her mood into words just now.

May 16, Lindsey, Ashley, Deiter, and their Dutch students once more took off on a week long sightseeing trip around the country. They spent a day hiking the Appalachian Trail, visited Disneyland, and a host of historical sites, including Gettysburg. A good time was had by all. As before, Professor Delius had them randomly pick which place to visit first, insisting Disneyland not be the first, for that would be too predictable.

Before long, their final grades were posted. Lindsey did far better than normal, acing every course, except a C in Dutch. "I just never took enough time to practice," Lindsey admitted.

Kathy surprised everyone by pulling the highest A in Potion Making I in the last ten years. With all the help everyone had this past year, no one got below a B in any of the major subjects. Yes, Deiter managed a B in potion making, but only just barely.

With graduation coming and the formal end of term ball coming up, the girls began preparing for the fancy gala. Ashley couldn't decide what to wear, but in the end, joined the others wearing their very expensive gowns they had worn to the Inaugural Ball. Ashley lent Katja and Jeannette two of her fancy new dresses she had worn for her photo shoot, which pleased both girls immensely. All day the teens primped and prepared for the graduation and ball. Lindsey couldn't figure out why this year it took her so much longer to get ready for the dance.

At the formal dinner, Ashley, Lindsey, Amanda, Fern, Audrey, and Pam went together to get Jim a graduation present. Jim was shocked when they surprised him. When they sat down to dine, all dressed in their finest, they presented him with it. Ashley's card read: May these come in handy. Inside the box were a semi-automatic pistol and a very fine high-powered rifle.

"We took a hint from our mother. Wizards can be stopped the old-fashioned way, Jim. Now you have an edge; please stay alive," Ashley told him. His would be a dangerous profession. Jim was speechless for a time, and then he hugged each one in turn.

A few minutes later, Jake Rattlebeam did his last official act as Yellow Hall team captain. "I hereby appoint Lindsey as your captain next year. Again, if you all don't like my choice, then you are free to elect whomever you wish. It's a shame the Nationals were canceled, but we all know that we would not have done as well there as last year. However, we did win the school trophy and that's fine with me. You've all been terrific, thanks."

A bit later, Monique arrived, wearing her fancy ball gown, as well, instead of her boyish suit. Pam, Ashley, Amanda, Ellie, Audrey, and Lindsey gave Monique her special graduation present. They had all chipped into buy her a dozen healing potions in a nice doctor's carrying case, which protected the sealed vials from breaking.

This was the first time that Lindsey saw Monique lose her composure. She broke down and cried. "Thank you all so much. This means a lot to me—to be able to help someone in dire need. Thank you." She then had to visit the restroom to touch up her makeup, which was now streaking from the tears.

At the graduation, the Yellow Hall team received the school soccer trophy and a round of applause. Lindsey was surprised to see both Deiter and Peaches clapping loudly for them, quite a change from four years ago, she thought.

Governor Alister gave a short speech, thanking the Dutch students for coming to Bradbury's. "It has been our great pleasure having you. We have all made many new friends and have many fond memories to remember." Everyone gave the standing twenty students a loud round of applause.

One by one, the graduating sixth years had their name called. Each walked up to receive their two diplomas, one for high school, and one from magic school. After the last one received theirs, the place erupted into a thunderous applause. Quickly, the tables and chairs were relocated for the formal dance.

At the dance, Lindsey sensed Pam was having a problem. Many of the Red Hall graduating boys wanted a last dance with Monique. Lindsey wondered how Pam was taking this. She was continually being interrupted, and Pam finally gave up trying to dance with her dear friend. Deiter noticed it as well, possibly because Lindsey was constantly trying to see the two. "You think they'd let Pam and Monique enjoy their last dance," he commented, slightly annoyed.

"Oh, look, other boys are whisking Pam onto the dance floor. I guess it is okay, but I wonder if I should check?"

"What are you going to do? Hang a sign on Monique and Pam, saying 'Do not interrupt?' I say leave them alone." Deiter kept Lindsey from interfering, though she wanted to say something, though she did not know just what. She had never really asked Pam or Monique just what their relationship actually was or their plans, for that matter. Still, she felt concerned that the boys just didn't leave the two alone.

At last, Lindsey could stand it no longer. She had Deiter move them closer to Pam so she could at least see her face better. Pam was smiling. "See, told you to leave it alone. She's not crying or anything." Lindsey finally relaxed and let Deiter lead. The next thing she knew Alister was announcing the last dance. She closed her eyes and danced. Strangely, she felt comfortable and secure with him. Why? She couldn't really say, only that she did.

When they got to their room, everyone was talking about the dance, but Pam. "Was ok," was all that Pam muttered. A bit later, just as Lindsey was going to suggest they go for a walk or something, Pam said, "Well, tomorrow we get our schedule for this fall. I wonder why it is so late this year?" Lindsey decided against making the suggestion.

The next day, eagerly, all examined their fall schedule

as fifth year students.

```
 8:00 English Literature
 9:00 PE and First Aid
10:00 Advanced Earth Science
11:00 Beginning Calculus
 1:00 Spell Research I
 2:00 Potion Making II
 3:00 Spell Casting Grade 6
 4:00 Spell Casting Grade 6
 6:00 Elective
```

Emilio groaned, "Oh no! More math!" Kathy giggled, but felt the same way. Would the math never end? For once, Pam said nothing to him.

"Advanced Earth Science, now that could be fun," Andy commented.

"Perhaps we will get to read novels," suggested Amanda, musing over the literature possibility. "We've not read many to date. Jim did say that he had very little free time in his fifth year."

"What I want to know is what is this Spell Research all about? Are we going to be inventing our own spells?" Lindsey asked.

"Say, Monique never had this class," Pam suddenly realized. "I wonder if it is a new course?"

"Now that you mention it, neither Jim nor Tom had it either," Amanda added. "Must be a new thing. Sounds interesting though. I thought that we were going to have Alteration Theory III—at least that's what Jim and Tom had."

"Why do we have two periods for Spell Casting?" Ashley wanted to know. "Are there lots more Grade 6 spells than any other grade?"

"Dunno, but let's go get our books," Pam suggested. "Then we can take a peek." They did just that. An hour later, the group examined their Standard Grade 6 Spells book. "Gosh it's heavy and thick," Pam commented.

"Golly, there are pages and pages on each spell! They must be really hard spells!" Amanda commented. "I bet we have to spend lots and lots of time trying to learn these. Hey, look; here's the one that Dominus used on Lindsey her first year, DNA Morph into Another. Right, it says you have to have a bit of their DNA, and they must remain alive. Ah, look, it says the spell doesn't end until you choose it to end or the person dies. Our usual Morph spell only last a few hours at most. Cool!"

"Oh, look at the time, we had better get packing!" Lindsey called out. Hastily, everyone began packing for their trip back home for summer vacation.

Two hours later, Lindsey and Pam began their Floor Monitoring duties once more, whisking their ever-growing number of duffle bags down to the bus.

"Look at this!" Fern proudly displayed her new patch on her school dress. "Your newest Yellow Hall Floor Monitor. Now I can Move Objects too!" She'd been bringing down the first, second, and third year's things.

Amanda gave her little sister a hug. "Way cool, sis!"

"Welcome to the elite club," Lindsey said, "we do get a work out, but it's fun. Good going, Fern."

"Yes, and Ellie is one too, for Red Hall, that is," Fern added.

Three hours later, Lindsey's large group arrived at her front porch. Monique had been crying the whole time. "This is my very last bus ride!" she wailed. Pam did her best to comfort her, however, but she failed. It was her last bus ride.

Lindsey realized that she too would be leaving Bradbury's in just two more short years! She sympathized with Monique. Bradbury's had given her a total new life! That it would all end in two years scared her more than a little. Though she didn't know why, she told Deiter this fear, just before he had departed at Colorado Springs.

Chapter 25—Dutch Farewells

"Welcome home everyone!" Lena exclaimed, as the troupe got off the bus. Hugs and kisses were the action of the moment, as the parents welcomed their teens back home for the summer.

Quickly, those heading over to the Whitewater ranch began using the teleport pad. While Monique was waiting her turn, Lottie Blackburn dropped an unexpected bombshell on her. "Dear, the medical school sent us a notice that you are to report to orientation and testing tomorrow morning. Your father and I will be accompanying you. We leave at nine in the morning. So you had better tell your friends goodbye and get packing yet this afternoon."

Monique looked shocked, but there wasn't anything she could do about it. Pam volunteered, "If you need any help, holler. Let's at least have supper together tonight."

"Of course, it's all arranged," Polly explained to her daughter. "We are giving Monique a sendoff party at five tonight. You can help us with the last minute details. Lottie didn't tell Monique before now, because she knew her daughter would have been a basket case, fretting and worrying." Pam grinned, knowing that her friend certainly would have.

Jonathon was now nearly a year old, and Lena gave her daughters the responsibility of looking after him during the daytime so that she could get back to her ranching duties. The girls unpacked and got themselves organized. Lindsey, with Jonathon in tow, helped decorate the dining room and living room for the party, while the others assisted Polly in the kitchen. Nearly everyone was chatting continually about what all had happened at school and what was going on around the ranch.

Doctor Blackburn came home early in time for the party, as well as Fred Betts. Monique's eyes were red, but she was now all re-packed for the morning's departure. She had hoped to have some time with Pam, but that was not to be. Her emotions continued to get the better of her all that evening, though she did have an hour alone with Pam before she returned home to get some sleep before her first day at her new school.

Over the supper, Henry explained, "Since the presidential election was over, the amount of trouble seems to have drastically subsided. Hence, Lottie and I have decided that we will return to living in our own home. However, if more trouble comes, we will graciously accept R. B.'s offer to return at once. Ellie wants to be with her friends this summer, so it is going to work out fine."

Fred Betts added, "Don't fret Pam; we're staying put here. I can't do my job if I have to worry about you and your mother's safety. Though crime seems to be down, I don't trust Dominus any farther than I can throw him. So we stay put for now, unless you really want to go back to Sterling for the summer."

"No, dad. Here is really much better and safer. I don't really have any friends in Sterling much anyway," Pam admitted, grateful that she was staying put here on the Compton ranch.

Fred replied, "Excellent. Oh yes, Jeannette, Katja, tomorrow at noon we are to meet your parents in Denver. We will bring them here for two days so that they can meet your host families. Then you will be returning to Utrecht with them. Hence, we all should get some sleep tonight. Everyone will have a busy day tomorrow."

"Geesh, any more surprises?" Lindsey chuckled.

"We have added two more horses, one cow, and ten chickens. Does that count?" Lena teased her daughter. The girls giggled.

The next morning, Pam had to cast Emotion: Calm on Monique who was already a basket case, and they had not yet left! The two hugged each other tightly. "I will never forget you, Pam. You are the best thing in my life," Monique whispered.

"Become the best mag doctor possible," Pam whispered back. A tear trickled down Pam's cheek after the Blackburn's teleported away, carrying over a dozen bags.

After doing their chores and cleaning up, Lindsey gave a

farewell present to Katja, a magnificent music box that sounded like a harpsichord. Her name was engraved upon the box as well. Ashley gave Jeannette and Katja a farewell present. She gave them the two dresses she had worn for the photo shoot and which they had worn for the formal dance. This pleased the two immensely! Both insisted on wearing them to meet their parents. Indeed, Jeannette's arms and shoulders were highly visible in this spring evening gown. Ashley knew that her parents would love to see her like this.

As noon approached, the small party assembled. R. B. and Jim were taking Hans, Monane, Wilma, while Lloyd and Fred were taking Lindsey, Ashley, Jeannette, and Katja. Pam and Audrey stayed behind to help Lena and Polly get things ready on this end. Two bedrooms needed to be created from two workshops, to say nothing of the fancy evening meal.

Two very excited twins and Jeannette waited impatiently for their parents to deplane at the huge Denver airport. "There they are!" Jeannette called out and pointed to her folks, waving her arms over her head, showing them off to her folks. They rushed forward, hugged, and kissed their daughter. The twins and their parents hugged as well, before turning to look at Jeannette and her arms. By the time the introductions came, both Falco and Marga were flowing tears of happiness over her arms.

"Mom, dad, this is Lindsey Barron and her sister Ashley Stokes-Compton and their dad, Lloyd Compton. These are my folks, Falco and Marga van Ravinstijn."

Both shook Lindsey's hands. "Words cannot express how we feel for what you did for our precious daughter, Jeannette," Falco said speaking slowly, probably rehearsed words so that he didn't error. "We cannot ever thank you enough for giving our daughter her quality of life. If you ever want or need anything, please let us know."

"Ja, dankuwel, thank you, thank you," Marga added.

"Mom, this is the dress that Ashley wore on the Teen Fashion photo shoot. She's given one of them to me and to Katja," Jeannette explained.

Katja introduced her parents, "This is Baren and Gonda van der Veer, Hans and my folks." Again, more handshakes.

Jim and R. B. were introduced next, followed by Wilma, Monane, and Fred. Everyone chatted furiously, while Fred led them to pick up their baggage and then to the teleport platform. A minute later, they arrived by the front porch of the Compton's ranch.

Lena, holding Jonathon, came out to meet them, followed by Pam, Polly, Audrey, Luci, Fern, and Amanda. After more introductions, Lena showed them to their rooms so they could stow their bags. Next, Jeannette and Katja just had to take their parents on a tour of this incredible ranch house, designed by R. B. himself. Hans wanted them to see the Whitewater ranch; plus all three wanted them to see the teleport pad they'd used so frequently. Hans and Jim gave them a tour, though Amanda and Fern tagged along behind them.

When they returned, they finally sat down to a light, late lunch and talk. Jeannette asked her dad, "Did you bring it?" He grinned and went to his suitcase and brought out a small box, which Jeannette snatched up. Of course, Katja was in on it, and she stood right beside Jeannette.

"Lindsey, we wanted to give you something to thank you for what you did for me. We know you love the harpsichord, even though you don't play it so well yet. So here, Cancel." The box suddenly enlarged many fold. Inside was a handmade harpsichord of the highest quality.

Katja, the harpsichord player, explained, "It has an automatic tuner system, because as you know, they are always going out of tune. This system continually keeps it in tune. This switch tunes it to A440 or A415, whichever you need at the time. We hope that you like it and now have no excuse not to practice."

Lindsey thanked them profusely. "Katja, please play us something so I can hear how it is supposed to sound, not like my plunkings." Katja needed no second request to play on this fine instrument. She played six pieces before she exclaimed that she ought to save up and get one of these herself.

"If you practice lots, then you can sound like this too," Katja encouraged Lindsey, who promised to practice every chance she had.

When there was finally a lull in the conversation, Jeannette asked Pam to explain to both set of parents what she had found out about the murders of their grandfathers. All four were fascinated that finally the stones had been found, at least a few of them. "So far, the serial number of every diamond that has been recovered has matched one on your list that was stolen." Pam continued her explanation.

Both men were relieved. Finally, the stones had appeared. Dominus was guilty, and the two men had closure after all these years. Pam felt good that she was able to do this for them.

After the feast for supper, the adults sat around the table discussing what was going on in the States. Both sets of parents were most interested, particularly how Dominus had gained such a powerful control over the running of the United States. After they heard the details, both promised to see that he could not use that same trick in the European countries. They speculated that Interpol could still try and convict Dominus for the theft of the diamonds and the two murders; there was no statute of limitation on murder in the European Union.

Fred thought that this was interesting aspect. Now Dominus could be tried and convicted in two other countries, even though he was apparently getting off entirely free here in the US. He sent Alister a Message concerning this.

Jeannette told Lindsey and the others, "After you all and we graduate, you must come over to the Netherlands for a visit and see our country. Just let us know when you can come, and we will be ready." They all promised to come if it was possible.

The next day, Fred, Wilma, Monane, and Jim escorted the Dutch visitors to the airport and saw them off. Meanwhile, the girls re-did the house, cleaning up and re-arranging things. That evening, Jim came to say farewell to Ashley. He was off to Security training on his new job.

"I promise to write to my Princess every day," Jim said, though Amanda wondered if Jim actually would.

"You'd better, or I will have to track you down and kick your butt!" Ashley teased him. They kissed passionately, and he, too, left.

At last on June 6, things finally quieted down into the long summer. With Jim now gone and the Blackburns as well, Amanda and Fern spent most of their time at the Compton's. Their house seemed terribly empty with both of their brothers now gone. Both felt strong pangs of loneliness, never realizing until now just how much their brothers had meant to them. However, the remaining teens all went swimming in R. B.'s pond nearly every day.

Lindsey finally relaxed. All the hustle and bustle was gone. Life seemed peaceful now. She settled into ranch life once more, caring for their animals and her little brother.

Audrey spent her days carving, trying to catch up on the many orders she had from her website business. Pam spent hours on her computer researching, as she said. Ashley helped around the house and doted on her little brother, especially while Lindsey attempted to practice on her new harpsichord. For a time, the evils of the world seemed a distant thing of the past.

The End.

A Favor to Other Readers

How about helping other readers? Many readers rely on reviews to make the decision whether to buy a book. You can help them make their decision by leaving your opinions and viewpoint in a short review of the positive things of this book. Writing the review and expressing your opinion only takes a few minutes, and other readers will appreciate your efforts.

Click this link: Volume 4 Dominus for President
scroll down to Customer Reviews; click on Write a Review, and enter your review. Thank you.

Author Information

Visit My Amazon.com Author Page
Vic Broquard Author Page

Follow My Blog
Vic Broquard's Blog

Follow Me on Social Media
Facebook
Google+
LinkedIn
YouTube

Other Books by Vic Broquard

Without Warning (fantasy)

The Trident Series: (fantasy)
Volume 1 The Trident and the Book
Volume 2 The Trident and the Scepter
Volume 3 The Trident and the Resurrection

The Adventures of Elizabeth Stanton Series: (science fiction)
Volume 1 The Evolution of the Path
Volume 2 The Great Messiah
Volume 3 Of Kings and Queens and Troubadours
Volume 4 Chaos in the Aftermath
Volume 5 Power Plays
Volume 6 Age of Exploration
Volume 7 Abducted
Volume 8 The Emperor and Empress
Volume 9 A Job Worth Doing
Volume 10 Degradation
Volume 11 The Second Crusade
Volume 12 When Worlds Collide
Volume 13 Dark Ages

The Lindsey Barron Series: (fantasy)
Volume 1 The Rod of the Apocalypse
Volume 2 The Board of Governors
Volume 3 The Crown of Moses
Volume 4 Dominus for President
Volume 5 The National Health Care Program
Volume 6 States Justice
Volume 7 Cross and Double-cross

Zoran Chronicles Series: (fantasy)
Volume 1 A Dragon in Our Town
Volume 2 Dragons, Power, Courts, and War

Planet of the Orange-red Sun Series: (science fiction)
Volume 1 When Kingdoms Fall

Vic Broquard

www.ingramcontent.com/pod-product-compliance
Lightning Source LLC
Chambersburg PA
CBHW070903260626
47162CB00007B/2541